DANGEROUS

LEO SULLIVAN

Compilation and Introduction copyright © 2007 by
Triple Crown Publications
PO Box 6888
Columbus, Ohio 43205
www.TripleCrownPublications.com

Library of Congress Control Number: 2007901203
ISBN: 0-9778804-4-3
ISBN 13: 978-0-9778804-4-7
Cover Design/Graphics: Aaron Blackman Davis -
www.elevado.us.com
Author: Leo Sullivan
Typesetting: Holscher Type and Design
Associate Editor: Cynthia Parker
Editorial Assistant: Elizabeth Zaleski
Editor-in-Chief: Mia McPherson
Consulting: Vickie M. Stringer

First Trade Paperback Edition Printing April 2007

10 9 8 7 6 5 4 3 2

Printed in the United States of America

IN LOVING MEMORY
OF MY MOTHER
EVETTE L. SULLIVAN
AUGUST 7, 1947 – JUNE 9, 2006

May your beautiful soul rest in peace
and the legacy of your loving grace live on.

Dear Mama,
I never had a chance to say goodbye,
to tell you just how much I love you.
My mind still refuses
to accept the fact that you are gone.
This is the most difficult writing
I've ever had to indite. Incite?
Through misty eyes
my pen flows ink in tears.
God only knows
how many times I've attempted to write this…

It's hard Mama.

Some say my mother died from malpractice,
a hospital's negligence.
Some say she died from an internal illness…
I am sure my mother died
like millions of other Black women,
from a lack of love, loneliness and a broken heart.

I, her only child, should have been there for her.

THREE CAN KEEP A SECRET

IF TWO ARE DEAD

Jack and Gina

They were illegally parked in front of the Galaxy Hotel in Brooklyn. A million and one thoughts presented themselves in Jack's mind – thoughts born from the sheer determination to survive in a vortex of hell, in a place called Brooklyn. Like most young gods, Jack had gotten most of his education in a 10' x 12' cell, haunted by white angry faces and blatant racists, in a place where men learned to be men. The system had brilliantly orchestrated a plan, a mental murder for hire. They tried to kill his spirit, break his soul, but in the end they were forced to admit: young black men were resilient like an army of project roaches. They say one of the worst things you can do is lock a man up all day and have him do nothing but think. Think about how he got caught. Think about how to get away next time. Think about revenge. Think about the crazy statistic that said 74% of black men who got out of prison came back within eighteen months of their release. Damn!

While they plotted his mental demise, Jack created a disguise by reading lots of books that taught him how to outwit the man. He read books on revolutionaries like George Jackson, Malcolm X and Nat Turner. Jack read so many books that the words would come to life and talk to him. They sharpened his mind, showing him how to avoid ever coming back to prison. Soon Jack learned that a man who doesn't plan, plans to fail. For some reason everyone started calling him a Thug Revolutionist. That was around the time Jack won his appeal and was released from federal prison where he had been serving a life sentence. It was on!

ONE

It was five o'clock in the morning and Gina had just built up enough courage to tell Jack that she was tired. Her feet hurt from walking all night in stilettos. She wanted nothing else but to go home, take a long, hot shower and get into her comfortable bed. She looked into his handsome face, but his eyes were trained on the entrance of the hotel. Etched on his face was an expression of deep concentration, unblinking, unfailing.

"There! There!" He spotted his target. "There the nigga go right there," Jack said, exercising extreme calm, the kind an experienced hunter uses when stalking prey. Gina's body perked up and she became alert and focused as she slid her eyes off of Jack over to Damon Dice, one of the richest niggas in New York City. Instantly, she felt a rush of high-octane adrenaline. She was about to become the kind of weapon a man uses when he'd rather have court on the streets. Court would soon be in session, with Jack being both judge and jury.

"Listen Gina," Jack spoke, never taking his eyes off of Damon. "You gotta get this nigga to walk you close to the car so I can get his testifying ass in the trunk." His tone was hushed and his forehead knotted.

For the past three days they had been tailing Damon Dice and his entourage. Earlier that night they had been in a club called *The Tunnel* in Manhattan. It was the spot where all the ballers, shot callers and entertainers were known to mingle. That night the place was jam-packed. The music was pumping bass so hard that Gina could feel its pulsating rhythm in her chest. Somehow, it seemed to hype her up as all the colorful lights strobed throughout the club. She strained her eyes in search of her target. Finally she spotted him and the big-ass platinum chain around his neck. Scantily dressed in a chic tight miniskirt that showed off all of her goodies and accentuated her plump round ass, she slowly sashayed toward him, sensuously moving her hips from side to side. She wasn't wearing a bra and her see-through silk blouse gave little to the imagination as her gorgeous breasts rose upward in salute to her youth. Boldly, Gina strutted into the VIP section of the club as if she belonged there, walking right up to Damon Dice and his crew. All eyes were on her. Show time! All their mouths dropped like old folks with lockjaw.

Get the nigga to follow you out da club, Gina heard Jack's words in her mind as she neared Damon, never taking her eyes off him. She arched her back, thrusting her mouth-watering nipples forward, parallel to Damon's eyes. He sat in his seat staring at her, mouth agape, drink in hand. As she approached she held him spellbound. All the members of his crew were also entranced. Her sweet perfume marinated their nostrils as she bent down showing them some peek-a-boo cleavage. Coyly, she whispered in Damon's ear, her lips brushing against his earlobe, "Nigga, I'll suck that dick so good your balls will get jealous." Damon choked on his drink, accidentally spitting on his boy sitting next to him, who erupted in laughter.

Damn, this chick is bold, he thought as he watched Gina.

"I got the world's best pussy." He could have sworn he saw one of her nipples wink at him as he took in all of her audacious, shapely curves. That was around the time he got an erection.

They struck up a conversation and the drinks began to flow. She cozied up to him, flirting and touching, doing all the things that Jack had told her to do. She played her part well.

Stealthily, Gina would reach her hand under the table and play with his dick, stroking him as she poured a heavy dose of her feminine charm all over him. Finally, she had cast her spell. She could see it in his eyes. He was filled with lust and enchanted by her beauty. If she wanted to, she could have fucked him right there on the dance floor.

Ever so gently she took his hand, the fox leading the chicken, and moved past his bodyguards and crew of henchmen. She led him toward the dance floor with him palming her ass like two basketballs. Drunk, he followed as if he were a lost child. As they passed through the crowd, they headed for the exit. Slyly, Gina smiled as she thought about Jack waiting outside.

All of a sudden, five yards from the door, all hell broke loose. A salvo of gunshots rang out causing pandemonium. Like a scared rabbit, Damon Dice didn't even try to protect her. He just took off running back to the safety of his bodyguards.

"Punk-ass nigga," Gina cursed as she ducked down and headed for the exit door.

TWO

Damion Dice

Damon staggered out of the Galaxy Hotel, intoxicated by a cocktail of exotic drugs. He wore so much heavy jewelry that when he walked he made loud metallic clinging sounds.

Animated, he wobbled over to the wall and grabbed hold of it as if he were trying to stop the building from falling. The front of his pants were soiled with a large piss stain that ran the length of his left pant leg. That night he was faced with one of the biggest dilemmas of the day – should he take his dick out and piss right there in front of the hotel or vomit first? With his world spinning, his bodily functions didn't give him a chance to decide. With his dick in his hand, he began to vomit and urinate uncontrollably. It truly was a sight to behold.

Afterward, with his mouth ringed with vomit, he staggered away while trying to place his joint back into his pants. He looked up, and through bleary eyes he saw Gina floating toward him. He tried his best to stand up straight, but the damn building kept leaning to the side.

Damn, she fine as a muthafucka, he thought as she sauntered up close. He tried to wipe his mouth with his shirt sleeve and smile. Even in the dim light, he could still make out the symmetry of her body. He staggered slightly in a failed attempt to gain his equilibrium.

"Heyyy fella!" Gina caroled seductively in a breathy voice as she walked up to him, enrapturing him with the wiles of her charm.

"Damn … you the broad … I mean … ahh … uhh," Damon

stammered as he recalled seeing her. His mouth was still partially ringed with vomit. Everything was still spinning, but starting to slow down. He let go of the wall, his legs wobbling unsteadily like a child just learning to walk. Gina came closer. He reached out and fondled one of her lovely breasts. She rewarded him with a giggle as jubilant as a young schoolgirl on her first date. She furtively glanced over her shoulder at Jack hunched low in the car watching her every move.

"Shorty, you wanna come inside the telly? A nigga got everything you need. You like to smoke? I got … I got …" Drunk, Damon lost his train of thought as he scratched his head. "I got what you need," Damon said, causing Gina to tentatively take a step back.

Goddamn! His breath smell just like horse shit, she thought as she noticed a puddle of vomit on the ground in front of him. It took everything in her power not to frown as he once again caressed her breasts. Talk about being an actress—she deserved an Oscar.

"I would love to come inside," she drawled. "You still want me to suck that dick?" She licked her lips and reached down to rub him. As she did that, she felt a wet spot. *Nasty muthafucka,* she thought to herself as she removed her hand and placed it on her shirt, slyly wiping her hand. "Big daddy, why don't you walk me to my car first, to lock it up … tight," she cajoled, puckering her luscious lips, showing him one of her sex faces.

"Wha … wha … where ya parked at, shorty?" Damon asked.

She giggled innocently, taking his hand and walking him toward Jack in the parked car. He staggered a few steps and suddenly stopped in his tracks. His eyes popped open as if he'd seen a ghost. He stared at something in the distance. Whatever it was spooked him, causing him to sober up quickly.

"Naw shorty. I just saw something across the street. A light went on in that van." He squinted his eyes as if trying to focus in his inebriated fog. Damon pulled away from her hand and started to backpedal out of her grasp.

Not again, Gina thought as she remembered the scene back at the club and how mad Jack was with her for letting him get away.

Think fast! Think fast! Trick-ass nigga getting away! Her mind churned. She reached into her purse and pulled out an elegant gold-plated .357 Derringer pistol. It was the size of a Bic lighter, but powerful enough to drop an elephant. "Take another step, bitch-ass nigga, and I'ma blow your whole fuckin' back out. Now try me!" she said coldly between clinched teeth. Her face was a mask of deadly intent.

For some reason, in her mind, everything moved in slow, surreal motion. A lavender sky was starting to peek over the pitch-black horizon as dawn, like a dirty sheet on the canvas of the night, exposed the good, the bad and the ugly. In the distance birds were starting to chirp, summoning morning.

"Pah-pah-leese don't shoot me!" Damon begged. They were standing only inches apart. A lone car passed, and its luminous headlights traced their bodies stalled in the night. The air suddenly turned cool with the imminent threat of death. Sweat gleamed on Damon's forehead as he stood panic-stricken, overcome with fear. Gina could tell he was thinking about bolting. There was no doubt whatsoever in her mind—if Damon tried to get away, she would kill him.

The lobby doors opened and out walked Damon's bodyguard. The man was huge. He stood about six feet, seven inches, three hundred and something pounds. He had broad shoulders like a mountain. The man's name was Prophet. He was an ex-con and a well-known killer. As soon as Prophet got out the joint, Damon Dice gave him a job as head of DieHard Security. Next to Prophet stood G-Solo, who was slightly built, with a baby face and long eyelashes. He resembled the rapper Chingy. Both men were strapped with guns.

"Yo, son! What the fuck is going on out here?" Prophet asked suspiciously as he took a step closer. His deep, throaty baritone voice seemed to resonate with the timbre of a man that commanded authority.

Playfully, Gina laughed and hugged Damon as she placed the barrel of the gun against his rib cage and whispered in his ear as Prophet approached, "Tell them you'll be inside in a second."

"I'ma ... I'ma ... I'ma be inside in a second," the frightened man said, raising his voice.

"Nigga, you know you got on too much ice," Prophet warned as he stepped closer. He was only a few feet from Gina now. "Come on man, let's go."

"You fitna be shittin' in a plastic bag, rollin' around in a wheelchair," Gina whispered in Damon's ear, feeling Prophet's presence was too damn close. She pushed the gun harder against his ribs.

"Man! I told 'cha, I'm fuckin' coming! Leave me the fuck alone!" Damon yelled at his bodyguard, causing him to exchange looks with G-Solo. They both shrugged their shoulders as if to say, "fuck him, let him have his way with the bitch" as they walked away. Gina could feel Damon's arms shaking like leaves on a tree.

"Pah-pah-pahleese don't kill me," Damon pleaded.

"Shut up, nigga!" Gina said as she peeked over in Jack's direction, huddled in the car. Just then, a weary crackhead prostitute walked up. She was dressed in raggedy clothes – a pair of blue jeans that looked like they had not been washed in days, sneakers and a once-white halter top that was now gray. Her eyes continued to dart suspiciously back and forth across the street as she smacked her lips as if she had just bitten into a sour lemon.

She jerked her long neck, snaking it from side to side hyperactively with her hand poised on her body as she patted her foot on the concrete. On a crackhead's impulse, her eyes began to search the ground as if this was the sacred ground where she had lost her rock the other night. Her foot did a casual sweep of the pavement as she made a face, twisting her lips as she said matter-of-factly, "Girlfriend, I think that's the po-po across the street parked in that van." Hearing that caused Damon's body to flinch uncontrollably.

"Shit!" Gina muttered as she glanced over at the white van. *Why didn't I recognize it earlier?* she thought.

"I'ma scream if you don't let me go," Damon whimpered. Something about hearing the word "police" had emboldened him.

"Nigga, you stunt if you wanna, and I'ma leave your punk ass slumped right here with a hole in your chest!" Gina hissed as she cocked the gun and pressed it harder against his ribs. Damon was standing on the balls of his feet as if that would ease the explosion if the gun went off, shattering his rib cage and blowing his whole back out.

The prostitute continued to look back and forth in all directions, including the ground, akin to a junkie's perpetual paranoia. Once again Gina glanced over at the car with Jack in it and then looked at the undercover police van.

"Shit!"

THREE

"Unit six to Captain Brooks …"

"Go ahead, this is Captain Brooks," an authoritative voice returned over the sporadic crackling of the police radio.

"Lieutenant Stanley Goldstein is trying to reach you on your cell phone."

Brooks turned on his cell and it rang instantly. The Lieutenant spoke urgently. "The suspect and his entourage have just turned off Pennsylvania Avenue onto Linden and Stanley. They're at the Galaxy Hotel."

"You're in fuckin' Brooklyn now?" Captain Brooks shrieked over the phone, thinking about the friction it would cause with the 75th Precinct. They already had a bad rivalry, and this would only make things worse.

"I want you and the rest of the unit to stay clear of the suspect until I get there and give the order to take his black ass down," the Captain barked over the phone.

"Captain?"

"What?" Brooks answered brusquely.

"Sir, there appears to be a white Cadillac with a black female driving. There is also another individual in the car that we can't seem to make out. They have been trailing the suspect all night long. The car is now illegally parked in front of the hotel. How shall we proceed?"

"Leave the car alone. We don't want to risk tipping off the 75th that we're on their turf about to make a major bust. They're probably harmless groupies. Tell your men to hang tight. I'm on my way." Brooks hung up the phone and made a U-turn in the middle of the street.

As he drove, his mind went over every detail as it related to how he was going to make the bust. Damon Dice was actually out of Brooks' jurisdiction, but since his department had tailed him from Manhattan to Brooklyn in violation of possession of drugs, the arrest was going to be perfectly legal. Now all Brooks had to do was plant the dope.

The good thing about what he was doing was that the Mayor himself was behind the special task force to arrest as many rappers as they could, and so far so good. His department had been having a field day. The only thing that kept Damon Dice on the streets for so long was the fact that he was a police informant and had been giving Brooks information for a long time. That was until he turned music mogul.

Damon Dice had switched hats from hustler to entrepreneur in the blink of an eye. He now felt he was invincible and refused to provide Brooks with any helpful information. Brooks hated that he didn't bust Damon earlier. Now he was selling hit records just like Suge Knight and J. Prince.

This fueled Brooks even more as his nondescript Ford sliced through the night. What really pissed off was to see a black man making so much damn money, legally. They were becoming a threat. Hell, the rapper 40, one of the hottest in the industry, had just bought a mansion with forty rooms, a bowling alley and a movie theater. Another was partial owner of a basketball team. It was becoming a trend. *How do they do it?* he pondered.

His knuckles were white as he tightly held onto the steering wheel as the car reached speeds of over a hundred miles per hour. He was consumed with the anticipation of the bust. He felt the adrenaline of a policeman's head rush – the set up, the chase, the capture and then the arrest. Just the thought of it gave him an erection. He would teach the fucker who he was playing with. Besides, Brooks wanted to please the Mayor. He was already told to treat all rappers as potential drug dealers until proven differently. Now all he had to do was follow the first law of police work—if there isn't a crime, invent one.

◊ ◊ ◊ ◊

Captain Brooks made the excursion from Manhattan to Brooklyn in seventeen minutes flat. Lights out, he cruised past the White Castle restaurant where a few prostitutes loitered. Unbeknownst to him, somewhere, somehow in the hub of this naked city, the streets were watching, waiting, listening. Brooks eased his car behind another unmarked car. As he exited, a dog barked in the distance. A crescent moon, embellished with stars, hung from the night sky like a lucid scratch on the underbelly of the black canvas of the night.

A weary prostitute ambled by. The woman took one look at the supposed undercover cop and decided he damn sure was not a trick. She took off walking fast, looking over her shoulder as if to make sure the cop made no attempt to tackle her.

The night air felt crisp and cool against Brooks' pale skin as he walked toward the surveillance van. He realized that he was starting to sweat under his cotton shirt, causing it to stick to his skin. The foul odor of rotten garbage mixed with New York air pollution only seemed to enhance the moment. Eyes alert, he could feel his senses tingling as he felt for the ounce of crack he had in his pocket. He intended to plant the dope on Damon Dice. That would get his ass to talking.

Lieutenant Goldstein opened the van door. Brooks grunted as he squatted, struggling to get in. The forty or so pounds he had picked up over the last few years were starting to take their toll on him. There were four other undercover officers in the cramped van.

"Captain, I just received word from the 75th Precinct. They want to know what we're doing on their turf. They're asking us to back off and let them handle the arrest."

"Handle my ass! I'm in command here. My authority comes all the way from the Mayor's office," Brooks screeched. He thought about the dope in his pocket intended for Damon Dice.

12

"Tell whomever it is that I said to fuck him and the horse he rode in on!"

"Holy shit!" one of the undercover officers lamented as he looked through the night vision binoculars. Brooks snatched the binoculars and peered out the window. As he bent down he accidentally hit a light switch causing the inside of the van to light up. And as usual, the streets were watching.

FOUR

Jack and Gina

Gina stood in front of the Galaxy Hotel paralyzed with fear as she held the gun against Damon's ribs. The prostitute had just warned her that the police were parked across the street in the van. Jack had spied everything from the confines of the car, but he had no idea that the police were parked nearby watching them.

Don't panic, Gina thought as her mind frantically searched for a way out, but it was useless, at least for her. Now her main concern was for Jack. They both didn't have to go to prison, if she could help it. She fully intended to save him by any means necessary. Suddenly, she had an idea. "Give her all your money," Gina ordered, shoving the gun harder against his ribs.

"What?" Damon asked.

"Nigga, you heard me!" Gina raised her voice. The prostitute continued to look on. Three people walked out of the hotel, a woman and two men. The woman saw what was going on, but played it off as she quickened her pace and nudged one of her partners. They saw, but didn't see. In the real world of the ghetto, a hero gets punished, sometimes even killed, for interfering in other people's business.

The threesome passed on their way to the parking garage. Damon's hands were shaking so bad when he handed the prostitute the wad of cash that the diamond platinum bracelets on his arms chimed like bells. He gave the junkie a little over six thousand dollars.

"Listen, you got a family?" Gina asked the prostitute.

"Yeah, I got a three-year-old girl," the junkie replied, eyes as big as silver dollars as she licked her dry lips.

"I have a family, too," Gina said as she spied the van across the street. "That's my family parked in that white car across the street over there." Gina pointed with a nod of her head. "I want you to promise me that you'll take that money and do something for your kid. But first I want you to walk over there and tell that dude parked in the car…tell him to go. Tell him the police are watching us, like a set up. Tell him the spot is hot. Tell him…" Gina's voice cracked. "Tell him I love him."

Why Gina just didn't walk away and let Damon go was a mystery. It was as if she couldn't stop, not even if she wanted to. Since Jack had gone away, robbery was in her blood and rushed through her veins. Every fiber in her body needed the feel of command over another's soul. Damon was the fix for her addiction.

Hauntingly, she was often reminded of a story she had watched as a small child on television, on PBS. It was a horrific story about how African monkeys are hunted, trapped and killed. The hunter merely places a shiny object inside a cage and the monkey reaches inside the cage to grab the shiny object. It's too big to get out of the narrow bars of the cage, and when the hunters come to trap him, even at the risk of his own life, the monkey is too dumb to let go, and is ultimately killed for refusing to let go. Like the monkey, Gina refused to let go, and she knew some day it would cost her her life.

She spun Damon around and made mock laughter like the two of them were lovebirds having a friendly frolic. She walked him toward the parking garage. There, she intended to strip him like a stolen Chevy.

Inside the dark garage, the stench of piss was strong. As she continued to walk him like a dog in the dim light, her mind raced. How was she going to pull this off? The entire time Damon whimpered and pleaded for his life.

Suddenly up ahead, car lights flashed and tires screeched. Startled, she braced herself as she held Damon by his shirt, leveling the gun at his kidneys. The car continued to accelerate toward her, its headlights engulfing them like deer standing in the middle of the road.

Police! Gina feared.

The car came to a screeching halt, only inches in front of them. Jack jumped out wearing a ski mask and a bullet-proof vest. He rushed over to her and pointed the AK-47 at Damon's head. For the second time that day, Damon pissed in his pants.

A few yards away a woman screamed. It was the same woman that had passed Gina earlier with her two companions. They were about to enter a cream-colored Lexus. The woman continued to scream. Jack rushed over to her and smacked her upside the head with the butt of his gun. Silence. She dropped like a sack of rocks as her two companions grimaced in horror.

"Gimme your car keys and wallets!" Jack commanded. His voice echoed. Terror-stricken, both men complied. Jack was moving fast as Gina looked on. "Remember, I got your IDs, so I know how to find you. Lie on the ground and be quiet for five minutes." Both men obeyed and lay down on the pissy concrete. Jack quickly moved to the back of the Lexus, opening the trunk with the car keys. He pointed the gun at Damon, waving for Gina to come on. Damon was moving too slow so she shoved him so hard he nearly fell as he stumbled. Gina marched him over to the open trunk.

"Girl, what the fuck you tryna do? You fuckin' death struck or somethin'?" Jack said as he hit Damon in the head with the butt of his gun. As Damon fell, Gina tried to grab him by his shirt, but it tore and Damon hit his head on the concrete with a thud. Moving swiftly, together they hoisted his body into the trunk as they both heard the blare of police sirens. Alarmed, they looked at each other. Jack threw her the car keys. "It's on you, Ma. If they open up the trunk I'm comin' out blastin'." He dived into the trunk next to the unconscious Damon Dice. Gina slammed the trunk shut, ran and jumped into the front seat. Placing the key in the ignition, she took a deep breath in an attempt to calm her nerves. She pulled off and headed toward the exit.

In front of her, lights bleared as sirens shrilled in her ears. Up ahead a caravan of police cars raced toward her. *It ain't gonna fuckin' go down like this,* she thought as her heart pounded so hard in her chest that it felt like it was going to explode.

A police car pulled in front of her, blocking her path. Gina clinched the gun in her hand as she thought about Jack in the trunk. Two police officers hopped out of their patrol cars with guns drawn, aimed at her head. "Get out of the car! Get out of the car, now!" One officer was white, the other black.

Gina palmed the small gun in her hand. Her life flashed before her eyes, the monkey that couldn't let go. Her mind churned, *Think fast! Think fast!* "Nooo! Nooo!" she cried hysterically. "There's a masked gunman back there! He tried to kidnap me! He already has one hostage back there with him." She pointed with her hand as the other clasped the gun between her legs as she continued to cry the way only a black woman could to save her man and herself. She manufactured an ocean of tears, with a "please help me, woman in distress" face to match.

Somehow, Gina was able to melt the heart of the white cop, but the black cop looked at her quizzically. The white cop looked behind Gina to the other end of the parking garage as he spoke, "I want you to drive out of here to safety and park your car on the side of the building. I'll send an officer to get a description of the gunman."

Gina nodded her head as she listened to the officer give her orders. A dry lump formed in her throat as she swallowed. "Okay…" she muttered as she listened to the cop call for backup on his radio. He asked for the SWAT team. Gina did as instructed and drove slowly through the throngs of police cars and flashing lights, all the while unconscious of the fact that she was holding her breath and praying to a God that had never listened to her.

FIVE

Captain Bill Brooks

"What the fuck is going on?" Brooks shrieked, his face flustered as he watched from the concealment of the van. The pretty black girl and Damon Dice flirted and touched on each other. Then two men walked out. There was an exchange of words. The two men left, a few other people passed and suddenly the crackhead that Brooks had seen earlier was talking to the couple and the pretty black girl walked Damon Dice to the parking garage. *She's probably going to suck his dick,* Captain Brooks thought.

Moments later the white car followed the girl into the garage and the next thing Brooks knew all hell broke loose. A woman's scream echoed from the garage and police came from everywhere. What the hell was the 75th Precinct doing there? The scene was pure madness. The streets were cluttered with police cars from both precincts.

Brooks watched the Lexus slowly drive out of the garage and weave through the congested streets.

"Sir, that's the 75th Precinct," Lieutenant Stanley meekly said to his superior, Captain Brooks.

"Thought I gave you orders to tell them to back the fuck off!" Brooks spat angrily.

"I did," Stanley barked back, making a face as he scurried to get out of the van.

"Motherfucking bureaucratic bullshit!" Brooks yelled as he got out of the van and stormed over to the handsomely dressed, plain-clothes officer who had just arrived on the scene and was giving orders.

"Who's in fucking charge here?" Brooks huffed.

"I am," the handsome black man said as he turned to meet the other man's stare. "And you've just fucked up for not getting permission from 75th."

"Fuck 75th buddy, and you with it. Who the hell are you?"

"Lieutenant Anthony Brown." He pulled out his badge.

"Well, by the time I'm finished with you, you'll be Lieutenant of fucking chicken shit, working somewhere in Alaska!"

Just then, the police radio crackled to life. Lieutenant Brown signaled for one of his men to pass him their radio. "Lieutenant Brown, go ahead."

"There are two males and an unconscious female in here," the voice on the other end replied urgently. "One of the males said an armed gunman hit his girl upside the head and stole their car. The other male claims he doesn't remember what happened. Be advised, a woman and a man were seen placing an individual in the trunk of a stolen beige Lexus. These individuals are to be considered armed and dangerous."

Lieutenant Brown looked over at Captain Brooks as the irate man kicked the side of a car. The voice on the other end of the radio continued, "One of the suspects, the woman, talked her way past a couple of officers. She's driving the Lexus. There is also an abandoned white Cadi—"

"White Cadillac?" Brooks retorted as his eyebrows shot up as he thought about the girl. *She wasn't a groupie,* he thought. He now realized she was part of some elaborate robbery scheme. He looked up to see the beige Lexus turning the corner. "There they go!" he shouted.

As Gina slowly drove away with her human cargo in the trunk, she had no idea of just how bad her day was going to get.

SIX

The Gentlemen's Club
Monique Cheeks - Fire

Curvaceous hips and sensuous brown thighs gyrated as her soft, honey-colored complexion glistened under the shine of bright lights. Sleek, sable velvet skin radiated beneath perspiration. Monique Cheeks was nude, bare as a baby's ass, as she danced ever so gracefully like a black swan, with the agility of an athlete and limberness of a cat. She bent over backward, lower ... lower ... each rhythmical beat of the music seemed to challenge her body. She arched her spine. Her titillating body hypnotized the men as she held them, and a few women, spellbound.

With her head nearly touching the floor, she raised her arms flailing like a mermaid in water. Then slowly, as naturally as a kitten yawns, she raised her leg as she held the bottom of her foot with her hand ... higher ... higher ... until finally she had placed her leg on the back of her neck. The room became quiet, lulled to silence as if time stood still. On one leg, Monique pivoted on the ball of her foot, then her toe. Magnificent! She raised her head to the heavens in a statuesque pose, while her small breasts jetted forward.

The jubilant crowd of wealthy white men erupted with raucous applause that stemmed into a standing ovation. Large streams of money were tossed on stage. The next show had to be delayed as Monique retrieved all the ten, twenty and fifty-dollar bills. There were even a few hundred-dollar bills balled up.

At twenty-one years of age, Monique Cheeks was the first African American woman to ever be given a chance to dance at the prestigious Gentlemen's Club. She did it with an urban hip-hop flare. At first the establishment had no intention of hiring a black woman, but under state laws, for the record, they at least had to make a show of practicing equal employment or risk losing their license. Monique auditioned and danced for the management. They were in awe of her style of dance. The black girl from the Marcus Garvey projects was hired that same day.

For the first time since college she was doing something that she truly loved—dancing. Three years ago, she had won a scholarship to attend the prestigious School of Modern Dance at Yale University. That same year she had become pregnant and was forced to drop out. She and her family were devastated, as the incident stalled what looked like a promising career.

She ended up taking a part-time job at a bakery and hating every minute of it, until one day she saw an ad in the paper: "Dancers wanted. Must be professional." Desperate to climb out of poverty's perilous grip, in search of a future for her child and herself, she applied for the position. To her surprise, out of twenty women, she was chosen. Now she would have the money to pay for college and move out of the Marcus Garvey projects, where she and her family had lived all their lives, generation to generation.

For the first two months at the Gentlemen's Club she was treated like an outcast by her co-workers, all except one white girl and she only spoke casually in passing. It didn't really matter to Monique what the rest of the girls thought about her. She knew that she had one clear advantage over them—soul. Monique danced with the soul and rhythm of a black woman and that wasn't something that could be learned. You either had it or you didn't.

However, Monique was forced to notice that some of the most beautiful women in the world worked at the club. Women of all races. Monique started to wonder, "When did white women start having bodies like black women?" Often the white girls danced so off-beat and out-of-sync with the music, it made Monique laugh as a few of the girls actually tried to imitate her.

One thing Monique promised herself was that she would

never disgrace herself by opening her legs and dancing nude for a table dance, ridiculing herself like the rest of the girls did for the love of money. She kept it strictly on stage, with the exception of a few select customers, and that was by her own choice. The establishment didn't go along with it at first; however, when they saw that she, alone, could pack a house with urban dance, they were forced to go along with it. Monique made almost three times the money that the rest of the girls made. On a good night she could easily bring home $3,000. She was also painfully aware that some of the girls had open disdain for that.

◊ ◊ ◊ ◊

One night after she had just finished her show to a standing-room-only crowd, she gathered her money off the stage floor and went to the ladies' dressing room with the rest of the girls. As usual, some of them spoke and some didn't.

As she passed a few girls to get to her locker, she was horrified to see the words "Nigger Bitch" scrawled on her locker in bold red lipstick. Stunned, Monique stood there as her eyes filled with tears of despair. She wanted nothing more than to be friends with the rest of the girls. *How could someone be so mean?* she thought, her heart full of hurt.

Slowly, she turned around in search of the culprit. The hum of a hair dryer droned loudly. A door opened and then shut. Monique heard herself say, "Which one of you wrote this on my locker?" Her voice quivered, as she fought for control, willing herself not to cry, not here, not in front of all these white girls.

Of the twenty or so women in the room a lone giggle tauntingly resonated from the back of the room. Monique's eyes roamed to see where the cackle came from. It was the tall Russian blonde who looked like a man. She had large breasts that looked as stiff as a board and round like balloons.

Her name was Tatyana Fedorov. She was once the headliner of the show, that was until Monique Cheeks came along and took her spot, earning the stage name "Fire" because everyone said her show was hot. Gingerly, Monique walked over to the middle of the dressing room floor as she studied the woman. Not only was she about ten years older than Monique, she was at least a full foot taller.

Monique spoke curtly, "You may not like me, but you're damn sure gonna have to respect me." Her tone was measured in an attempt to bridle her anger. "Just like most of you, I came here to feed my family, my child." Her voice cracked with emotion as her eyes rimmed with tears. As her shoulders slumped she suddenly thought to herself, *Maybe this whole thing would just go away if I acted like the better woman and walked away.* She did what her mind told her but as she did, Tatyana and her friends' stinging laughter filled the air. Automatically, Monique spun around and stared all three of them down.

"One of you bitches find something funny?" Monique pointed in the big Russian's direction as the girl stepped forward. She had narrow shoulders with long wiry arms. "Yes, you need to leave here … leave us … alone … go back to your watermelon and fried chicken," Tatyana spoke in broken English. What disturbed Monique most was the pure hatred the woman carried in her eyes.

"Naw bitch, you need to leave me alone! You don't know who you fuckin' with!" Monique turned and walked away, but the women continued to laugh.

Monique was from Brooklyn. All the girls in her rough neighborhood had grown up fighting boys. It wasn't even an option. Fighting back was a way of survival.

Leisurely, Monique strode over to her locker with her mind on the matter at hand. The rest of the girls in the dressing room went back to what they were doing, gossiping and getting dressed. Monique could hear the big Russian using the word "nigger" like it was standard everyday language for her and her pals. The sound of the word infuriated her. Never in her entire life had a person outside of her race called her a nigger.

With her back toward Tatyana and her clique, furtively, Monique opened a pack of razors, peeled one from the pack and placed it in her mouth. Quickly, she dressed into a white T-shirt, blue jeans and sneakers. She then reached for the Vaseline and put it on her face. At a demure 5 feet, 6 inches, she strolled over to the big Russian and her friends. "Which one of you bitches called me a nigger?" Monique asked tersely, while her brown eyes sized up the Russian.

Tatyana looked down at Monique and smirked devilishly as three other girls came and stood next to her. They made no secret of their attempt to jump on Monique. It was now six to one. They began to surround her. One of the girls had something she was trying to conceal in her hand. Tentatively, Monique took a step back as her mind hurried to evaluate the situation. It was simple: she had fallen for the oldest trick in the book. Tatyana had set her up by taunting her to walk right into a trap. Instantly, she looked over her shoulder for the door and realized that she was in great danger. Timidly, she took a step back. Even with the razor in her mouth she knew that it would be a difficult task to fight all the women.

They began to close in. "Nigger, what you gonna do now?" Tatyana threatened. Doomed, Monique braced herself as they closed in on her.

"Uh-uh, it ain't gonna go down like that! Not today!" Monique turned her head toward the sound of the voice. It was the white girl who casually spoke in passing. She elbowed her way through the crowd. In her hand she had a black can of mace and aimed it at Tatyana's face. "I'll air this bitch out first before I let all y'all jump on this girl."

Fear showed in Tatyana's eyes as the rest of her girls stood back, intimidated. In that split second, perhaps it was fear, or just the willpower and desire not to be defeated, Monique seized the moment and lashed forward, striking Tatyana on her long beak nose, breaking it in three places. The rest of the girls quickly decided they didn't want none of Monique and got the hell out the way.

In a whirling blur of motion, Monique punched Tatyana like she was a man. It happened so fast. Monique then kicked Tatyana in the stomach. Tatyana screamed in agony as her tall, lithe body keeled over. Monique lassoed her fingers through Tatyana's long blond hair and yanked it hard as she brought her knee up to meet Tatyana's face. The bone collided with the soft tissue of her face. The sound was like a baseball bat hitting wood. Blood squirted like a faucet as three teeth slid across the floor. Tatyana fell in a heap, face first on the floor.

The rest of the women in the room looked on in pure shock. Monique spit the razor out of her mouth, causing the girl that had come to her rescue to take a step back. Monique did a full circle in the room as she stood over the unconscious Tatyana lying at her feet, blood streaming from her face. "Do the rest of you bitches want some of this nigger here?" She scanned the room, looking for a response.

The white girl who had come to her rescue smiled. As most of the girls scrambled to get away, one of Tatyana's friends rushed to her side and felt for a pulse. She immediately reached for her cell phone and dialed 911. As she requested an ambulance, Monique thought about what had just transpired. Not only was she sure she would lose her job, but even worse; she feared she might be arrested for assault. She left the scene in a hurry without even saying thank you to the white girl who had come to her aid.

The next night when she came to work, Monique was surprised to learn that management had learned of the incident and was shamed by it. To learn that racist epithets had been scrawled on Monique's locker and that it had caused an altercation was bad news. The kind of news that would not only be bad for publicity but it could have warranted all kinds of civil law suits for racial insensitivity.

To her utter surprise, Monique was given her own private dressing room. Also, management paid for Tatyana to have reconstructive surgery on her face. She was also given a handsome sum of money to drop any future lawsuits. However, Tatyana's beautiful face would never be the same. She was forced to find employment elsewhere.

◊ ◊ ◊ ◊

Three days after the fight with Tatyana, an executive from "*Gentlemen's Magazine*" approached Monique. He had just so happened to be in town and had seen one of her shows. Although she was black, her beauty mesmerized him.

After the show, he approached Monique with a proposition. It was a long shot, but he was willing to try it if she was willing to invest a little time. He asked her if he could fly her to California to do a photo session for the magazine. If the photo session went well, Monique would be offered a seven-figure contract to be a model and possibly a chance to be Model of the Year. Her picture would be viewed by millions of men all over the world. If worse came to worst, she would still be paid $2,000 for her time.

Monique was awestruck beyond words. After all, she was a twenty-one-year-old Brooklyn chick, still illegally receiving welfare checks. *Damn, white folks got it going on,* she thought. Now her only problem was Rasheed, her baby's daddy. He would go berserk! For two months she had been leaving him at her house, taking care of their three-year-old son, acting like she was working the midnight shift at the bakery. He never questioned her. God, he was going to be crushed when he found out she was a stripper.

The bad part was, she had no plans to stop working any time soon. And now, the offer to pose nude for Gentlemen's truly blew her mind. She fought with herself about how to tell him without breaking his heart. Then it dawned on her – there's no way a woman can tell her man that for the past two months she has been dancing nude as a stripper.

As she drove home that night to face Rasheed, she was determined to tell him about her deep, dark secret. She pulled into the parking lot of the rough, crime-ridden, drug-infested Marcus Garvey projects. If by some uncanny fate you lived there, you would be considered family. Unfortunately it was family of the worst kind. The family of shattered dreams and broken promises, where tomorrow never comes and the days are always too late. Monique Cheeks was determined to find a way out, maybe even at the expense of leaving her man. Maybe?

◊ ◊ ◊ ◊

She closed the door behind her as she walked into the sound of the TV blaring. Rasheed and baby Malcolm were asleep on the living room couch. One of Rasheed's long legs hung over the armrest. The two of them were beautiful together, father and son, as they slept. *Malcolm is the spitting image of his father,* she thought as she peered down at her man and child. The moment was gentle as the two slept. For Monique it was one of those Kodak moments.

Even in sleep, Rasheed's potent masculinity was vibrant and strong. Monique resisted the urge to stroke his cheek. Instead she took off her shoes and placed her purse on the table. Roaches scattered in every direction. She decided to place her purse on the floor next to the couch.

Rasheed stirred in his sleep. She drew in a deep breath as she fought the urge to smother his handsome face with kisses. At 6 feet, 9 inches, she pictured him running up and down the basketball court. She thought about him, his dreams and his aspirations. Although he would emphatically deny it, Rasheed loved basketball more than he loved life itself.

Rasheed Smith wanted to be a professional basketball player. He attended a small college, St. John's University, and for two years in a row he had led the nation in scoring and assists. In his senior year of high school, all the major colleges recruited him; however, that same year he got caught riding in a stolen car with drugs in it.

He was arrested and went to jail for a few months. The only reason he was released from jail and given a light sentence of probation was due to his high school coach, a man by the name of Dan Reeves. He and the judge were friends. Rasheed's arrest made headlines across the nation in the sports section and suddenly all of the major colleges that had expressed interest in him dropped his name from the list.

Rasheed was forced to attend a small college where every night he lit up the scoreboard with as many as fifty points a game. Sure, the NBA scouts were watching, but would they take a chance on a troubled black kid that had never known his mother or father? His elderly grandmother had raised him as best she could, and many in the community felt she had done a good job.

With her hands clasped in front of her, Monique looked at the sleeping Rasheed as images flashed before her eyes – images of herself dancing nude. If only God would give her the courage to tell him so she could finally get it over with. Again, she wondered if he'd leave her or even worse, kick her ass.

She bit down on her bottom lip with a feeling of deep despair and guilt. She thought about the $2,700 she had in her purse; money she had made that night. Not only that, but she had $22,300 stashed in the closet in a shoebox. In less than a month she was scheduled to fly to California for a photo shoot for the magazine. If she passed the initial screening, the rewards would be many, the money would be huge, and the opportunities would be endless.

"Oh, baby, please don't be mad at me," she whispered in the dim light with her nerves on edge. This night she decided she was going to tell Rasheed and let the cards fall where they may. Suddenly his eyes fluttered open. A beacon of light shined through the worn out curtains accentuating the brown flecks in his eyes. Rasheed reached up to grab her. Startled, she screamed. He laughed. Playfully she hit him on the chest as she fell onto the couch into his arms. They kissed passionately as the baby stirred in his sleep with his body now wedged between his parents.

"You scared me, musty breath." Monique wrinkled up her nose and playfully hit him on his chest again. He frowned, making a face as he looked at her.

"You smell like cigarette smoke," he replied.

"I … I … uh gave a girlfriend a ride home from work. She smoked in the car," Monique lied and changed the subject. "Did you miss me?"

"Yeah, I missed you," he said groggily.

"How much?"

"This much." Rasheed threw back the covers showing her his morning erection outlined in his boxer shorts.

"Wow, you could hurt a girl with that thang, daddy," Monique said flippantly and reached down to caress his penis ever so gently with long, even strokes.

"What time you gotta go to basketball practice?" she asked with a husky timbre of lust in her voice.

"Seven o'clock."

"We got time for a quickie?" She began kissing his neck below the earlobe.

"Only if you let me hit it from the back." He smiled sheepishly.

"Aw, you want a little doggy style," she chimed as she felt his hands fondling her breasts, unbuttoning her blouse. With his forefinger and thumb he freed one of her breasts and leaned forward, taking it into his mouth and savoring the taste. She released a sigh, beckoning him to take her.

"Go put the baby in his bed … and you can have all the doggy style you want, sweetheart," she said, feeling her nipple harden with the sensation of his tongue. As he attempted to get up to honor her request, she sucked in a deep breath and her tone changed. "I need to talk to you about something. Something I've been meaning to tell you for quite some time." She was determined to look him in his eyes.

Rasheed detected something in her demeanor that alerted him something was up. He rose up on his elbows with his brow knotted and looked her in the eye.

"Tell me what, Mo?" he asked suspiciously. She eased up off of him and walked over to the window. She could not bear seeing the hurt on his face for what she had to say next. She inhaled deeply. She could feel her heart pounding in her chest so hard it felt like she was having trouble breathing.

"My job …" she said, trying to figure out how to start the conversation.

"Yeah," he said as he waited for her to speak again.

She turned toward the window searching for the words to say. Rasheed immediately walked toward her and put his one free arm around her waist and pulled her into his body. "Baby, it'll be alright. We'll get through it," he reassured. Rasheed thought she had lost her job. She knew this and his comforting words and gestures were making her admission harder.

"Baby ... remember I told you I was working at the bakery?" Rasheed didn't answer. "Well ..." She made a face and swallowed the dry lump in her throat. Suddenly a gust of emotions overcame her. "I don't work there anymore." He held her with a blank stare. "I've been dancing."

"Dancing?" he retorted. "What kind of dancing?" he asked, raising his voice so loud it made her flinch. Monique wondered if he would hit her. He stepped away from her, looking at her as if it was his first time really seeing her. For some reason his nearness was starting to make her feel uncomfortable; she wanted to run out of the house, but she had come too far to turn back now.

"I've been dancing at the Gentlemen's Club," she blurted out as if to get the evil words off her tongue.

"YOU WHAT!?" he bellowed angrily as he stepped a little closer to her, giving her a look of disbelief. "Tell me you're joking," he said, his brown eyes holding her captive. Somberly, Monique shook her head slowly from left to right indicating she wasn't joking. She cast a long stare down at the floor refusing to meet his eyes. Her hands repeatedly washed over each other. She was a bundle of nerves.

"I've been working there for over two months now," she revealed, feeling a surge of emotions like a floodgate that was finally released. "I make more money in one night than I did for an entire month at the bakery."

"You're a fucking stripper? Is that what you're telling me?" Rasheed said indignantly, causing Monique to turn and glare at him. Frustrated, he mopped his face and raked his hands through his curly hair. She had hurt him to the core of his being, as only a woman could.

Monique wanted to hold him desperately, to assure him that all was going to be okay. "It's really not all that bad," she said softly. I dance for mostly rich older men."

"Mo, that makes it betta 'cause you dance for white men?" he shouted as he placed his feet firmly on the floor, giving her a look of disbelief. The baby awakened and Rasheed sat back down on the couch, letting the baby crawl into his lap.

"What about your dreams?" He pointed at her. "Our dreams?" He pointed at himself and their son. "Since the first day I met you, you talked about wanting to be a dancer. What happened, Mo? This the kind of dancin' you dreamed of?" he asked curtly with the strain of the situation showing on his face.

Something about the way he said that dug deep under her skin causing her to lash out with words. "You think I wanna do this?" She peered at him. "Those were dreams, Rasheed, dreams! In the real world you got me pregnant at eighteen years old and that's when I learned that my dreams wouldn't put food on the table, or pay the bills." She looked around the apartment and saw a roach making its way into a crack in the wall. "I'm living here in this roach trap and you living with your grandmother. When was the last time you had a job, Rasheed? It's been over two years," she reminded him. "You got the nerve to talk about *my* dreams? What the hell am I suppose to do? Yo' ass ain't helpin' me none!" Her words hit him like a sledgehammer.

"Helpin' you none? Helpin' you none?" he yelled at her. Innocently the baby looked on with those eyes, undecided if he wanted to cry or not. "Every day that I go to school I'm helpin' you. Every day that I step foot on the basketball court and an NBA scout comes out to watch, I'm helpin' you." And then, as if on his second wind, with a furrow in his brow he asked, "You don't believe in me no mo'?" She didn't answer, but the cold expression on her face said enough. "You're gonna quit that fuckin' job and take yo' ass back to the bakery!"

"And suppose I don't want to? What you gonna do, make me?"

Her words were bold as she crossed her arms over her chest and narrowed her brown eyes at him in defiance.

Momentarily, he was stunned by her reply. Lost for words, he just stared at her with his lips pressed tightly together in an attempt to control his temperament. Then suddenly something washed over him causing his features to soften to the face of a defeated man.

"Mo … Mo, you my woman, not some freak show for other men to get their thang off. My woman …" He sat down and lowered his gaze to the floor. Like a broken man he asked, "Mo, why you doing this to me … to us?"

She heard the pensive tremor in his voice and saw how his bottom lip began to quiver. He was experiencing the pang of humiliation that a man experiences when he realizes his woman and his world are about to crumble down right before his eyes. His pain affected her in the worst way. She knew it was a man's bravado that would often not let them see past their egos. Right then she knew she needed to try a different approach, something subtler.

"Listen, baby," she said with compassion, her voice terse and filled with intent. "Me and my child, we can't live like this." Monique began to cry as she spoke barely above a whisper. "We gotta get out of here." She paused as she looked around the room, then continued, "This ain't livin. You're gonna have to put your pride and ego to the side." She looked at her purse. "Look, I have $2,700 in my purse and over $22,000 stashed in a shoe box in the closet." She stopped and mopped at her eyes with the palm of her hands. "Rasheed, baby, we got enough money to move outta here." Her voice was now a desperate plea. He just looked at her and shrugged his shoulders. It was hard for her to read his thoughts.

Silence. They both just stared straight ahead as dawn started to creep through the window. She could hear the rustle of air as he sharply expelled a deep breath through his nose, as if he was fighting something deep within his soul. The moment lingered awkwardly with the still quietness of lovers who had found out they did not really know each other. Monique wept. A stream of tears ran down her cheeks.

"Rasheed, I love you … but so help me God, if me and my child can escape from this hellhole then I fully intend to. Why do I have to live like this if I can help it? My mother was raised in these projects and so was I. I don't want my child to inherit this," she said, gesturing with her hand. Monique swallowed hard as she continued, "The other day at work I met a man, a white man, who is an executive at Gentlemen's. He's seen my show and wants to fly me to California for a photo shoot. If I pass I'll be in the magazine." Rasheed just looked at her with a blank stare. She continued, "I know it's a slim chance, but if I accept it, it would be the opportunity of a lifetime."

"Nude? They want to take pictures of you nude?" he asked, making a face at her.

She rolled her eyes up at the ceiling, giving him a look that might have said, "no dummy, they want me to pose in an Eskimo suit." She didn't answer his question. The baby, now getting restless, lassoed his arms around his father's neck and for some reason both father and son turned and looked at her accusingly, with the same pair of hurt-filled eyes – two against one. She couldn't help but feel guilt-ridden as she watched Rasheed kiss their son on the forehead and whisper something into his ear. Slowly, he looked up at her. The dark circles under his eyes, along with his sulking face, told her his disposition.

His voice trembled as he spoke, "Mo, I could love you if you were fat, old and gray. I could love you if you worked at a bakery for the rest of your life. I could love you with my very last breath, 'cause a nigga love you to death," he said with a frown tugging at the corners of his mouth. Hurt was smoldering in his eyes like a dark volcano about to erupt. "But I can't love you if you selling your body by dancing nude, degrading yourself for the love of money." With that, his shoulders slumped. For the first time he was exposing a side of him that she had rarely seen before. "Love shouldn't have boundaries or limitations in the form of financial expectations. You're putting a price on our love. Please don't do this to us … to me, Mo."

"What part of this don't you understand?" she interjected with steel in her voice. "I'm not selling my body, nor am I trying to hurt you and your manly ego. We need the money. I could care less about those men looking at my body. Hell, you even said it yourself, I have a beautiful body." He narrowed his eyes at her, optic slants that could kill. Instantly she regretted what she had said, all the while she wondered how to get through his thick skull to his brain. Men!

"I'm not going for it," he said loudly. The baby began to cry as he reached for his shirt and grabbed his car keys off the table and headed for the door.

"Rasheed! Rasheed! Please don't go," she pleaded with her voice filled with the dread of losing her man. Now she regretted even wanting to tell him, but in her heart and soul she knew that she had to—for the sake of her future and the opportunity at a ticket out of the ghetto. The problem now was, would she take it?

Rasheed turned around at the door. "I don't think I'm coming back," he said over his shoulder, not bothering to look her. "I need time to think about this."

"Think about what?" she volleyed in an attempt to stall him, hoping he wouldn't leave. She needed him to stay, not just now, but forever. She asked, "Are you going to watch your son tonight?"

He turned and looked at her long and hard. Finally he answered, "No," as he kissed Malcolm on his forehead and gently shoved him into her arms. Malcolm immediately reached for Rasheed, which tugged at his heart. And then on second thought, he said, "Just bring the baby by my grandmother's house tonight." With that he looked at her with bitterness in his eyes and walked outside, closing the door to their lives.

SEVEN

Jack and Gina

Gina drove the Lexus from the Galaxy Hotel. Palms sweaty, she steered the car slowly, weaving through the crowds of scattered police cars and foot patrolmen. An officer waved, signaling for her to turn his way. Gina ignored him. She could feel her heart pounding in her chest so hard that she felt nauseated. She gulped down air into her lungs as she tried to take deep breaths to soothe the urge.

The officer in the garage had ordered her to pull over to the side of the building so that she could give a description of the gunman. She drove to the corner even though the officer called for her to stop. All she could think about was Jack's last statement, *If the police open this trunk I'm coming up blasting!* She was sure he meant what he said.

Making a left at the corner, a beautiful morning dawn stared her in the face as a pack of stray dogs roamed the street, crossing directly in front of the car causing her to pump the breaks, barely coming to a stop. She thought she heard something thump in the trunk causing her to gaze up at the rear view mirror. She saw the bright lights of approaching police cars racing toward her.

She pushed the pedal to the metal. The luxury car leapt forward, pulling away so fast that it threw her neck back. At a hundred and ten miles per hour she headed down one of Brooklyn's main thoroughfares, Linden Boulevard. The early morning streets were nearly deserted. The chase was on! Gina ran through all red lights as a caravan of police cars with flashing lights followed her in hot pursuit. Up ahead to her right, she saw a speeding Amtrak train headed in the same direction as she.

She glanced in her rear view mirror again. The police cars were gaining on her with alarming speed. Suddenly Gina had an idea. It was dangerous as hell. With a determined look scrawled on her face she focused all her energy on the speeding train as she passed it.

The passengers gawked at her in horror as Gina zoomed by. Up ahead was a train crossing, with its wooden red and white gates lowered, and a red light blinking a warning sign flashing: DO NOT ATTEMPT TO CROSS! Once she felt she had distanced herself enough from the train, she stepped on the brakes causing the car to go sliding … sliding … sliding, fishtailing, as she frantically fought for control. She came to a stop in front of the train's crossing section as it approached.

The speeding locomotive was only a few yards away with the police cars even closer, fully intent on ramming her car. Then she did the impossible. She punched the accelerator and plowed through the red and white wooden gates, shattering them into pieces as she drove in front of the oncoming train. Suicide?

◊ ◊ ◊ ◊

After her death-defying escape she drove the short distance to Coney Island to a house that Jack had her rent under an alias. She parked the car in the garage. With her heart still racing, nerves on edge, she still could not believe she had pulled a stunt like that to get away. No wonder so many people got killed trying to outrun the police. The adrenaline rush along with the sheer desire to want to get away will make you do some crazy shit.

Gina walked out from the dark garage to see if the coast was clear. A light breeze played in her hair as the bright morning sun felt hot on her cheeks. To her surprise, she felt her body trembling as she looked in the sky and saw a police helicopter hovering at a safe distance. For some reason she laughed out loud and ducked back into the garage. With a feeling of exhilaration, she popped the trunk of the Lexus. Jack aimed the AK-47 at her head, ready to fire.

Damon Dice was still unconscious. He had a bleeding six-inch gash on his forehead. Jack hopped out the trunk. His clothes were soiled and dirty. Gina detected the rank smell of urine mixed with fear coming from the open trunk as she looked at Jack. Elated, she wanted to hold him.

"Bitch! What you tryna do? Get a nigga kilt?" Jack pulled the ski mask up over his face to reveal an angry expression which punctuated his wrath as he stepped toward her, causing the smile on Gina's face to freeze as she braced herself for the slap across her face she was sure to come.

"You were s'pose ta just walk away if anything went wrong!" He said angrily as he reached out and grabbed her by her throat, nearly cutting off all the air to her lungs. She had never seen him this irate in her entire life and just stood her ground, her nostrils flared and eyes bulging with a glint of defiance. "Girl, I dunno what the fuck has gotten into you since I went away. You fuckin' crazy or some shit now? And where in the fuck you get that gun? Huh?" Jack screamed in her face as he began to choke her. No answer. Her eyes began to fill with tears.

"Where did you get the fuckin' gun?" Jack asked again. "I thought I heard a fuckin' train when you was racin' up and down the street wit' me in the trunk. Girl, let me find out you was doing some dumb shit," he yelled as he looked at her face. Still no answer. He watched her green eyes rim with tears. Then suddenly something about her unnerved him as he watched her delicate bottom lip tremor. She wasn't afraid. And not just that, Gina wasn't the little girl that he had left to let the streets raise while he was in prison.

Gina spoke calmly and directly, "If you think a bitch fitna run off and leave you, you got life fucked up." She spoke audaciously, completely taking Jack by surprise. "And if you wanna know the truth, it was you that taught me this lifestyle. You," she pointed at him, "showed me how to survive on the streets and then you went away." Gina began to cry in sobs that racked her body. Jack released his grip on her throat and stared at her, stunned. "You took me out the house. You made me the woman I am today."

They heard a moan and both turned and looked down into the trunk of the car. Damon Dice was starting to regain consciousness. Jack raised his eyebrows at her, a slight warning, as he leveled the gun in Damon's direction. "When you left you told me to use my body to juice niggas out their paper. I wasn't going to sell my pussy for no crumbs."

"I also told you to take your ass back to school. I didn't tell you to start robbing niggas."

"Well, regardless of what you say, this is how you taught me to survive. While you were in prison serving a life sentence I held you down to the utmost like a thoroughbred bitch is suppose ta. All the while your so-called friends was tryna holla at me, saying you had a lifetime in the feds and you was never gettin' out." Wrinkles creased in Jack's forehead as what she was saying started to soak into his brain. Gina slid her eyes away from Jack as her hand absently rubbed at the red welt left on her neck from his grip. "I had to hustle my *ass* off to come up with the forty grand for your lawyers!"

As he looked at her he wondered how many men she had robbed to come up with that kind of cash. He thought about the diamond Rolex watch she had given him. Suddenly he squinted his eyes, frowning as she looked at him, and it dawned on him: Gina had indeed changed. It wasn't just that her body had blossomed and her features had become sharper, defining her femininity. It was her interior, her mind. She now possessed the great enigma that had baffled men since time immemorial—a woman's brain.

Just then Damon Dice opened his eyes. Jack pulled the ski mask back down over his face. "Get yo' punk ass out the trunk nigga," Jack ordered as Gina looked on. It was something about this gangster that she just loved. To watch Jack do his thing, for her, was a sight to behold.

Jack stripped Damon of all his jewelry and then his clothes. Completely naked, he made Damon lie on the gray, rusty, steel workstation in the garage. There were small pieces of wood chips all over the table as if someone had once used the table for a wood crafting. With his palms up, shivering, Damon pleaded for his life like a man about to go to the gas chamber. "Shut up nigga!" Jack ordered calmly as Gina looked on. The dank garage suddenly turned deadly quiet as in the distance a helicopter could be heard overhead. "Bitch-ass nigga, I'ma give you a betta chance than you gave me."

"Who ... who are you?"

Jack's eyes squinted and he turned his head to the side. "Didn't I tell yo' punk ass to stop talkin'," he said through gritted teeth.

Damon nodded his head up and down like a frightened kid.

"I'ma give you two choices," Jack said as he held up two fingers. He continued slowly and methodically. "You niggas left me for dead, and in so many ways, I was. Now I've risen like Lazarus and it's time for you to pay your debt to not only me, but also to society. I want the first installment in blood. You think very carefully about what I'm about to ask you." Jack wet his lips with his tongue in anticipation of what he was going to say next. "Now, you can either give me an eyeball or your rat-ass snitch tongue. That's a better choice than you gave me."

Damon Dice began to cry, sobbing as he lay on the table naked pleading for his life. "I don't even know you. Please!"

"Nigga, save the rap. Court is back in session and the jury has reached its verdict. It's either an eyeball or your snitching-ass tongue. I ain't got all day." Jack looked over at Gina as she stood impassive, unmoved by all Damon's pathetic babbling and crying. *Why couldn't niggas just die like men?* she thought to herself as she turned and walked away.

"Where you goin'?" Jack called behind her.

"To the bathroom to put on something more comfortable." She continued to walk.

Jack turned back to face Damon. "Nigga, you don't know who I am?"

Damon shook his head "no" as he sniffled tears.

"I'm the nigga you took the stand on. The nigga you lied on. Them crackas gave me a life sentence, but now I'm back! Your eyeball or your tongue?" Jack drawled and removed the ski mask. Damon Dice pissed a small stream on the table once he saw Jack Lemon's face.

◊ ◊ ◊ ◊

About thirty minutes later, Gina returned. Her mood was jubilant as if the earlier friction with Jack had never occurred. She bounced into the musty-smelling garage, ponytail swinging, hips swaying. She always made it a point to look sexy for her man, because if she didn't, she knew another woman would.

She now wore a number twenty-three throwback jersey and a pair of blue Enyce low cut coochie cutter jeans. In her right hand was a blunt filled with purple haze. In her other hand was a glass of Hennessy.

There was an oil slick on the dirty floor that almost caused her to slip as she walked through the door. A splinter of sunlight streamed through the dusty windows into the garage while Hot 97 blared from the car radio. The controversial host, Wendy Williams, was on the air talking about gay rappers who act like they're gangsters.

Gina's "oh shit" startled Jack, causing him to turn around and look at her. He had duct taped Damon's mouth shut as he lay on the ancient-looking workstation butt-ass naked. As she scanned his body, she could see that he was brutally beaten. The lower left side of his chest was caved in grimly, causing the broken bones to protrude, pushing the skin into what looked like a hellish, deformed contortion. Working her way toward his face, she saw his left eye partially dangling from the socket as blood oozed out. Muffled guttural sounds escaped from Damon's taped mouth.

"Oh my god! Oh my god!" Gina exclaimed, horrified by the sight of Damon's body.

"Girl, get the fuck outta here!" Jack said with the bloody screwdriver in his hand that he had used to gouge out Damon's eye. On the floor was a bloody brick. Jack's clothes were spattered with blood all the way down to his Timbs.

"No." Jack turned and looked at her like she was crazy. "I wanna stay and watch," Gina confirmed with her eyes wide open as she staggered, slightly nauseated. Suddenly she felt the urge to vomit. She took a long swig from the glass and frowned as the strong drink went down. That didn't help the nausea so she took a deep pull off the blunt and passed it to Jack.

Plaintively, Damon moaned as his eye found hers. He pleaded for his life. Hesitantly, she looked over at Jack and wondered what could have happened to him in prison to make him want to cause someone so much pain and suffering. As he filled his lungs with purple haze, he handed the blunt back to Gina then gave Damon his undivided attention.

"Nigga, this gonna hurt me more than it's gonna hurt you. You got one good eye left, you tryna donate that muthafucka too?" Jack threatened as sweat gleamed off his forehead. He bent down over Damon, placing the screwdriver under his good eye, tracing it. Gina looked in horror.

"I wanna know a few things from you," Jack said evenly as he pressed the screwdriver harder on his face, causing Damon to flinch uncontrollably. "First, I wanna know why you took the stand and lied on me? I also wanna know where your man G-Solo lives. And last …" Jack said, taking a deep breath as he wiped at the sweat from his brow with the back of his hand. "I wanna know who is overseeing you at the company with the seventy-five mil budget, and where you got all the cash stashed at, the dope money you was hustlin' wit'."

"What's that?" Gina asked, pointing. From the sound of her voice Jack could tell she was still intimidated by the sight of Damon's battered body. Jack turned and looked at her, annoyed. She was talking about the contraption Jack had placed on Damon's head

"It's called a vice," Jack answered as he turned the vice causing Damon to let out a muffled agonizing scream. Gingerly, Gina stepped closer, examining the nigga-rigged torture contraption. It looked like a solid steel clamp. Next to him his jewelry was piled high, like maybe someone had robbed an Egyptian mummy. As the horrid scene started to crystallize in Gina's mind, she felt a scream about to erupt in the pit of her gut. This was the real sordid world of a gangsta. Damon's eyeball lay on his cheek as blood poured slowly from the hole that was once its home. On the radio, eerily, Biggie Smalls' song, *"Ready to Die,"* played. Gina took another swig of the Henn as she willed herself not to vomit.

Jack snatched the duct tape off Damon's mouth causing him to whine. "M ... M ... My eye," Damon groaned in agony.

"I got more where that came from." Jack nudged the eyeball with the screwdriver. "Now tell me, why did you take the stand and lie on me?"

"I ... I ... I had to. They made ... me ..." Damon croaked in agony.

"Listen nigga, the faster you talk, the faster we can get you to the morgue, oops, my bad dawg. I meant to say emergency room." Jack made a face at Gina.

"The cop ... Brooks ..." Damon's voice was barely above a whisper. "Brooks ... 40 ... Vito ..." Damon's words were not clear.

"You talkin' 'bout Captain Brooks from Manhattan and the rappers 40 and Vito? Was they all behind the set up?" Jack asked, agitated because none of it made any sense. It was true them cats looked up to Jack, but 40 and Vito had major beef.

"No, Captain Brooks showed me a picture of you ... said they needed to get you off the streets." Damon winced in pain.

Jack snapped, "Nigga, on everything God love, if you complain one more time about your punk-ass eye, I'ma pull the otha one out. Now finish!"

Damon swallowed hard. "Captain Brooks and the feds wanted you, 40 and Vito off the streets."

"What, me?" Jack said out loud, as if talking to himself.

"Too ... many dudes was ... coming up ... missing. Your name was ... out there ..." Damon drawled. Jack was caught off-guard. Brooks would have to be dealt with, but how was he going to get word to 40 and Vito before the feds spun their insidious web of corruption?

For the next fifteen minutes or so Damon told all, including info about a powerful man by the name of Michael Cobin. He was over at Tony Records and responsible for how the money was spent on DieHard Records. Jack made a mental note to pay Mr. Cobin a visit, too. The white man was the Don King of the rap music industry. He could make or break a career with a simple nod of his head. Mr. Cobin was also connected to the mob; that alone made him dangerous.

"Now tell me where all that dope money at. The money you used to start the record label," Jack asked as he looked at Damon closely. He motioned for Gina to give him the blunt again. He took a long drag and blew the smoke in Damon's face.

"It's ... it's ... in the bank," Damon clamored painfully as Jack placed the screwdriver underneath his good eye caressing it as he talked.

"Nigga, you brought this shit on yourself. You didn't have to get on the witness stand and lie about me, saying I told you about a body."

"I ... I ... sorry," Damon whimpered, feeling the pressure of the screwdriver underneath his good eye. He didn't flinch when the ash from the blunt dropped on his forehead.

"Yeah, I'm sorry, too, sorry that our society is starting to breed a whole generation of niggas like you. Back in the day they had a code—keep your fuckin' mouth shut!" Jack yelled as a dribble of saliva slid from the corner of his crooked mouth. Gina bit her nails as she looked on.

"When you go to work with them crackas you can never come back, 'cause they make rats outta niggas by sellin' they soul for another man's life. And you know what hurt? It was thousands of niggas doing life just like me and we were all there because of rats like you. Nigga, you didn't even know me from a can of paint and you took the stand on me," Jack said with a menacing scowl on his face.

"They … made … meee!" Damon screeched with the passion of a man that knew his time was coming to an end.

"Uncle Toms is what they called niggas like you back in the day. Niggas that sell out their race for their own personal gain."

"No … No … No …" Damon cried.

"Son, you betta tell me where dem chips is at or I'ma dress your punk ass up in a box and send you back to your mama." Jack applied more pressure on Damon's face with the screwdriver.

"You gotta believe me! All the money is in the bank!" Damon pleaded.

"Fuck dat nigga!" Jack hissed with his top lip snarled in disdain as he shoved the screwdriver into Damon's face with so much force that blood squirted nearly a foot in the air. Damon howled in pain. Jack heard a loud thud. He turned around to see Gina sprawled on the floor. She had fainted and was lying on her back in a large oil stain. Awkwardly, one of her legs was underneath her as if it may have been broken. Her hands were extended at her sides like a bad impression of Jesus nailed to the cross. Jack shook his head. *Women. And she wanna be gangsta*, he thought.

Turning his attention back to Damon, painfully Jack thought about the promise he had solemnly made to all his homies in the joint, his heroes, the cats that stood up like men and did their time—giving the ultimate sacrifice, their lives, rather than betray the street code of ethics. Men knew that snitching on a man was no different than committing genocide because you're not just killing the man, you're killing the family, too. Somebody's father, son, brother, or husband.

As Jack looked down at Damon, he knew that he must be made an example of, but he was also smart enough to realize that his feelings were much too involved. He had done more damage to Damon than he should have, but still the dying man refused to tell him where the money was stashed. Maybe Damon didn't have the money after all but Jack knew that would be going against the grain.

All real hustlers had a stash spot. Even when they do get legit, it's in their blood – you never know when it'll be time to get ghost. The problem was making them talk. Jack had long reasoned that that was the whole purpose behind kidnapping. Ironically, in a world where discrimination was prevalent, kidnapping crossed all barriers. Men, women, children of all races were fair game for the fine art of abduction.

Frustrated, Jack turned the handle on the vice, tightening it on Damon's skull causing him to scream loud enough to wake the dead; if not the dead, the neighbors for sure. The pain was so excruciating that Damon almost welcomed death. Once again, Jack thought, *why won't this nigga tell where that cheddar at?* Jack had damn near cracked Damon's skull, and he had lost a lot of blood.

Jack had recalled reading literature somewhere dealing with a Chinese technique of torture. It involved teeth and the very sensitive nerves at the root of each tooth that are connected to the brain. Jack knew that he had to think of something fast.

At the end of the workstation was a pair of old rusty pliers. He reached over and picked them up. Taking a long drag off the blunt he looked down at Damon as thick smoke smoldered, curling out of his nose. Jack said mildly, "Open yo' mouth." Damon's one good eye stretched as wide as a silver dollar as he realized what Jack intended to do with the pliers.

"Ahh, uhm," Damon mumbled, clamping his bruised lips shut tightly, making a face to show he refused to open his mouth. Jack turned the handle to the jaws of the vice on Damon's head, causing him to open his mouth to scream. Jack shoved the pliers inside his mouth grabbing teeth and gums, twisting and pulling— a crunching sound of teeth being torn away violently from the root.

"Nigga, where dat muthafuckin' money at?" Jack yelled as he teetered on the ball of his toes, yanking and pulling. Damon experienced more pain than he had ever felt race through his brain. Finally, Jack yanked out two teeth matted with gory, blood-dripping gums that resembled a chunk of hamburger meat.

"Two down, thirty mo' to go," Jack chimed as he dropped the teeth on the floor, wiped his hands on his pant leg and prepared to go back into Damon's mouth. Damon choked and gagged as blood poured from his mouth. His lips moved, but no words came out. He was trying to speak as he drifted in and out of consciousness. Jack knew that sleep was the cousin to death.

"Mama's ... house ..." Damon muttered as he dreamed of his body at peace in a closed casket. He welcomed it.

"Nigga, what did you say?" Jack asked, leaning over, placing his ear near Damon's lips.

No answer.

Jack reached for the bloody pliers again, determined to make him talk.

"Stop! Stop!" Gina hollered. She was terrified as she wobbled while holding her stomach. "Baby, I think he's tryna tell you something."

"Well, I'm glad you finally woke the fuck up," Jack said sarcastically as he glared at her. She ignored him as she forced her eyes away from the horrific sight of Damon's bloodied body. Damn, how much pain can one man take? His face was barely recognizable as blood poured from both his mouth and eye. The right side of his chest was now caved in from where Jack had beaten him with the brick. Simply said, it was just too much for her to bear.

"The money ... is ... at my ... ma's ...house," Damon whispered in a hoarse voice. The one secret that every hustler knew he was supposed to take to his grave. Jeopardizing the life of his mother, Damon began to cough and spasm. He was choking on his own blood. Gina frowned as she felt her knees about to buckle and she held onto the nearby table for support.

"That's mo' like it, nigga," Jack said with a smirk as he took a long pull off the blunt, rubbing his hands together anxiously. It suddenly dawned on him why Damon had refused to tell where the money was—a man's love for his mother. Being the rat that he was, Damon had told on her, too, with no remorse.

To Gina, her brief exposure to the other side of the life of a real gangsta was something she would never forget. In the years to come she would adopt Jack's style of torture, just like she had been emulating everything else about her man. However, what she didn't know was, under the dirty apple standards of kidnapping and holding them for ransom policy, Jack's demonstration of torture to make them tell was the soft version. Normally body parts were sent to the family members as evidence that they were dead serious about their money. So far, Jack had not cut off any body parts, at least not yet.

Damon spilled his guts. He told Jack about the money he had stashed at his mother's house. It was a little over a million dollars. Damon pleaded the best he could for Jack not to kill his mother. Jack assured him he wouldn't, under one condition – Damon had to get on the phone and tell his mother that a woman was coming over to get the money. Damon agreed. He made the call on one of the many cellular phones that Jack had just for the occasion. The phone was stolen, so it couldn't be traced back to the caller.

To all their amazement, Damon was able to talk to his mother. Instantly his mother knew something was terribly wrong as her son gave her instructions to give the two duffel bags of money that were stashed in her basement to a woman that was coming to retrieve them. The entire time he spoke, his mother's intuition kicked in and like most mothers with a son in the game—she knew the territory. She was living proof of that. Her son had taken her out of the ghetto and placed her in a big house in the suburbs. She drove a Benz. She knew the risks of her son's lifestyle were great, but what she didn't know, as she held the phone with her hands trembling, was that it would be her last time ever speaking to her oldest child.

◊ ◊ ◊ ◊

Gina put on a disguise – a blond wig, dark shades and a baseball cap – and walked up the street to catch a cab to go pick up the money. One thing was for certain, Damon's mom would never call the police unless she was sure that her son was in harm's way. With the help of the cab driver, Gina lugged the money to the cab. When Damon's mom asked about her son with tears in her eyes, Gina could not dare look the woman in her face as her mind flashed back to the horrific scene at the garage with Jack standing over Damon holding a bloodied screwdriver. "I'ma dress your punk-ass up and send you back home to you mama in a box," she remembered him saying.

"Yes, ma'am, your son will be back home soon. He just had a hangover, told me to come," Gina lied, not bothering to look at the older woman. After she had picked up the money, everything went as planned. Now came the really hard part – the takeover of DieHard Records.

They say one of the worst things you can do is lock a man up with him having nothing but time to think. Jack had carefully orchestrated an elaborate plan. Now all he had to do was focus on the key players: Michael Cobin and G-Solo. Jack knew that G-Solo would temporarily replace Damon Dice and that Cobin would be overseeing the operations of DieHard until they found a replacement. Jack needed to move fast on G-Solo. With all the helpful information he had gotten from Damon Dice, he went along and put his plan in motion. He was going to have to recruit Gina one last time for the most dangerous task of all.

Jack contemplated his plans as Damon lay on the workstation table looking like a human science project gone bad. His lips moved, gurgling blood, as he struggled to talk. Jack bent down, nearly placing his eye to his mouth.

"Don't … leave … me … like this … kill …me …" Damon pleaded plaintively in a dry hoarse voice as blood dripped from his ears. The claw-like clamps of the vice grip on his head were so tight that it was slowly crushing his skull. As Damon begged to be killed, Jack furtively nodded his head with sympathy as he reached down to the floor retrieving a pair of shears used in lawn mainte-nance. The sharp instrument was for cutting through thick bush but Jack had another purpose in mind.

"I'ma need one mo' thang from you," Jack said matter-of-fact-ly, ignoring Damon's pleas for death. "I want your lyin'-ass tongue for a kind of souvenir, a special memento to send to the good Captain Brooks and the rest of them hot-ass niggas to let them know that us real gangstas is still runnin' shit."

"You ... fuckin' crazy!" Damon spat between breaths.

"I know, I know," Jack said in a singsong voice, "and that's why I promise you I'ma send a lot of niggas to join you." With that, Jack turned the vice causing Damon to open his mouth for the last time. He violently shoved the shears into Damon's mouth in order to cut his tongue out.

Afterward, tired and bloody, Jack needed a handsaw and some garbage bags. He was determined to make a grand statement: Keep your fucking mouth shut!

EIGHT

Rasheed Smith

. Rasheed drove an old, raggedy, brown '86 Ford Mercury. The passenger door was dented with rust spots underneath the paneling. He affectionately referred to his car as "The Batmobile." Disdainfully, his girl Monique called his hoopty a piece of raggedy-ass junk. For some reason, whenever she said it, it always struck his funny bone and gave him a good hearty laugh.

When they were in high school, Rasheed would pick her up from school during forth period lunch. She would be embarrassed as hell to be seen getting into his raggedy car but Rasheed was the captain of the basketball team. Tall and lanky with a mane of curly hair and dimples and skin the color of roasted peanuts, Rasheed Smith could have had any girl he wanted in high school. Even back then, scouts, along with the media, were coming to watch his games. Rasheed was gifted in all sports, but he chose basketball, regardless of whether or not basketball chose him.

At fifteen, he was already 6 foot 5 and growing. Every major college in the United States was trying to recruit him. One even offered his grandmother money. She flatly turned it down. She had earned her profession as a nurse the hard way—making it through college during the Jim Crow era of blatant racism and "whites only" signs. But in some ways that had made her stronger and she wouldn't expect anything less from her grandchild. Call it Black pride, but she was determined that Rasheed would stand on his own two legs and not be given benefits because he was a gifted athlete.

◊ ◊ ◊ ◊

Rasheed drove away from practice with a heavy heart and dampened sprits. As usual, the media was there snapping away, taking pictures of him. Rasheed even noticed French Stuart, the NBA scout for the Chicago Bulls. The draft was less than two months away, but all Rasheed could think about was Monique dancing naked. That day, Rasheed was all thumbs. He couldn't catch a pass, his man kept beating him off the dribble and most of his shots were air balls. The one day that he needed to impress, he looked pathetic.

After practice, Coach Jones chewed his ass out and told him to meet him in his office. Hesitantly, Rasheed knocked on the coach's door. A voice from the other side summoned him.

The coach was a middle-aged man in his forties. He had a cherubic face with deep aquamarine eyes that always appeared to smile at the corners. His neatly cut salt and pepper hair was starting to recede at the top. With a wave of his hand he gestured for Rasheed to take a seat at the front of his desk.

The coach was seated behind a large oak desk that looked like it dated back to the ancient civil war days. The desk was cluttered with papers and other items, including a coffee mug with the school's emblem on it. The coach cleared his throat as Rasheed removed a folder off the metal folding chair and sat down. He felt uncomfortable. The coach cleared his throat again and pulled in a deep breath like a man about to enter uncharted territory with words.

"Son, you know my job is to basically teach you the fundamentals of basketball, also the importance of team sports."

Rasheed nodded his head. The coach sighed audibly as he reeled back in his chair.

"Today you played like shit!" the coach said, raising his voice and pointing a finger at Rasheed. "Once you realize you have a gift, you enhance that gift. Not just that, you must make it a habit to practice like it's your work. These people invest millions of dollars in a person's athletic ability and you sho'll better be able to produce. Today may have been your last chance." The coach's voice was hard like steel. Rasheed's shoulders slumped as he dropped his head looking at the floor.

"I'm having family problems," Rasheed muttered.

"Kid, is it your grandma?" The coach asked with concern.

"Naw."

"Your son?" the coach asked with his brow raised. Rasheed swallowed the lump in his throat and answered, "It's my girl. She started dancing naked."

"Whaaat! That's what you're all worried about?" The coach screeched as he stood with surprising quickness and walked around the desk to grab a handful of Rasheed's T-shirt.

"That's what this is all about? You're worried 'cause your girl is stripping? Let me tell you something and you better not ever forget this," the coach huffed, red-faced. "A woman will do anything in the world when it comes to taking care of her child," he said, looking at Rasheed as he released his hold on Rasheed's T-shirt. "Listen son, you can't really blame her. Trust me when I say she could be doing something a whole lot worse, not to say that stripping isn't bad, but, if you want her to stop providing a livelihood for her child by dancing, you need to start earning some money. Get signed by the NBA and I promise you, if she loves you, she'll stop dancing. Other than that, self-preservation is the first law of nature."

"But not like that, coach," Rasheed said brokenly.

"Yes, like that, and that's why a man will never understand the ways of a woman. Don't even try it son, it will drive you crazy." The coach chuckled. "Just take what I have given you today and remember, the climate is right for change. You," he pointed at Rasheed, "just got to make it happen."

The two men just looked at each other before Coach Jones looked at the calendar on his desk. "We've got one more practice before the big game. You better show up. Your future depends on it." The coaches were like mentors and Coach Jones was no exception.

At least now Rasheed felt he had a solution—get drafted into the NBA. It was a lot easier said than done. Still, after he left the coach's office, all he could think about was the love of his life, Monique Cheeks. As he drove through traffic, he ruminated on her poignant words, "… and yo' ass ain't helpin' me none!"

Rasheed slapped the dashboard. "Shit!" He cursed as he thought about what the coach had said. He looked at his hands on the steering wheel, thought about all those white folks that came to watch him entertain them. Could what the coach said have been true?

NINE

It was such a beautiful day that Rasheed decided to drive to Coney Island. He knew an Arab-owned store that had a sale on ice-cold beer. As he stopped at a red light at a busy intersection, he gazed up at the sky. Terry-cloth clouds lingered, contrasted by a hue of heavenly blue, the kind of picturesque splendor that makes a man wonder about the crafty architect of the universe. Of God?

As Rasheed sat at the light he was sure to keep one foot on the gas, manipulating the pedal and the other foot on the brake, or else his old hoopty would stall. A homeless person, a vagabond, pushed a shopping cart across the street. The old woman must have had on six coats and other articles of clothing. It was close to one hundred degrees in the sweltering heat.

Rasheed's old car sputtered and coughed. "Come on baby, don't you act up on me!" Rasheed muttered under his breath as he felt a ball of sweat running down his chest. Hot weather and old cars make for bad days. Just then, he looked up into the sweltering heat to see what looked like a mirage walking across the street in front of his car. He blinked his eyes as the ardent sun partially blinded him. Rasheed cupped his hand over his forehead to shield the sun.

He could recognize that Brooklyn walk anywhere. It was more like a bounce from side to side, arms swaying, pants sagging, shoulders thrust forward, thug style, like a man on a mission. That was his best friend, crazy-ass Jack Lemon, but how? It couldn't be. Jack had a lifetime in the pen for a lot of bodies that were never discovered, but still he was convicted by other people's testimonies.

Rasheed blew the horn frantically and damn near scared Jack Lemon out of his skin, causing him to jump nearly a foot off the ground as he reached for the pistol at his side. The light turned green. Rasheed jumped out of the car and called his friend's name as he smiled broadly. A look of relief washed over Jack's face as he took his hand out of his pocket and flashed Rasheed a smile. They met each other in the middle of the street and rough neck hugged in a jovial dance as cars tooted their disapproval. Jack gave the car behind them the middle finger as Rasheed opened the car door for him since the passenger's door didn't open. Jack slid inside the car—just as the vehicle stalled at the light.

"Fuck!" Rasheed cursed, hitting the dashboard and making a face of a spoiled kid, causing Jack to erupt in laughter.

It's good to see my old friend again, Jack thought as he looked up to see a huge black man with a short-cropped afro and thick mustache. He had a stump of a cigar in his mouth. In his eyes shined the pure rage and pent-up hate which New York motorists are notorious for. The big man peered inside the car looking Jack directly in the eye.

"If you don't hurry up and move this piece of shit I'ma—"

Jack pulled up his shirt and flashed the chrome-plated nine.

"Yo, son! Don't make me bust a cap in yo' fat ass over some stupid shit. Now fall back!"

The big man's eyes got as big as saucers. "I didn't mean any harm, sir," he shuddered in an humble tone. Quickly, he backpedaled, stumbled and nearly fell as he walked back to his black SUV. Rasheed turned the ignition and the motor fired to life.

"Nigga, you still got this raggedy-ass car?" Jack chided his old friend in a poor attempt to play off what had just happened with the big man.

Rasheed pulled away from the red light, leaving a trail of gray smoke behind. Rasheed just shrugged his shoulders as he looked in the rear view mirror and made a turn at the corner. Jack didn't even have to tell him what to do—keep his eyes on that black SUV. They both watched the vehicle as it drove straight ahead. Rasheed sighed in relief as he turned to Jack and smiled genuinely.

"Damn son, I didn't think I would ever see you again." Rasheed smiled and punched Jack in the shoulder. "When did you get out?"

"A few weeks ago," Jack said as he glanced in the passenger's mirror.

"Damn, and you didn't holla at my fam?" Rasheed questioned with a frown. He was barely able to contain his disappointment as he glanced over at Jack and saw what looked like blood on his pants and Timbs.

"You know a nigga got mad love for ya, but you know how the streets is with all these niggas tellin' now-a-days. Niggas find out I'm back and they get larcenous 'cause they know my resume is impeccable for putting in work in this town. This time I'm on the element of some surprise-type shit."

Rasheed understood, nodded his head and made a left at the corner.

"Man, it's good to see you. I still can't believe this." Rasheed beamed with joy and then added, "I'm about to enter the NBA draft."

"Get the fuck outta here," Jack gidded.

"No shit." Rasheed smiled proudly.

"You got an agent?"

Rasheed made a face as he shook his head "no."

"I'ma buy you an agent. What's that waterhead dude name … ah … ah …" Jack thought for a few seconds. "David Stern!" he said and snapped his fingers. Rasheed cracked up in laughter.

"Man, David Stern is the Commissioner of the NBA."

"What the fuck ever. You just as good as Kobe. You just need a shot at the pros."

"Yeah, me and about a million other brothas," Rasheed acknowledged as he hit the brakes to avoid hitting some kids who ran into the street. The car stopped at a red light. Jack peered over at the gas gauge.

"Damn son! You driving 'round on fumes in this bucket." Rasheed ignored him as the car started to shake and sputter. A chocolate sista with generous curves strutted by pushing a baby stroller. She wore a floral sundress with laced shoulder straps. She made eye contact with Rasheed and smiled. Both men watched the sensuous sway of her hips as her plump behind moved from side to side.

"Yo, son, shorty lookin' for a baby daddy. With an ass like that she won't have to look too hard." Jack waved at the young woman. She waved back, smiling like she knew him. The two old friends erupted in laughter as Rasheed pulled away from the red light.

Moments later, as they rode, Rasheed turned to Jack and asked, "Where you headed?"

"To the hardware store to pick up a few items."

"Items like what?"

"A handsaw, cement and some garbage bags."

Rasheed turned and looked at his friend just as an ambulance raced by, startling both of them. High in the celestial sky, a Goodyear blimp sailed by. Jack smelled burning oil and wondered how Rasheed could ride around in a raggedy-ass car like this. But it touched him as he thought about his best friend's loyalty.

"Yo, B, I got the magazines and all the articles you sent to me on your scoring titles. Oh, and thanks for the chips you sent me, too."

Embarrassed, Rasheed felt his cheeks flush. The most money that he could ever send was twenty dollars at a time. Jack read his best friend's thoughts. "Listen my nigga, don't ever get it twisted. You and my shorty Gina was the only muthafuckas that held me down. I got mad love fo' y'all. It's cats in the joint that don't get no mail, no one comes to visit them, people won't even accept a phone call, basically they don't get no love. When you sent me those twenty dollars with pictures of your shorty and the baby, that shit touched me right here, B," Jack said, pounding his chest with his fist so hard it sounded like a bass drum. "You'd have to experience the shit to know what I'm sayin'. Shit was crazy. They had niggas packed in cells the size of a small closet, while up the street they had animal activists picketing at the zoo, talking about cruelty toward animals 'cause the gorilla's space was not big enough. Should have been cruelty against niggas. Cats in there serving life for twenty dollars worth of dope." Jack made a face as he shook his head like he was reliving a bad moment in his mind.

Rasheed parked the car in the Ace Hardware store parking lot. The humidity was so high that you could see the heat vapors rising from the scorched concrete. A youngster with neatly French braided hair, dressed in an orange apron with Ace Hardware stenciled across it, raced by as he collected shopping carts.

Rasheed turned off the ignition. The old car sputtered as the engine continued to run. Jack snickered, "Damn son, you want me to get out and shoot this muthafucka?" Rasheed peered over at him, his mind elsewhere. Finally, the car turned off.

With a serious expression on his face, Rasheed spoke. "What was it like in there?"

Jack turned his head away from Rasheed as he gazed out the window. "Death before dishonor is dead. It's legalized slavery now. One nigga get popped by the feds, he tell on twenty other niggas, most of them he don't even know. The judge told me in the courtroom, if I didn't cooperate he was going to give me life. That old cracka did just that when an all-white jury convicted me of five homicides where they never found any bodies."

"How did you beat the case?" Rasheed asked.

"Gina got me a lawyer. I beat it on appeal. They arrested me with an illegal search warrant."

"It figures," Rasheed huffed.

"They got factories in all the federal prisons," Jack continued. "The judges have investments in the factories like some kind of stock. They give niggas these big-ass fines that they know they can't pay and send them to work in the factory. Dudes working twenty-four-hour days, making less than four dollars."

"Damn, why won't the public or the people that can do something about it, do something?" Rasheed asked innocently.

"I dunno. Niggas on some bling-bling time and all the churches is exploiting so much money. Shit, in prison, ninety percent of rats claim to be Christians. Sayin' Jesus told them to go back and testify and shit. Don't care who they tell on."

"Get the fuck outta here," Rasheed said as he opened the door to let some fresh air in.

"One thing I did learn in prison, religion and the so called 'Holy Bible' are the biggest brainwashing tools on the earth. Fuck, was we heathens in Africa before they brought us over here and gave us Christianity? Teaching that bullshit about you gotta die to go to heaven where the streets is paved with gold. If that was true them crackas would be lined up killin' each other just to get there. Instead, they lined up killin' us, sending us to mythical heaven, while they enjoy themselves right here on earth." Rasheed raised his eyebrow like he wanted to say something. "A white man's heaven is a black man's hell."

"Man, you know I'm a Christian," Rasheed said, disturbed.

Jack retorted, "Nigga, you the one who asked me what prison was like." Just then a beautiful butterfly with an array of pastel colors – purple, blue and yellow – flew into the car. With surprising quickness Jack smashed it with the heel of his hand against the windshield. Startled, Rasheed looked at the wounded butterfly as its wings still fluttered. "Did you know that 'God' spelled backward is 'dog,' and that we all are gods in our own way? If need be, a nigga cross me, I could kill another man just like I killed that bug," Jack said ominously, causing Rasheed to shudder. As he looked at his best friend, it dawned on him that Jack had indeed changed. He wondered what could have happened to him to make him adopt such a mentality.

"Did you know that Jesus was a black man, a revolutionary? And that white men, the Romans, killed him 'cause they said he conspired against them? Just like they killin' niggas in the joint now-a-days and charging them with conspiracy. In John, Chapter

10 of your Christian Bible it says, 'Ye are gods.' Jesus said that when the Jews were getting ready to stone him for blasphemy, for claiming he was God."

"Man, you trippin'. You done let that place get inside your head," Rasheed said.

"Son, we all got God-type qualities in us. We just gotta find them. Ain't nothing wrong with religion, especially Christianity, but it has to be practiced from a black perspective."

"Why is that?" Rasheed asked, wishing he had never asked the initial question.

"'Cause the people in the Bible was black, and they don't want you to know that. That's why crackas use fear and God in religion, all in one."

"Man, what the hell does fear and religion got to do with you being god?" Rasheed questioned, with his brow knotted in frustration. Jack sighed audibly as he placed his foot on the dashboard, giving his friend a weary look like, "you just don't get it."

"Peep game, playa. All this religious shit started out of Egypt. The Bible is only six thousand years old. Egypt is in Africa. It's over hundreds of thousands of years old—"

Rasheed interrupted, "Damn nigga, what you is, a historian now?"

Jack glowered at him with a face that said "don't disturb me." "Naw, I'm no fuckin' historian. I just read a lot while I was in the joint. It's true what the crackas say about us. If you wanna hide something, put it in a book."

"I hope you read something other than history books 'cause you 'bout ready to start selling bean pies," Rasheed joked in a bad attempt to ease the tension that Jack created with his new far-fetched prison theories.

"Yeah, I remember this one book I read where some lame was quoting Machiavelli. Don't get me wrong, he was a sharp cat, but niggas read that shit and took it literally. He said, 'It is better to be feared than loved. Fear you can control, love you can't.' That's some straight bullshit! There's a lot of good niggas in the joint with six-number release dates. Son, don't never forget this, real niggas don't deal in emotions. Period! Neither fear, nor love, because fear is what started witness protection. Fear is what makes good niggas go bad, flip the script, turn snitch on they men," Jack said vehemently, his face full of anger. As Rasheed looked at him he was now certain that Jack had spent too much time in the joint.

"Son, I left a lot of good niggas in the joint. I know you ain't feelin' me on this. You probably think a nigga crazy buggin', but just ask Boy George and McGriff and all them niggas that was down with the Preacher Man Crew what fear will do to a nigga when them crackas start talking 'bout a lifetime in the joint or tell. See, like I was sayin', fear, religion and God are all used the same."

"Man, I don't know!" Rasheed said, throwing up his hands. "Y'all cats go to the joint, read a few books and become chain gang scholars or some shit." A Mexican woman walked by. She glanced in the car and held her purse tightly as she picked up her pace. "I'm just tryna raise my seed, be a man, do the right thing," Rasheed confessed somberly.

A yellow school bus passed slowly with children playfully laughing and screaming out the windows. Jack smiled dreamily and pointed at the bus. A beautiful little black girl with two pony-tails, hair parted down the middle, frantically waved at them.

"That's our future right there. Them babies. I'm willing to die for what I believe in. Son, shit gotta change. We gotta start being self-sufficient and independent. We need to start running all them Arabs and Chinese stores out our communities."

"Jack, you buggin' for real now."

"No I ain't. Shit, they don't spend no money in our stores, nor will they let you put a store in they hood 'cause they smart enough to know betta."

Rasheed felt his heart skip a beat as his eyes roamed down Jack's pant legs. Once again he wondered about the blood and was tempted to ask. Instead, he used another tactic.

"What do you think about brothas killin' brothas?" Rasheed asked as he glanced at the butterfly on the windshield. It had stopped moving.

Jack fanned hot air with his hand as he considered the thought. "This is how it works in the so-called American diplomatic society. You got the rich and the po'. Well, the rich, they steal from everybody and the po', we steal from each other, but that shit fitna change. All these modern day Uncle Tom-ass niggas is going to be dealt with. Back in the day they had a code of ethics – keep yo' muthafuckin' mouth shut and give somethin' back to the hood or else get a vicious beat down, and the next time you fuck up they leave you leakin'."

"Why you wanna kill black folks?" Rasheed interrupted, barely able to contain his distress over his friend's state of mind.

"'Cause we can't keep blaming this shit on the crackas when niggas is gettin' millions of dollars now-a-days and ain't investing it in our children's futures."

"You can't change that," Rasheed countered. "Niggas like to dress and buy fancy cars." Rasheed glanced over at Jack. He had his eyes closed as if in a trance. When he opened his mouth to speak it was eerie.

"Sometimes … sometimes when I close my eyes I hear voices, see faces, a river of blood, screams." As Rasheed looked at Jack, a tiny drop of sweat glistened as it cascaded down his forehead onto the bridge of his nose and teetered there. "I … hear my father's voice." Jack's lower lip trembled as he frowned, reliving the moment in the dark crevice of his mind.

It was 1975. Jack Lemon was a small child. He and his dad had stopped by the Black Panther branch in Harlem, where his father was a member. They intended to spend some quality time together that day. They had only stopped at the Harlem branch to take some food to the brothas and sistas. Jack's father was the Minister of Defense for that particular Panther branch. It was a festive occasion. Jack had on his black beret like all the Black Panthers were wearing at the time. Barely able to look over the pool table, Jack ran, enjoying himself with the rest of the children. As was typical, most of the Panther members were barely in their twenties. However, that never stopped them from debating about politics and laws that affected their plight as a people.

The James Brown song, "*Say It Loud—I'm Black and I'm Proud,*" played while the young adults debated and the children ran and played. There was a loud knock at the door. Suddenly, the music died and panic-filled voices could be heard outside where the police lined the streets in full force. The entire street had been surrounded as people gawked out their windows, waiting for the drama to unfold. It was the police against the Black Panthers.

"Come out with your hands up and no one will be harmed," the police demanded from a loudspeaker. Jack Lemon's father, known as Big Jack, went to the door and opened it wide enough for the police to see that he was unarmed.

"Pig, if you have a warrant to arrest any one of us, let me see it. If not, you're in violation of our constitutional rights."

"YOU! Black male standing in the doorway! Disrobe and come out with your hands in the air where we can see them! This will be your last warning," the officer bellowed orders. As the police spoke, inside the Black Panther's headquarters, members armed themselves in preparation to go to war. Young men and women determined to live or die for their human rights and to be treated as the Constitution of the United States says. Besides, they really knew what the police were doing. This was an old police tactic used to humiliate and harass blacks. The same tactic was being deployed all over the United States to eliminate all pro-Black movements that the government deemed a threat because young blacks had started resisting police brutality and other forms of oppression.

Lil' Jack watched his dad as the moment lulled with suspense, his eyes barely above the pool table. As Jack spoke to the police, a pretty pecan-colored woman with a big Afro stood guard as she had been trained.

"Pig, we got women and children in here. We ain't lookin' for no trouble. If you got a warrant that says we're in violation of any of your laws we'll honor that, but—"

POW! A single shot rang out. Jack watched as his father keeled over in what looked like slow motion. The blood poured from the gaping hole in his neck. His father's dark sunglasses caromed off the wall across the room. The sista with the big Afro opened fire in self-defense as she screamed at the top of her lungs, "Die muthafucka, die!" With marksmanship skill, she killed two officers. Soon a fusillade of shots rang out.

After an eight-hour gun battle with the authorities, the National Guard had to be called in. Twenty-seven Black Panthers massacred – men, women and children. The woman with the big Afro was a revolutionary by the name of Adia Shakur. She placed Lil' Jack inside of a metal cabinet, saving his life. Somehow she escaped. They were the sole survivors. To that day the government had a million dollar bounty out on her head, dead or alive.

Jack opened his eyes. "Sometimes ... I see my father's blood. I know y'all think I'm crazy, but have you ever seen a product of its environment? It looks like me."

"So, I guess you must be on some revolutionary time now, huh?"

"Whatever." Jack smacked his lips. "All I know is muthafuckas gonna start dying."

"Have you seen Damon Dice yet?" Rasheed asked.

"Naw, I ain't seen dude," Jack lied as he peered at Rasheed, eyes full of mischief. "But in due time, I'm sure he'll pop up some place."

"What did he say against you at your trial?"

"Nothing that an eye and a tongue couldn't pay fo'," Jack responded.

"Huh?" Rasheed muttered, confused.

"Listen, I'ma keep it gangsta wit' 'cha 'cause I fucks wit' 'cha like dat. I just hit a lick on some shit that I've been plotting for years. And you know what, it feels good! Wasn't it Tupac that said that revenge is sweeter than pussy?"

Rasheed raised his brow at Jack.

"Son," Jack lowered his voice to a conspiratorial tone as he leaned toward him. "Shit fitna get hectic. Niggas gonna start dying. I caught a nigga slippin', so I gripped. Know what I mean? I'ma bring the pain in the worst way and the residue ... well ..." Jack had a menacing grimace on his face. "You just stand the fuck back and let me do me."

"Shit, man. You know that I got your back," Rasheed replied.

"Naw, you just stay in school and let me do my thang." He patted Rasheed on the back. "I made my first mil today and it's more where that came from."

"What?"

"Yup, and it was as easy as pulling teeth." Jack added his own personal humor as he thought about how he had punished dude. "Tomorrow I'm gonna stop by your grandma's and we going shoppin' for a new whip for you." He looked at Rasheed's ride and continued, "Son, you gotta get rid of this ancient-ass bucket."

Rasheed gave his friend a quick once-over, like maybe he had doubts about Jack's tale of newly found riches. Once again he swept his eyes over Jack's gear. Jack picked up on his thoughts.

"Nigga, don't let my appearance fool ya! These my work clothes. Chuck-a-nigga-in-the-trunk clothes. Ain't much change. I'm still dressing niggas in cement shoes, sendin' them back to they maker if they don't break bread. No mo' crumbs this time 'cause I got a Brooklyn crew of niggas that hungry, know what I mean?" Jack drawled.

"Shit done changed a lot since you been gone, Jack. Them cats got big bodyguards."

"Gina been sayin' the same shit about 'shit done changed.' Shit, as long as niggas still bleed like me, ain't a damn thang changed," Jack said and winked his eye as he took his foot off the dashboard. He then reached into his pocket and retrieved a large wad of cash. Rasheed's jaw dropped as he looked at all the money. Jack peeled off five one-hundred dollar bills and extended his hand. "Here, give this to Monique." All Rasheed could do was smile.

◊ ◊ ◊ ◊

Afterward, Rasheed dropped Jack off at an old, dilapidated house and watched Jack's Brooklyn gait as he bounced, shopping bags swinging from side to side with his determined strides.

As Rasheed drove away, for some reason his mind drifted back to Monique. The confrontation was inevitable. She was scheduled to pick up the baby that night at his grandmother's house. Rasheed felt the five hundred dollars in his pocket and thought about her posing nude for the magazine and all the money that it could bring. He was forced to admit, the money sounded tempting.

TEN

The Gentlemen's Club

In Brooklyn, the wind moaned outside like a million pipes playing as the air gusted against the window panes. Monique Cheeks sat in her dressing room chair looking at herself in the mirror. She was clad only in her lace panties and bra. An old school R. Kelly CD played from the other side of the room. As she stared at herself in the mirror, she brought a delicate hand to her face, tracing her cheek and the bags that were starting to form under her eyes. She felt she was too young for this stress. For the past month, self-doubt and despair had consumed her. Outside her window, gaudy lightning ricocheted across the sky as torrential rains flooded the city.

Today had been one of them days, she realized as her mind reflected back to Rasheed. She didn't mean to hurt him the way she did. After she got off work she was scheduled to meet him at his grandmother's house to discuss their future, or perhaps their break up. Rasheed was all the man that she could ever want—the only man that she had shared her body with, the only man that she had ever loved.

Her eyes got teary as she stared at her crestfallen face in the mirror. She thought about Malcolm, their three-year-old son. He was the spitting image of his father. The last time she took him to the bathroom, Malcolm urinated all over the toilet seat as he tried to shake his wee-wee, emulating his father. Monique smiled through her teary eyes, then the smile waned, turning upside down as she thought about Rasheed. It caused her heart to pound in her chest. If he would only just let her dance one more month

67

she felt they would have enough money to move into a nice neighborhood, and she could go back to college. She knew the photo shoot for the magazine was a long shot, like Rasheed's dream of entering the pros. Hell, he had a better chance than she did. But still Rasheed was being stubborn and too damn unreasonable. She made a face in the mirror.

"Rasheed!" she screamed at the mirror. Just then she heard the loud roar of applause as a wave of clamor rose. The noise, the applause, continued for so long Monique had to go take a peek to see who the competition was getting all the noise on her stage. She threw on her robe and hurried out to catch the show.

To her utter surprise, the place was jam-packed. Monique wasn't the only dancer to come out from the dressing room. All the other girls had come up to find out what the loud commotion was all about as well. The women, like everybody else in the club, gawked at the stage in awe of the performance. Monique had to stand on her tiptoes just to get a view of the show. On stage a beautiful array of colorful lights flashed as G-Unit's "*Magic Stick*" played. It was Monique's first time ever hearing rap music played in the club and the lighting was new, too.

What she saw on stage blew her mind. It was the white girl who had come to her rescue when Tatyana and her girls set her up to get jumped. The white girl had an audacious body like a thick black woman with butt for days. Monique was rattled because she still couldn't recall the girl's name. On stage, nude, except for a silver and black glittery thong, her nimble body was deep copper toned, covered with a filigree of silvery sparkles. She walked on her hands, adroitly displaying the skillful acrobatics of a talented gymnast, as she approached the pole in the center of the stage. With her thick, brawny thighs she used her buttock muscles as she spun on the heel of one hand grabbing the pool with the mounds of her succulent butt cheeks, causing a ripple of gasps to erupt throughout the audience.

Everyone was astounded, including Monique, as she watched the white girl steal her show. While still on her hands, she did a scissor move spreading her legs wide, the lips of her vagina displayed like crown jewels in the luminous stage light as she made her butt bounce doing upside down push-ups on the pole – something that required enormous strength and agility. Then, she gracefully wrapped her long legs around the pole. In suspended animation she removed her hands from the floor and raised, using only her legs, until her body was in an upright position. Then she spread her legs, grinding her crotch against the pole as she slid down. The lights went dim and the audience went wild. Even Monique was forced to applaud. Money was tossed at the stage.

Suddenly there was a loud clap of thunder and the lights went out, along with the music. The normally passive crowd started to get rowdy. The emergency lights came on. The tempestuous weather had knocked out the electricity, forcing the rest of the performances to be cancelled for the night.

Monique walked back to her dressing room in a funk. The canceling of the show meant she would make no money. "Damnit!" She couldn't get the awesome stage show out of her mind. *What is that girl's name?* she pondered as she walked back into her dressing room and closed the door behind her. "Georgia Mae? Yeah, that's it," she said out loud. *What kind of crazy ass name is that?* she thought as she began to dress. Everyone called her "Game" for short, and she understood why. The few times Monique had spoken to Game were only in passing and she had wanted to go to a black club and meet some brothas. She must have made it because she could dance her ass off. Monique had never seen a performance like that before; and not just that either, Game had a body like a sista with one of them big round ghetto booties.

There was a knock at Monique's door followed by a loud clap of seismic thunder that made her flinch. The lights blinked causing R. Kelly to skip a note on the CD player. She plodded to the door, now fully dressed, opening it. To her surprise the white girl, Game, stood outside. Monique smiled as she invited her in. Game's blond shoulder-length hair was cut short in the front into ringlets that stylishly hung above her eyebrows. She had a beautiful oval face with enchanting green eyes.

"Fire, I need to talk you about something," Georgia Mae said, calling Monique by her stage name.

Monique twisted her lips to the side of her face as she said, "Girl, I know you ain't come in here on this messed up night to ask me about taking you to some black club so you can meet some men." The two of them giggled. In some ways the two women were compatible. They were both considered outcasts. Mostly it was by choice. Just as Monique had started disassociating herself from the rest of the women who worked at the club, so had Georgia Mae. There was just something about her that Monique couldn't put her finger on. Georgia Mae was sophisticated and she dressed real fly in all the latest designer clothes. However, when it came to picking men, she really didn't have a choice. Black men chose her because of her freaky round behind, shapely curves, taut waistline and large breasts. At 5 foot 9, she was considered a brick house that could give any black woman a run for her money.

Georgia Mae wasn't all body; she had ample brains. She graduated from Harvard with a 3.97 GPA. She had a Jurist Doctorate in Law and a Ph.D. in Psychology. Since the age of three, her mother had entered her in every beauty pageant and talent show she could find. It was as if her mother were trying to relive her failed beauty pageant years through her child. At the age of eighteen, Georgia Mae Hargrove entered the Miss USA Pageant. She came in a disappointing third place.

Her mother felt she knew why she didn't win. It was because her daughter did not have the physique like most of the white women she was in competition with. However, her physique mimicked those of the few black women that were chosen as finalists, and truth be told, Miss USA wasn't ready for a white woman with a black woman's body. Georgia Mae had enough when her mother suggested she have a surgery to reduce the size of her behind. Instead of concentrating on her physical assets, she decided to develop herself mentally and she enrolled in college. That was also the time the dancing bug bit her.

In college she met a smooth brotha by the name of Ozzie King, known to his friends as Big O. One day as she lay on the campus grass reading a book, he walked up and sat down beside her and made a comment about the book she was reading. She instantly found him strikingly handsome and intelligent, not to mention funny. Two weeks later he stole her virginity along with her heart. He introduced her to the world of strip club dancing, rap videos and eventually cocaine. All of Georgia Mae's life she had secretly been attracted to black men. It wasn't just black men, it was the culture – the music, the food, the dance, the style and most definitely, the sex.

On the other hand, it seemed like white men shunned her because of her curvaceous figure, one that they would expect on a black woman.

Monique scanned Georgia Mae and saw that she was dressed sexy and provocatively in a cream-colored Baby Phat jacket with matching jeans. Underneath she wore a vanilla lace see-through blouse that highlighted her double-D breasts, along with her diamond navel ring and heart-shaped tattoo. Her feminine high-heeled Timberland boots seemed to accentuate her long bowlegs, exposing an eye-opening sensuous gap between her thighs. As Monique took in the shapely curves of the white girl she couldn't help but feel attracted to her in some way, and for a fleeting moment she wondered if she could be gay. She quickly flung the stupid idea out of her mind. Georgia Mae was just one of them rare crazy-sexy-cool white chicks that could comfortably blend right in with the sistas.

As Monique looked at Georgia Mae she noticed her damp hair, fringed at the ends like she had just gotten out of the shower. Once again, Monique thought of the several occasions she had hinted at going out partying together. She was half-expecting her to ask again as she gazed up at her, but for some uncanny reason, images of the stage show flashed in Monique's mind. She couldn't help but ask, "Georgia Mae, girl, where did 'ja learn how to pop your coochie like that?"

The white girl smiled brightly. "Ever since I was a little girl my mother had me entering mostly black talent shows because she said black folks had natural soul and that made them the best in the world at singin' and dancin'. She said if I could compete with them I could compete with anybody."

"Did you win any?" Monique asked out of curiosity.

Georgia Mae made a face and answered, "I lost more than I won, but at seven years old, growing up around black kids was a positive experience for me." For the first time Monique noticed the beauty mark above her right cheek as Georgia Mae continued to talk.

"My mother said that Elvis Presley used to sneak backstage and watch the blacks perform. He would steal all their routines. That's how he got so famous."

"Did your mama tell you that Elvis said that all a nigger could do for him was kiss his ass and shine his shoes?"

Georgia Mae raised her brow at Monique causing her to instantly feel bad about letting that roll off of her tongue. Suddenly, the elements outside made a mighty rumble, causing both women to shudder.

Silence.

Monique turned and tensely glanced out the window.

"Uh ... anyway, for some reason the black girls at the talent shows nicknamed me 'Game.' I thought it was kind of cool, so it's stuck with me ever since."

Monique nodded her head in agreement. "I never would have thought your name would be Georgia Mae."

"Me neither," she laughed. "When I was born my daddy showed up at the hospital drunk and unmanageable. He's a very big man; actually he's a damn fool when he's drunk. That was the first name that came outta his mouth after I was born. My mother wasn't one to argue with him while he was drunk, so Georgia Mae he said, and Georgia Mae it was."

Monique got a good laugh out of that as she turned away from the window and the pouring rain. She saw cash stuffed in Game's Gucci handbag. It painfully reminded her of the money she was going to miss due to the storm outside. She couldn't help but wonder, with all Game's education and talent, not to mention her natural beauty, why would she want to dance at the Gentlemen's Club?

"Fire," Georgia Mae spoke, remembering her reason for being there. "There's a gentleman here to see you. He's very affluent and generous with his money." She raised her eyebrow. "He wants to meet you."

"Affluent?" Monique frowned.

"Meaning he's very rich," Game said, taking a step closer. As she talked, Monique noticed a gold tooth inside her mouth. It looked kind of fly, even though she was sure it was fake. "He wants you to dance for him personally."

"I'm flattered," Monique said with genuine sincerity as she drew back in her chair, her hand over her heart, "but the show has been cancelled."

"No, he wants you to perform for him personally." Game walked over and sat on the edge of the dresser, partially blocking Monique's view of the mirror. She leaned forward and lowered her voice. "Fire, the man has more money than God." With her forehead wrinkled for emphasis she said, "He says he loves your show and that he's never been with a sista before."

"It figures," Monique laughed.

"The man is eighty years old. The last time I went to his place he wanted me to dress up in leather and beat the shit out of him."

"What?" Monique huffed, raising her eyebrows.

Game fidgeted as she continued, "He's what they call a masochist. It's a sexual perversion where people get pleasure from being abused."

"No shit," Monique hissed, ill-tempered with Game for trying her like that.

"I ... I ... told him we would do a combo if he had the right amount of money." Game became a bundle of nerves as she ground the heel of her boot back and forth on the floor.

"Girl! I know the fuck you didn't!" Monique exclaimed, raising her voice.

Game removed her rear end off the dressing table as she rubbed her behind and stretched her neck from side to side. The fatigue from dancing wore heavily on her face. "I apologize, but since they cancelled your show I figured you could use the money."

"I can't believe you would do something like that without asking me!" Monique said hotly.

"The limousine should be here to pick us up in a few minutes. He usually pays three grand, but you can ask for five." Game slyly threw the gambit of money at Monique.

"Fi ... five grand?" Monique stuttered as she sat straight up in her chair. Game had her attention now. She saw her reflection in the mirror ... then Rasheed's. She blinked twice and saw dollar signs. "Five grand, huh?" Monique drawled slowly. Game smiled with mischief as she walked up to the dresser and retrieved something from her purse, a packet of white powder. She poured a small mountain on the dresser tabletop and removed a crisp hundred-dollar bill from her purse. With long manicured fingernails she delicately rolled the bill into a tube.

"What's that?" Monique asked.

"Coke. Want a toot?"

"Nope." Monique looked at Game as she slid her chair back. "When did you start using that?" Monique asked with feeling.

"Let's just put it like this," Game said, her eyes rolling to the back of her head after taking a snort of the powder. "I met a handsome black man that introduced me to a white girl with no legs. Her name was Cocaine. Since then, the brotha left, taking my money and stealing my heart. She's my new love. She loves me and says that she'll never leave me," Game mimicked in a singsong voice.

Monique instantly picked up on the gnawing hurt. Game was still suffering, trying to get over a broken heart. Drugs will never repair the ruins of love's demise. Monique started to tell her so, but it was not the right moment.

"You know you're gonna have to stop that," was all Monique said as she watched Game snort another line.

"Yeah, I'ma stop when you hook your girl up with one of them fine brothas." She leaned forward, snorted the last line and rose.

Monique could see the coke in her nose. Game was becoming a cocaine junkie and didn't even know it. Just then, there was a loud knock at the door causing both women to jump nervously as they exchanged looks. Quickly, Game placed the coke back in her purse. Monique walked to the door to open it. An elderly white man stood at the door. Monique instantly noticed something formidable about his features. He was dressed in all black, donning a matching hat and gloves. His clothes looked wet from the rain. Game perked up. "Hey Johnson, you're early!"

Looking in her direction, the chauffeur slightly nodded his head. "Ma'am, if you ladies are ready, the car is waiting."

Game became excited as she looked in the mirror, wiped at her nose and checked her appearance. Satisfied, she buttoned up her jacket and briskly headed for the door as she gestured with a wave of her manicured hand. "Ta-ta love. You stayin' or you trying to get some of this free money?"

It took Monique less than a second to make up her mind. Five grand was a lot of money by any standards. "Damn girl, wait for meee!" Monique grabbed her purse and ran behind them.

E LEVEN

With umbrella in hand, the old chauffeur swayed slightly under the turbulent winds as he struggled to open the door. A strong gust of wind took his hat away, exposing his bald head. He looked down the street at his hat blowing in the wind as the wind further threatened to take him with it. Game's blond hair swirled around her face as she ducked to get inside the limousine. Monique exhaled slowly before she got into the spacious car. Classical music popped from the speakers as they drove down the streets of New York in the early morning.

Game crossed her long legs, one over the other, as she took out a miniature make-up case. She pursed her thin lips as she looked into the mirror to apply her lipstick. "He lives in the Belleview Towers. It's a high rise that overlooks the city. Oprah and Bill Gates have suites there along with a few other celebrities."

"Who is this guy?" Monique asked.

"His name is Dr. Hugstible."

As Game talked Monique leaned forward, craning her neck, eyes adjusting to the passing lights of the city and of cars passing by. Game's demeanor was tense, but still sophisticated.

"What I'm about to introduce you to is a world within a world. The filthy rich and the famous. In other words, the freaks and the shameless."

"You sure he don't want me to have sex with him or any-thing?" Monique asked nervously.

"I'm sure." Game laughed as she reached into her purse and retrieved her MAC pressed powder compact. She continued, "He just wants you to dominate him. He's into bondage—leather and whips and shit. The last time I was there I beat him while he wore pink panties and a bra."

"Get outta here!" Monique's mouth was wide open forming an incredulous O. The car veered to the right, making a sharp turn. Georgia Mae patted the sponge on her face, making sure her skin was flawless. "Why is he so interested in me?" Monique questioned as she looked out of the window watching the rain pour down.

Game snapped her compact closed with such force that it got Monique's attention. She ran her tongue over her teeth as if she was considering her words carefully. "The old man has been asking about you for quite some time, I just never told you. I told him that you weren't interested and figured as such. The truth is, in this business, when you find a gold mine, you don't tell everybody else. Hell, the old fart might die and leave me his entire estate," Game reasoned. "When they cancelled your show tonight, he went ballistic, saying he had to see you. It was real bizarre, like something straight out of the twilight zone, but then it dawned on me ... something I learned my sophomore year of college."

"What's that?" Monique asked.

Game pulled in a deep breath and frowned with her tight lips forming a thin line across her face. "In college I was fortunate enough to have a black professor for my African American studies class. It started with twenty other white students in the class, including me. In two weeks I was the only white person there." Game made a face as she continued, "When you learn black history from a black perspective it's totally different than the watered-down version that teaches Christopher Columbus discovered America and how civilization started with Rome. Anyway, girl ..."

Baffled, Monique looked at Game wondering what the hell she was talking about.

Game continued, "During slavery it was a big thing for a white man to own female slaves, even poor whites, but the majority of rich white men had a harem of female slaves just for their own personal satisfaction. Even back then, the white man had sexual lust for black women. They maintained their powerful positions because of all of the money they made off of slavery. The profit was something like 1500%. A white male with a black female mistress was an acceptable part of Southern life, even a rite of manhood. A young white man wasn't a man until he had sex with a black woman. Unfortunately, the majority of the black women were raped. Some of the stronger black women openly chose suicide rather than continuing to be raped, molested and degraded. We were told that one black woman even cut her master's head off."

"And?" Monique said. She was clearly disturbed by what Game was saying, but wondered what all of this had to do with her.

"Well ..." Game shrugged her shoulders uncomfortably. "I feel like an outsider lookin' in. Dr. Hugstible is the grandchild of a rich former slave owner. It just seems like white men have this secret fetish for black women that dates back so far, but they try to hide it."

"Girl, please. They don't try to hide that shit. It's taboo and they love it. Just like white women who openly have a thing for black men." She looked at Georgia Mae with a raised eyebrow.

Game had to giggle because she did prefer a black man over a white one any day. She swatted Monique's arm, hitting her as the two women laughed like old friends. Then with a serious expression, Game added, "I ain't no white woman, at least I swear to God I don't feel like one. I'm a black woman trapped in a white woman's body."

Monique corrected her by playfully saying, "Naw girl, you mean a black woman trapped in a white woman's skin, 'cause you damn sho'll got a black girl's junk in your trunk." They laughed. Monique fixed herself a strong drink from the bar and for the first time in her life she listened to, and enjoyed, classical music as she watched Game remove a Philly blunt from her purse and expertly bust it open with her fingernail. They rode the rest of the way in silence as they blazed the blunt in the back seat of the limo. The dark rainy night welcomed them to a destination of the freaks and the shameless.

◊ ◊ ◊ ◊

Dr. Hugstible greeted them amicably at the door. He pecked Game on her cheek as they entered the penthouse suite. Monique was in awe of its grandiose splendor. She was also taken by surprise at the stature of the doctor. He had wide thin shoulders, bony hands, and narrow hips. He stood a little over six feet tall with lank gray hair and a large fleshy nose with spider veins in it, but there was something about his eyes – the glint of a sparkle. In his day, the doctor used to be a ladies' man. Now his body was riddled with age. His old, wrinkled skin barely hung on his bones. His shifty eyes and thick gray eyebrows twitched as he spoke to Game. Monique stood stoic with a generic polite smile plastered on her face as she tried to mask her discomfort. She slid her eyes off the doctor over to Game.

"Fire, I'm honored to meet you," the doctor said, catching her off-guard. He extended his hand out to her. Hesitantly, she shook it. His hand felt moist and clammy as he smiled with teeth fit for a horse, too big for his narrow mouth and shrunken head.

An older Mexican woman, the maid, entered the room. She was dressed in a white A-line skirt with a black apron. They followed the doctor into the main parlor. The walls were adorned with expensive antique oil paintings. Next to a large picture window sat a white grand piano. In the corner to her left was a seven-foot-tall knight in shining armor. For some reason the huge statue spooked Monique. It reminded her of the horror movies she used to watch when she was a little girl. Outside the window, the thunder clapped and lightning lit up the night sky. Monique flinched.

"I've always enjoyed the aesthetics of beautiful women, especially black women, but you, my dear, are beyond beautiful. You're like an exquisite African rose in the summertime," the doctor said as his eyes undressed her. *Was that a white man's version of putting his mack down?* Monique thought as she watched the doctor crinkle his nose at her while he scratched his privates and continued to let his hand linger there, touching himself. Game looked on, annoyed, as she strutted to the other side of the room and placed her purse on the floor and began to undress. Somewhere in the distance a clock loudly chimed.

"Honey, you never did say a price for both of us," Game said, in an attempt to jock for position over Monique. It was as if Monique had some kind of spell on the doctor. Game arched her back, thrusting out her supple breasts. The doctor continued to ignore her while staring at Monique like a hungry wolf. He licked his lips and rubbed his hands together anxiously.

"Fire, what do you feel is appropriate?" he asked with a strained smile on his lips. His teeth were so large they overlapped in his mouth. He walked up closer to Monique as she stood aloof, even though she felt his nearness like a second skin. Every nerve and fiber in her body was alive, alert, tingling. She knew that she was totally out of her element. From across the room, Game looked on with contempt.

"Sugar, we have every intention of serving every one of your needs and desires, as only you want us to serve you, but I'd rather you make an offer and I'll let you know if the price is right," Monique said in the sweetest voice she could while doing her best impression of a strip tease as she slowly undressed. As the doctor watched, a trickle of saliva dribbled from the corner of his mouth. Monique eyed Game, searching for her approval. Game slyly winked her eye, but her face was smug. She was sending Monique mixed signals.

The doctor reached out and touched Monique on the shoulder. His bony fingers were cold as his hand trembled. He rubbed at her skin almost as if to see if the color would rub off. The doctor was fascinated with Monique. As she removed his hand, Monique realized that she had been holding her breath.

"I'll pay you seven thousand dollars."

At the sound of the money Monique kicked her shoe off with

so much force that it sailed across the room, landing next to the knight. Game shot Monique a warning stare as she walked toward the doctor with her arms folded over her breasts.

"Surely, you can't be talking about seven thousand measly dollars for us to split?"

The doctor turned, giving her a look as if she were an intruder. "No, I was thinking more to the tune of five thousand for Fire and two for you."

Taken aback, Game threw her head back like she had been slapped in the face. "That's bullshit!" she screeched, shooting daggers at the old man with jagged green eyes.

Instantly Monique caught on to what was happening and decided to play her hand with a straight poker face. Taking a step forward she boldly announced, "We came here together and we leave here together. Either you accept our price and pay the same for both of us or we walk," Monique said adamantly with her hands on her hips.

The old man bunched his lips to talk as a muffled groan escaped from somewhere deep in his throat like a man lost for words. Game couldn't help but smirk with joy as she struggled to suppress a smile. The old man took a step back and placed one hand in his pocket and the other underneath his chin, as if contemplating his next thought. Slowly, Game started to get dressed as she watched the drama unfold. Now she felt like an outsider. The moment lingered. Monique realized she had played her hand and lost. She padded across the carpet to retrieve her shoe.

The old man, disgruntled, responded, "Okay ... okay, as you wish. Five thousand a piece."

Monique stopped in her tracks, looking at the spooky statue as she reached for her shoe. She thought about a man being behind the steel cage of the mask. She turned around and smiled so broadly it hurt her cheeks. Amused, the doctor couldn't help but laugh. Monique Cheeks had played the game well, so far. Game just looked on, confused, as once again she wondered about the forbidden taboo, the white man's lascivious lust for black flesh.

◊ ◊ ◊ ◊

Game was familiar with the boudoir inside the doctor's suite. It was about the size of a small chic clothing store. An assortment of brand new clothes and costumes lined the walls. Monique did a full turn in the middle of the floor, mouth agape. There were even a few designer clothes with the tags still on them – Gucci, Louis Vuitton. She saw some Rocawear and Dolce and Gabbana also. Instantly she regretted not bringing her big purse. She was sure the old man wouldn't miss any of the stuff if it came up missing.

"You go girl!" Game exclaimed joyfully as she gave Monique a high-five. "Five thousand a piece. Wow! You damn sure got guts."

"You said he was willing to pay five grand."

"I lied. I was just trying to persuade you to come," Game said, still excited about the money. Monique just shook her head at Game as she continued to look at all the beautiful clothes and exotic costumes.

They quickly got dressed. Monique had on a black, leather, crotchless catwoman outfit. She refused to put on the mask. As it was, Game was cracking up laughing at her. Game wore a skin-tight red devil outfit. The pants were too small for her big butt, so she had to wear her thong instead. Game continued to chuckle as they exited the room and headed down the hall.

"Bitch, what's so damn funny?" Monique asked, amused by Game's humor. They were both still high from the blunt they had smoked earlier.

Game was curled over in laughter as she held her side. "You ... you ... look like a cat burglar dressed up in ... that get-up," Game managed to say as she roared with hysterical laughter, grabbing at her sides like she couldn't breathe.

"At least I found clothes I could fit into and my ass ain't too big to get into my costume."

"Aw, bitch, stop hatin'," Game said with a giggle as she fought for control of her laughter. "Once we walk through that door ..." Game looked down at Monique's clothes and giggled. Monique rolled her eyes as she promised herself that this would be her last time ever smoking with this chick. Game tried to speak again as her eyes sparkled with giddy laughter. "Once we step through that door it's showtime."

Monique swallowed the lump in her throat. Unlike Game, she still had the jitters and regardless of how much she tried to relax, the creepy old white man still disturbed her.

"The last time I was here he wanted me to beat him. It was really disgusting." Game made a face at the memory as a wisp of blond hair fell over her eyes.

"I don't know about you, but for five grand, girl, please, I'm about ta beat all the pink off his peanut-head ass."

Game burst out laughing, placing her hand over her mouth.

"I swear, I'll never smoke with you again," Monique huffed as they slowly walked. Up ahead, at the end of the hall, the doctor appeared. He had changed into a simple black robe with gray loafers. Monique stutter-stepped when she saw him.

Game giggled at her antics as she nudged Monique. "Look!" The doctor stood with his hands inside his pockets, his eyes glued to Monique as both women approached. His left eye twitched as if he was in some type of pain. Game sobered up fast as she wiped at the tuft of hair in front of her forehead with the back of her hand. "Here comes the perverted part. Watch this."

"Huh?" Monique said as she watched the doctor bow his head and disrobe. Underneath he wore a pink garter belt with matching bra, sheer panties and black stockings. Game barbed a giggle that threatened to erupt into a boisterous cackle.

"Goddamnitmuthafuckingsonofabitch! Look at him!" Monique intoned as her jaw dropped, aghast by the sight of the old man. The doctor's body was covered with long, prickly gray hairs. His skinny ribs were visible and he had dense patches of hair on his chest and private area. He looked like a starved bear with a bad case of mange. A bush of furry hair protruded from between his scrawny legs. His withered penis was about the size of an infant's.

"Oh, mother of punishment, I have been a bad boy, please don't hurt me," the doctor mimicked in a child's voice. Monique made a face as she exchanged glances with Game. The doctor fell on his hands and knees groveling in mock penitent tones. Monique could see his skinny backbone through all the hair and his sickly pale skin.

Game strutted over to him with all the confidence of a woman who was used to playing the sick game of sadomasochism. On the floor the doctor had an assortment of toys that he liked to be punished with – a whip, something that resembled a water hose and even a thin chain that looked like it was made of gold. Game picked up the flexible hose and began to lightly swat the doctor on his fanny as she smirked at Monique who was barely able to contain her laughter. Acting, the old man shuddered and whimpered at her feet as Monique looked on in disbelief.

"Bad boy ... bad boy," Game said with animation as she played the charade.

The doctor looked up at her. "Harder! Harder!" Tightly, Monique closed her eyes and then opened them. She was overcome with grief and despair. This old white man had all this wealth. Just looking around at all the opulent splendor, it disturbed her in a way that she could not explain. She thought about what Game had said on the ride over. *A world of the filthy rich and famous ... the freaks and the shameless.*

Once again Monique looked at Game frolicking with the doctor as she lightly tapped him on his rear. He didn't appear to be enjoying the game. Monique couldn't help but think to herself, *white folks are crazy.* She felt something deep within her stir, a combination of envy, jealousy and even rage. All her life her family had been struggling just to survive. She thought about the neighbor next door, the fifteen-year-old girl who had a baby and dumped it in the dumpster and all the single mothers she knew who were struggling. She thought about herself and what she was doing, all because of shattered dreams. At twenty-one she should have been about to graduate from college, but no.

A world of hatred began to swell inside of her, in that sacred place that she had tried to shelter from the cold and bitter world—that place in her heart. To her utter dismay, she watched as the doctor groveled toward her, crawling on all fours like a dog. Disgusting! He was at her feet. Game made a swinging motion with her hand, indicating to Monique to hit the doctor. Paralyzed with fear Monique just stood there, frozen. The moment lingered like a clock whose hands had stalled.

"Mother, don't hurt me," the doctor said.

"Pst, hit him, hit him!" Game persuaded with a concerned look on her face.

"Punish me," the doctor clamored and looked up at Monique sideways. In the corner of her eye she saw Game gesturing with her hand for her to strike the doctor. Monique realized she couldn't do it as she looked down at the pale ghastly skin of the doctor with his butt tooted up in the air. God, she wished this grotesque scene would go away.

"Pst, Monique, damnit girl, do it!" Game hissed with her voice on edge.

"Punish me." The doctor's voice sounded like a plea. Two voices both urged her on in a world within a world, the freaks and the shameless.

"I can't do this," Monique said to herself. She looked at Game with an apologetic face. Just then, she felt something wet and clammy on her foot. She looked down to see the doctor licking her feet. Something inside her snapped as red flashed behind her eyes. Images of a baby in a dumpster flashed before her eyes, just as she had seen it on the news. She picked up the thick whip a few feet away from her and totally lost control.

She watched herself go crazy as she brought the whip down hard on the doctor's back. It made a deadly whistling sound in the air as it connected with flesh. The doctor opened his mouth to scream, but no words came out, only a pained expression of pure agony. Finally, from somewhere in the pit of his gut, a simmering guttural sound segued into a protracted howl that ended in a haunting scream. Frantically, he began to rub the area where she had just struck him as if it were on fire. Monique brought the whip down again, this time with more force, causing the doctor to howl.

She struck him, again and again. Violently she swung the whip causing it to whistle in the air. Her face was a mask of fury, lips pulled back with malice scrawled across it, intent on inflicting as much pain as possible. With each blow she felt like she was releasing pent-up emotions as she escaped into of a part of her mind that she did not know existed—she crossed the thin line between sanity and insanity.

She never knew that inflicting so much pain could feel so good. Too good. Tears began to fill her eyes. Once again she thought about the baby in the dumpster, this life and the brutal ways of the world for a single woman trying to raise a child. *Whip! Whip! Whip!* The doctor began to wither and retreat as he put up a weary hand to ward off the blows. His body was grossly covered with red marks with a few of the marks now bleeding.

"Stop it! Stop it!" Game yelled loudly as she placed one of her hands over her mouth in shock. In a trance-like state Monique continued to beat him in a fit of rage, drawing blood from the doctor's back and lower extremities. He desperately attempted to get away from her. She was a raving maniac and was giving him more than his five thousand dollars worth. She was trying to kill him.

The doctor crawled under a table. Monique wasted no time grabbing one of his scrawny legs and yanking him so hard across the floor that she gave him rug burns. She began to violently punch and kick him in the face and in the head and arms, whirling in a blur of motion.

The doctor stopped resisting and lay there motionless as she continued to pummel him. Game rushed over just as Monique was about to swing again. She caught her fist in mid-air, spun Monique around and placed her in a bear hug. They tripped and fell down with Game on top. Monique was panting loudly and her body was covered in sweat.

"Monique, you're going to kill him, for Godsake!" Game said as she looked down at her. She could feel her heaving. It was the only sound that echoed in the stillness of the parlor. Dr. Hugstible lay motionless at the other end of the floor as blood trickled from both his nose and his mouth. One of his large horse-sized teeth lay in the middle of the floor as a silent reminder of the tragedy that had just taken place.

"Oh my God! Listen," Game's voice quivered. She could feel Monique's heart beating against her chest.

"Listen to what?" Monique asked, still winded. For some strange reason she looked up at the artwork on the cathedral ceiling—a nude boy with angelic wings, aiming a bow and arrow.

"It's too quiet." They both sat up, eyes alert, ears astute, listening to the unnerving silence. They helped each other up and tiptoed over to the doctor.

"He's dead! You killed him," Game said. Her face was a ball of anguish. "Feel his heart," she whispered.

"Uh-uh, I'm not touching him," Monique replied, taking a step back. They were both startled by a noise. It sounded like someone clearing their throat to get their attention. Standing ominously in the shadows at the end of the hall were the chauffeur and the maid. Their gloomy figures frightened them.

"Oh, shit, look!" Game uttered. "Please go feel for his heartbeat. We need to see if he's still alive. Maybe we can get him to a hospital."

Slowly Monique walked over toward the doctor. She could feel her heart racing so fast in her chest that it felt like she was going to faint. She bent down and reached out to feel his neck for a pulse. Her eyes darted all over the place like she expected someone to grab her. Gently, with two fingers, she touched the doctor's neck as a million ideas ran wild through her head. The two figures stood at the end of the hall watching. How was she going to make an escape? Was it possible for a black woman in a crotchless catwoman suit to catch a cab in the wee hours of the morning in

Belleview Heights?

Rasheed's face appeared on the screen of her panicked mind. Her hand trembled as she searched the doctor's neck for a pulse. The chauffeur started to walk toward them briskly. He had something in his hand. A gun? A phone? "Aw, shit," Game muttered fearfully.

Monique couldn't feel any pulse. The doctor was dead. Monique looked up just as the chauffeur entered the room. As if on cue, the doctor reached up and grabbed Monique's hand. "Boo!" Monique leapt up so fast that she stumbled and fell on her butt.

The doctor roared with laughter at the antics of the black girl. His tooth was missing, one of his eyes was partially swollen closed, black and blue bruises covered his body and his gray hair stood up like he had stuck his finger in a light socket. He began laughing like a man that truly got a kick out of playing a prank on someone. After he caught his breath, still giddy, he said, "My dear lady, that was mar-ve-lous. I got 'cha, huh?" He laughed some more as he cupped his jaw with his hand, twisting it from side to side to see how badly it was broken. He winced noticeably.

"She almost killed you!" Game stepped up and screamed at the old man. She was infuriated. A thick blue vein protruded from her forehead as her jagged green eyes flashed optic slants of anger.

"On the contrary, my dear, she merely facilitated me in a game I immensely enjoy playing. Frankly, you need to take lessons from her."

"Whaaat!?" Game screeched. As Monique looked on, a wave of relief washed over her. Thank God the old man was alive. As Game continued to curse out the doctor, Monique's heart rate began to steady. She opened and closed her fist, examining her knuckles as all she could think about was getting her money and getting the hell out of there.

◊ ◊ ◊ ◊

They rode in the back of the limo in total silence as the rain pelted the car windows. The car stopped at a red light across the street from a liquor store. Vaguely, an orange neon light flashed inside the car, illuminating Game's face. Monique tried her best to ignore her ill disposition since they had left the doctor's residence.

"That cracka blew my high," Game said hotly, causing Monique to glance sideways at her. Sometimes Game talked just like a black person and it continued to amaze Monique. The car pulled away from the light causing them to lean back in their seats. Monique shuffled through the new, crisp hundred-dollar bills in her hand. Five thousand dollars, just as the good doctor promised.

"I'm never going back there again," Game said as she reached into her purse for a Philly blunt that she quickly began to break open. "What about you?" Monique's mind was someplace else. Game leered at her as she twisted the blunt. "I said I'm never going back there. What about you?" she asked a little louder this time.

Silence. Speeding, the car veered as it changed lanes. Monique looked up from the money. "I almost killed him," she said out loud. Her comment was totally out of place.

Somehow Game seemed not to notice as she replied, "Sometimes my own people, white people, embarrass the hell out of me." Game lit the blunt with a gold cigarette lighter and inhaled deeply on the potent weed.

"Umph, you can say that again ... about your own people embarrassing you," Monique said, her voice distant.

"What happened back there anyway?" Game took a pull off the blunt. "At first you were scared to death to hit him and then you just went the fuck off."

"I dunno." Monique shrugged her shoulders. "At first I was scared, then something about him provoked me. I think it was when he was licking my feet. Not only was I disgusted, I felt violated. Once I hit him with that whip it felt like I was releasing all my hurt and anger ... about the baby in the dumpster."

"Huh?"

"Yeah, I almost killed him. What you said about this being a world within a world. Well, I've never had this much money given to me at one time in my entire life," Monique said, holding up the money. Game arched her brow at her and took another pull off the blunt. Monique continued, "In fact, in my world, crackheads would beat the brakes off that white man for much less than five grand. They would do it for five dollars, on an installment plan."

Game chuckled and gagged on the blunt as the aroma filled the car. She attempted to pass it to Monique, but she declined. Game tossed her blond hair back as headlights passed, lighting up her face. "You had that same wild look in your eyes that night you fought Tatyana in the dressing room."

"What look?" Monique questioned with a raised brow.

"The look of a person possessed by demons."

"Yeah, well, it may have looked like I was, but the little move you did by grabbing my wrists and placing me in whatever kind of hold that was ..." Monique remembered how Game had held her.

"I have a black belt in karate. Sorry, I wasn't trying to hurt you. I told you my mom had me entering all kinds of talent shows. She had me practicing martial arts at seven years old." Monique thought back to Game's awesome stage performance. Her walking on her hands and grabbing the pole with her butt.

"You would have killed that old man if I hadn't stopped you," Game said, mentally pinning Monique against a brick wall of reality. She leaned forward and poured herself a drink from the bar as Monique let the window down. The cool night air whooshed around the car with its tiny raindrops. Monique licked the rim of her top lip, savoring the taste. She closed her eyes and saw Rasheed's face ... again. *How can I make him understand?* she thought as Game spoke.

"I told you I was a black woman trapped in a white woman's body, and now I've introduced you to the white world. Now it's time for you to introduce me to the other world, the black world." As Game spoke it dawned on Monique that she was dead serious. She was actually trying to replace a broken heart with a broken heart. That was what was going to happen if Game got what she wanted—a brotha. At least that was Monique's opinion.

"Girl, trust me when I say that these men today ain't shit. They just wanna hit it and move on to the next piece of ass. Stay on your side of the tracks. They'll run through you like water."

Game was instantly offended. "What? I know what I want," Game shot back.

"Are you willing to deal with the changes, their instability?" Monique questioned as she thought about Rasheed.

"I had your back in more ways than one, Monique." Game waved her envelope filled with money in the air. Monique then looked down at her envelope. She was right, if it weren't for Game, she wouldn't have five thousand dollars in her hand.

"Well, I guess I do owe you that much." Monique had to admit, Game not only talked black, she also dressed and behaved just like a black woman, so it shouldn't be any problem. "You know you my girl. I'ma see if I can hook you up."

Game smiled in acknowledgement as they rode the rest of the way in silence.

TWELVE

Rasheed Smith

A bright moon held Rasheed's spirit captive as he stared up at the sky. A lone star in the galaxy sparkled. In the distance a cat screamed and a door slammed. Across the street an old Marvin Gaye tune blared from one of the neighbor's houses, "*What's goin' on?*"

As Rasheed stared up at the celestial heavens, a full moon stared back at him with a sly grin. It was 4:47 a.m. He sat on his grandma's front porch. The old decrepit house was the only home he had ever known. The house was so old that when anyone stepped on the porch, a slight noise would be heard inside the house, a poor man's burglar alarm, always causing Grandma Hattie to wake from a sound sleep.

Rasheed fanned mosquitoes absent-mindedly as he was lost in his thoughts, thoughts that barged their way into his twenty-two-year-old mind. Monique dancing nude, parading her body for other men to see. All for the love of money. "Damn!" He thought about his future. What if he didn't get drafted into the pros? His prospects didn't look too bright then. He was a convicted felon. He worried about his son, his needs, life's basic necessities, school clothes and education. "Shit!" Rasheed cursed as he raked his fingers through his curly hair.

He looked up to see a dope fiend walking down the sidewalk doing a reconnaissance mission through the neighborhood, looking for something to steal. Rasheed recognized the man as Tyson Harmon. He lived a few blocks away. He and Rasheed played ball against each other. Tyson was a better athlete than Rasheed at one time. That was until he started hanging with the wrong crew. Just then, in the opposite direction, Rasheed looked up to see headlights approaching. It was Monique's car, a late model Honda.

The brakes squeaked as she pulled into the yard. One of her headlights was dim. Rasheed sat in the darkness as he watched her, a girl he had loved since she was fourteen years old. As she got out of the car, he watched her bounce up the walkway on the ball of her toes. Monique Cheeks was born to be a dancer. She even walked like a dancer. He fought to contain his breathing as he realized he didn't know what to say or even where to start.

"Mo," he whispered, softly saying her name, careful not to startle her as he stood.

She stutter-stepped, surprised. "Baby, what you doing out here?" For some reason her words seemed to stir his emotions as the incandescent moon's glow shimmered off her shiny black hair and delicate features, causing her silhouette to appear like an enigma in his mind. He needed to see her face up close, touch her, and feel her, his woman.

"I couldn't sleep … had a lot on my mind," he said, answering her question.

Instantly she recognized that his voice was filled with hurt. Her heart sunk in her chest as she watched him sit back down. She walked up to him and stood between his legs, embracing his head in her arms, pressing his face against her bosom as she rocked him.

"I saw Jack Lemon today," was all Rasheed could think to say.

Monique pulled away from him. "He's out?"

"Yeah, and crazy as hell this time."

"He's always been a little off if you ask me."

"Naw, but it's worse this time."

"I don't know how it can be that much worse. Even though he's our friend and we've known him since high school, Jack has killed a lot of people. How did he get out this time?"

"He won an appeal. He gave me some money to give to you, too." Rasheed cleared his throat. "Dude on some serious death before dishonor shit."

"What about Gina?"

"I dunno, but he's acting like he's god of the universe. He told me she got him out of prison. Tomorrow he's going to stop by here—"

"I'm sorry for what I said," Monique blurted out, changing the subject, taking both of them to that place that neither wanted to go—the present moment. "My son has a father and I have a man. I love you so much," she whispered in the dark as her words stuck in her throat. She blinked back tears as she spoke. Reaching in her purse, she removed a wad of cash, placing the bills in his hand.

"What's this?" he asked.

She took a step back and looked at him. "It's five thousand dollars." She couldn't muster the courage to tell him how she earned the money and he knew better than to ask.

"I'll stop dancing and go back to the bakery, but I'm beggin' you please just let me work two more weeks and then I'll stop," Monique pleaded as she gently held his handsome face in her hands. "Baby, it's up to you if you want to let me do the magazine shoot. Chances are they won't accept me anyway, but if they do, I'll have enough money to go back to college and maybe buy a house, or at least put a down payment on one."

"Two weeks, huh?" Rasheed muttered, tossing the idea around in his head.

"Uh-huh ... ouch!" she screeched, slapping her arm. "Damn mosquitoes."

He chuckled as he palmed her butt. "Two weeks and you promise you'll quit?"

"Yes, yes." Monique beamed with joy and pulled him close to her. "Baby, I promise I'll quit. I know how bad this whole thing hurts you. You've always liked to watch me dance. I never wanted you to lose respect for me." She looked into his eyes and the starry night suddenly took on a whole new meaning. "Rasheed, can I make love to you?" The timbre of her voice was soft as the night breeze, mellow like a song. She grinded her torso against him, closing her eyes, envisioning him deep inside of her.

Up the street a police car cruised as its searchlights rudely disturbed the night, illuminating the streets like a miniature sun, bouncing, roaming from place to place, in search of something. Finally, the light settled on Rasheed and Monique, causing her to flinch and turn around to see what was going on. Rasheed stood up, shielding his eyes from the intrusive light with his hands. Suddenly two officers got out of their cars with their guns drawn.

"You, the black male, slowly come off the porch with your hands in the air where we can see them," an authoritative, deep baritone voice commanded. Rasheed could tell it was a white officer. The lights blinded him as he squinted his eyes at the bright lights and went for his wallet.

"Officer, there's a mistake. I live—"

"Freeze!" a voice ordered on the fringe of panic. Rasheed heard the distinctive sound of guns being cocked. The deadly sound resonated in the still of the night.

"Please, no. We live here!" Monique shrieked. She knew all too well about the excessive force of the NYPD.

"This is bullshit!" Rasheed mumbled under his breath.

"What's going on out there?" Grandma Hattie asked from inside the door. "Ra, baby, you alright?"

"Yeah, Ma, I'm alright. Go back inside," Rasheed was able to say without letting on to his fear.

"No, he ain't alright! These damn fools out here got guns pulled on us," Monique belted out, gesturing with her hands as she stomped her foot in frustration.

Tentatively Rasheed walked down the steps with his hands high in the air. The officer rushed him in an attempt to slam him to the ground.

"Hold up, hold up, man!" Rasheed said, resisting being slammed to the ground.

"Stop it! Stop it!" Monique wailed.

"You women go back inside and let us handle this situation," the officer commanded.

"My boy ain't done nuttin' ta nobody. Y'all leave him be!" Grandma Hattie said, walking onto the porch as she clasped her old threadbare robe around her. When Rasheed saw his grandma walk onto the porch he stopped resisting and let the officer slam him to ground.

Monique screamed, "Rasheed!" He hit the hard pavement in a thud, unsettling dirt and dust in the artificial smoggy haze. The officer jumped on Rasheed's back, kneeing him in the spine, shoving his face in the dirt. Rasheed grunted in pain as the officer struck him in the head with his fist and placed the gun to his temple.

The officer whispered in a gravelly voice, "Nigger, you move again and I'll blow your goddamn brains out right here in front of your granny and that loud-mouth bitch. You didn't know who you was fuckin' wit', huh?" The officer attempted to show his partner just how to control one of them "wanna be bad niggers."

This was not Rasheed's first encounter with the boys in blue, the power hungry demons who were supposed to serve and protect him. What made this painstakingly humiliating for Rasheed was that it was a black officer who held a gun to his head threatening to kill him in front of his family. He was obviously trying to impress his white buddy. Rasheed hated for his grandmother and Monique to see him like this. A sour taste shocked his taste buds as blood co-mingled with dirt covered his palate.

"What do we have here?" the officer said as he snatched a wad of cash out of Rasheed's pocket.

"Hey, that's my girl's money!" Rasheed yelled.

"Yeah, and I'm motherfuckin' Santa Claus," the officer retorted derisively, kneeing Rasheed in the back. Monique couldn't take any more of the madness. She attempted to run down the steps but Grandma Hattie grabbed her arm with surprising strength and shot her a warning glance that told her to let her take over.

At eighty-eight, she had seen more than her share of brutality and abuse of her people. There was a period in time when there was such a thing as "strange fruit hanging from trees." That was during a time when young black men and women were lynched and hung from trees, merely because of the color of their skin, for some festive occasion. Some say that is where the word "picnic" was coined, from "pick-a-nigger."

Grandma Hattie ambled to the front of the porch. A few neighbors trickled out of their houses onto their front porches after being awakened by the commotion. An elderly black woman in slippers and a housecoat who had a large German Shepherd at her side watched her neighbor of over forty years talk to the police.

Grandma Hattie said vehemently, "That's my grand boy, he ain't done nuttin' ta nobody. His name is Rasheed Smith. He plays basketball for St. John's." She had focused all of her attention on the white cop because she knew a black man trying to impress whites was the most dangerous person on the face of the planet. "Sir, my boy is a good boy," she spoke in a small voice as she cast her eyes down at the ground, a submissive posture to go with her poignant plea. The white cop went for it.

As he searched his memory bank for the recollection of the name, he spoke, "Oh, I know 'em. He's the kid who scored sixty-one points a few weeks back. They had him on SportsCenter."

"Yes sir, that's my boy," Grandma Hattie said, slightly nodding her head. People began to gather around, gawking. A van and an SUV pulled up with young adults who had just left a party.

The white officer frowned at his partner. "Ma'am, we had a call for a prowler in the area." He then walked over to his partner. "Tate, that ain't him. Let him up."

The youngsters got out of their cars and walked over to the melee. "Hey, that's Rasheed Smith on the ground." The officer was still on top of Rasheed, whispering threats into his ear when the bottle came whistling by, barely missing the black cop's head. The cop leapt off Rasheed, eyes ablaze with fury as he searched the crowd for the culprit who had thrown the bottle.

An angry voice vociferously yelled, "Y'all leave that man alone!"

Rasheed got off the ground slowly. To his horror, he saw his

Lil' Malcolm standing in the doorway beside the dog with a terrified expression on his face. Something panged in Rasheed's chest. God, why did his son have to see him like this? This evil tradition, police brutality in the ghetto, was handed down from one generation to the next. Two other police cruisers drove up as more people started to gather around.

Lieutenant Anthony Brown got out of his car to the raucous sound of hecklers, a sign that trouble was brewing. As he weaved through the crowd of onlookers, he politely urged the people to go back to their houses. He was taken aback by the sight of Grandma Hattie. Then his attention focused on the kid, Rasheed, all covered in dirt with blood coming from his mouth. "Hi Grandma Hattie, what's going on here?" he asked the woman who had single-handedly raised an entire neighborhood with love and affection.

She hobbled down the stairs. "This Sambo nigger here is harassing my boy!" she said, pointing a scrawny finger at the black officer.

"The boy tried to resist when I told him to raise his hands."

"You tellin' a damn lie," Monique interjected as she walked down the stairs.

"I took this money off of him." The black officer showcased a satisfied grin on his face as he talked to his young superior.

"That's my damn money. I worked for it!" Monique screeched.

"If you don't have a receipt for it, I'ma have to take it."

"Can he do that?" Monique turned toward the Lieutenant. Her eyebrows knotted together. Her voice had given way to a hint of fear.

The young Lieutenant shrugged his shoulders nodding his head, indicating "yes."

"I guess he also can walk up here on private property and beat the hell out of an innocent man, too, huh?" she said indignantly as she boldly got in the black officer's face. The Lieutenant raised his brow with the word "beat." Monique had his attention.

"He just came on my property and threw Rasheed to the ground and placed a gun to his head," Grandma Hattie said.

"That's a lie," the black officer barked. The commotion heated up as vulgar words were exchanged back and forth. For some reason, Rasheed just stood there impassive with his brown eyes transfixed on his son, the child who was destined to inherit a torn legacy of broken promises and shattered dreams, handed down from father to son, from generation to generation.

Rasheed felt numb and dehumanized as rage and humiliation consumed him. He was powerless to act on this most profane violation, denied a man's right to defend himself and his family. Rasheed felt that if he couldn't kill the officer for the egregious violation of dishonoring him in front of his family, then what was the use of giving the officer the satisfaction of knowing that he was humiliated to the point of being tormented with anger – a conscious man's logic in dealing with defeat.

As Monique and the officer argued, Grandma Hattie sneaked alongside the black officer and with surprising quickness, snatched the money out of his hand. The crowd roared with laughter as the old woman placed the money in her brassiere. The black cop moved toward Grandma Hattie like he was going to take the money back. Rasheed stepped in between them, bumping his chest against the black cop. "I'll die for that old woman right there. Now you put your hands on her, try me, you sell-out-ass nigga," Rasheed threatened, his nostrils flared, eyes bulging with disdain. The right side of his face was covered with dirt.

"Back off, Tate, and you, Rasheed, take your butt back into the house," Lieutenant Brown said sternly.

"But what about the money?" the cop asked with a frown on his face.

"What about we press charges on your sorry ass?" Monique huffed.

The white cop walked up. It was obvious by his flushed red cheeks that he didn't want anything to do with the abuse of the kid. "I'm sorry about what happened—"

"Sorry about what?" Monique cut him off. "The NYPD give a black man a beatdown on the regular, twenty-four seven, like fuckin' recreation. Now you got brain-dead-ass niggas doin' all the dirty work. The worst thing that white folks could have done was give a black man a little authority because he becomes worse than them." Monique cringed when she realized she had cursed in front of Ms. Hattie. "Oops," she said, covering her mouth.

"I could not have said it better, child," Grandma Hattie admitted.

The white cop looked at Lieutenant Brown. "Sir, there may have been some excessive force on the part of Tate. You know how he gets at times." He looked at his partner who angrily stalked away. Lieutenant Brown turned to Rasheed with a raised brow as if to ask a question. Rasheed stood on the porch, now holding his son. The expression on his face was that of a man determined to hide his wounded pride.

"You want to file charges or should I report him to Internal Affairs?"

"No! You don't file charges on a man that steps on your land and disrespects you and your family by physically abusing you in front of your woman and kid." Rasheed raised his voice, one of his eyes red as if he had fought to control his emotions. "You file 'vengeance to kill by any means necessary' whenever he crosses your path again." Rasheed's jaw was clenched tight. "And *you*," Rasheed addressed Officer Tate, "Grandma Hattie raised you. You grew up right down the street from here. You used to call yourself a Black Panther back in the day and now this is what you bring back to your very own community? You a mad-dog-ass nigga." Rasheed had a pained expression on his face as his voice cracked.

"I took this job to help y'all from getting hurt," Lieutenant Brown reminded Rasheed. "You can't hold one bad cop's actions against all the good cops who are trying to help the community."

Monique and Grandma Hattie just watched the exchange of words. The crowd started to leave as a murmur of shallow voices announced their departure. A patrol car pulled up in front of the yard. Rasheed recognized Tyson Harmon in the back seat, the junkie who had passed the house earlier. A white officer called from the patrol car window, "Lieutenant, we found the prowler. The suspect was trying to break into a car a few blocks from here."

It dawned on Rasheed that Tyson was the cause of all this mess. The ironic part was, Tyson Harmon was Lieutenant Brown's nephew. Rasheed watched Brown peer into the car and then kicked the dirt in disgust. "Shit!" he muttered under his breath and turned to Grandma Hattie. "I'll stop by for dinner after church." He didn't give her a chance to answer as he turned and walked briskly toward the patrol car with Tyson in the back seat. The crowd had already dispersed. For the first time the old dog tried to bark—a sound that could have passed for a human cough.

They walked inside the old house. As expected, Grandma Hattie preached about right and wrong. She said she knew that something bad was about to happen because all night her right leg had been bothering her and the last time that happened was when they tried to evict her out of her house due to a tax error. Finally, she yawned and gave Rasheed his money back and shuffled back to her room, humming an old church hymn. The baby had fallen asleep in his father's arms. Monique spied the soul of a battered man as Rasheed limped away to put their son back to bed. She could sense his pain as only a black woman could.

◊ ◊ ◊ ◊

They hadn't spoken since Rasheed placed the baby at the foot of his bed and disrobed in the semi-darkness of the room, the same room she had lost her virginity in when she was seventeen. With his shoulders slumped, she watched him trudge to the bathroom to take a shower. She hated to see him hurt like that. She knew that he carried the weight of the world on his shoulders.

Monique eased the door shut to the bathroom as the dense steam engulfed her. She could see the shadow of Rasheed's nude body as he showered. She quickly undressed and opened the shower stall door. Rasheed stood under the water with his eyes closed with a bar of soap in one hand and a washcloth in the other.

He must have felt a draft because he opened his eyes just as she stepped into the shower with him.

Her nubile breasts gently brushed against his stomach, causing him to inhale her feminine scent. She looked like a midget standing next to a giant as she stared up at him. The water ran as the steam fogged them in a hue of gray. Monique searched for the right words to fill the void of love's passion that was missing from their relationship. On tiptoes she leaned forward and kissed his nipple. "Ra," she spoke. Her delicate voice echoed in the backdrop of torrential waters. "You're my man, my king, my everything." She gently began to rub his muscular chest, his six-pack abs.

"Mo, you think I should have kicked his ass?"

"Shh ..." she whispered, placing her finger over his lips, feeling the two-day stubble of a beard on her wrist. She reached down and held his manhood, which responded to her gentle touch. He closed his eyes and allowed her sultry voice to relax him as the hot, torrid water tranquilized him, relieving all the pent-up anger and frustration like a knotted rope being released from around his neck. A protracted sigh escaped from his lips. "You like this? Does this feel good?" Monique cajoled in a husky, seductive voice as she stroked him, causing him to relinquish a part of himself that will forever be a woman's true conquest—his body.

"Remember when I asked you if I could make love to you?" she asked in a breathy voice, whispering against his skin as the water drenched her face. The fahrenheit only seemed to increase as she deftly continued to stroke him with both hands, rubbing his penis on her erect nipples. Her lubricious tongue began an exploration across his wide, brawny chest, tasting the sweet taste of his brown skin like he was molasses.

She sucked on his nipple, feeling it grow hard on the tip of her tongue, causing him to shudder and moan. Her mouth traveled down south leaving a trail of hot saliva to be erased by the waters that bathed them. She made a stop at his belly button. She now held his enormous penis in both hands as she primed him with even strokes, feeling the thick veins that ran along the shaft.

Gently he placed both of his large hands on her shoulders, a silent gesture beckoning her, willing her. His body quivered. Finally, just about when he felt he could not take any more, she slowly got down on her knees. Stroking him, she gently kissed the head of his member. He was hard as a rock. She meant just what she had said when she asked him if she could make love to him.

Her love was the only thing a black woman could give freely when all else failed and reconciliation was the only form of redemption. Slowly her tongue rode the head of his penis then down the long sleek surface as she leaned back against the wall, taking him with her. A towel fell in the water as she drew him in her mouth, causing him to exhale deeply. She slowly deep-throated him, letting him fill her completely as she bobbed her head up and down ... up and down ... lips and tongue sucking and massaging with warmth from her mouth. Her saliva lubricated him, willing him to deposit his seed deep within her throat.

Her rhythm quickened with a fervid intensity. Loud slurping, sucking noises resonated as she devoured as much of him as her mouth would allow. He palmed her head gently and groaned with pure ecstasy at the feel of her mouth. Her hand manipulated his balls, gently tugging at them. The rhythm grew faster, almost on the fringe of a fanatical climax, causing him to moan. He was ready to explode with an enormous orgasm. Monique held on to his penis with both hands and sucked greedily. He lost control as he cursed God and called to Jesus with what felt like oceans of jet streams filling her mouth. Getting his dick sucked had never felt so good in his entire life. Then she pulled away, leaving him to dangle as a dribble of cum glistened off her pursed bottom lip.

A tuft of matted hair stuck to her face and eyes as the water splashed her body. Ever so gently, Rasheed wiped at the water obscuring her face and eyes. He wondered, as men seldom do, why his woman was going through such great lengths to please him. He knew her knees had to hurt and she also had just gotten her hair done.

Monique smiled up at him starry-eyed as his penis dangled in front of her face. She blinked back the water and caressed him one more time as she took him back in her mouth and hummed. She used all the force in her jaw muscles to stimulate him with her tongue. A young girl can learn a lot from X-rated movies. And indeed she had.

She pulled her mouth away from him again. This time he asked in a croaked, strained voice full of passion, "What's wrong?" She ignored him like she was in a world of her own. She caressed his penis, enjoying the feeling of controlling his lust for her, the feeling that only a real woman felt when she had really mastered the art of loving her man, causing him to crave her, need her, long for her in only a way such that only she suffices.

She rubbed the head of his penis on her breasts, savoring the moment for when she planned to have him deep inside of her. With his hardened shaft between her breasts, she squeezed them together, causing him to whisper words that not even he understood. She stood and turned the water off. Her firm pendulous breasts bounced, her quarter-sized nipples aimed at him.

She took his hand, soaking wet as they padded from the bathroom, leaving a trail of water behind, along with their inhibitions. The baby lay at the end of the bed asleep. They were careful not to disturb him. This would not be their first time stealing love while the baby slept in the same bed.

Monique gently placed the condom on Rasheed as he sat on the bed, leaning back on his elbows. She smiled to herself. His penis looked like a crooked light pole. Monique whispered, "You know you're going to have to go slow with me. I wanna ride it." He nodded his head as she stood in front of him. He watched the lovely patch of hair between her legs. It looked like she was trying to hide a small monkey.

"Remember, I'm making love to you, my king," she whispered with a twinkle in her eyes, as succulent beads of water cascaded off her body. His throat was thick with passion as again, he bobbed his head as he listened to his woman's sweet command. Slowly she mounted him like she was climbing a mountain. He lay back on the bed and watched. With his latexed penis she spread the lips of her vagina and eased the head in slowly.

From his vantage point, the view was great. Monique was positioned like a jockey on a horse as she slid a painful inch in and made a face that he knew all too well. He had no choice but to aid her. Even though she desperately wanted to make love to him, she was too tight –actually, he was too large. That depended on who you asked. With her heat smothering him he humped in a deep upward thrust, so deep that it felt like she could feel him in her chest cavity. She moaned and groaned as she thrashed her head from side to side.

He palmed her ass and went deeper, causing her eyes to roll to the back of her head as her body French kissed his. He continued to palm her ass, squeezing it, guiding, controlling her like a rag doll as he plunged deeper, faster, seizing control of what should have been her dominance over him, all for the benefit of giving him her love. She wanted to ride him to that place of pure ecstasy, but his thrusts turned almost violent as he moved inside of her using her body like she was a joystick.

In the fitful pounding, he pulled her down on him, filling her with all eleven inches. It felt like she was being torn in half as her supple breasts bounced in the air. She held onto his hairy chest and repressed a scream as his pace quickened. A slippery sound of flesh resonated as her body was heaved up and down with so much force she no longer had any control over his wanton lust.

"Ra … sheed … stop … you're … you're … hurting meee," she droned as he continued to pound away inside of her like some crazed maniac. Her body bounced in the air. Finally, he exploded in convulsions as he pressed her vagina tight against his body and cursed as the ebb and flow of love-making finally subsided. Exhausted, her body collapsed to his side, her right leg on top of his left. His panting echoed throughout the room as his muscles began to relax.

He thrust one more time for the sake of having a semi-hard erection. Monique began to move with his slow strokes inside of her. He assumed the position on top which forced her legs to open wide. He watched as he slid in and out of her slippery opening, still not fully erect. Monique loved his fervid passion when it grew weak like now, as long as he was still hard. She closed her eyes, enraptured. Her sex was strange; it was always hard for her to achieve an orgasm, but then tears spilled over onto her cheeks as he slowly moved inside of her, not as a beast, but as a lover.

She began to cry tenderly, lovingly, as he looked at her confused. Tears? She read his mind and smiled through her tears and shivered. "It feels sooo good. You feel so good inside of me. Oh God, please just go slow … like that, yeah … yeah …" She had awakened something inside of him, but now he was the aggressor. Then it happened. As she opened her mouth to scream to the heavens, another cry of terror caused them to both turn and look.

Lil' Malcolm was wide awake, his doe eyes filled with fear as he stared and pointed at his father with his little stubby fingers. "You hurtin' mommy," he cried.

Rasheed quickly pulled out of Monique and dived under the covers.

"What's wrong, lil' man?" Rasheed asked his son. Monique giggled under the covers. He turned and glowered at her as she pulled the cover down to her chin, smiling, satiated from sex as only a woman can describe.

"You hurt mommy," Malcolm said, causing Monique to laugh. Rasheed threw a pillow at her. She ducked, placing the covers over her face as her body continued to rock with jubilant spasms of laughter. *Women!* Rasheed thought as he tore his eyes away from her.

"No, Malcolm, daddy was not hurting mommy. I was making love to her," he said affectionately.

"Don't tell him that!" Monique said, popping her head from under the covers.

"What you want me to tell him?" Rasheed asked, making a face at her. "I sure as hell ain't fitna lie to him about the birds and the bees, so he can come home at thirteen telling us that he got his twelve-year-old girlfriend knocked up or worse." He turned back to his son, "Come here, lil' man." The child sniffled and crawled into his father's arms. "I wasn't hurting mommy. Watch this," he chimed playfully as he leaned forward and kissed Monique on her lips.

Surprisingly, she reached up, grabbing both of them in a hug. Malcolm squealed with delight, wedged between his loving parents as they both tickled and smothered him with kisses until his belly hurt from laughing. Moments afterward, Rasheed and Monique dozed off to sleep. Malcolm stealthily eased out of the bed and rambled through the house until he found Grandma Hattie in the kitchen cooking breakfast.

THIRTEEN

Jack the Ripper

The luxurious platinum package, limited-edition Mercedes had a customized front grill. The inside was handsomely decorated in black leather and sheepskin with a host of gadgets found throughout. The state of the art Alpine stereo system thumped so hard that it vibrated the ground. Quiet as it's kept, within the car's interior design was a hide-away compartment, especially designed to conceal guns and drugs.

Jack Lemon sat comfortably in the passenger seat with the air conditioner blowing, one hand on his pistol and the other on Gina's thigh. The smoldering smoke from the blunt wedged between his lips made him snarl as he tried to keep the smoke out of his eyes. A sense of satisfaction enveloped Jack and he smiled as he thought about Damon's decapitated body. An example of what happens to snitch niggas. He wondered how long it would be before they found him.

◊ ◊ ◊ ◊

Monique staggered from the bed to the sound of loud music outside the window. She strained her eyes against the sunlight as she looked at the clock on the nightstand next to the bed, 1:28 p.m. She groggily rose from the bed, placing her feet on the wooden floor. She looked out the window and saw the large automobile gleaming in the ardent sunlight. She couldn't tell who was inside because of the dark tinted windows. Then she looked around. "Malcolm?" She called his name. Rasheed stirred in his sleep. One of his long legs came out from under the covers. It reminded her of the sex they had. She was sore down there.

She put on Rasheed's T-shirt and headed for the door. On her way out she glanced in the mirror. *I look like shit,* she thought, as she brushed her hair down with her hand. The potent scent of their love-making was still in the air, or was it just her?

On the kitchen table she found a note from Grandma Hattie. It said that she and Malcolm went grocery shopping with Aunt Esta. There was a knock at the door. As she padded her way through the living room, she once again patted at her nappy hair as she opened the door thinking about her ruined relaxer.

She was surprised to see Jack standing there. He had a shit-eating grin on his face. "Jack Lemon!" She smiled broadly, happy to see him, while at the same time regretting she had come to the door looking like a real chicken head. Once again she mopped at her hair with her hands. He hugged her and laughed. He smelled like a marijuana factory and, painfully, that reminded her of his criminal past. They had been friends since high school, but it was mostly because of Rasheed. Jack was Jack. He loved to flirt with death, amongst other things.

"Did you get the money I gave Ra to give to you?" he asked.

She nodded and cast a glance out the door and looked back at him. "Whose car is that and how did you get out of prison? They said you had life in the feds." She delivered a rapid fire of words. If Jack was anything, he was trouble in the worst way.

"Damn shawty, why the twenty questions? Yeah, that's my whip," he nodded nonchantly toward the car. "A nigga doing big thangs. I'm fitna put this thang on mash! Shit gonna be different this time."

"Really," she said, curling her lips as she arched her brow.

"Where that nigga Ra at? I told him I was gonna take him shoppin'."

She drew in a deep breath. "J, Rasheed's asleep and he told me not to wake him up for nobody," she lied. Her gut was telling her to protect her man. Jack was cool, but she knew that he was up to no good. She needed to express this to him in such a way as to not offend him, but let him know what was up. "We got a three-year-old son now." She tried to smile.

"I know, he sent me pictures of y'all when I was in."

"No, you don't know, Jack," she said with calm emphasis. "I love you like crazy, but you're the reason that Rasheed was not able to go to a major college. He might have even been in the NBA by now."

"Me?" Jack huffed, pointing a finger at his chest.

"Yeah, you. The last time you came 'round here in a new car, it was stolen and Rasheed took the fall for it."

Jack exploded. "Bullshit! We rented a car from a crackhead. I gave him six rocks to rent it for the entire day. Later that day I went to the store to buy some beer. We didn't know that junkie had reported the car stolen. I came out the store, five-O all over the car. They found the weed and the burner in the car. What could I do?" Jack threw both of his hands up.

Monique shook her head. She had nothing against Jack, but damn.

"The next thing I know, the shit was all on the news and in the papers."

"Jack, please just understand what I'm sayin'. I got mad love fo' ya, that's word, but you're gonna end up dead or back in the joint if you don't change."

"I ain't never going back to the joint," Jack said with a dead serious expression on his face as he adjusted the gun on his waist. "I'ma be a'ight this time. I'm a seven figga nigga now, Ma. I ain't gotta grind no mo' if I don't want to. Know what I mean?"

A car horn blew. Monique strained her eyes as she looked out the door at the female getting out the car. "Gina!" Monique recognized her old friend. They had not seen each other in years. "Gina Thomas, girrrl, come here!" Monique hollered with glee, causing Jack to make a face as he placed his fingers in his ears. *All that damn yelling like they still cheerleaders,* he thought. Gina went inside the house. The two women danced jubilantly as they exchanged hugs. She was wearing a fly Baby Phat blue pantsuit that accentuated all her curves, giving her ample cleavage the attention it deserved. She wore a pair of Versace sandals to match her purse.

Rasheed came in the room with a look on his sleepy face wondering what all the commotion was all about. He took one look at Gina and Monique hugging in the middle of the floor and smiled as he scratched his privates and yawned. He wore a sheet around him like it was a toga. "What's up son?" Rasheed said, stifling a yawn.

"Mo was just telling me that she was 'bout to wake you up," Jack said as he cut his eyes at Monique. She made a face at him. They all talked for a minute then the girls went into the kitchen to fix the guys something to eat.

Once the girls had left, Jack said to Rasheed, "Mo still got a little hate in her blood for me."

"Yeah, kinda, but that shit go back to high school since the day we ran a train on Sha-Sha at Brenda's party."

"B, her pussy smelled like rotten fish and some mo' shit," Jack chuckled, causing Rasheed to crack up in laughter as he walked over to the front door, opening it. The system in the Benz was so loud that Rasheed could feel it reverberating under his feet.

"Daaamn, whose whip you done stole this time?" Rasheed droned, half serious. The car was beautiful. It must have cost over a hundred grand. As Jack reached into his pocket, Rasheed noticed a platinum and diamond Rolex watch on his wrist. Jack pulled out a small black device about the size of a pack of cigarettes. He pushed a button and the stereo system's music lowered. They could hear the girls in the kitchen rattling pans and gossiping like schoolgirls as they laughed.

"Damn, Gina looks good, son. What happened to the bracelets and ponytails she used to wear back in the day?" Rasheed asked.

"Kid, she doing her own thug thizzal now-a-days. Straight gangstress. When I took her out the house she was a foot dragger with potential. Now, she's a thoroughbred, game tight."

Rasheed pulled at the sheet around his waist as he listened to his friend. The front room of his grandma's house was cluttered with all kinds of trophies and plaques. Jack reached up and caressed a gold ball atop a trophy that stood almost six feet tall, trophies that went back to when Rasheed played junior basketball at seven years old.

Guilt-ridden, Jack wondered for the umpteenth time, if he hadn't gotten that car from that junkie that day, would Rasheed be now playing in the pros? He, along with everybody else, knew the answer to that. Like some invisible demon, the two never talked about it, they always managed to walk around the subject. In his heart it pained Jack miserably and he had sworn to himself, if it was the last thing he ever did, he would make amends with his friend.

"Think fast!" Jack said, tossing Rasheed a wad of money wrapped in a rubber band. The sheet almost fell off of him as he grabbed the money out of the air and gave Jack a facial expression that read, "what's this for?"

"Nigga, we fitna go splurge Jack the Ripper style." He then added, "That's twenty G's, stack it like you like it."

Rasheed felt the corners of his cheeks pull back into a smile.

"Nigga, is you tryna roll to the lot for a new whip or not?"

Rasheed scratched his head as he vaguely heard the women in the kitchen.

Monique stepped into the doorway. "Food ready!" her voice sang. She knotted her brow, grimacing at the money in Rasheed's hand. "Baby, can I see you in the bedroom for a sec?" She tried to keep the disgruntled apprehension out of her voice. Once they entered the room she snapped. "Don't you let that nigga get you in trouble."

He spun around and grabbed her shoulders. "I don't care what you say. You ain't never liked none of my friends."

"That's a lie." She frowned as she pulled away from him. She took a step back and stretched, arching her back like a cat. "Personally, I don't have nothing against Jack. I just don't want him to get you in trouble again. All this money, Ra ... it just feels like he's trying to buy your friendship," she said in a small voice as she turned away from him. He thought he saw tears in her eyes.

"Ma, I'm going to be okay." With that he went to take a shower. Afterward they ate breakfast together. The girls exchanged numbers and Rasheed left with Jack and Gina. Monique declined to go.

◊ ◊ ◊ ◊

Rasheed picked out a Cadillac SUV with expensive 22-inch rims. He had other accessories added to the car like tint, a customized grill and another DVD player especially for Malcolm. The dealership owner asked them to come back the following Monday. They had to take extra precaution with the paperwork since the vehicle was paid for in cash. They didn't need the feds sneaking around.

As they drove away, Jack thought he detected something in Gina's eyes – jealousy. As Rasheed rode in the back seat, he noticed all the fine handmade oak craftsmanship that went into the design of the car. There was a bar, two telephones – one on each side of the car – and televisions in the headrests. Rasheed looked down at the floor. Wedged in the front seat was a chrome-plated nine. His heart leapt in his chest, pounding so hard he could hardly breathe. He leaned back in his seat. That's when he saw the pound of weed inside a Ziploc bag. It had a purple tint to it. Gina saw his expression in the rearview mirror and danced her eyebrows at Jack to get his attention. Jack turned around and saw something in his friend's eyes—fear.

"Son, I could have put the brink and burner in the stash spot, but I learned when a nigga riding dirty and them folks pull a nigga over with the K-9 unit, I can just get out and run." He reached back and hit Rasheed on the leg reassuringly. "Son, I promise you, I'm never goin' to let you get fucked up again." Gina suddenly put on the brakes at the stoplight, causing Jack to jerk forward. He shot her a glare that said "what the fuck you doing?"

Jack continued, "Besides, I ain't even gonna front. I been in this grimy-ass city too long, seen to many niggas get caught slippin'. I'd rather get caught with my heat than without it." Rasheed nodded his head and swallowed the lump in his throat. In the back of his mind he could hear Monique's voice, like some evil incantation.

Moments later they dropped the drugs off at an old, run-down house that Gina had rented in Coney Island. Afterward, they decided to ride through their old stomping grounds in BK, flaunting the luxury car. They were drinking Hennessy and Coke as Jack puffed on a large blunt. He had the burner under his seat as they all exchanged war stories and laughed. The atmosphere was relaxed as they rode along getting high off blunts and drunk on nostalgic memories.

The night was alive and vibrant in New York City, the hub of the world. Gina drove, Jack navigated, telling her where to turn, what dope hole to visit. This was the part of the game that Gina loved. Jack Lemon was that nigga and just about every spot they stopped, cats showed love to him by giving him cash. It wasn't no military secret, Jack was the nigga you wanted on your team.

Niggas broke bread out of love and some did it as a way to renew their payments on protection fees. Jack Lemon was back out. To some, that was mind-boggling, because many hated him, most feared him, but all respected him. *Damn, it feels good to be a gangsta,* Jack thought as they rode around, bending corners in the Benz. Shit was looking lovely, even by his standards.

He glanced over at Gina as she snapped her fingers, jamming to the music on the radio, going to that place where women go when they're truly relaxed, looking sexy and don't even know it. DJ Clue stopped the music and began to speak in a somber tune. "To all my hip-hop fam out there, G-Solo and Big Prophet just walked into the studio."

"Yo … yo … what's up, son?" Prophet and G-Solo said in chorus as chairs and microphones could be heard moving around in the background.

DJ Clue continued, "It's really an honor to have these two double-platinum-selling artists in the station." After the small formalities ended, DJ Clue spoke to the listeners. "Everyone listen up, this is important. There's a hundred thousand dollar reward for the whereabouts of Damon Dice of DieHard Records."

"Hold up!" Jack said, throwing up his hand, spilling his drink on his pants and on the seat.

Gina turned her head and glanced at Jack. Like hers, his expression was intense as he wrinkled his brow in concentration, listening to the radio.

"This is for all the heads out there that have been supporting DieHard Records." G-Solo was talking. "My man Damon Dice was abducted the other night. As usual, the police ain't tryna do $%&* about it." The radio station bleeped out the curse word. "However, they do say that foul play is suspected. That's bull#*%$ 'cause we know for sure that at the time of his abduction the police had Damon under surveillance, and they let this atrocity happen right under their noses. Now we're offering a one-hun-dred-thousand-dollar reward for any information, no matter how small it may be, as long as it helps us find him."

DJ Clue cut in, "I hear that y'all have a significant lead already."

"Yeah, yeah, a bitch hit him up." The station wasn't quick enough to bleep that out. "She got a tattoo on her breast of either an apple or an orange. It could even be a lemon with the initials J.L. or J.M. underneath it. I can't be too sure 'cause we was all drinkin' that night."

Jack bolted straightforward in his seat and looked at Gina's breast. Her clothes concealed her tattoo. From the back seat Rasheed watched their reaction. *Could Jack have abducted Damon Dice?* Rasheed wondered. He thought about the blood on Jack's pants and his most recent purchase of a handsaw and cement. Rasheed gulped down the rest of his drink.

Big Prophet was on the mic talking now. "She followed us from the club to the hotel. That's when I saw her again, in front of the hotel lobby with Damon. Some time after that, he was abducted at gunpoint and placed in the trunk of a car, and the whole time the police just sat around watching."

"We already got the mysterious deaths of Biggie and Pac," DJ Clue reminded the listeners. "Not to mention Jam Master Jay, God rest their souls. What is it that our listeners can do to help?"

"Somebody out there has seen something. This same chick picked up a large sum of money at Damon's mom's crib. We can't be sure that it was her, but I got a gut feelin' it was. Also, we're pretty sure she got into a high-speed chase with the police and they let her get away."

Jack Lemon grinded his teeth as he disdainfully listened to Big Prophet. The same nigga that used to sit in the courtroom smiling and laughing with Damon Dice when the rat was on the stand lying on him. Jack slammed his fist into the dashboard. Gina cringed. Jack remembered the big man smiling and exchanging daps with Damon Dice when the judge pronounced a life sentence and the officers led him away in shackles to die in prison.

"So, if y'all saw the woman again do you think you could pick her out of a lineup?" The radio host asked.

"Hell yeah!"

"Damn right!" The two men answered in unison.

"It's these coward-ass niggas these days that put they bitches on the front line to do all they dirty work," Big Prophet offered in a thick baritone voice dripping with venom.

"Personally, I believe it's a nigga in BK somewhere. Anyway, son, I got a message for you," G-Solo challenged. "When I get my hands on your bitch's ass, whoever it was that set this whole thing up, I'ma punish you, bad. Yeah, I'm putting you on blast, 'J,' whatever your name is."

Visibly shaken, Gina pulled over to the side of the road. Rasheed sat in the back seat, stiff as a board, with a fresh drink in hand. Earlier he was sitting in the back seat plotting how he was going to sneak to Monique's job to see how she really earned all that money. Now he was racking his brain trying to remember what kind of tattoo Gina had on her chest. He knew better than to open his mouth. Something had gone down, and it had something to do with Damon Dice, the man who had testified against Jack.

"Move over! I'm driving," was all Jack said. He had that glassy look in his eyes that she knew all too well. Murder, murder, murder was the theme that rung in his head as he got into the driver's seat. Jack did a U-turn in the middle of the street. They listened as a caller called in. He had a heavy foreign accent. To their utter shock he said that an attractive female came into his jewelry store. He went on to describe the tattoo on Gina's breast and what she looked like to a T.

"The woman told me that her old man had just gotten out the joint and she wanted something really nice for him. So I told her a Rolex would be nice. She had me inscribe 'G loves J.L.' on the back of the watch."

"Did you get her name and number?" Prophet asked with excitement in his voice.

"Yes, but it's at the store," the caller offered. "I'm at home now. I just so happened to be turning the radio station and I heard you asking about this woman."

Jack glared at Gina as he drove.

"I'm sorry," she mouthed quietly with a fearful look on her face. They both listened as the man gave the address to his establishment.

"First thing in the morning, I'm going to see dude. A jewelry store, huh?" Jack said aloud, talking to no one in particular as he drove with both hands on the steering wheel.

"I'ma hafta drop you off at the crib. Somethin' just came up," Jack snapped over his shoulder as he turned down the radio. Rasheed nodded his head in the dark as he looked out the window watching the world go by. He knew what Jack was about to do. Rasheed's thoughts went back to the blood on Jack's pant legs. He took another sip from his drink and leaned back in his seat. *Shit!*

As Jack turned down 4th Avenue, the block that Rasheed's grandma lived on, he noticed an unmarked Caprice pull up behind him. Jack had the pistol in his lap. The unmarked car was all on his rear bumper. Furtively, he passed Gina the burner. She placed it in the hidden compartment.

"You a'ight?" Rasheed asked from the back seat as they pulled into the driveway.

"Yeah, the po-po right behind us. Hold that drink down." Rasheed turned around and saw Lieutenant Brown getting out of his car. He walked up and tapped on the driver's window. Jack lowered it slowly. Brown fanned the air as the scent of weed drifted from the car window into the gray haze of the streetlights. Lieutenant Brown did a double take at seeing Jack behind the wheel of such an expensive car.

"Hot damn! Jack Lemon. How in the hell did you get out?"

"They slipped, I gripped, same ole', same ole'. You know how it goes," Jack said nonchalantly as he popped his collar. They were having the traditional cops and robbers dialogue. Brown ducked his head down to get a better look into the car. He saw Gina in the passenger's seat. She had her arm on the armrest with her hand poised under her chin. Her manicured fingernails glistened as she rubbed her chin.

"Hello, young lady," Brown said. She didn't answer. One thing that Lieutenant Brown had to admit, Jack Lemon was a seasoned hustler and maybe even a cold-blooded killer. Even a police lieutenant was forced to respect that.

"What, it's your turn to beat me this time?" Rasheed questioned sarcastically, reminding Brown of the situation the night before between him and Officer Tate.

"Listen Ra, that officer was reprimanded. Why don't you let that go?"

"Like hell," Rasheed retorted as he got out the car, his height towering over the lieutenant.

"One day you'll find out I'm one of the good guys. It's going to take black police officers to stop white police brutality."

"Yeah, and what is it going to take to stop black cops from doing more harm to their own race than white cops?"

Lieutenant Brown, lost for words, stood there and looked at

Rasheed. "One of the worst things in the world they can do is give a nigga a job overseeing his own kind. He worse than a cracka."

"You need to let that go," the lieutenant said again, with steel in his voice.

Rasheed refused to back down. "My grandma helped raise you. You used to talk all that black power junk." He looked at Jack and continued, "This nigga went to school with your old man."

"Chill, nigga," Jack said, frowning with just enough of a hint to remind Rasheed there was a gun in the car. The front porch lights came on. Monique walked out. She had her hair re-done. It reminded Rasheed that he was going to sneak to her job that night and watch the show.

"Just because I'm a cop doesn't mean that I don't understand the plight of my people. I promise you one of these days you're going to find that out. Oh, and by the way, one of the reasons I was tailing you was because the light over your license plate is out. That's reason enough for a routine traffic stop," he spoke and raised his eyebrows. "Better me than them." Lieutenant Brown smiled, knowing they got his point. "Y'all have a nice day ... and Jack, get that light fixed." Jack nodded his head at Lieutenant Brown as he walked back to his patrol car.

Jack turned to Rasheed, "Man, you gotta learn how to finesse dude."

"Fuck 'em!" Rasheed said, walking up to Jack, giving him a dap. "Be careful, man."

With that, he walked away to let Jack go handle his business. Jack got back into his car, turned up the stereo and exited the driveway.

◊ ◊ ◊ ◊

G-Solo and his bodyguard, Big Prophet, left the radio station in somewhat of a hurry after DJ Clue was immediately called into the program manager's office. He knew he was going to get reprimanded for the language the two exhibited a few moments ago. Once they exited the building, they stood in silence. It was one of those starless Saturday nights with a full moon in the sky, and the

119

air was beginning to turn cool. They were thankful, for once, that there weren't any groupies waiting outside the radio station.

The parking lot was small, for security purposes. A few cars dotted the parking lot as they headed for the Maybach limousine parked a few feet away. The motor was idling as they got into the car. G-Solo picked up the car phone. "Steve, drop Prophet off at the club first, then you can take me home to Jersey." A grumbled reply came from the other end of the phone as the car pulled onto the streets.

"Listen, whoever this chick is, I promise you I'ma find her." Prophet was continuing their conversation.

"I dunno, I got a bad vibe about this whole thing. You heard what dude said back there at the radio station. He compared Damon's kidnapping to Biggie and Pac. Besides, Damon used to say it himself, the mob had their hands in about 90% of the rap game."

"That's bullshit! All we gotta do is find this red bitch with the tattoo on her chest. Money talks. I betcha for a hundred G's that hoe's own mama would drop a dime," Prophet said in an attempt to console G-Solo.

G-Solo frowned and said, "Then how in the hell does a nigga like him get kidnapped when he got mo' police 'round him than the President? Dude was s'pose to be under surveillance."

"I can't answer that, but my man that works at the police station pulled my coat, told me keep it on the lo-lo, but Damon was working with the Chief of Police, cat by the name of Brooks. Some kind of way they had a fallout, and the cop had a hair up his ass for Damon."

"Damon workin' for the police? Man, I don't believe that shit!" G-Solo shook his head in disbelief and slumped in his seat.

"Hey, I'm just telling you what was told to me by a good source."

They rode in silence for a moment as they both considered what to do.

"Did you see the way the phones lit up back there at the station? Dude that called in said he owned the jewelry store—that's our man," Prophet said reassuringly as he watched G-Solo slump further into his seat. One thing was for damn sure, G-Solo had no intentions of ever taking the lead. He was a follower. They both knew that with the looming possibility of Damon Dice being dead, DieHard Records was in serious trouble. Even though G-Solo rapped about being a gangster – his money, his hoes, his cars and his clothes – personally, he had never lived this lifestyle. He came from a middle-class family and attended Catholic school.

Suddenly the limousine came to a stop. "Where the fuck we at?" Big Prophet yelled, looking out the window into the pitch black darkness.

The window divider that separated the chauffeur from the passengers opened. A woman wearing a New York baseball cap, ponytail and dark shades stuck her head in the window and announced tersely, "Somebody said you was lookin' fo' me." The red beam from the .44 bounced around off the two men's foreheads as it ominously stabbed at the darkness until it finally settled on Big Prophet's forehead.

"Oh shit!" G-Solo screeched as they both recognized the woman at the same time. The door opened next and a masked gunman got inside the car. Everything was moving fast as both men looked on, startled.

"Big man, you like to rap a lot. Just be careful what you ask fo'," Jack said as he pressed his nine-millimeter against Prophet's throat while at the same time relieving him of the gun under his coat.

"Wha … wha … the fuck's going on?" Prophet stuttered.

Jack sat down opposite of both men, his composure dangerously cool and calm. "Bitch-made nigga, you gonna go on the radio and sell death to me," Jack said with a menacing scowl on his face, his voice sounding like dry ice being dragged across a wooden floor.

"Man, I don't even know you," Prophet responded, his voice hinting at a plea.

"Aw, nigga, you know me. I'm the nigga you was looking fo'. You called me out, so I'm here, J.L. in the flesh."

His neck snapped back like he had been slapped when he realized who was sitting across from him with a gun leveled at his head.

"Listen, man, I ain't got nothing against nobody," Prophet said, knowing that the first real law of the streets was to never buck a jack.

"Take whatever you want," G-Solo said timidly as he took off his Rolex. For some reason, G-Solo focused all of his attention on Gina as she moved the beam in intervals, dancing it off both men's foreheads.

"You ain't gotta tell me that," Jack said, aiming the gun at G-Solo. "I plan to take what I want. And since your man here," he pointed the gun at Prophet, "got a slick-ass mouth, he just earned himself a closed casket. I'ma dress your punk ass up."

"Hold up, man! Hold up! I didn't mean no harm," the big man said with his palms raised in the air. G-Solo cowered next to him.

"I didn't say nothin'," G-Solo chimed in somberly. All the manliness was gone from his voice. He almost sounded feminine on the verge of tears.

"Both of y'all shut the fuck up," Jack said.

Silence.

"You might have a chance," Jack said to G-Solo, pointing the gun in his direction. "But you, fat boy," Jack spoke to Prophet, "this is your only chance."

He reached into his pocket and removed a large water pistol. "Nigga, I'ma let you choose your weapon of death, which is better than the chance you gave me."

Prophet looked at Jack, narrowing his eyes at him and said, "What, you crazy or somethin'?"

Jack smirked as he calmly aimed the real gun at Prophet's kneecap and fired. The blast from the gun was deafening in the small confines of the car.

The big man hollered. "Aw shit, aw shit, you fuckin' shot me!" He grabbed his knee with a face stricken with both pain and terror as he looked at the madman sitting across from him. The red beam from the light continued to tease his mind as it roamed across his face and eyes. G-Solo whimpered as he looked on with his hands clasped in prayer.

"Okay, I'ma ask you one mo' time, and this time be careful how you respond. Know what I mean?"

Prophet grimaced in pain as he nodded his head up and down. "Which weapon of death do you prefer?" Jack reiterated.

Prophet pointed to the water gun and croaked hoarsely, "The water gun." *How in the world can a water gun kill someone?* he thought. For the first time, Jack displayed what could have passed for a smile as he raised the water pistol, taking aim and then lowered it.

"First, let me tell you a lil' joke." Gina sucked her teeth impatiently. Jack knew he had made the wrong decision in bringing her, but he would deal with her later. She rolled her eyes at him and let the smoked glass divider separate them while Jack continued with his business.

"Where was I? Oh, the joke," he said as if talking to himself. Prophet moaned, holding what was left of his shattered kneecap. "Ever heard any of them white man, Chinese man, black man jokes?" Jack Lemon asked, his voice sounding sinister as he continued looking out the window.

No answer.

He pointed the gun at Prophet's other knee. "Nigga, you hard of hearin' or somethin'?

"No, no please!" Prophet begged as he covered his good knee with his hands and pushed his back against the car door. G-Solo looked on with fear-filled eyes. In an attempt to distance himself from his wounded friend, he slid his body as far away as the limited space would allow. He mumbled something about the Lord being his Shepherd. Again, Jack furtively glanced out the window. The muffled sounds of the chauffeur screaming in the trunk disturbed Jack. The man had promised to be quiet. Jack made a mental note to blow a hole in the trunk of the car before he departed.

"Okay, there was this African king," Jack said rhythmically, causing his voice to fluctuate in tune as he reached over and started squirting Prophet in the face with the water pistol. "The big black king's name was Mutoto. He was the most feared king in all of Africa." Jack glanced out the window again. "He had a harem of beautiful women that lived not too far from the village. Three men from the village had got caught sneaking into the harem. They had been sexing the king's wives. So, his loyal servants brought one of the men before the king. This was the Chinese man. The king asked, 'Boungy or death?'—Boungy meaning that a big, black Mandingo African would bend the little Chinese man over and fuck him in the ass with a two-foot dick or else choose death. The little Chinese man happily chose Boungy." Jack snickered like the Devil himself at his own crude joke as he squirted Prophet with the water gun.

"Next was the white man. The king asked him, 'Boungy or death?' 'Boungy,' the white man said, happy to walk away with his life." Jack continued to squirt the water pistol as they looked at him, sure that he was insane. "Last was the black man. He was all cool and shit, walked with a pimpish limp. The king asked, 'Boungy or death?' The black man frowned and said, "Fuck you, king. I muthafuckin' choose death!" The king chuckled with amusement and said, 'Okay, that's fine with me.' He pointed at his servant and ordered, 'Boungy until death!'" Jack smiled with his eyes hooded in mischief as he leaned over again and squirted. It then suddenly dawned on them what Jack was up to as he placed the water gun down and lit a cigarette. The perilous fumes of the gasoline thickly permeated the air. Prophet's clothes were soaked. His eyes grew wide with fear.

"Nooo!" he screamed at the horror that was yet to come.

"Nigga, this ya Boungy, this water gun right here. You picked it as your weapon of death." Jack looked out the window again and turned back to the big man. "I told you you got a big fuckin' mouth, plus you got snitch in yo' blood." He then turned to G-Solo and stated, "Son, this thang bigger than me and you. The earth fitna shake. A lot of niggas fitna fall through the cracks, know what I mean?" Jack drawled, winking as he casually leaned over and shot Prophet's other knee. The big man fell in a heap on the floor, folding up like a crushed can. He writhed in pain. Jack took the honor of squirting him in the face.

"We … got … to … make sure that … the casket stays closed," Jack said with malice as he squirted the gun, emphasizing each word. Prophet groaned in pain on the floor. Jack now focused his attention on G-Solo. "Somebody wants you alive, people in high places. You might be the next golden boy at DieHard. That might get your bitch ass a pass. If I had it my way, you'd be dead." Jack stopped talking for a dramatic effect. The light from the cigarette glowed in the dark. He wanted G-Solo to marinate in fear as a duet of death sang in the car – Prophet's moaning along with the chauffeur's muffled screams from the trunk of the car – a mantra of sour melodies.

Jack spoke with determination in his voice. "In order for somebody to live, somebody gotta die. You wanna live?" Jack asked G-Solo. The frightened man nodded his head vigorously. "Take this cigarette. I want you to do your man." Jack placed the empty water gun on the seat and removed the dangling cigarette from his lips. "If you wanna live, dude gotta die," Jack said, pointing the gun at Prophet. "If you do the job right, just maybe my boss will let you hang around at DieHard and be the next golden boy."

Just then Gina slid the window down again. "We got a problem," she informed. "The police are headed in this direction."

"Fuck!" Jack cursed under the ski mask. He knew that if they suddenly drove off it would surely get them pulled over, and if they stayed, the police would look into the car. Gina got out of the car and walked right toward them.

FOURTEEN

The Gentlemen's Club

He watched her svelte figure as she danced on stage as beautiful as a ballerina. His palms were sweaty and for some reason he was nervous. Monique was completely nude, and for the first time in his life, Rasheed Smith had to admit, as he looked around at all the white patrons in the club, the place was extremely tasteful in terms of its handsome décor and atmosphere. It wasn't what he had imagined. All the waitresses wore cute little bunny outfits. For the most part, the women that worked there were drop-dead gorgeous. Monique was the only black person that he had seen in the entire club.

Rasheed ensconced himself in a dark booth in the back of the club. He accepted the few looks that he received when he first walked in the door, but other than that, everything was going better than he had expected.

"Hey sexy, want a table dance?" Georgia Mae asked as she sauntered up so close to him that he could see the diamonds in her belly ring as the light cast off it. She wore a royal blue transparent sarong. Her wide hips spread so far apart that he could still see parts of Monique's show through the gap in between her legs. He tilted his head up at her and smiled as the white girl intentionally blocked his view. He couldn't help but wonder when white girls started having fat asses like the bodacious one standing right in front of him. Damn!

Seductively Georgia Mae licked the rim of her lips as she first bobbed her head, then her body and started rhythmically grinding the air. She grabbed her hair and humped her pelvis in his face causing him to lean back in his seat. She turned around and hiked up the thin material. Underneath she was nude as she bent all the way over. She made one butt cheek dance, then the other, then to his amazement, like it was on some kind of hydraulics, her ass rose and her butt cheeks clapped. She dropped to the floor, doing a split, and got back up.

"Godmuthafuckindamn!" was all Rasheed could drawl as he sat with his mouth wide open. The white girl had lips on her kitty that looked like human lips, only smaller. She had mesmerized him and he did a poor job of playing it off. She could see the large print in his pants.

"Naw, I'm good." He smiled as he politely tried to wave her away.

She saw the light beads of sweat starting to form on his forehead. Her vanity was slightly wounded—she had never been turned down by a man before, especially a black man. She narrowed her eyes at him as she walked up closer. "Gee, I've never seen you before," she said.

"This is my first time," he answered as his eyes, with a mind of their own, roamed her luscious body. Forcefully, he tore his eyes away from her and looked at the stage.

"First time, huh?" she said in a dreamy voice as she placed a finger in her mouth and toyed with her tongue. He crossed his legs one over the other. Two white men walked by. They both gave Rasheed a prolonged look, nothing disrespectful, but just enough to remind him of where he was.

"Since this is your first time here, how about a free lap dance? You never know, you might get lucky," she said with all the charm she could muster as she let the thin material she was wearing slide to the floor. She stood in front of him, pigeon-toed and bow-legged, with a heart-shaped patch of fur between her thighs.

For the first time, he noticed her round breasts, how they curved upward, firm and succulent with an amber tint. Suddenly he had the urge to reach out and touch one of them. Instead, he reached into his pocket and removed a few bills. "Seriously, I'm a'ight." He tried to pass her the money, but she looked at him as if she were offended by his response. Georgia Mae's mouth smiled but her green eyes didn't as once again he slid his eyes off her body to look behind her at Monique on stage.

"That's Fire on stage. She's hot. You like her?" she asked as she bent down to retrieve the sarong and replaced it on her body. She walked around and sat in the chair next to him at the table.

"Who?!" Rasheed asked, as he raised his eyebrows and craned his neck to hear her over the loud music.

"That's my nizzle-fo-shizzel on stage. Her real name is Monique," Georgia Mae said with a broad smile. There was raucous applause as Monique's show ended. Men started to throw money on stage, lots of it. Rasheed knew that he had violated the sanctity of their trust by coming to the club without telling her, but his male curiosity had gotten the best of him. Rasheed felt something crawling across his thigh. It was Georgia Mae's hand. It came to rest on his penis. She squeezed it and made a face. "Damn, baby, you're huge," she gasped in surprise.

Delicately he removed her hand. "Don't do that," he said sternly, placing emphasis in his voice. She licked her lips and frowned, making a pouting face at him like a woman who was used to having her way.

"Honey, you know what they say, once you go white yo' life will always be right," she rhymed giddily as she flirtatiously pushed her large breasts, pink nipples like missiles, directly at him. The talkative, fly white girl had forced him to smile with her bold antics.

"Listen, the girl on the stage, you said her name was Fire?" he asked just as the waitress appeared, dressed in a low-cut black and white bunny outfit designed to show off lots of cleavage. "Rum and Coke, please."

"Yeah, that's my girl. She got a man and a baby though." She crossed her legs. The lights dimmed as Monique started picking up money off the floor.

"I know you've been told this many times before, but you're a very handsome black man." Rasheed blushed and smiled politely as he cut his eyes away from her to the stage. Georgia Mae was admiring his luscious, thick brown lips, his deep chiseled dimples and his skin the color of roasted pecans. She noticed his hands were large and he was tall, too. Game was determined to do everything in her power to take this black man home with her and seduce him, one way or the other.

He watched her as her jagged green eyes held him with a piercing stare. She had the most beautiful eyes he had ever seen.

"I just came here to relax and get my thoughts together," he finally said, pulling himself away from her seductive wiles.

"You say you just came to a strip club to get your thoughts together?" she reworded his statement, making it sound lame even to him. "If that's the case, sugar, I got more bounce to the ounce." She gave him a seductive stare, causing him to squirm in his seat. The room suddenly felt like the temperature had risen as he mopped at his brow with the back of his hand. She was driving him crazy, sitting in front of him partially nude with her breasts displayed like proud trophies.

He took a deep breath. "The establishment don't trip when you're sitting down propositioning the customers?" This time it was her turn to laugh, vibrant and throaty. As her head reeled back he couldn't help but enjoy the way her pendulous breasts bounced.

She remarked spontaneously, "As long as your sexy ass is buying the drinks I can sit here as long as I want. And if you keep up the resistance it's going to be me offering you money." With that they both erupted in jubilant laughter. He had to admit, she was funny as well as strikingly gorgeous. Her nearness made him feel vulnerable. He had never cheated on Monique in his life.

"After the show, do you wanna come home with me?" she asked. The expression on her face had changed. She was now dead serious as she leaned forward, as if peering inside of him. Like a woman shipwrecked, she could sense this was her last chance at grabbing land. She went for it all. "I love old school music—the Isley Brothers, Luther—I got all their CDs, plus the new ones.

You like Usher?" He nodded his head like a two-year-old.

"We could snort a couple lines of coke and fuck like rabbits. I can show you a trick or two with my ass ... things you ain't never experienced before. If you think I'm joking, wait for me in the parking lot for a trial run." She was desperately determined. Georgia Mae had turned huntress and he was the hunted as she held him enthralled with her sexual charm. She reached under the table and caressed his need. She found his penis, long and hard. It made her exhale a deep sigh as she felt moistness between her thighs.

"Please, come," she paused, "home with me." She spoke in a sultry, breathy voice, waving a pink tongue across her lips as the promise of pure ecstasy was sealed with puckered lips. She squeezed his penis, causing him to groan. She moved closer to his earlobe and whispered as she ran her hand down the length of his penis, "Do you wanna come—"

She stopped in mid-sentence as she was interrupted by some-one calling her name. It was Monique.

◊ ◊ ◊ ◊

Outside the Gentlemen's Club, three people sat in an old Ford truck. One of them was Tatyana, the Russian girl who Monique had beaten up in the club. Her face was still partially disfigured, and because of that, her career as a model was ruined. With smol-dering hate she blamed it all on Monique. She was back with vengeance on her mind and a score to settle.

Since her career had been ruined, the only work she could find dancing was at sleazy, run-down clubs in the black section of town. The patrons were all drug dealers, shady characters who pre-ferred to pay in drugs. It wasn't long before she started experi-menting with drugs—crystal meth and crack. One of the most hellish sights in the world was to see a white girl in a black world turned out on drugs, addicted and not even aware of it. The drugs had ravaged Tatyana's mind.

In the truck with her were two huge rednecks. The malodor-ous funk of unwashed bodies and stale cigarettes permeated the air. The old truck was littered with Budweiser beer cans and wine bottles.

"I want you to cave her face in and break both her legs so she can never dance again," Tatyana shouted, spraying the dirty window with spittle.

One of the rednecks responded, "I'm gonna whack her in the face with this hurr ball bat and Jethro gonna run her over with the truck a coupla times." Tatyana crinkled her reconstructed nose at the man. *God, he stinks,* she thought. The other redneck, Jethro, snickered as he took another hit off the makeshift crack pipe made out of an antenna. His teeth were rotten. A tuft of dirty blond hair fell over his eyes. His shoulders were broad, taking up most of the room in the cab of the truck. He passed the crack pipe to Bo. Tatyana had found the men at a Salvation Army residence for the homeless. She had promised to pay them five hundred dollars and all the crack they could smoke.

"I promise you that gurl will never work again," Bo said, taking a hit from the pipe, inhaling deeply. The dope made a crackling sound.

Tatyana smiled devilishly. "If you don't do a good job, I'm not going to pay you," she said in broken English. She looked to her left at Bo, then to her right at Jethro and continued, "If you do a really good job you can stay at my place tonight and I will personally bathe both of you." Her voice hinted at a drug-frenzied ménage à trois. Both men laughed excitedly as if she had just tossed a bone to a hungry pack of dogs.

She reached inside a plastic bag that used to contain a fifth pack of cocaine rocks. She pinched off one of the rocks, getting just a crumb just like the blacks used to do her and passed it to Bo. "Here's another twenty dollars," she said, with surprising quickness. Jethro grabbed the rock and at the same time he farted so loud it vibrated the seats.

Together, they waited outside the club, hidden in the backdrop of darkness. It was like Tatyana had planned, dreamed of. Now all she needed was for the black bitch to walk out.

"Please, someone open up a window," she complained as she waited patiently. The wait wouldn't be much longer.

◊ ◊ ◊ ◊

Rasheed turned his head long enough to see Monique walking toward the audience. Thank God she hadn't seen him yet. She was now adorned in a red robe.

"Here's your chance to meet the lovely Fire," Georgia Mae said as Monique walked straight for them. Rasheed held his breath as he slumped down in his chair. An elderly white man stepped in front of Monique. He had a dozen red roses in his hand for her, causing her to smile brightly.

Georgia Mae rolled her eyes at Dr. Hugstible. The old man seemed to be infatuated with her, and from the looks of it, so was the handsome man sitting across from him.

"Hey! Hey! Can a girl get a break? Damn," Georgia Mae barked. "I've done everything but propose marriage to you and your eyes have been roaming ever since I sat down." She was slightly pissed by his actions, but had to admit, Monique was an attractive woman. Finally Georgia said, "It looks like you would like to be one of her fans. I'll introduce you to her." Georgia Mae stood.

"No! No!" He raised his voice above the music for the first time as he grabbed at her arm. Too late. She was gone.

Briskly she walked to the front of the stage, almost colliding with a waitress that was balancing two trays of drinks. A few customers tried to get her attention as she reached Monique. "Girl, I got a man as fine as Denzel Washington, with a body like Usher." Georgia Mae said enthusiastically as she leaned closer to Monique. "I swear to God, his thang's this long." She used both of her hands to indicate how long. They both giggled like school girls. Another woman was about to take the stage. A few men were trying to get their attention. The lights suddenly dimmed as Georgia Mae took Monique's hand and led her to the table. It was empty. The handsome man was gone.

"I swear to God he was here a moment ago," Georgia Mae said

with a frown on her face as she searched the crowd.

◊ ◊ ◊ ◊

Rasheed walked briskly to the parking lot, ignoring the valet. He had parked his old hoopty way in the back of the lot. The cool air made him take notice of the night breeze. His shirt was soaked. He glanced over his shoulder and almost walked into a parked car. *Talk about a close call,* he thought. His ears still buzzed from the horrible music from the club. Once he reached his car he noticed the raggedy truck parked next to it, and not just that, but the awful smell that came from one of the open windows.

The three people inside the truck watched him closely. He could feel their eyes on him like a second skin. His instincts gnawed at him – a signal – just like the smell in the air told him they were smoking crack. He got in his car. As he fumbled with his car keys he thought he heard a woman's voice yell, "Nigger!" as he pumped the gas and turned the ignition. The batmobile sputtered and coughed, but finally the car started. He drove off with a gut feeling that something terribly wrong was about to happen.

And indeed something terribly wrong was about to happen.

◊ ◊ ◊ ◊

Georgia Mae walked into Monique's dressing room with her thoughts whirling, creating a riveting string of emotions. Even though she had never seen the handsome black man before, it was the first time in her entire life that she felt like it was love at first sight.

"Game, why you looking at me like that?" Monique asked with a half smile as Georgia Mae came in and straddled the chair beside her. Dreamy-eyed, Georgia Mae watched Monique take off her makeup. Georgia Mae had changed clothes. She wore simple white, low-cut jeans, a white halter top and boots with fur on the inside of them. "I was just wondering what it feels like to be in love with a fine black man with a dick down to his knee," she said before exhaling like she was blowing out candles. Monique turned and looked at her friend quizzically.

"Now, where did that come from?" Monique asked.

"I want to marry a black man and have his babies so bad, I don't care what people think," Georgia Mae continued, ignoring Monique's question. If you could have seen that fine motherfucker tonight, girl." Georgia Mae hit Monique on her leg. She continued, "You should have seen him though! He was just like I like 'em, tall, dark and handsome. The last man that loved me was a black man. He took my money and turned me out on sex and drugs. Gave me my first orgasm, and it wasn't from my vagina—"

"Stop! Okay, you're getting a little too vivid here," Monique said with a halting hand in front of Game's face.

"Somebody loves you, baby ... somebody loves you, baby," Georgia Mae began to sing beautifully, melodically hitting all the high notes just like Patti LaBelle.

"Girl, where did you learn to sing like that?" Monique asked, surprised. Before Georgia Mae could reply, Monique answered for her. "Oops, I know, I know. In all the talent shows your mom used to have you in."

Georgia Mae nodded her head. "Yup, I sang that song at the Apollo Theater. I came in second place."

Old Man Smitty, the janitor, knocked on the door and stuck his head in. "Sorry to bother you ladies, but you two are the only ones left in the building. I'm just about finished with the floor."

"Okay, we'll be out in a minute," Monique said. She then hurried to get dressed while Georgia Mae sat and hummed a tune. She gazed around the room and stopped when her eyes saw the roses Dr. Hugstible had given to Monique. She reached out and touched one of the rose petals. The image of the unnamed black man flashed through her mind. At that very moment in time she decided she didn't care what it took, she had to have him.

◊ ◊ ◊ ◊

Old Man Smitty walked with a bad limp, like maybe he had broken his hip at one time. Monique and Georgia Mae stood by the door and waited as he limped toward them. He had a mop in one had and a worn handkerchief in the other. He wiped his brow and placed the rag in his back pocket as he began to fumble with an enormous set of keys on a ring. It looked like it must have had over a hundred keys on it. Monique noticed the McDonald's hamburger toy on the chain. For some reason it reminded her of her son.

Outside the club the night was still and a constellation of bright stars embellished the black sky. A light breeze played with Georgia Mae's hair as she turned to Monique.

"Call me in the morning," Georgia Mae said as she reached out to hug Monique.

Monique pulled away from her. "I'll call you. Maybe we can go shopping."

"Yeah, that would be great." They each walked to their cars parked at separate sections of the parking lot. The parking lot was almost empty except for one truck and one other car. As Monique approached her car, she fished around in her purse for her keys. She normally walked with them out and carried a small knife concealed in her hand for protection, but tonight she didn't. As she found her keys, she attempted to open her door, but just then, someone grabbed her arm with brute strength, spinning her around.

Her key chain fell to the ground. Terrified, she looked up at what looked like the Devil himself bearing down on her, a white man. He was huge with broad shoulders, wide like a mountain. His silhouette was cut out of the darkness by the lurid moonlight. Monique could detect a foul odor coming from the man. Her first instinct told her to kick the giant in his balls. To her right, in the darkness, another figure appeared, taller, causing her heart to slam against her ribs with panic. Her eyes darted around frantically looking for an escape. One of the men had something in his hand as he neared. It suddenly occurred to her that it was a baseball bat. The shadows closed in.

"What do you want? Get the fuck away from me!" Monique said with her back against the car door. The man with the bat raised it, causing her mind to switch into overdrive. Fight, scream, run! Instinctively she went into fight mode.

"You must pay for what you done to me," a female voice said in broken English. Instantly Monique recognized the voice and it sent shivers through her spine. Tatyana nudged her way between the girth of the two big men and the two finally stood eye to eye. When Monique saw the tall Russian woman, it was hard to believe it was her. Tatyana had lost a lot of weight. Her once beautiful eyes were now gaunt slits of hate. Her cheeks were sunken and her hair was a shade of dirty blond.

"I never meant to hurt you." Monique's voice sounded like a plea, the tremor in it gave way to her riveting fear. To her right she could see the man inching toward her with the baseball bat.

"You have no fucking idea what you have done to my life, my career. Look at my face. Look!" Tatyana hollered as she spoke with a Russian accent. Boldly, she walked up on Monique. The two women looked at each other.

"Tatyana, I swear, I was not trying to hurt you," Monique said in a small voice with her back pressed against the car door. She could feel her legs shaking.

"You lie," the Russian spat as she hauled off and slapped Monique hard across her face with so much force that it nearly knocked her down.

"Break her fucking legs. Make sure she never dance again," Tatyana commanded, pointing at Monique's legs.

Just then, a pearl-white BMW sports coupe pulled up. The tires screeched to a halt as Georgia Mae hopped out and ran over. "Run, Monique! Run!" she yelled as she crunched low, legs extended, arms apart, waving as if her every movement was based on timing. And it was. Bo swung the bat at her with so much velocity it made a whooshing sound in the air. Georgia Mae timed it perfectly by spreading her legs. She ducked and came back up as swiftly as a cat, and using her momentum, she kicked him in the face, causing the bat to fly out of his hand. The blow caused him to stagger then fall backward. Hard.

In that split second Monique knew she had to react. She kicked the other man in the balls with all her might. He doubled over as her actions caught him off-guard. As she drew her leg up to kick him again, she looked over and saw Georgia Mae kicking the shit out of his partner. Tatyana screamed like a madwoman and charged toward her. With all her might Monique kicked, scratched and fought as Tatyana ran into her like a train. Monique felt her fist connect to Tatyana's jaw. She dropped. It was then that Monique saw the big white man grab Georgia Mae from behind like she was a rag doll and slam her, head first, on the hard concrete. It made an eerie thudding sound that Monique would never forget.

Monique reached for the key chain on the ground with her knife on it. The other man was only a few feet away. He was still stunned from the blow to his testicles, but not enough to stop him from going after Monique to accomplish the mission he had come for—to break her legs, five hundred dollars and all the crack he could smoke. He grimaced in pain as he reached to pick up the bat. For big men, they were surprisingly quick. They were, in fact, young men, but both had an old appearance from too much drinking and drugs.

Tatyana, as if possessed, teetered on one knee as she tried to get back up. She screamed at the top of her lungs, "Get her!" The big man had the baseball bat in his hands. He came at Monique. Off balance, he swung the bat at her legs. She tried to hop out of the way using her arm to ward off the blow. *Crack!* The bat hit her arm causing pain to explode throughout her body. She cried out.

Directly in front of her, Georgia Mae lay on the ground. The delicate figure of her body curved out in crimson blood as her life spilled onto the concrete. Monique held her arm as her assailant once again prepared to swing at her legs. She somehow managed to sidestep him as Tatyana stood up wearily. Monique took off running as fast as she could. To her horror, Jethro, the younger of the two men, came after her as she ran screaming for help. She held her wounded arm at her side as if it were a package she was carrying. They were in an isolated rural area in the wee hours of the morning. No one could hear her screams as the big man chased behind her. She could hear his labored grunts as he gained on her. "Bitch, I'ma kill yer."

Her arm was in excruciating pain. He was only a few yards away from her and gaining with each strong stride. Fear tormented her mind as she glanced back. She stumbled and fell. He was almost upon her as she scrambled to get back on her feet. The first blow landed on her buttocks. It came with so much force that she fell back down.

He was now upon her, there was nothing she could do. Her strength was depleted as perspiration poured from her forehead. Her breath fogged in the cool air. The moon was the only witness to the hideous assault on this night as it cast its gory shadow on them. She closed her eyes and said a prayer. Maybe the next blow would be to her head and it would all end painlessly. Images of her son, Malcolm, flashed in her mind. *Lord, no. Not like this. Who is going to take care of my baby?*

FIFTEEN

Jack and Gina

Jack watched as the two patrol officers neared. The damn chauffeur continued to make noise in the trunk of the car. Jack held his breath as they approached. All he could do was watch and wait. With his mind racing as to what to do, he reached over and turned up the volume on the radio. He almost slipped on the blood on the floor as both men, G-Solo and Prophet, watched him intently, searching for any possibility of escape or flaw in his character. They both heard Gina when she said the police were nearing.

"What da fuck y'all niggas lookin' at me like dat fo'? If the po-pos get hot, y'all gonna be the first muthafuckas shot. Word is bond. Ya'll goin out execution style," Jack barked, pointing the gun back and forth at them. His baritone voice was husky with the promise of death. Once again he strained his eyes to see Gina approaching the two officers.

The park was dimly lit. An occasional bush or tree outlined the nocturnal landscape. To her left was a garbage can, next to it was a water fountain that ran continuously. Clinched in her hand inside her leather jacket was a Desert Eagle. Gina had cut a hole in the lining of the jacket and positioned the gun at one of the officers' chests. Her palm sweated as she approached them. There was little doubt in her mind that if shit got out of hand, she was going to blast first. A lone car passed, the headlights streaked across the officers' faces. She was relieved that it wasn't backup. Gina went into a spell.

"My girlfriend's pregnant! We can't find her. We've looked

139

everywhere," Gina said as she began to cry instant tears.

"Hold on. Hold on, ma'am," the smaller of the two officers said as he raised his hand to comfort her. She drew in a deep breath as her shoulders heaved as if she was a distraught woman trying to seize control of her emotions. A cry of despair ripped past her lips. The younger officer had rosy cheeks and the pleasant smile of a man still in his youth. His square chin and sloping forehead gave him the appearance of a much older man. Gina would have shot him dead in a heartbeat if he acted up.

The other officer was tall and astute, the older of the two. His watchful blue eyes held her with suspicion. He frowned with a knotted brow at her. *Something is wrong with this woman*, he thought. He just couldn't put his finger on it. Gina detected his suspicions and turned toward him, the gun now leveled at his chest. "You say your girlfriend's lost and you can't find her, huh?"

"Yes, yes," Gina said, now in control. She pointed in the opposite direction of the limo parked up the street. They were about to turn in the direction she was pointing when a muffled shout resonated in the darkness. Along with it came the sound of loud music. The taller of the two officers reached for his gun and cautiously walked toward the sound of the noise. The limousine was sheathed in complete darkness up ahead, just like everything else in the park at night. Gina cocked the gun in her pocket as she raised her voice. "Those are my babies in the car, what are you doin'?"

The younger officer turned to his partner. "Bob, a pregnant woman is missing. I think we need to call in a K-9 unit." He then turned to Gina. "Ma'am, if she has not been missing for over twenty-four hours there's not much we can do," he said with genuine sincerity in his voice. The other officer continued to strain his ears, listening to the night noises. He turned and walked back toward them. His demeanor was impassive. Her tears did not affect him at all. "Go wait in the car with your kids, ma'am. We'll retrace your steps," the younger officer suggested with kindness. "I have a pregnant wife at home. If your friend is out here, we'll find her. Does she normally come out here alone?"

"No. She and her boyfriend had a fight," Gina responded between bouts of sobs as she turned and walked away.

The taller officer, the older of the two, called after her, "Hey, you, stop!"

Gina felt her heart pounding in her chest because she knew what was next—gun play. She touched the gun in her pocket as she slowly turned.

"What did you say your friend's name was?" the officer asked.

She had to think for a fleeting second that seemed like an eternity. "Umm ..." she paused. "Evette ... Evette Yates, that's her name." Her voice cracked as she slowly eased her hand out of her pocket. To her relief she watched both officers turn and walk briskly back toward their patrol car parked up the street. Gina sighed as she took off in a trot, headed back to the limo. The police turned on their searchlight as they did a U-turn in the middle of the street.

"They're gone," she said, nearly out of breath once she reached the car. The encounter with the police had somehow left her feeling fatigued and weary. Jack could see she was visibly shaken. Her fake tears had caused her mascara to run and she looked like a sad clown. As she stood outside of the car, she inhaled the strong fumes from the gasoline and made a face at Jack.

"Get in and drive the car to the school near the Marcus Garvey projects. Park in the lot." Jack ordered.

"But ..." she was about to complain.

"Just do what da fuck I just said," he hollered.

Prophet continued to moan as he writhed in pain on the floor.

Jack spoke to G-Solo as the car headed to its destination, a killing field. "You're the sole beneficiary of a million dollar empire. With Damon Dice gone, everything falls into your hands, everything that you and him built together, know what I mean," Jack said in an attempt to make G-Solo see the master plan.

"I don't know if Damon is gone yet," G-Solo said somberly. The car hit a bump in the road. Prophet moaned in agony.

"Big man with the big mouth, it's fitna be over in just a minute," Jack said, looking down at him. He turned back to G-Solo and said to him ominously, with his top lip curled, "Trust me when I say Damon Dice ain't never comin' back. My nigga, believe dat. Now, if you play your cards right you can inherit the reigns to your seventy-five-million-dollar part of the DieHard throne, or tonight you could lose your life, too," Jack whispered as he leaned over and kicked Prophet in the knee. "You don't wanna be like big mouth here, do ya?" Jack asked.

G-Solo shook his head vigorously like a man who wanted to live.

"The only thing better than the double cross is the triple cross," Jack said, his voice harsh like gravel. "Meaning, three can keep a secret if two are dead. And if Damon and Prophet are gone, the world is yours," Jack said persuasively.

"Don't listen to him," Prophet yelled from the floor.

"Nigga, that's why I'm fitna make your bitch-ass extra crispy," Jack exhorted angrily as he turned back to G-Solo with a feral grin. "Nigga, you tryna die or what?" Jack asked, pointing at G-Solo's head.

"Ye … ye … yes, I wanna live! I want to live! Please don't kill me," G-Solo pleaded with his animated palms shaking in front of him like he was about to go into convulsions. The car suddenly stopped. Jack peered out of the window and then calmly leaned back in his seat with gun in hand. Casually he lit another cigarette and placed it in his mouth. Gina opened the car door allowing the crescent moon's sinister glow to cover Jack Lemon's ski mask as he held the chrome-plated nine.

"Gimme your gun," Jack said, gesturing to Gina with his hand. She hesitated and passed it to him. She watched as he took all the bullets out, except one. He got out of the car carefully, checking the infrastructure and its surroundings. They were in the parking lot in back of a school. Jack ordered both men out of the car. Prophet complained that he couldn't walk.

"Okay, have it your way," Jack said nonchalantly as his eyes continued to survey everything around them. The last thing Jack wanted was a witness to the gruesome horror he was about to inflict on his enemies. He raised the gun to G-Solo's head.

"Dawg, here's the deal. I'm gonna give you the gun with one bullet in it and you're gonna shoot your man in the head with it and give it back to me with your fingerprints all over it. From this day forward you gonna be partnas with some big people in big places. When the police arrive you'll just say you were robbed. Know what I mean?"

G-Solo was shaking so badly that his lips were starting to tremble with the rest of his body. Large beads of perspiration cascaded down his forehead. He managed to nod his head tremulously with a frown on his face, like a man watching doctors perform open heart surgery on him. Jack passed him the gun as Gina looked on in utter shock.

"No! No!" Prophet screamed as he somehow managed to crawl out of the car. Jack threw the lit cigarette onto Prophet's gasoline-saturated clothes, igniting them, making Prophet a human fireball, an orange blaze lighting up the night. The heat was warm against Gina's arm, causing her to take a step back, aghast at the sight of the burning body.

"Shoot muthafucka, shoot!" Jack yelled at G-Solo. As G-Solo's hand trembled, he grimaced while tears spilled down his cheeks. *POW!* The gun roared as the bullet caught Prophet just above the right cheek, causing him to roll across the pavement. Suddenly the night had taken on a new meaning. It was wild and primitive as if a beast had been awoken. Prophet continued to thrash about. Jack stepped into the fray and fired five quick, successive shots into Prophet's burning body.

"Die muthafucka, die!" Jack's bestial voice sounded almost inhuman as it resonated throughout the ghetto like a lion's mighty roar or a young gangster staking his claim to the next throne of the streets.

Finally, Prophet's body stopped moving. The fire continued to burn as the awful scent of burnt flesh filled the air. Gina thought she was going to vomit. The fire flickered off G-Solo's teary eyes as Jack forcefully turned him around. He violently struck G-Solo and shoved the barrel of the gun in his mouth, breaking several of his teeth and possibly his jaw in the process.

Jack spoke with his jaws clenched tightly together as the smog from the smoke bathed both of them. He was intent on getting his point across to G-Solo. He need to get inside the terrified man's head to make him do as he said.

"Pussy nigga, you said you wanna live. Here's your chance. When the po-pos come, you can tell them you was robbed and your man got killed. You'll spend the rest of your life as a million-aire, not to mention, I'm rewarding your bitch ass with your life. Or you can explain how you murdered both men, Damon and big mouth," Jack said, nodding toward the smoldering body of Prophet. "Remember, I got the gun to prove it."

G-Solo listened carefully as he choked on the blood spilling from his mouth. He ran his numb tongue over his gums where his teeth used to be. He was certain that at least seven teeth were missing. "I swear to God, if you let me live, sir, I'll keep my mouth shut. Pleeeeeaze don't kill me," G-Solo gibbered as best he could. "I'll do whatever you want me to do."

Jack realized that G-Solo was dangerously near delirium. He hoped he hadn't pushed him over the edge. There's only so much terror a mind can take.

Jack spun G-Solo around. "In a week or so when you get out of the hospital from the gunshot wound, a friend is going to pay you a visit at the Tony building."

"Gunshot wound?" G-Solo mouthed.

"Yeah, I gotta make this look real," Jack said. He nodded toward Gina and she stepped up and removed G-Solo's Rolex. Blood from his mouth fell on her wrist.

"Dawg, I know mo' than you think I know 'bout 'cha. Yo' mama live in New Jersey with the rest of them fake-ass, wanna-be rappers," Jack added, making yet another threat as he looked around, his eyes alert and his mind telling him he had been here too long. He took a step back and shot G-Solo in the ass. He screamed and fell to the ground. Jack was just about ready to trot off when he remembered something. He quickly walked over to the trunk of the car and fired two shots into it. He and Gina jogged off into the night, holding hands. Together they had left behind a human wreckage, the mayhem of a prominent up-and-coming young gangster who's motto was "Black love first." And, as usual, the streets were watching. Young nigga on the come up.

◊ ◊ ◊ ◊

G-Solo hobbled over to the phone inside the car and dialed 911, reporting that he had been shot and robbed and that his bodyguard had been murdered. As he spoke into the phone, a cinder from the fire was still burning. G-Solo reached over and pushed the button to open the trunk. The chauffeur had somehow managed to survive. He had been shot in the legs.

Moments later the authorities arrived. Lieutenant Anthony Brown was with them. Three men had been shot, one of them fatally. One of the victims had actually been burnt to a crisp. Leonard Green, better known as G-Solo, had clearly developed a bad case of amnesia. All he could remember was a masked gunman and a woman. Judging from the evidence at the crime scene, Lieutenant Brown recognized an execution-style hit. He had been living in Brooklyn long enough to see that right away. Now he just wondered why G-Solo hadn't been killed. Someone wanted to keep him alive, but why?

◊ ◊ ◊ ◊

Monique lay on the ground in a heap, lungs on fire, depleted of oxygen as the formidable shadow towered over her. His breathing was labored like that of a pack-a-day smoker as he gasped for air. Hunched over her, he pulled back to swing the baseball bat, his face grimacing with malice, intent on doing serious bodily harm. Suddenly, an ardent light shined across the parking lot.

A woman's voice screamed, "Bo, hurry!" The voice belonged to Tatyana as she called out to her accomplice. The other had already jumped back inside the truck. Rasheed's car headlights illuminated Monique's body as she lay there. She screamed just as the car came to a halt.

He couldn't believe what he was seeing. It was like a living nightmare, his woman being attacked by a white man. Rasheed hopped out of the car and rushed over to her. The redneck swung the bat, causing it to whistle just inches from Rasheed's head as he ducked and rushed the big man. Rasheed swung wildly and connected with an overhand right that caught the redneck on the bridge of his nose, sending him spiraling backward. The baseball bat fell to the ground.

Bo threw one punch, nearly falling. Rasheed was up on Bo as he rained blows down on his face and mid-section, opening up a deep gash on the white man's pale forehead, and another, as Rasheed drew back, striking with all his might. For some reason, the white man would not cover his face. A truck sped up behind Rasheed in an attempt to run him over. Monique screamed a warning. Rasheed dived out of the way in the nick of time and rolled on the ground near the bumper of his car. Punch drunk, Bo was barely able to stagger over to the truck to get in, his face a mess. The truck sped away, burning rubber, leaving behind a trail of smoke.

"Are you okay?" Rasheed asked Monique as he got off the ground, winded. She saw blood on one of his knuckles.

"My arm hurts, bad. I think it may be broken. When I fell I hurt my ankle," she said, biting down on her bottom lip, making a feeble attempt to hold back her tears, as her body became racked with sobs. He looked at his woman and it felt like a part of him was dying. It was unbearable to see her in so much pain. She tried to sit up, but winced.

"Shit! Shit! Shit!" he cursed, enraged, as he balled up his fists. He sat on the ground beside her. His heart was a river of emotions about to overflow its banks.

"Ba ... baby, I'ma hafta pick you up and carry you to the car so I can get you to the hospital," he said in the voice of a broken man. He was failing miserably at keeping the hurt out of his voice.

She rested her head on his shoulder and sighed deeply. In the distance a siren blared. In the sky, a lavender dawn was starting to peek over the starry horizon, morning's attempt to steal the night away.

"Oh Lord, Game!" Monique shouted as she suddenly remembered she had come to her rescue once again. "Ra, you gotta go check on Game. She's hurt bad, please," Monique cried pungently as tears fell down her cheeks.

He frowned as he looked at her. "Baby, who you talkin' about?"

"Game, my friend. She's hurt real bad. You gotta help her." Monique pointed with a trembling finger as she wailed. Rasheed strained his eyes in an attempt to locate who she was talking about. Vaguely he could see a figure sprawled out on the pavement. Monique tugged his shirt. "Rasheed, you gotta help her!" she pleaded. He stood, eyes still focused on the spot in the distance. He took off running.

Game lay on the ground in a pool of her own blood, her body in a grotesque position, like a discarded baby doll that had been slung to the ground. Rasheed wasn't a doctor, but he knew instantly something was terribly wrong. *She looks familiar,* he thought to himself. It then dawned on him – it was the flirtatious girl from the club. He swallowed the lump in his throat as he timidly crouched down to check on her. He could tell from the bubble of blood that rose from her nose that she was breathing. He rubbed at the back of her head to find the source of the pool of blood. "Damnit man!" She had a hole in the back of her head about the size of his fist. He pulled his hand away. It was covered in blood. She was dying.

"I got to get her help. The girl is almost dead. It looks like her neck or somethin' is broken," he said to Monique as she sat on the concrete cradling her arm. She grimaced in pain.

"Mmm, my cell phone is dead, but Smitty the janitor should still be in the club," she said, panting, swaying back and forth in an attempt to find the fortitude to deal with the pain.

"I'll be back," Rasheed said. This time he headed for the club.

Moments later he was banging on the glass door. After Rasheed told the old janitor what happened to the girls, Smitty called the authorities.

SIXTEEN

Rasheed & Monique

The police arrived in large numbers, enough so that they instantly made Rasheed nervous, the way they did lots of young black men. Monique sat in the passenger seat of Rasheed's car. Her arm was bruised black and purple. It had already started to swell. The sirens blared a raucous symphony in her ears as a sea of police cars surrounded them in the parking lot. For a fleeting second she thought she saw fear in Rasheed's eyes.

"What happened here?" an authoritative voice asked. He looked to be in his late fifties. He was of medium height with salt and pepper hair. His long nose was crooked as if it had been broken before. His blue eyes were hard to read, like a man who had been on the force a long time.

Monique did all the talking, but for some reason, the cop's eyes stayed on Rasheed. The atmosphere was quickly turning into pandemonium. The mighty roar of a police helicopter reverberated in the sky. Rasheed couldn't help but notice that all the medical attention was being focused on Game. Sure, the white girl needed it, but so did Monique. Off to his right Rasheed could see Old Man Smitty, the janitor, talking to a plain-clothes officers. The old man pointed in his direction as one of the officers jotted down something on a note pad.

"You say two white males and a female approached you in the parking lot, and it was over there that one of the white males struck you with the baseball bat?" the officer asked with one eyebrow arched.

"One of them picked her up," she pointed at Game, "and

slammed her head on the ground," Monique said. It was evident that she was in serious pain as she attempted to talk. At one point it looked like she was about to pass out. As Rasheed looked on, he was disturbed as once again like another day in the life of a Black man, he was confronted with one of his deepest fears, like some damn phobia—white men in blue suits. He pulled in a deep breath as what seemed like a thousand eyes bore through him with lingering suspicion.

The officer said, "Young lady, could you repeat that again?" His icy cold blue eyes continued to dart back and forth between them. It was all but evident that he was not buying her story. Monique looked up at him with a wrinkled forehead as she held her arm.

Rasheed looked around helplessly. On the other side of the parking lot, three ambulances sat parked as they attended to Georgia Mae. A few more moments passed and finally Rasheed's temper flared. Monique was in so much pain tha tears cascaded down her cheeks as she retold her story for the third time. Rasheed could feel the blood rising in his face. The impulse to hit the officer in the mouth began to taunt him. Somehow it felt like he was being humiliated by watching Monique suffer and not being able to act.

Finally he had enough. With eyes blazing with fury he spoke through his teeth, jaws clenched so tightly his chin seemed to jet forward.

"My fiancée needs medical attention and it seems like she's being interrogated instead of aided as a victim of a crime." Rasheed's words caused the officer to jerk his neck back as he turned and looked at him. The officer was in his thirties with a chubby face and a hunched, rotund body.

"First off, you need to shut up and speak only when spoken to, and second, I need to see some identification."

"What the fuck does me having ID gotta do with her being assaulted?" Rasheed asked indignantly as he frowned. It was then that he noticed that he and Monique were completely surrounded as if the police expected them to make a run for it. They were victims of an assault, yet they were somehow being treated as suspects in a crime. All the smug faces and callous grins said more than a million words. A white woman had been assaulted and he and Monique were the next best things to an arrest.

In the distance, paramedics scrambled to get Georgia Mae into the waiting ambulance. She had a gauze wrap around her head and one of the medics was holding an IV bag that dripped a clear liquid into her arm.

"Okay, buddy, let's see some ID," the cop asked again, waving his fingers at Rasheed. Rasheed looked at him with narrow, slanted eyes as he shook his head in disbelief and fought with everything in his power not to lose his temper. He reached into his pocket for his ID. The officer hollered to one of the other officers, "We're gonna need a female officer to search the girl here."

That was it. Rasheed exploded. "Y'all ain't puttin' a muthafuckin' hand on her. She needs medical attention. NOW! Fuck you, man!"

"Calm down, these are normal procedures."

"Calm down?" Rasheed said, making a face. "Calm down for what, so you can continue to violate my fuckin' rights?"

One of the officers standing around commented eagerly, "You want me to place him in cuffs?"

Rasheed turned around to see where the voice had come from. It was then that he realized that the rest of the police were closing in. He prepared for the inevitable as he imagined the unfathomable, a white girl dying and he and Monique being accused of a crime they did not commit.

"Place your hands up, spread your legs," another officer said, walking up on him. He had an attitude with Rasheed, and judging from the hate written on his face, he looked forward to seeing Rasheed attempt to resist arrest. Rasheed retorted with a face of pure contempt.

"I didn't do shit. Put my hands up for what?" Rasheed challenged.

Monique pleaded as she sat in the car sideways with her feet on the ground. She reached out to him, her voice cooed a warning, "No, Ra, no." She winced in pain as the tears continued to streak her ebony cheeks. But, Rasheed's mind was gone to that place where a man's mind goes when he finds his back against a wall. If he allowed these evil men to handcuff him and place him in the back seat of a patrol car he would be considered guilty until proven innocent. For impoverished people that lived in the ghetto, that had always been the real law.

"I said, put your hands up, turn around and spread your legs!" the officer said, raising his voice. He was about five inches shorter than Rasheed and that made it all the better. It justified him using excessive force if need be, just like the Rodney King beating, only in this case, a white woman had been brutalized.

One of the plain-clothes detectives who had been talking to the janitor walked over, nudging his way into the crowd of officers that were about to pummel the tall, willowy kid.

"What's going on here?" he asked after making his way to within a few feet of them.

Rasheed spoke first, his eyes instantly recognizing that the detective in the suit must have ranked higher than the rest of the officers in uniform. "Sir, please help me," Rasheed said, his voice cracking as he swallowed the dry lump in his throat. Rasheed continued as he cast a glance down at Monique. "My fiancée and her girlfriend work here at the club. They were attacked as they left work." Rasheed went on to tell him the entire story—start to finish—as the detective listened. What he couldn't tell was what he didn't know, that Tatyana was one of the assailants. The way Monique was raised, she wouldn't tell on her unless it was absolutely necessary because, as crazy as it may sound, it was looked upon as snitching, and besides, Tatyana hadn't gone to the police on her when Monique had whooped her ass.

After Rasheed finished talking the detective looked around at the rest of the police standing nearby. His opaque green eyes were hard to read as he shook his head and walked over to Monique. He crouched down, establishing eye contact with her, and said in a compassionate, fatherly voice as he gently touched her leg with the tips of his fingers, "Fire, are you alright?" He called her by her stage name. He had learned it from talking to the janitor.

"Nooo, my arm ... I ... I think it's broken." There was something about his caring voice that pulled a string inside of her, causing her emotions to spill over. Rasheed turned away and stomped his foot on the pavement as he glared at the cop who had been so anxious to put the cuffs on him.

"I ..." she said, trying to move her foot, "twisted my ankle when I was running," Monique sobbed. The detective looked down at her badly swollen arm. He mumbled something under his breath and then pressed his thin lips so tightly together that they formed one line across his face. He looked at the poor kids; they were probably frightened to death. Gently, he patted her on her legs.

"I'm going to help you. How about we get you to the hospital, okay?" He spoke with kindness. He stood back up, his cheeks flushed red as he twisted his face angrily. How could people that were supposed to help be responsible for so much hurt? There was no doubt in his mind what would have gone down had he not approached.

"Get a fucking ambulance over here. Now!" he barked. Heads turned to look at him. "Why the fuck are y'all standing around gawking? MOVE!" Just then his partner approached. With two fingers he held up a baseball bat, careful not to destroy any fingerprints that might be on it.

"Have this dusted for prints," the officer said as his eyes searched the ground for any more evidence.

Visibly shaken, Rasheed sighed in relief. As he leaned back against his car it felt like a large boulder had been taken off of his back. For the first time in his life, he looked at the police with real gratitude for coming to his aid.

"If you like, you can ride in the back of the ambulance with her," the detective offered. Wearily, Rasheed raked his fingers through his hair and exhaled, "Thanks."

SEVENTEEN

The Murder Scene

Lieutenant Anthony Brown bent down to examine the charred body of the victim. The horrible smell of burned flesh permeated the fog around the smoldering human remains. The doors to the Maybach limousine were open. Next to one of the doors was a discarded gym shoe. For some reason Lieutenant Brown stared at it, as if it could give some kind of hint as to what had happened.

"Lieutenant, there appears to be a bullet hole in the victim's right cheek, and judging by the markings on the ground along with the blood smear, it looks like the victim didn't die immediately. In fact, he may have tried to put up a struggle." Mario Rodriguez was a Mexican detective with a reputation for busting cases. He had a thick mustache with bushy eyebrows and a tan complexion. He was in his late forties and worked out daily at the gym.

"Do you think he was shot after being doused with something to make him burn like this?" Rodriguez asked as they both looked at the badly burned body.

The Lieutenant frowned as he cupped his hand under his chin. "This place looks death struck. There's a cold-blooded killer runnin' around this city. This wasn't just a murder; this was a message," Brown summarized.

A police officer walked by. Rodriguez made a face as he complained, "For Christ's sake, could you please walk around the other way? Don't they teach you guys how not to contaminate a crime scene? Shee!" he exclaimed derisively.

"Sorry, pal," the officer said with a smirk, gesturing with his hands as he tiptoed away.

Lieutenant Brown touched the body with his latex-gloved hand and smelled his finger. "Gasoline?" Two more officers walked by. Rodriguez shot them both mean glares. Brown stood looking at the crime scene. Dawn was starting to brighten the sky with an orange, Indian Summer glow. A piece of trash blew in the wind and once again Lieutenant Brown looked down at the dead man's gym shoe as if, in some way, it could tell the tale of what happened to its owner.

Rodriguez said, "We got three victims, one fatally wounded. The paramedics say the chauffeur is going to make it. He was shot twice. He made a statement that a woman pulled a gun on him while he was outside of a radio station. He also said that a black male wearing a ski mask forced him in the trunk at gunpoint. The guy told him he'd better keep his mouth shut or else he was going to shoot him."

Lieutenant Brown walked over and looked at the bullet holes in the trunk and commented, "Guess he didn't keep his mouth shut." Brown took a second look at the holes in the trunk of the car. He raised his brow and walked over to the bullet casings on the ground. The evidence technician had tagged and numbered each casing with orange markings, one through five. Lieutenant Brown removed a pencil from his breast pocket, reached down and picked up one of the casings with its tip. He examined it closely.

What he saw disturbed him greatly. He determined the caliber of the gun to be a nine-millimeter. However, the ammunition was deadly, a Teflon-coated KTW metal-piercing bullet, better known as a "Cop Killer." For years the ammunition had been outlawed in New York ever since two armed bank robbers had held two entire police stations at bay, killing several officers and bystanders. The ammo was powerful enough to go through twelve telephone books with ease and still hit its target. Brown deposited the shell in an envelope and placed it in his pocket as he vaguely heard

Rodriguez talking in the background.

"The other victim was shot in the ass," Rodriguez said.

"Did he tell you anything?" another officer asked.

"The only thing he could tell me was that the gunman wore a black mask. Other than that he couldn't remember anything." Rodriguez licked his thumb and flipped through pages on a small pad to make sure he hadn't missed anything.

"Someone had to drive the car while the gunman held the two victims captive," Lieutenant Brown reasoned as he approached Rodriguez and the other officer. "And not just that, the kid, G-Solo, is not leveling with us."

"Why do you say that, Lieutenant?"

"He never mentioned the woman that the chauffeur spoke of. The first thing that runs through a person's mind when they're being abducted is, 'where are you taking me?' so his mind would have been on the driver. Remember, the dead man wore expensive jewelry and had over a grand in his pocket."

The two officers looked at Lieutenant Brown as if to say, "And?"

He continued, "G-Solo said he was robbed. Why didn't the robbers take anything from his bodyguard ... other than his life?" Brown asked on a somber note. As he looked across the school parking lot, police vans, cars and various other police units scurried about like a small army. Bright yellow crime scene tape with black letters stretched the entire circumference of the lot. Brown paid close attention to the herds of media that had already begun to arrive. He looked up overhead where a news helicopter hovered.

"Lieutenant Brown," one of the techs called from inside the car. Brown walked over and peered inside. The technician was a middle-aged man with thick glasses and a large balding head. He wore latex gloves which were visible as he pushed his glasses up on the bridge of his nose. He pointed with his other gloved hand. "Here." Brown squatted down. The inside of the limousine, on the right side, was stained with blood. Underneath the seats in the leg area, the tech had found two bullet holes and the casing to match. Brown bent down to examine the bullet holes. He reasoned that the victims had been shot inside the car as well. He briskly walked back over to the dead body. The pant legs were badly burned, but he could still make out the gunshot wounds to the victim's knees.

"Damn, you must have pissed somebody off bad," he said to the corpse as his mind churned. Finally, the stench from the body overwhelmed him. He crinkled his nose and rose to his feet. "Rodriguez!"

"Yes, sir," he answered from a distance.

"Get the DNA lab to analyze the car. Then have a profile run through the database to see if we get lucky and get a hit. Also, have the blood checked on all the evidence, especially everyone's clothing. Sometimes the killer injures himself." Brown bit down on his bottom lip as Rodriguez jotted down notes on a piece of paper. Brown added, "Also, don't forget to get traces of hair and fibers. Find out who the limousine service belongs to and get their phone records. I wanna do a house-to-house check in this area. Somebody had to have seen or heard something."

"Why did someone shoot G-Solo in the ass, at close range, but kill his bodyguard?" Rodriguez asked as if talking to himself.

"He let G-Solo live for a reason," Brown confirmed. "I have a feeling this may be connected to the Damon Dice disappearance. It's just too close for comfort." As he talked, something on the dead body caught his attention. On he right side of Prophet's shirt was an outline of a bloodstain. It almost looked like a signature on a child's drawing. Brown took out his pencil and eased the dead man's shirt back out of the way to get a better look at the markings exposed in the charred flesh. Carved next to his nipple were skewed markings. Lieutenant Brown knotted his brow quizzically as he jotted down the letters on a piece of paper.

"Don't look now, but we got trouble comin' this way," Rodriguez warned. Brown's mind was elsewhere. Like all good cops, his instincts told him that the dead man had scribbled on his body with his fingernails; letters that could be just the lead he needed to break the case. A dead man talking.

"I need to speak to you," a curt voice said, causing Brown to look up. He eased the shirt back over the markings and stood to match glares with Captain Brooks.

"Damn, why don't you just try putting in an application for a job at 75th? It'll save you time and trouble from making the trip all the way out here," Brown said without humor as he placed a hand inside his pocket.

"Good news travels fast," Brooks said, looking down at the body on the ground with a satisfied smirk on his lips. "Especially if it's one of your good men at the 75th who tips me off."

Brown ignored the last remark. "So what gives you reason to barge in on my territory this time?" Brown asked, barely able to contain his disdain for the man. Just then, the medical examiner arrived. Both men turned to watch Dr. Wong. He was a very small man, about five feet tall with shoes on. He wore spectacles as thick as pop bottles. In the strange world of police work, Dr. Wong was considered a multi-genius. He held several different degrees. He was also a lawyer, amongst other things. Momentarily, both men stopped talking and nodded their heads toward the doctor, acknowledging him.

"Morning, gentlemen," the doctor said, bowing his head slightly. He and Lieutenant Brown were close, having even sat in the morgue on a few occasions and drank beer as they talked about the gory details of a case.

The doctor placed a pair of latex gloves over his child-sized hands and squatted down, going right to work. To some in his profession, Dr. Wong was an odd man. Some would even consider him a little off his rocker, but all agreed that when it came to the science of crime scene investigation, he was a genius. As he reached down to examine the body, he frowned and spoke to it as if he expected an answer back. "A bullet entered your right cheek. I can't be sure until I get you on autopsy table, but it look like the temporal, occipital, parietal and frontal bones of your skull have been shattered." Wong made a face and peered closer at the body.

"Jesus, what he shoot you with, an elephant gun?" The doctor's eyebrows stretched upward.

"This homicide may be connected to the disappearance of Damon Dice," Captain Brooks was saying to the lieutenant. Their volley of words were heated, nearing a shouting match. Brooks continued, "If that's the case my department needs to be abreast at all times of the goings-on of this case, no matter how small they may be."

Brown looked the Captain in the eyes and stated bluntly, "Didn't you just tell me earlier that you had a spy in my department in the 75th?" Brooks arched his brow at the lieutenant as Brown finished his statement. "Then I think it would be in your best interest to use him, because until my superiors tell me so, I ain't tellin' you shit about this case."

As the two officers argued, Dr. Wong continued to meticulously go over the body, talking to it as if it were a dear old friend. He discovered more gunshot wounds as he pulled back the deceased's shirt. The doctor looked up to get Lieutenant Brown's attention and Brown just so happened to look over at Wong. He silenced him with a warning look. The last thing he wanted was for Brooks to know the dead man had left a clue as to who the murderer was.

"I take it you haven't seen this morning's paper?" Brooks shouted with his finger in the young lieutenant's face. "The media, along with certain people in high places, including myself," the angry Brooks got up in Brown's face causing him to take a step back, "believe the disappearance of Damon Dice is connected to the East Coast, West Coast beef. The same beef that took down them criminals Tupac and Biggie Smalls. You know, a rivalry."

Brown made a face at the white man as he shook his head. "Listen man, this ain't got jackshit to do with a fuckin' rivalry. You and I both know it. There's a madman on the loose running round this city, and I got a feeling that until we find him, there are going to be a lot more killings," Brown said, fuming over the Captain's ignorance.

The two men continued to argue. Everyone around them stopped what they were doing to watch. Lieutenant Brown, the younger of the two, didn't intend to back down. Dr. Wong looked on as the Captain made the crucial mistake of jabbing Brown in the chest with his index finger, not once, but twice, causing Brown to look at the finger and frown, as if it were a deadly disease. Brooks lifted his finger a third time to jab Brown in the chest, but before he could, Brown drew back and knocked the older man out cold.

"Oh shit," Dr. Wong said as he looked on.

That was the day Lieutenant Anthony Brown made one of the biggest mistakes of his life.

EIGHTEEN

Jack and Gina

Gina Thomas lay awake in the darkness listening to the old house settle as it cracked and shifted, making noises as gusts of wind could be heard throughout, like ghosts rumbling through it. She pulled the thick quilted blanket up to her chin.

So much was going through her young mind. Jack had called her a bitch the other night while they were pulling off the lick with G-Solo. It wasn't just that, he had gone on a tirade about her being dumb for buying the watch in her real name. She admitted to herself that it wasn't the brightest move. She remembered him saying that he was going to stop by the jewelry store in the morning, personally, and retrieve the information from the Arab jeweler. She knew what that meant. Murder. But not if she could beat him to it. She reasoned that all she had to do was get the information out the cabinet where she remembered seeing him file it. She didn't want Jack to take the risk of going into the store. He was moving too fast, taking too many chances. Now this.

Jack stirred in his sleep, lassoing his arm around her. The security of his arms felt so good. Like him, she had waited a long time. She felt his hot breath on the nape of her neck as his large hands began to roam the contours of her body. He eased up her Victoria's Secret nightie. She wasn't wearing any panties. She lay still, faking sleep. Just about every night it was the same thing. Since he had gotten out of prison, Jack was like a sex fiend. At one point she even had to buy some K-Y Jelly for lubrication. He was beating in her guts so much she stayed sore.

His hands palmed her ass. She could hear his breathing, feel his breath on her back. Then she felt his dick on her butt cheek, probing. He asked in a husky voice dripping with lust, "Boo, you 'sleep?" She didn't answer, not yet. He eased closer. He kneaded her breasts. She felt his dick crawl between her thighs as she lay on her side. She turned over and faced him in the dark.

They both felt the cold draft at the same time. She had accidentally pulled the covers off their feet. Jack pulled the covers back down. Her hand came to rest on his hairy chest, more so as a divider, a quiet request for him to desist. She needed to talk, but Jack needed sex. That was the one thing she had never denied him, her sex or "his pussy" as he liked to call it. He had trained her, taught her so much, even showing her how to use the muscles in her pussy to contract and tighten so that she would know how to milk him, please him. She wondered if he was going to ask her to give him head. Of course, she knew she would comply. Gina knew the secrets to keeping her man. What she wouldn't do in bed, another woman would.

"Jack, we need to talk," she said, feeling his dick jabbing her in the stomach.

"Talk?" he repeated as he squeezed her breast so hard that she almost screamed. Instead, she sucked in a deep breath as she felt her nipples grow hard at his touch.

"You called me a bitch the other day."

Silence.

Finally, Jack spoke, "Ma, that was my head speaking, not my heart. Things was movin' fast. I was frustrated. I needed to bust them niggas' ass, you know, make a statement."

"Jack, it hurts when a nigga refer to his lady as a bitch," she said suddenly. "Yeah, I know, I'm that ride or die bitch, your gangsta bitch, a bitch that know how to rock a nigga to sleep, but it hurts in a way that I can't explain when a nigga call his shorty a bitch," she said in a small voice. Jack's hand sailed across her nipple as two fingers gently caressed her breast. He inched closer, his mind considering the right words.

"I know you wanna take over DieHard Records and put the

whole industry on smash, but in the process you gotta respect me. And in the end, I'ma let you do you," she said as Jack walked his fingers down her breasts toward her stomach. He ran his hand across her pubic hairs as he inched a little closer. "I'ma play my position," Gina said, talking in the darkness, her voice slightly muffled by the thick quilted blanket.

Quiet awkwardly consumed them. With Jack, Gina could be sure when she had overstepped her boundaries for pillow talking.

She continued, "You hungry? You want me to go downstairs to fix something to eat?"

"No."

"You want me to roll you a blunt?"

"Naw, I'm good," Jack said, taking his hand off of her and turning onto his back. Gina could sense that Jack's mind was now elsewhere as she bit down on her lip. She tried to read his thoughts, but came up blank. Like most women who are determined to do anything to keep their man, she wondered if she had said the wrong thing or perhaps hadn't said enough.

She reached down and grabbed his dick. He was semi-hard. She stroked him to life. She could feel him grow in her hands – veins thick as her fingers. She squeezed his dick and it pumped back like it had a mind of its own, responding to her hand manipulation. Jack released a deep sigh of pent-up energy as she placed her thigh over his legs. He reached down and palmed her butt cheeks, spreading them so wide that two of his fingers nestled comfortably in her pussy.

They were on their sides, face to face, and she responded to his touch by licking his chin like he was ice cream. She nibbled on his lip, grinding her torso against him as her tongue drove down his neck. Hot saliva mingled with the moisture that was starting to form on his body. She licked his hairy chest like he was something sweet. As he moved his two fingers expertly within her, she moaned against his flesh. The room was no longer cold, they were on fire as the covers fell away from her backside. Slurping sounds escalated as moans serenaded the darkness. Even though she was still sore she dared to want more of his sex. Boldly she started talking like a teasing lover.

"Jack," she said, her voice a breathless whisper against his skin. "I want you to fuck me ... fuck me hard." She said it like a command as she humped his hand. His fingers stroked her clitoris, stirring her passion. She was so wet and slippery inside, the sensation almost drove her crazy.

"You think ... you think I don't appreciate you ... us," Jack said with his words slurred like he was drunk off of lust. Gina had a way of doing that to him. She had a way of doing that to any man. Not even he was immune to the wiles of her feminine enticement. But tonight he was going to entirely flip the script on her. His fingers were dripping with her juices like honey.

"Now, how 'bout I serve you?" he asked, taking her completely by surprise. He reached over and pulled her on top of him. His nature was so hard that it felt like a steel pole against her stomach as the warmth of their bodies smothered his dick. She raised her body slightly as she licked his chest, beckoning him. Gina's thighs were almost as thick as his; her ass bounced as he heaved her upward. He was interrupting her rhythm until she realized what he was doing.

"I want you to sit on my face," Jack said, not waiting for her answer. Gina giggled. Jack imagined seeing her face in the dark as he positioned each one of her thick thighs on the side of his face while she sat her ass on his chest. He buried his tongue in her as his fingers spread her lips. He lapped and licked as her pubic hairs tickled his nose. He found the little man in the boat and just sucked and tongue-lashed it until Gina started to grind on his face.

"Oh, shiiit, that's it. Yeah, yeah that's it. Hmm, suck it! Suck it!" He spread her lips wider, burying his tongue as deep as it would go. "Oh, my ... oh, shit ... shit. I'm gonna cum in your mouth." Jack grabbed her butt, making her pussy press tightly against his mouth. With his teeth he gently bit her clitoris and used his entire face to rub across her sex while he took his tongue

164

on a trip down south in a circular motion and dipped it in and out. Gina threw her neck back as he massaged her labia, his mouth dripping with her juices. He returned to her clitoris, mounting an assault of pure ecstasy.

He sucked on her greedily, non-stop, until finally she exploded with his mouth still locked tight on her pussy. She released a stream of cum that flowed in what felt like an ocean. Her orgasm rocked her body in spasms. He continued to suck as his tongue molested her like it was taking more than she could give, thrashing, exploring. "Oh, Jack, that's enough, that's enough! I ... I ... I can't take it ... any ... more," she intoned, throwing her head back like she had whiplash.

Jack held her in position with his arms tightly holding her thighs in place, pussy center to his face. He worked her G-spot until she screamed. It was like some kind of gravitational pull. His hot mouth sucking on her clit. How could something that felt so good drive her insane? "Oh, Jack, I'm cumming again!" she exclaimed as her eyes rolled back. She rode his motions as they ebbed and flowed, her body trembling and shaking. He never ceased or slowed. If anything he went faster ... faster. Deftly, his hands spread her skin and his tongue found another spot, a wall. *God, where did he learn that from?* she thought in the back of her mind as she pleaded out loud to deaf ears. "Oooh wee, you're torturing meee, yesss!" A tear spilled from her eyes. One more orgasm like that and she would be climbing the wall.

With all her might she threw her body back, and she pulled away. Like some gigantic suction cup, she was released. Her supple breasts were covered in sweat. Her hair was matted to her face and she sucked air like she had just run a hundred yard dash.

Gently she grabbed his dick, placing it into her mouth. Instantly she tasted his sweet pre-cum, savoring the taste on her tongue. She tried to deep throat him, but gagged, he was too big, so hard. She deep throated him again, up and down ... up and down. Her arm felt numb from the uncomfortable position she had landed in when she threw herself off his body. She turned around with him still lying on his back and straddled him in a sixty-nine position.

She continued to take him into her mouth while her hands played with his balls, saliva dripping over her fingers. He dug into her sex. Leaning up he bit down on her butt. The sensation only seemed to excite her more. She worked him with the same determination to bring him to ecstasy as he had her.

With her hands she waxed his penis up and down with the juices from her mouth as she sucked hard. She traced his dick with her tongue as he moaned and grabbed her head, placing his dick back into her mouth, a silent signal to her that he was about to cum. She wanted him down in her throat, but Jack enjoyed cumming on her chest, massaging his load all over her large breasts. She found her rhythm as her pace quickened. "That's it. Suck that dick. Uh … watch your teeth."

He moaned with his hand on her head, forcing her to go deeper—and she did. Gina wasn't the best at giving head, but she got points for swallowing. Suddenly, she stopped as she turned around to face him. She heard him take a deep breath and curse in the dark. "Gina, what did you stop for?" he asked vexed as he groped for her in the dark. He felt her take hold of him as she shifted her position.

"Please baby, cum inside of me." Her mellow voice quivered with a hint of a plea. He swallowed hard, determined to bridle his sex. He could feel her move next to him on her back. She had never taken her hand off his rigid hardness. Slowly, he rolled onto her, spreading her legs wide with her thighs wedged against his. He placed one of her legs on his shoulder. Gina gasped in anticipation of what was coming next. With dick in hand she could feel him prodding, searching her pubic hairs.

With her legs wide open, the scent of her sex was in the air. He eased inside of her hot spot as his mouth greedily came down slobbering on her breast as if he really thought he could force her whole titty in his mouth. Inch by inch he was sliding right in. She was so hot and wet that his first deep stroke, flesh against flesh, sounded like a French kiss. He went deeper with her legs spread wider. She squirmed and wiggled as her claws dug into his hairy, muscular chest. She tried to scoot up, but there was nowhere to go.

"You wanted me to fuck you hard," he stated as he eased inside of her a little deeper. She bit down on her lip and threw her head back on the pillow as she arched her spine to meet him with a thrust of her own. He followed her invitation and drove his dick in as far as he could. Gina stifled a scream as she grunted and groaned with each one of his powerful thrusts. She clung to him as if he were a black stallion she was losing control of. He was so deep in her body that he was hitting a spot that felt like a nerve.

"Oh Jack, oh Jack. Ba … baby gooo slooo," she pleaded. His pace was so fevered that it felt like someone was pounding a battering ram inside of her. Then it happened, his body turned into a human volcano. Saliva trickled from his mouth onto her breasts as he shivered and shook, back arched. He pulled out of her and cum squirted like a faucet all over her stomach, chest and face, enough to lotion her body with. Satiated, depleted, he plopped down on her body, winded, gasping for breath.

Sleepy-eyed, Jack rolled over onto his back as Gina reached down for the thick quilted blanket. She could feel the goosebumps on her arms. The room had suddenly taken on a chill, as she shuddered, teeth chattering. She needed to go to the bathroom. Instead, she snuggled into Jack's waiting arms, careful to avoid the cold wet spot in the bed, evidence of their lovemaking. She could feel his heart beating with a rhythm of its own, powerful and strong. His skin was moist and warm, soothing against her body. This was where she needed to be, wanted to be, in his arms, forever. She sighed tranquilly, like a woman who had just achieved multiple orgasms. She closed her eyes and was about to doze off.

Jack said groggily, "Wake me up in the morning. I'ma go holla at dude at the jewelry store. I don't like movin' like this." Jack's breathing was heavy as sleep toyed with his brain. "You know where the stash is, just in case…" he said.

Gina's eyes stretched wide open as she was brought back to the reality of her blunder – leaving her real name with the jeweler. She knew what he was talking about, just in case. In other words, he meant in the event he did not make it back.

Gina lay perfectly still listening to the noises in the old house. For some reason she felt the urge to cry. Everything was going so right. Lord knew they had taken so many chances and somehow managed to get away. With a million dollars stashed away, not including the jewelry they had taken, how could everything that was going so right, suddenly go so wrong? There was no way in hell she was going to let Jack take the chance of maybe walking into an ambush if the police happened to follow up on the lead at the jewelry store.

Sunlight was starting to stream through the window as she stealthily eased out of bed while listening to Jack's light snoring. The old wooden floor creaked under her bare feet as she crept over to the dresser. She picked up Jack's gun as he stirred in his sleep. Her heart pounded in her chest as she stood as still as a mannequin. There was only so much that any man could take. Jack was a thug. She knew that he was going to beat her ass when he woke and found she was gone with one of his guns. If she made it back home with the application, she reasoned, Jack would be relieved. She used the bathroom, took a quick shower and left for a place of no return.

NINETEEN

As Gina drove, she felt like she was racing against time. There was no way of knowing if the Arab who owned the jewelry store had already contacted the authorities, anxious to get the reward money. She knew she was taking a great risk, but it was better she than Jack, she reasoned.

She parked her car downtown, almost a block away from the jewelry store. With the pistol safely in her purse, she exhaled as she looked in the mirror and donned a pair of sunglasses. She adjusted the blond wig on her head. Her hand trembled as she puckered her lips to apply lipstick. She had a bad feeling she couldn't shake. Her intuition was telling her that something was going to go terribly wrong. She ignored it, took a deep breath and exited the car.

Showtime.

An elderly white man with a shopping bag brushed against her. She paid him no mind as she continued to walk briskly, looking straight ahead. Her eyes narrowed as she searched for anything unusual. She studied the jewelry store across the street. She could feel her chest tightening as she watched pedestrians traverse the streets. She could smell the sweet aroma of food coming from somewhere. It was 8:31 in the morning. *Suppose he has someone in the store with him?* she thought. As she neared, she realized that the security gate of the store was not opened yet. Her pace slowed, and for the first time, she thought about turning back.

A young man with freshly braided hair, so neat that it looked like it had been painted on, bumped into her, hard. He was talking on one of the smallest cellular phones she had ever seen.

"Damn. Yo, watch where you goin'!" he huffed, frowning. Then his eyes softened as he took her in. His gaze fell to her wide hips. He suddenly smiled as he watched Gina abruptly turn and walk away. She walked over to the newsstand, pretending to be interested in a magazine, something to do with Weight Watchers. She held the magazine in her hand and looked at the others on the stand. There was a picture of Oprah with big hair on her magazine, "*O*," and at the bottom of the magazine rack was a newspaper with a picture of Damon Dice's face splashed across the front page. Gina's heart did somersaults in her chest as she read the headline:

"*Music Executive Damon Dice still missing, presumed dead. Case may be connected to the East Coast, West Coast rivalry . . .*"

Just as Gina was about to reach for the newspaper, she saw the proprietor of the jewelry store arrive. With his briefcase in one hand, he opened the gate with the other while his shifty eyes looked around. Like most foreigners, the Arab was very conscious of his surroundings. Gina took off in a trot, her heart racing in her chest as her mind signaled a warning. She crossed the busy street with her hand in her purse and her mind paying no heed to the silent warning. As she neared and her pace slowed, her mind quickened with each step.

The Arab, with his back to her, opened the gate and took one final look behind him, but didn't seem to notice Gina as he entered the vestibule of the store. He had inserted the key into the door and was about to turn off the silent alarm when Gina walked up. Her shadow fell across him. Startled, he turned around and faced the black woman who had an icy cold demeanor. She wore dark shades and her lips slightly curved up to the right. The Arab noticed the gun poised in her hand, aimed at his chest.

"Do as I say, and you won't be harmed," Gina spoke calmly.

"Okay, okay," the frightened man said with his eyes bulging as he looked down at the gun. He raised his hands in the air.

"Put your hands down and open the door," Gina ordered as she waved the gun at him. The Arab complied. In doing so he triggered the silent alarm. Gina walked inside, remembering where she saw the man file her paperwork. At that very moment, police were already headed for the jewelry store.

Gina made the man lie down on the floor. A tuft of straight dark hair fell over his forehead as he took his time getting to the floor. He continued to hold onto the briefcase as if his life depended on it. He watched Gina with what looked like mischief on his tanned face. His thick beard, bushy eyebrows and piercing black eyes made Gina feel something was not right about his character. She had only come for the application with her name on it and was going to be out of there in a dash, but there was something about the way he held onto the briefcase as he lay on the floor. It wasn't fear she saw in his eyes, it was something else.

"Gimme that briefcase, Muslim!" she said, raising her voice, gesturing with a wave of the gun.

"No!" he said as he continued to shake his head adamantly and clutch the briefcase to his side. Gina leaned down and pressed the nine-millimeter to the back of his head.

"Let it go!" she yelled. He complied as he mumbled something under his breath about Allah. Gina opened the briefcase. To her disappointment all she found was an assortment of papers, a palm pilot and a thin calculator. The damn Arab was watching her intensely.

Just when she was about to close it, something told her to look inside one of the small side pockets. She did and found three black velvet pouches. Bingo! Diamonds, large and uncut. She quickly stuffed them into her pocket. In the back of her mind a voice was warning her.

On the floor, the Arab squirmed around as he began to curse in his own language. At one point, Gina was almost sure he was going to get up and try her. Time was moving fast, but the voice in her head told her she was moving slow, way too slow. Her inexperience would cost her as she turned away and headed for the filing cabinet.

The phone rang, startling her. As fast as she could she scanned through the "T" section in the filing cabinet, found her application, careful not to leave any fingerprints, and shoved it into her pocket. As she turned around the store owner pointed a gun at her and fired. The impact of the bullet knocked her backward. She staggered into the file cabinet. His next shot missed.

She crouched down and fired with her eyes closed. She was acting purely on instinct. She managed to get off a fusillade of shots, hitting the store owner in the upper chest and neck. He keeled over backward, his gun, a small caliber .22, slid across the floor. Gina took off hobbling. She could feel warm blood soaking her pant leg and running into the heel of her shoe. She grimaced in pain as she headed for the door with her gun concealed under her jacket.

Outside the police were arriving as tires screeched to a halt directly in front of her. She felt trapped as she held her jacket together at the collar. Underneath, with the other hand, she held onto the gun.

"In there! In there!" she screamed, pointing frantically like a woman terrified as she turned and back-pedaled. She had the best disguise in the world. Who would ever suspect a beautiful woman to be a cold-blooded killer? At least that was what she was relying on as she blended in with the rest of the people in the early morning on their way to work.

Lieutenant Brown got out of his Caprice. His trained eyes scanned the crowd as he entered the store. Immediately, his radio crackled to life, "There's a gunshot victim in here, a possible homicide. Secure the area!" He ran to the door and saw a woman with blond hair in the near distance who was hobbling badly, trying to get away.

"HEY ... YOU!" Lieutenant Brown called out to the woman. The woman took off in a trot. No one paid any attention to either the Lieutenant or Gina, as if they were in a world all their own. Gina tried her best to blend in with the morning commuters on their way to work as she weaved in and out of the crowd.

Gina tossed a look over her shoulder, praying that Lieutenant

Brown would not recognize her. She turned a corner. Her hip hurt something awful. She was almost at her car ... just a few yards more.

"Hey, you, stop!" Brown ordered. She turned around, surprised that the cop had gained on her. She thought she had lost him. He was too close. The crowd of people stood around her like a human barrier, protecting her from his capture, but still he was closing in fast. She needed to act quickly. With no other recourse, Gina came up firing two swift shots. Instantly, pandemonium erupted as people screamed and scurried in all directions, stumbling all over each other. Lieutenant Brown crouched down and aimed at Gina's back as she ran away. "Too many people. Fuck!" he cursed and continued after her. This time he ran after her with caution, haunted by the glimpse of her face.

Up ahead, at a busy intersection, the light had turned red. A middle-aged white man wearing a cowboy hat and leisurely smoking a cigar drummed his fingers on the door of his SUV. Gina approached him and flung open the door.

"Get out the car, cracka!" she hollered, with her wig on sideways.

"Huh?" he jerked his head around, looking at her dumbfounded as she pulled on his shirt collar. He resisted by holding onto the steering wheel for dear life as he bit down on his cigar.

Gina looked over her shoulder. "Damnit!" The cop was approaching fast. She fired two shots into the driver's face, causing chunks of flesh to fly in the air. She pulled him from the vehicle, throwing him to the pavement, and hopped in the SUV as a staccato of shots rang out, hitting the steel and fiberglass. Gina ducked down, punching the gas pedal. The vehicle leapt forward as the tires screeched and the car fishtailed. She ran the red light and barely avoided hitting a yellow school bus. She sideswiped an oncoming car. Gina sped away in a daring getaway in broad daylight in downtown Brooklyn. All she left behind was a trail of burnt rubber, empty bullet shells and dead bodies.

Lieutenant Brown ran up and raised his gun to fire at the

departing vehicle, hesitating as he looked down at the lifeless body of the man who had been snatched from his vehicle. He made a futile attempt to check for a heartbeat. The entire left side of the victim's face was missing. Brain matter and skull fragments were on the pavement. The revolting sight forced him to turn his head as all around him people scurried about in panic, on the precipice of madness.

An ambulance's shrill siren blared in the distance as patrol cars arrived. Lieutenant Brown happened to look at the ground next to the body and for the first time he noticed the bullet shell casing. Carefully he reached down to pick it up. His breath lodged in his throat. The ammo the woman was using was KTW. Brown had a gut feeling the bullet would match the ones they found at the homicide of G-Solo's bodyguard, Prophet.

"Did you get a good description of the shooter?" a voice asked, causing Brown to look up into the bright morning sun. The brief image of Gina flashed in his mind. He recognized her from somewhere, but where?

As sweat gleamed off his forehead he responded, "African American woman, light-skinned, blond hair—"

"Woman?" the officer retorted, surprised.

Brown shot him a glare for interrupting.

"She appeared to be wounded and to have lost a lot of blood. I spotted her leaving the scene at Hasan's spot."

A voice cut in. It was Detective Rodriguez.

"We found a body back at the jewelry store. The owner was gunned down. There's lots of blood. From the looks of it, it was a botched robbery attempt, but I can't be for sure. There's a surveillance camera in there, so I'm gonna have the tape taken down to the station to see what we can find." As an afterthought, Rodriquez added, "Hasan was determined not give up his property."

"Yeah, and it cost him his life trying to be a hero," Brown said on a more somber note. At least they had video of the robbery. Maybe that would be just the big break they needed. He hoped.

◊ ◊ ◊ ◊

A few miles away, police helicopters raced over the horizon through the dense clouds and thick New York smog. It spotted the red SUV and instantly lowered, careful not to touch any electrical wires in the small enclosure between the buildings.

"You, the occupant of the vehicle, get out with your hands up, walk ten yards and lie flat on the ground spread eagle!" the police ordered. Dust and debris stirred on the ground in small tornados as the powerful rotors lowered, descending on the vehicle.

Half a block away, Gina limped, dragging her leg as her eyes desperately searched for a place to hide. She used the side of a building for support. She continued to walk as best she could. Up ahead she saw a Laundromat. She was beginning to black out as she held onto the wall.

A police car sped past her. An old black woman folding clothes looked up at Gina, whose pants were soiled with what looked like blood. She frowned. "Lord have mercy." The old woman's hands never stopped moving as she watched the young black girl limp inside the Laundromat. Their eyes met, young and old. The older woman's five-year-old granddaughter sat in a chair, legs swinging. She played with a black Barbie doll. The little girl watched Gina struggle to walk.

"Ma'am … I'm hurt … bad. Could you please help … me?" Gina said as she held onto the edge of the folding table, blood caked under her acrylic fingernails. As Gina spoke, police cars zoomed up and down the streets. Overhead the roar of a helicopter could be heard.

"Oh my God, child. What have you done to yourself?" the old woman asked with tears in her eyes. Her voice cracked as she shook her head. Strands of unruly gray hair sprouted from her loose ponytail. Her skin was a deep, Hershey chocolate brown. She had deep age lines that formed creases and made her once beautiful face sag like a woman who was always sad, even when she smiled, which wasn't often.

"Ma'am, I'm in a lotta of trouble," Gina winced, looking over her shoulder as she spoke to the old black woman. The old woman looked at Gina with concern as she walked over to the door and looked out. The police had completely surrounded the block. She turned the orange sign on the door, "CLOSED." She then turned around to see Gina on her cellular phone.

"Jack! I'm hurt ... bad baby ... you gonna hafta come get me. I'm at the Laundromat on 27th and Main," her voice quivered.

"Fuck! Gina, I told ..." Jack was shouting into the phone, but realized it wouldn't do any good. He quickly got dressed, grabbed his .380 and was out the door. He drove his Benz to the area he knew all too well, it wasn't too far from where he was.

TWENTY

Jack Lemon

Jack drove while surveying the neighborhood. The spot was hot and the place was crawling with cops. The police had the block sealed off and weren't letting any traffic in or out as they did a door-to-door search with dogs. "Shit!" Jack cursed as he drove with the burner on his lap. Up ahead he saw the Laundromat. The sign in the window said it was closed. He prayed Gina was safely in there. *What the hell did she do?* he wondered.

A helicopter hovered overhead. It looked like some shit straight out of the movies as throngs of police, some of them wearing riot gear, marched down the street. "Ginaaa!" Jack droned as he pounded his fist on the steering wheel. "How am I gonna get her outta this?" he questioned himself. As Jack turned the corner, his mind raced against the clock in his head. Then he had an idea. It was risky as hell, but he had to try it. It wouldn't be long before the police made it to the Laundromat.

Jack drove around back about a block away and parked his car, leaving it idle. He got out with the .380 concealed in his pocket. He cut through an alley that led to a gangway which led to another. From his position in the narrow gangway he could see all the passing police cars.

With gun in hand, he hunched down, obscured in the shadows. He waited as a police cruiser passed. Jack raised the gun, aimed and fired three shots at the police car. He took off running back through the alley. By the time he made it back to his car he was walking casually as he watched police cars abandon their search and rush to the scene where the police car had been fired upon. The police car that

177

had taken the shots called in for help. "Officer down! Officer down!" was the cry on the police radio.

As Jack cruised back toward the Laundromat, he noticed a SWAT team van and a host of other police vehicles race by him, all headed in the direction of the infamous call for help.

Jack parked in front of the Laundromat and quickly got out. His eyes scanned up and down the street. As he walked up he noticed that someone had thrown a bleach solution on the ground. He pounded on the door. The old woman who opened the door wouldn't look him in the eyes. A little girl sat in a chair cradling a brown baby doll as she softly cried. Gina lay on the floor in a puddle of blood. Jack felt something in his chest tighten as he looked down at her unconscious body.

"Ah, fuck, Gina! Nooo!" Jack's voice choked up with emotions as he ambled over. His heart ached in his chest at seeing Gina this way. Taking a deep breath, he felt his eyes grow misty. The old woman and the child looked on. The little girl was crying in sobs that racked her little body. Jack made a face, that of a pain-stricken man. For some reason the old woman would not look him directly in his eyes.

Jack snatched a blanket off the folding table and began to carefully wrap Gina's body in it. She moaned softly, fluttered her eyes momentarily as he picked her up. Already, the blanket was soaked in her blood, him too. He picked her up and headed for the door. The old woman raced ahead of him, opening the door. Still they exchanged no words. He nodded his head; she wiped a tear, a simple gesture that conveyed so much. As he walked out the door he prayed like hell that they would go unnoticed. It was only a few yards to his car, but it seemed like miles.

Gently he placed Gina in the back seat and got into the front. He steered the car in the opposite direction of the police and headed for a destination where he was sure someone would look after Gina – Rasheed's grandmother. She used to help all of the wounded Panthers back in the day. Some say she even helped Adia Shakur when she was wounded, shot by the police when she came out with hands up, surrendering.

T W E N T Y O N E

Rasheed & Monique

The police had finally taken Monique to the hospital and they allowed Rasheed to ride along in the ambulance with her. Afterward her wounds were treated and she was questioned, at length, by two plain-clothes detectives. Her head spun. Monique wanted to scream at them because she felt like in some ways they were still viewing her and Rasheed with suspicion.

Now, as if in some kind of fugue, Monique stared down at the hospital's linoleum floor like she didn't know how she had gotten there. An elderly man with a walking cane sat across from her, sleeping with his mouth wide open. Monique was fortunate, neither her arm nor her ankle were broken, just badly sprained. The doctor told her she would heal within a week or two, but what about Georgia Mae? Would she make it? Rasheed placed his arm around her. She sniffled and dropped a tear as she scrolled her eyes up at him. In a small voice, she asked, "What made you come to the club? You showed up—"

"Monique Cheeks?" A husky, but polite, voice interrupted her question to Rasheed, causing her to tilt her head in the direction of the emergency room door just as a woman was pushing a small child by in a wheelchair. Monique raised her hand, wincing in pain at the motion, and the doctor walked over. He had an assortment of fancy pens in the breast pocket of his white jacket. His eyes, with bags underneath, looked tired. Patches of gray hair ringed his head. He talked with caring gestures, very animated with his hands and neck. For reasons unknown to her, Monique, with her lips pressed tightly together, stared at the pens in his pocket.

After the doctor had introduced himself he went on to explain that her friend Georgia Mae Hargrove had a concussion, a hairline fracture to her skull that required fifteen stitches and a bruised spinal column. The doctor arched his brow as he stated frankly, "Georgia Mae is a marvelous specimen of a female, her physique, her sinew. If she wouldn't have been in the shape she was in, she more than likely would have died from her injuries, or would have been paralyzed for life." With the doctor's statement Monique's hand flew to her mouth in shock.

As if having a second thought, the doctor scratched his chin and looked at Monique. "Are you a dancer, too, young lady?"

"Not no mo'," Monique retorted.

The doctor slightly nodded his head in agreement.

"Can we see her?" Monique asked as a woman walked by silently weeping. The doctor glanced at the woman with a genuine show of concern, and then looked back at Monique. For a fleeting second, she thought he was going to tell her no.

Finally he answered, "Yes, please follow me." He led them to Georgia Mae. As he walked away his coattail drifted behind him. Awkwardly, Rasheed stood behind Monique while she struggled with her crutches to walk toward the emergency room door.

◊ ◊ ◊ ◊

Silently, Monique sat in a chair next to the bed. Georgia Mae lay still, almost serene, under the crisp white sheets, arms folded, one over the other. The white bandage on her head was stained red. For some reason Monique could not get out of her mind, no matter how tight she closed her eyes, how Game looked like she was lying dead in a casket.

Monique noticed the bruises and lacerations on her face. "Shit," Monique cursed under her breath. *She came to my rescue again and now she's lying there like she's in a coma*, she thought. Once again tears rimmed in Monique's eyes. Suddenly Georgia Mae stirred underneath the covers. A hand with a broken finger-nail moved just a little, but enough to give Monique a signal.

"Game?" Monique called her name. The whole time Rasheed looked on. Georgia Mae's eyes fluttered open like butterflies. Monique scooted her chair closer. Georgia Mae turned and looked at Monique. A warm smile tugged at her lips.

"God, I thought you were dead," Monique said, taking a deep breath and rolling her eyes up at the ceiling.

"Child, pah-leze. ATL bitches don't get kilt, we gets crunk," Georgia Mae said in her best ghetto, countrified, but strained voice. She attempted to laugh, but instead she frowned. "Damn, my head hurts." Her eyes darted away from Monique to the figure who was standing away from the bed. Game smiled for the first time. She then looked at Monique. "Yo, what he doing here?"

Monique looked at Rasheed and asked, "Do you two know each other?"

Slyly, Rasheed shot the white girl a warning glare.

"No, we don't know each other. Do we?" Rasheed said, continuing to warn her with his eyes. Game just stared at him and made a face. Pain. Her pink tongue primed her thin lips as she swallowed hard like her tongue was made of sandpaper.

"Naw, I don't know you, dude." She turned her attention back to Monique. "Girl, are you alright?" she questioned as her hands drifted to her head, feeling the bandage.

"Just a few bumps and bruises," Monique replied.

"I can't believe I did some dumb shit like that. I could have taken both them rednecks out easy," Georgia Mae said balling her fist up. "I kicked that cracka square in the face. Thought he was out for the count, but that fucker got me from behind."

"It wasn't your fault," Monique said placing her hand on Georgia Mae's arm.

"Yes, it was. My instructor always taught us, when you get a man down, punish him." She shook her head and continued to touch the bandages. "I thought they were old. They were just old junkies with young bodies. And Tatyana, I got something for that long neck bitch."

"Yep, me too. I gotta admit, ole girl had intentions of killin' me," Monique said and then asked, "did you tell the police that she had something to do with this?"

"Hell naw," Game shot back. "She didn't tell on you when you got that ass at the club."

"Y'all mean to tell me y'all know who did this?" Rasheed questioned.

Monique and Georgia Mae exchanged glances with each other agreeing to keep his ass out of it. Rasheed was about to say something when his cell phone vibrated on his hip. He turned away to answer it and began speaking in hushed tones.

"The doctor says they're gonna have to run a few tests on me, hold me for a week or two," Game lowered her voice and pursed her bottom lip. "At first I couldn't feel nothing in my legs, now they're both numb with a slight tingling sensation." She had the kind of fortitude that let you know she was a strong-willed woman.

"You have any family here in New York?" Monique asked, her voice filled with sympathy. Game shrugged her shoulders and made a face like she was taking a stroll down memory lane.

"Naw, I don't have any family here."

"Who's going to take care of you once you get out of the hospital?"

"Ah, girl, I'm going to be okay. I've been taking care of myself ever since I went off to college," Georgia Mae answered.

"Nah," Monique sighed, "you're comin' to stay with me."

Game stretched her lips to the side of her face and rolled her eyes. "Girl, I couldn't impose on y'all like that."

Rasheed walked back over to the bed. His face looked like all the life had been drained out of it.

"Gina been shot," he said with a slack jaw, mouth agape like a man in shock.

"Oh my God!" Monique muttered as she exchanged looks with Rasheed. "What the hell is goin' on? Is she okay?"

Rasheed just nodded his head with a distant look in his eyes. Moments later they rushed out of the hospital and caught a cab to his Grandmother's house. Jack greeted them at the door. He looked terrible. The two old friends hugged each other. Monique hugged Jack, too. Rasheed had never seen Jack look so distraught in his entire life.

Jack raised his brow when he noticed Monique with the crutches and her arm in a sling. They sat on the couch and gave each other details of what had happened, each story more devastating than the other. Jack had relied on the fact that Grandma Hattie was a nurse who would always help people, black or white, if they needed medical attention. There was no way in hell Jack could have taken Gina to the hospital. By now they were all crawling with cops looking for a woman with a gunshot wound. The bullet had entered her thigh and come out. She had lost a lot of blood – too much – but Grandma Hattie said she would make it. She would take care of Gina for the next few weeks. She said being a nurse was a true gift from God, doing His will, healing the sick.

TWENTY-TWO

Two Weeks Later
Lieutenant Brown

Like someone piecing together a mysterious puzzle, Lieutenant Brown had started to fit all the pieces together from the murders that his department had infamously named the "Death Struck" cases, due to the particularly hideous nature of the deaths. He had been working on the cases around the clock for the past forty-eight hours. Finally, the first big break came. The security camera in the jewelry store where the Arab was robbed and killed had actually captured footage of the shootout and murder. However, when they went to view the video, to Brown's dismay, it was of such low quality that it was hard to discern the actual features of the person. One thing was for sure, the killer was a woman and she moved with confidence.

Brown drank black coffee from a Styrofoam cup and rewound the video over and over, as images of the phantom woman moved across the screen. Even after she was shot, she moved with a swagger as she removed some papers from the filing cabinet. There was something about her gait that disturbed Brown as he strained his bloodshot eyes at the snowy picture on the TV screen. After staying up all night in his office going over the video, about the only thing he was sure of was that the black woman wore a blond wig. In his mind he could still see her firing shots at him as he chased her. It was something in her eyes and not just that, the wig. The blond wig. Blond ... wig.

Brown's mind churned as he took a sip of his coffee. Suddenly it dawned on him. Did the mother of Damon Dice say that a young woman wearing a blond wig came to pick up the money as her dying son had requested? He frantically waited for the ballistic report to come back to see if the bullets from the jewelry store murders matched those of the brutal murder of G-Solo's bodyguard, Big Prophet. The bullets still weighed heavily on his mind. Brown had a hunch. It was a long shot, but he figured he had nothing to lose.

He got on the phone and had one of his men retrieve the records of the cab companies in the Coney Island area. There were a million cabs in the naked city. It was a job that could take months or longer, but if they found the cab driver, maybe he could identify the woman who picked up the money ... and maybe even locate the killer's location.

There was a knock at his office door. Detective Rodriguez opened it slightly and stuck his head in. His shiny hair was slicked back on his head, still wet from his morning shower. Sleep's shadow was cast on his face as he munched on a large glazed donut.

"We got a match on the jewelry store homicides," Rodriguez said in between bites of the donut.

"Yes! Yes!" Brown chanted and swung his fist in the air. Rodriguez then added, "The Chief wants to see you in his office ASAP."

◊ ◊ ◊ ◊

As soon as he walked in he knew that something was terribly wrong. He could tell by the long expression. Chief Daniel Steel, with his hound dog eyes and receding hairline, was a no-nonsense man.

"Have a seat," he said to Brown as he took off his spectacles. Brown sat down. As always, the picture on the cluttered desk caught his attention. It was of a little girl about ten years old. She was holding a soccer ball and standing in front of a yellow school bus. Her teeth were severely crooked, just like the Chief's.

Chief Steel exhaled deeply as he shuffled some papers around on his desk. "I'm going to get straight to the point. You're being taken off of the Death Struck case and suspended indefinitely."

"Whaaat!?" Brown screeched, bolting straight forward in his

seat.

The Chief silenced him with a glare and continued, "You struck a superior officer. If you had reported the matter to me, maybe I could have had it taken care of. However, it was reported to Internal Affairs downtown."

"That's bullshit!" Brown yelled, standing up, nearly toppling the chair over. "That man put his hands on me. I have a right to defend myself."

"No, you should have reported the matter to me. Promptly."

Brown frowned with disgust for his boss. "Chief, the man was trying to belittle me in front of my men and the entire 75th. Where I come from you don't put your hands on another man. Period!"

"Yeah, and where I come from you don't strike another officer, especially the likes of your kind."

"My kind? What the fuck is that s'posta mean?" Brown asked, enraged, taking a step closer, lips pressed tightly across his teeth. The two men stared at each other. Brown couldn't believe what he was hearing. Not only was it some racist bullshit, but he was being suspended and removed from a case that he felt he was close to cracking. "I just can't believe you'd take me off the case after all the hours I've put into it. It's bad enough that I'm being suspended, but what's the reason for removing me?"

Silence.

Brown went ahead and tried his last card. "Chief, I found a match between bullets found in the jewelry store murders and the ones found at the murder scene of the rapper's bodyguard. The connection may be a female. I'm having records of cab companies checked and a composite of the woman made. It's the same black woman, blond wig."

The Chief's eyebrow rose as he placed his elbows on the desk. He was obviously impressed with the progress Brown had made on the case. He looked at the younger man sternly. "You're a good cop, but you crossed the line and you have no one to blame for this but yourself. I want you to go clean out your desk," the Chief said as he reared back in his chair as if that were the end of their conversation.

Brown was filled with a stirring desire. He felt that it involved something bigger than what the Chief was telling him. Disgusted, Brown simply gathered his thoughts and walked out the door.

As soon as Brown was gone, Chief Steel picked up the phone and called a friend. Fate may have finally shone favorably on him. He couldn't wait to deliver the information he had just learned from Brown. Certain people in high places were always looking for a little free publicity. Everything he had just learned, he relayed to his friend, assuring him that Brown had been taken off the case. Now it was just a matter of time.

Scrambling to check with the cab companies, the Chief ran a ballistics check himself. Now that he had learned that it was a woman in both cases, he would send the video of the jewelry store murder to Washington, D.C. where the best crime scene technicians in the world would have the picture of the woman enhanced and quickly identified. The payoff in the end would be great, just as his friend Captain Bill Brooks had promised him. Brooks would get the glory in front of the media for cracking one of them thug-rapper murder cases and he would get a bonus, along with his retirement from the Mayor's Office. That was an offer he couldn't refuse.

TWENTY-THREE

Jack

Jack pulled up into the Marcus Garvey Projects driving Gina's sleek black Jeep Cherokee with tinted windows, sitting on 22s. He sipped on an Olde English 800, while a blunt smoldered between his fingers. On his lap was a new chrome-plated nine. He placed the pistol in his waistband and turned up the bottle to take another long swig. He belched like a frog, wiping his mouth with the back of his hand.

As he got out of the Jeep, he left behind a trail of Chronic smoke. Jack waved to a few heads in the parking lot who he knew. A chick wearing blue jeans and a white halter top called his name. Instantly he recognized her from back in the day – big booty Pam. She was now a smoker. Some said she was on that shit, and by the frantic way that she waved at him, her large double D's threatening to expose themselves from the confines of her halter, Pam was definitely on something. If it wasn't crack then it damn sure was dope boys.

◊ ◊ ◊ ◊

It was Saturday night, and a brilliant full moon hung in the majestic sky like a waxed coin embellished with scattered stars. Jack had a nice buzz from good weed and drink, but not enough to make him lose his focus as he walked. In the back of his mind, he couldn't help thinking shit was lookin' lovely. As he liked to say, shit was bubbling. He hadn't been out the joint a minute and his grind had come up big time. He thought back to Gina and how she took a bullet. At first he was pissed at her for doing some dumb shit, but when she gave him the diamonds, well, a nigga had to give her props. Like no other chick he had ever known, Gina kept it gangsta to the utmost. The stones she stole were probably worth close to a million dollars.

As Jack walked, bopping through the Marcus Garvey Projects, he felt like a big ole pimp stacking paper, pulling capers, plotting on not just the rap industry, but the entire game.

Jack knocked on a door while carefully checking his sur-roundings, still conscious of where he was. He watched everything in his peripheral vision. Nina, his nine, was snug in his drawers. Just as he looked over his shoulder, the door opened. An attractive white girl was standing in the doorway. Jack did a double take at her then turned to look at the number on the door. "428," he muttered and scratched his head, craning his neck to look at the next door. He knew the weed he had just smoked was good, but damn. "Ah, mmm. Yo, I got the wrong address," he mumbled with his eyebrows knotted together in confusion.

The girl giggled. "You looking for Rasheed and Monique?" she asked with a glint of humor in her eyes. She sounded so much like a black woman that if Jack had closed his eyes he wouldn't have been able to tell the difference. He nodded his head. He couldn't help letting his eyes roam her full figure. She was thick, with a fat ass so wide that you could see it from the front. Her green eyes sparkled with some kind of feminine mischief as she looked at him, almost daringly flirting with him, as if sizing him up. Her eyes strolled across his gear and then the lump in his pants from the gun.

"You got the right place. Come on in," she said, opening the door wide. Jack glanced over his shoulder, adjusted his stride and casually walked in. He thought he smelled the faint aroma of weed. He tried not to stare, but couldn't help it. She was stacked like a brick house, with sharp curves all the way down to her sculptured calves. Her large pineapple-sized breasts jutted forward and her strawberry nipples hardened, like tiny faces watching him through the thin material of her wife beater. Her stomach was rip-pled with feminine muscles. A navel ring pierced her belly. Over her wide hips, she had on a pair of short shorts, the kind that mostly white girls wear, with the stringy threads hanging everywhere, the top button undone.

Jack tried not to look at the fat pussy print that was so big that it would be a shame to call it a monkey. It looked more like she had a gorilla in her panties. He continued to watch her. With a delicate finger she pushed a ringlet of curly blond hair from her forehead. With that movement her soft breasts jiggled, straining against the sheer, thin fabric. She shifted positions from one leg to the other. For some unknown reason Jack's mouth watered.

She was checking him out, too. As usual, Jack was rocking the latest gear – a Sean John suede jacket with matching baggy pants outfit, a pinky ring and a simple platinum chain that hung down to his stomach. Underneath his New York baseball cap he wore a black doo rag.

"Have a seat," Georgia Mae said with a smile. "Rasheed and Monique stepped out for a minute. You know tomorrow is the NBA draft, plus Fire is scheduled to fly to California."

"Damn, that's right!" Jack said as he tore his eyes away from the white girl's body as it suddenly occurred to him who she was. Jack snapped fingers trying to recall her name. "Your name is ah, ah …"

"Georgia Mae," she said with a curt smile.

He frowned at her. She knew what he was thinking, so before he could ask she said,

"… but you can call me Game."

"Game," he repeated.

"Yup." She turned and slowly walked away, tossing her wide hips from side to side, ass shaking like jelly.

Jack grimaced, "Gotmuthafuckindamit," he muttered under his breath. One side of her shorts rode way up the crack of her butt. It looked like she was wearing a partial thong as she moved across the room, causing a miniature earthquake. The motion in her ocean made Jack's eyes bulge. He also noticed the patch on the back of her head.

Suddenly she turned around, catching him watching her. A lock of unruly hair fell over her eyes. She arched her foot on her toe and looked as if she wanted to ask him something. Her look was untamed, almost wild in a sexy kind of way. "You want something to drink?" she asked in a throaty voice with a smirk on her face, the way a woman looks when she's loving every minute of a man checking her out.

"Yo, you can get me a beer," Jack said with a hard voice, trying to play it off. He knew he needed to stay focused. He had come to ask a favor of Rasheed. Jack had been so busy the past few days that he had forgotten about the draft. Jack also wondered why Rasheed had not told him the girl was staying with Monique.

He sat down on the couch as a roach crawled across the floor in front of him. On the wall hung a Malcolm X photo with Malcolm pointing an angry finger, his top lip slightly curled with disdain. Jack shifted the gun in his pants to a comfortable position and reached for the PlayStation on the table. He noticed the half burnt blunt in the ashtray as Game sashayed back into the room with drinks in her hand. Jack forbade his eyes to look in between her legs as she stood in front of him. He pretended to be interested in the game.

She set his drink down. Her perfume was a strange kind of musky sweetness. He sucked in a deep breath and let out a small sigh. She was standing too damn close. It felt like her nearness was suffocating him as he felt her eyes on him.

"Yo, how long have they been gone?" he asked for the sake of conversation. His mind had already convinced him it was time to leave. Jack was faithful to Gina. Besides, he didn't do white chicks, period!

Game padded over to the loveseat and sat down, crossing her long legs, one over the other, Indian style. "They've been gone a couple of hours." She took a sip from her drink, eyeing him over the rim of her glass. "You smoke? I got some skunk weed. That's it in the ashtray, or if you like I can roll you a fresh one."

Jack looked up at her, tempted to take her up on her offer, but decided against it. "Naw, I'm good. I gotta bounce anyway."

Game fidgeted and stirred her drink with a manicured red fingernail as the ice clinked with glass. "Psss … what's up with all you good lookin' black guys? Got a sista on lockdown, smokin' on the solo. Chile, pah-leez, wha' da world comin' to?" Game sassed, rolling her eyes like she was dead serious.

Jack found himself smiling at her antics. She sounded so much like a black girl that he looked at her amazed. "What, you raised around blacks all yo' life or some shit?"

Game tossed her mane of hair over her shoulder and pushed her breasts forward. "Yeah, I was raised around blacks. I'm black. Trust me, Jack, you wouldn't know the difference with the lights off." She gave him a slight grin. A thin mustache of beer ringed her top lip. Jack burst out laughing. She smiled, too. He stopped playing the game and looked at her closely, like it was his first time really seeing her. She caught him off-guard by calling him by name.

"You know my name?" he asked with a raised brow. This time it was her turn to smile during the exchange of words. Purposely, she let the moment linger, while secretly enjoying the attention he was giving her. She took a sip from her drink and pursed her lips.

"Saw your picture in the photo album over there." She pointed. "It looked like you was in jail posing with all them tattoos on your arms. You were cute, so I asked my girl Fire who you were."

"Fire?"

"Oops." She placed her hand over her mouth and giggled. "I mean Monique. Fire was her stage name."

"Damn, that's right. Both y'all used to dance before—"

"Nope, I'm still a dancer," she confirmed.

Playfully, Jack corrected her. "You're a scripper," he said, pronouncing "stripper" like the rapper Lil Jon.

"Whateeevah!" she said, snaking her neck from side to side, giving him her bent wrist with a sweep of her hand and a snap of her fingers. They both laughed. She was mad stupid. Jack reached for the partial blunt in the ashtray as she stood up on wobbly legs and pulled her shorts out of her crotch. Jack shook his head. One thing he had to admit, she damn sure had a bangin' body. Foolishly, he heard his voice say, "All scrippers have a certain dance move. What's yours?"

"I don't know 'bout all the dance moves, but I can do a trick or two with my anus. Heard it drives the guys wild. You wanna see it?" she asked like a challenge, again turning the tables on him with her quick wit. He was completely at a loss for words. "You got a girlfriend, Jack?"

"Yeah, I got a shorty." Just the thought of Gina brought him back to his senses. "She been down with a nigga for a minute." Game noticed the change come over his face like the sun coming out from behind the clouds. Jack's mind drifted back to Gina, his down-ass chick. Jack shook his head and glanced at his watch. In doing so, his mind was released from the thought of her and when he glanced up, Game was standing over him with her coochie in his face. In the dim light her olive skin seemed to radiate and glow. For the first time he noticed the tiny pubic hairs climbing up her belly, looking like a golden spider web.

"Yo, a nigga gotta blaze up outta here," Jack said, looking up to see the now sour expression on her face. He saw something else, too, something he would later regret he did not recognize. Somehow, again, it felt like she had inched closer. Her perfume mingled in his nostrils. Her pink, pointed nipples swayed with her movement as she reached out and touched his arm. Fiery hot, he fought the urge to pull away from her. It felt as if somehow she was seeping into his soul like liquid fire. With her milky white skin against his brown skin, they looked at each other as the moment stalled like giant hands on a clock, only it was her hand on him.

"Aw, man, don't go," she pouted with petulant lips. "Rasheed and Fire will be back in a minute. I've been cooped up in this joint for the past two weeks, bored. I got some pizza in the fridge, got mo' beer and whatever else you want. Please stay." She rubbed her hand up and down his arm.

"A'ight!" He pulled away. "Yo, but only for a minute." He was glad she had taken her hand off of him. He glanced down between her thighs. She was fat as a muhfuh. A smile appeared on her face as she picked up his empty glass.

"Hey, you like sports?" she asked out of the blue, causing Jack to slightly tilt his head as smoke from the blunt filtered the air like a small cloud from his mouth into his nose—the sign of a real weed connoisseur. She continued, with three fingers of her hand inside her pocket, standing with her hips leaning to one side. "Well, in sports you got the first-string starters and the second-string, just in case one of the players gets hurt." She looked at him with a hint of something written on her face. "I can play all positions when the first-string starter gets hurt." Her words hung in the air. "Only thing is, I can play my position much betta."

Jack wondered if she was talking about Gina being hurt. He took a long drag off the blunt, gagged and frowned as he licked his dry lips, looking at her through the smoke and haze. For some reason, his lips were numb and so was the tip of his tongue. He had been smoking all day and night. One thing was for sure, he needed to get something straight with this fly-ass white chick. She was nice on the scale of dime pieces, but he was not tryin' to cut. He cleared his throat and took another puff of the blunt. For some reason his lungs were hungry for the weed that numbed his mouth.

"Dig, Ma, no disrespect, know what I mean, but a nigga loyal to the wifey, plus I don't do white chicks."

Game's neck jerked back as her eyes narrowed at him. "Uhmph!" she muttered, like he had just hit her in the chest with his fist. Somehow she managed to keep her composure. Placing her right hand on her hip, she looked at him. "I guess since you don't do white girls you don't do cocaine either? That's white and it makes you feel good, too."

"Hell, naw. I don't fuck wit' that shit! It's for suckers," Jack said as he took another long toke off the blunt and held the roach between his fingers.

Game grinned at him like a real vixen. *I got a trick or two for his ass,* she thought as she watched him greedily suck on the blunt laced with coke. She spun on her heels with a mischievous look and strutted out of the room.

Once in the kitchen, Game peered around the corner back into the living room. Jack was rolling a blunt with his face twisted to the side. He was trying to chase the white girl, cocaine, that had invaded his body and left him craving her.

She began crushing two white Ecstasy pills to put into Jack's drink. One pill was enough to stimulate the body, making a person experience a kind of ultra-sensitivity, a sensation like the body was one big orgasm. But two pills could be more than dangerous, depending on the individual's temperament. Not only could the drug enhance the sex drive, but it could do the same thing for rage if a person wasn't used to it. Little did she know that Jack Lemon was the wrong nigga to be fucking with. When it came to rage, a quick death was better than feeling his wrath.

Her back was to the door as she poured the crushed pills into his drink. The only thing going through her mind was what she was going to do to him—maybe even show him the trick she could do. She smiled as she thought about her coochie in his face. As she made sure all of the powder was in his beer, she swirled it around with her finger. "So, you don't do white chicks, huh," she said to herself. "We'll see."

"What you doin'?" Jack asked, scaring the shit out of her. She spilled some of the substance on the counter as she flinched. As she turned around her breasts stood at attention with her nipples aiming at him as she held onto the edge of the counter. Her breath was lost in her throat. For some reason she focused on the knife mark on Jack's neck from where he had been cut before.

"What you doin'?" Jack asked again, this time with more authority in his voice.

"I … I … I'm fixing you a drink," Game stuttered, her heart fluttering like a caged bird was inside of it. She turned back around within the limited space between them. She quickly retrieved their drinks and passed him his. He took a step back and looked between her and the drink like he knew something was up.

"Let me find out you got some shit wit' 'cha." He eyed her carefully as his tongue danced around in his mouth the way coke heads' do. Game suddenly realized that her scandalous ways could finally catch up with her. Now, fearfully, she watched as he held the drink up to the light, studying it.

"You think you tried a nigga, huh?" Jack spit, looking between her and the glass. Game had already made her mind up – she was going to kick Jack in the balls and make a run for the door. She braced herself as he stared at her. "I thought you said you had pizza," Jack reminded, his now chapped lips curled into a smile. He swallowed hard against his cotton mouth. "A nigga got the munchies and that bomb-ass weed got me jonesin' for mo'." With that said, he turned up the glass and guzzled the beer.

Yeah, just like that, she thought to herself as she watched him intently, just like Eve did Adam after she was tricked by the serpent and then watched dude take a bite out that piece of fruit. A tiny dribble of Heineken dribbled from the corner of his mouth down to his chin. She resisted the urge to wipe it with her fingers as her hungry eyes watched his handsome face like he was her prey and she was a lioness about to pounce.

With a satisfied smirk she stepped closer, smiled and massaged her breasts seductively as she swayed her hips over to the refrigerator. She bent over to show him her assets and give him the "home of the gorilla with all this pussy in your face" pose. The life of a stripper had more than its share of advantages.

She turned, doing the same dick-teasing move at the stove. With each move her scanty clothes seemed to be more revealing. Jack now stood with a full erection. Just that quickly the drug was starting to take effect, or maybe it was her? The front of his pants looked like a large tent as he moved his jaw from side to side, his tongue slightly hanging out. He suddenly had this overwhelming urge to grind his teeth. Shit was crazy. The good weed was starting to take effect on him, or so he thought. His body and mind were starting to experience a slight tingling sensation.

He noticed that Game's shoulder strap was pulled down, exposing the soft, milky-white flesh of her breasts. Jack turned the empty glass up to his lips, he saw the powdery substance at the bottom of the glass. He felt the effects of something powerful invading his body like an electrical current. He shook his head and slightly staggered. It felt like a hundred soldiers were marching through his veins and a million angry voices screamed, "Kill the bitch!"

For some reason, only now could he read the deception in her green eyes as she stood before him, pants lower than he could remember, pubic hairs long and blond, now showing the forest, land of the gorilla. She saw him look at the glass, forehead wrinkled, frowning.

Something was smoldering in his eyes as his jaw worked from side to side, teeth grinding, rage stirring. Jack took a step forward, drew his hand back as far as he could and slapped the shit out of her. He hit her so hard that her neck snapped back causing her hair to fall into her face.

"Bitch, you put something in my muthafuckin' drink!" he yelled, taking a step forward, fist balled up. The millions of voices in his head all chanted in unison, "Kill her, beat that bitch like a man. Kill her!" She had taken him to the point of no return. It felt like he was having an out-of-body experience.

She had a large red welt on her face from his hand. She huffed as her breasts swelled defiantly, teeth streaked with blood. She said boldly, "All I wanted was for you to fuck me! So I put X in your drink."

Jack, blinded with rage, couldn't hear anything she said. He drew back to punch her with his fist. She was pinned between him and the kitchen table. On the table was a large butcher knife.

"If you like, you can hit me again. Punish me," she said as blood dripped from her mouth. Jack thought about all the tales he had heard about the drug X while he was in the joint. He had heard about the crazy maniac effect it had on chicks, but this shit was too crazy. To his amazement the white girl tore off the wife beater and her large, pendulous breasts flung free. Her small nipples were erect and pink. Tan marks outlined the contours of her breasts.

Next she stepped out of her shorts and white thong. Her vagina was so furry that it looked like she was trying to conceal a kitten between her thighs. She fell to her knees and unzipped his pants. Jack stood as if paralyzed, both fists balled up so tightly that his knuckles cracked. The bitch was past being bold. He had never experienced a woman like her in his entire life.

Somehow, unabashed, unrestrained, he took his gun out just as she bugged at the size of his dick, its length, its long, black, coiling thick veins. She could hardly get her hands around its girth. Her eyes grew wide. His dick was so dark it was like black-blue in contrast with her fair skin. It was as long as a small child's arm, but thicker. She stroked him up and down like a plunger, making the pre cum gleam in the head like pearls in a clamshell. She primed her lips with her tongue. He raised the gun to her head, pulled the hammer back. She glanced up, didn't even bat an eye as she opened her mouth wide, taking him in her throat. She had to stretch her mouth so wide it felt like she was going to get lockjaw.

Jack couldn't help it, his mind was gone to that place of no return. He had to humiliate her, hurt her, bad! Violently he shoved his dick down her throat, making her gag and choke as he grabbed a handful of her hair, pressing the gun to her temple.

"Punk-ass bitch! Dis what you want, huh?" Jack yelled with his top lip curled to the side. The drug had completely seized his body. Beads of sweat were starting to glisten on his forehead like shimmering brown gold as he continued to mash her head into his crotch, forcing his way down her throat. As he looked down at her through the fog of his mind, it looked like the more he dogged her out, the more she sucked on his dick, gagging and choking, saliva dripping off his penis onto her fingers and down his balls. Black and white skin, the combination a lethal curse, like the taboo, black blood with white.

"Shoot her! Shoot her!" the voices in his head exhorted as he held the gun to her head, forcing himself down her throat. Somehow in the frenzied dual, amidst the loud slurping sounds that seemed to echo, Game masterfully contracted the muscles in her throat as she took him in deeper, almost all eleven, thick inches as he humped her face. Now she was the aggressor. Her head bobbed up and down so fast, so deep, so hot. Jack's eyes rolled to the back of his head. He was losing himself, losing control to her tempo.

Jack felt his knees grow weak. Absent-mindedly, he placed the gun down on top of the stove. His eyes peeled open wide as she worked the juices in her mouth like some dance theme. Her tongue roamed up and down the ridge of his dick, while her lips trailed not far behind. Her mouth, succulent, moist, hot and wet, molested his organ, savoring every hypersensitive, tingling inch of him. It was three against one – lips, mouth and tongue, against his tool.

Jack heard a grunt, loud and bestial, like a wounded wild animal, then a moan that segued into a protracted groan. To his utter surprise, the sound was coming from deep within his throat, somewhere in the pit of his gut. He threw his head back and roared, opening his mouth wider. Spasms rocked his body, then a shudder. He felt chills run up and down his spine as Game's hot mouth worked him, pushing him past the brink of ecstasy.

The fuckin' dope had completely possessed him. He was about to cum down her throat and somehow the white girl knew it, sensed it. On her knees Game smiled with the huge black dick in her mouth. He reached down and pulled her up by her hair. Her mouth was still agape in awe and shock as she screeched in pain. His was dick dangling with a long string of cum seeping out of the head. Her large breasts bounced, swinging in front of him. Jack furrowed his brow when he saw cum, like honey, sparkling in the hairs of her vagina in the gap between her wide thighs. A line of cum ran down her inner thigh. Jack could have sworn he saw a glint of a smile tug at Game's lips.

Deep down, something about her infuriated him. Now he just wanted to dog this bitch out. She stood before him, unafraid, unrestrained and untamed. Perhaps it was the drugs, or the fact that she had tried a nigga big time, putting that shit in his drink. He grabbed her by the shoulders, spinning her around so hard that her hair twirled like an umbrella. He bent her over the table, forcing her head down, ass up. He spread her legs. She muttered something as she tried to look back over her shoulder. He slammed her head down hard on the table. She whimpered a dove's cry with her butt and furry pussy tooted up in the air. She had a forest down there, home of the gorilla.

"So you want me to fuck you, huh?" Jack said with a menacing scowl on his face, eyes ablaze with fury that he would later regret. He stroked himself long and hard, pointed his dick between her ass cheeks, intending to do serious damage. He couldn't help but admire her luscious backside. Like the Devil, the dope told him to. Bent over like she was, Jack slapped her hard on the ass, leaving a handprint. She cried out in pain and tried to raise her head. He slammed it back down on the table with a loud thud. Jack was deranged. Now his intent was to abuse her body by violently taking her from the back, in more ways than one. He spit on his hand, rubbed it up and down his long shaft, and aimed it as he grabbed a handful of her flesh, spreading her cheeks, opening the pink morsel of flesh dripping wet with her juices like dew on a watermelon.

He eased inside her. Slowly she wiggled her ass in an attempt to accommodate him. Once he got the mushroom-like head of his dick in her tight vagina he rammed it in, eight inches, causing her to cry out in pain. She looked back at him and for the first time she had pure torment written on her face. He went deeper, giving her his full length. She screamed to the top of her lungs, thrashed and bucked. "You're hurting me!" she screeched, pleading. "Go slow. Ohhh …" She reached back with her hand. He slapped it down and thrust deeper into her.

"Oh, oh, shit, yo … yo … you black motherfucker!" Game

was talking like a white woman now as Jack continued to fervidly pound away inside her guts. The table shook so hard that it felt like the legs were about to fall off. Sweat poured off both of their bodies as his balls banged against her. She could feel him deep within her, like he was rubbing against her ribs. He was frantic, like a raved maniac out of control. With each of his powerful thrusts the table continued to slam against the wall as she cried out for him to stop. He had the pussy on fire.

"Oh …You killiiing mee!" she pleaded. It only seemed to bring more of the animal out of him. Now for the first time she was concerned for her health. Jack only ignored her as he continued to grunt and fuck her from the back, making her pussy pop. Finally, about an hour later, he stopped and pulled out of her. She was red, irritated and sore. Soon as he withdrew his dick, her pussy farted long and hard. He squirted cum all over her back and hair. They were both winded, their breath echoing like chants of a song that neither of them had rehearsed.

"Naw bitch, you gonna rememba dis dick," he hissed, standing behind her. He reached for the Crisco cooking oil on the stove and squeezed oil between her ass and all over her back, his dick in his hand like a large battering ram. He looked down at the small hole of her anus. If the Bible mentioned something about a camel and the eye of a needle, then surely his dick could go through something the size of a dime. With his lubricated finger he eased it inside of her ass. To his amazement, Game jacked up one ass cheek, then the other, and spread her thick round ass wide, making it jiggle and bounce at the same time. The little pink hole in the center slightly winked at him as it opened like "open-sesame."

Jack did a double-take, blinking his eyes, like *what the fuck?* Then his mind flashed back to what she had said earlier about being able to do a trick or two with her anus. He placed the head of his pipe inside of her determined to do as much damage as humanly possible. Game took a deep breath, eased off the side of the table, bent all the way down, touched the floor with her hands, and made some kind of noise that Jack could not make out. He glided an inch or two inside of her. She groaned, he moaned and slipped in deeper. She raised her head, looking back at him. The tight sensation that was gripping him suddenly made him lose control.

He knew it had to be the drug. He plunged deep inside of her. She let out a shriek as her hands reached back to block some of the length of his penetration. He was building momentum, like riding down a mountain. His pace quickened. Jack rode her long and hard. She knew that he was trying to punish her. He had the right idea, but the wrong woman. Together they reached multiple climaxes, her breasts swinging back and forth as his body clapped against hers. She bit down on her lip, taking all of him. He pounded away inside of her with deep, long strokes. He had never fucked a chick in the ass before in his life.

Finally, they came together like two desperate people running a race, a fuck marathon. In the end, they both were drenched with sweat, panting. He pulled his dick out of her, leaving a swollen, irritated gaping hole the size of a small fist. Jack looked at his watch, 4:24 a.m. His dick was still rock hard! Game turned around and looked at him as she wiped her clit and made a face that stayed that way as she continued to feel around down there.

So many things were going through Jack's mind. He had failed miserably at punishing the white girl with his dick. For some reason, the drug made him stay bad-tempered, evil like the Devil. "Bitch, I should kill your punk ass," Jack said.

Game continued to rub her clit like it was on fire as she glared at him with dried blood on her chin. She responded tersely, "You already killed me. You killed the poonaney." Jack frowned at her and her slick-ass mouth. They were both high off X and still horny as hell. "Spend the night. You know you want to," Game said, looking at his dick, which was still hard and swinging from side to side. She was right, the drug made him want to take her again.

Instead, he walked over to the faucet and drank some water with his hands, thirsty like a homeless dog. She watched him with her thick legs spread and continued to rub her clit. It dawned on him just how freaky this white bitch was, for he had done his damnedest to punish her. He slapped the shit out of her, rough-housed the pussy and unsuccessfully tried to molest her asshole. The bitch must have loved every minute of him sodomizing the shit out of her. For a second, a voice in his head chanted, "Strangle the bitch! Strangle the bitch!" Jack took a step forward, teeth grinding, hands coiling, muscles tensing. He recoiled his fingers like claws, staring at the soft white fleshy tissue on her neck. His palm print was still on her face from where he had slapped her.

"W-w-why you looking at me like that?" Game asked, taking a tentative step back.

This shit is crazy, Jack thought. The dope was making him crazy. The bold, crazy-ass white bitch standing before him nude still rubbing her coochie with cum running down her leg was crazy. His fucking throat was so dry, his mouth was numb and why in the hell was he grinding his fucking teeth so damn much? It felt like he was going to crack them. His dick was so hard he had to shove it into his pants, but it had a mind of its own and didn't want to cooperate. Fuckin' dope! He grabbed his gun and turned to walk away, feeling like a nigga that tried to play, but had gotten played instead.

Then, for some dumb reason, he heard his mouth say, "I thought you said Rasheed and Mo was comin' back in a few?"

She rolled her eyes and sucked her teeth. *Why is he still asking about them?* she thought. Game took a step closer, one of her eyes was slightly red, and her hair was matted to her forehead with sweat. She placed her hand on the curve of her wide hip as she turned her leg outward. "I lied to you. They ain't comin' home tonight. They staying at a hotel." Then Game added, like some practiced cliché, "You know you comin' back for mo'. Look at the bulge in your pants," she said, pointing and taking a step forward. "You said you don't do white girls or coke. Well, two white girls name coke and Game just did 'cha." She chimed. "Touché!"

"What?" Jack grumbled as it dawned on him what the bitch had just said. He balled his fist up tight and took a step forward, fully intent on dropping her like a man. He went to swing, but she just stood there with her perfect white, feral teeth showing, rubbing her clit as she looked at him like a sex fiend. Jack unclenched his fist and turned to walk out the door. The cackle of her laughter followed him. From that day forward, Jack would never get high off anything but life. The white girl had taught him a lesson. And not just that, he went up in her raw. "Fuckin' drugs!"

TWENTY-FOUR

The Family

Jack parked Gina's Jeep in the front yard of Grandma Hattie's house. The yard was cluttered with cars. Across the street was a Channel Five news van. Two crackheads strolled by as Jack hopped out of the Jeep, giving them the screwface, like "don't even think about stealing shit out this yard." The junkies quickly focused their attention on the white woman and the two news reporters inside the van. They were obviously on the wrong side of town, but if it was announced that Rasheed Smith was drafted into the NBA, the reporter would rush the house for a story.

Jack walked inside the house. It was jam-packed with folks. The mood was festive. He saw cats he hadn't seen in ages, chicks, too. The television volume was turned up loud on SportsCenter. Rasheed sat perched in the middle of the couch as people mingled about all around him. He looked like a zombie with both hands nervously holding a forty ounce of malt liquor.

"Damn, nigga, you look like shit!" Rasheed said to his man Jack. It was the truth. Jack had been up all night and was still horny and extremely thirsty, still wired from the X pills. It felt like his jaws were cemented together. Jack ignored his friend's remark as he stared at the forty in his hands. For some unknown reason his right eye kept twitching. Jack sat down next to Rasheed. Rasheed took one look at Jack's chapped lips and frowned. He then sniffed the air and leaned away from Jack. He was about to say something, but Jack spoke first.

"Nigga, why didn't you tell me dat white bitch was staying at Gina's?" Jack asked with a snarl.

205

"Georgia Mae?"

"Yeah, Game," Jack said.

"Why ... how you know?" Rasheed asked with a little too much concern in his voice. "It wasn't important. What, you met her? She's dope, huh?" Rasheed said with a smile that conveyed more than appreciation for her.

The sportscaster started talking. J.T., from high school, started talking louder. "You know Rasheed ain't in the first round because of racism."

Someone else shouted, "But the rest of the players are mostly black."

"That only makes it worse. Why they only got mostly black dudes?" J.T. asked stupidly, staggering across the room.

"Hey!" J.T. yelled, looking around trying to find the culprit who threw a magazine at him.

"Sit your dumb ass down!" a voice yelled from amongst the crowd.

Everyone laughed as J.T. did just that.

As Rasheed sat on the couch nervous, with butterflies the size of bats in his stomach, his mind flashed back to the last game of the year, the AAA Championship game that he had played in against the Spartans. The big game that the coach had been preparing him for, the game of his life, the one that would help decide whether or not he would go pro. It seemed like everyone who had something to do with sports in New York had been in the house. The media was there in full blast; even a couple of basketball stars and their agents came out to watch the big game.

The entire first quarter, the opposing team was guarding him with two and three men. The defense was good. They kept changing it up. Finally, he was able to get a shot off—air ball. He missed everything. Running down court, the white boy, his opponent, shoved him and he fell hard. He looked up at the coach and the man was screaming at him. Them white boys was laying some serious wood. By halftime he had no points, and not just that, the opposing team managed to keep him off the boards—no rebounds. The referees refused to give him any calls. It was a game played at the opposing team's school.

At halftime in the locker room, Coach Jones screamed so much that he became hoarse. Rasheed was embarrassed. In his heart he knew that he was scared because of all of the pressure. It caused him to not just let himself down, but his teammates, too. They couldn't even look him in the eye. The Spartans were all white boys and regardless of what anyone said, them white boys could play some ball. They played rough and hard.

Finally, the coach turned to Rasheed, the team captain. "Maybe this isn't your team or your game. A true champion welcomes a challenge. That's the only thing that separates him from the rest, shows if he's the best. None of you deserve to go to the pros," the coach said angrily. Everyone in the locker room knew who the statement was really directed toward.

Rasheed rose to his feet so fast that the towel on his lap fell two feet in front of him. "Yo, I got this! We gotta start playing together like a team. Y'all standing around watching me! Move! Set some picks!" Rasheed looked at his coach. "Set some plays for me. Get me the damn ball in the post!" The coach grinned at the hypercharged attitude of his player. The art of good coaching was knowing how to motivate the players.

◊ ◊ ◊ ◊

Rasheed's team, the Wild Cats, started the second half off sixteen points behind the opposing team. The crowd was going wild. Rasheed saw Magic Johnson in the stands. Just like he had asked, the coach ran plays for him. Rasheed missed his first three shots with the lanky white boys guarding him. As he hustled down court, the coach gave him a pained expression as he yelled for another player off the bench to replace Rasheed. This was it, the biggest game of his entire life and he couldn't produce. Rasheed refused to come out of the game and mouthed to coach, "No." The coach shook his head, making a face at Rasheed that he was disappointed with his game. Rasheed stole a pass and ran the ball all the way up the court and pulled up in the white boy's face, hit a three – all net, and was fouled. The crowd booed.

Rasheed went to the line and for the first time that day, he talked shit to the white boys just like he did on the Brooklyn basketball courts. He was in his zone as he shot the free throw. He went on to score twenty-two points in the second half. He was hot, hitting fifteen straight points, and now with six seconds left in the game, they were down by one. The coach called a screen. Rasheed would come off his man and roll to the free throw line for a pass. It worked as planned. As his teammate passed him the ball, Rasheed pulled up for the shot and was fouled. He went to the free throw line knowing he could either tie the game by hitting one free throw or lose the game if he missed both.

There were two seconds left on the game clock. Rasheed knew he was a seventy percent shooter from the line. *A piece of cake,* he told himself as he dribbled the ball twice. *Bend your knees, use your wrist, deep breath … Swoosh!* The first shot sailed through the net. The score was now tied. Rasheed released a deep breath that he didn't even know he was holding.

The boisterous crowd had gotten louder. They were stomping their feet, waving orange flags and other paraphernalia in front of him. A fan was actually standing a few feet in back of the basketball goal yelling at him. Rasheed glanced over at the bench. Some of his teammates were holding hands huddled together. A few were actually on their knees with their hands clasped in front of them. All wore solemn faces, especially the coach. He had a towel in his mouth, gnawing on it. The future of this team rested on Rasheed's shoulders.

The ball left his hand as if in slow motion – a surreal moment. The world had slowed to a crawl as everyone held their breath. The ball hit the rim, bounced high, bounced … bounced … falling out of the rim. To everybody's amazement, Rasheed came flying high above the rim over everyone on the floor. With one hand, he palmed the ball and did a ferocious one-hand dunk with his nuts in the seven foot center's face! The clock shrilled! The game was over! His teammates went wild! They stormed the court, burying him with emotional hugs. They had won the championship game. For the first time ever they had made the front page of the "*USA Today*" sports section.

Now Rasheed sat in front of the television. Nervous couldn't begin to describe what he was feeling. He was past that, almost to the point of being frantic. Jack sat next to him grinding his teeth. He wasn't about to tell Rasheed about how Game had stunted on him by pulling that bullshit with the dope. Plus, everyone knew that he didn't mess with white chicks.

"I stopped by y'all's crib. Mmmm, uh, why you got that cracka broad stayin' with y'all?" Jack asked, raising his voice above the crowd in the room. Rasheed wasn't really paying any attention to him though. J.T. was drunk and dancing in front of the television.

"Move, nigga!" Rasheed yelled. "Me and Mo went to a hotel last night. In a few days she's leaving for Cali." Then he smiled. "So, you met Georgia Mae. She's dope, huh?" Rasheed said with a sly smile.

Jack was thinking, *She's dope alright,* but he could sense something else was going on.

"Gina's been asking about you. Said you was supposed to come back last night." Just then, the kitchen door opened. Grandma Hattie appeared, followed by Monique, Aunt Esta, Gina and a few more women that Jack didn't recognize. They all had trays of soul food – collard greens, fried chicken and barbecue ribs. Gina hobbled so badly that Jack had to resist the urge to get up and help her. Besides, his conscience was getting to him. Not to mention, the dope still had him dry-mouthed and horny.

Gina's long hair was in a ponytail with curls hanging on each side of her face. She wore a white sundress with flowers, looking like the average attractive black woman. As she looked at Jack her eyes sparkled and a light smile tugged at her cheeks. Her cinnamon complexion seemed to glow. One of the women turned and whispered something, causing all the women to erupt in giddy laughter, an indication of the jovial mood in the old house.

Suddenly the bright smile on Gina's face froze as her eyes narrowed looking at Jack. He rose to greet her, genuinely happy to see his woman. The room was full of noisy chatter as he bopped over and kissed Gina on the cheek with his dry chapped lips. He continued to grind his teeth as he tried to speak. Gina reached out and pinched him hard, grabbing a fold of his skin underneath his shirt.

"Ouch!" Jack screeched.

"Nigga, where you been?" she demanded with a frown on her face so intense that Jack took a step back, at the same time trying to remove his tongue from the roof of his mouth. The room suddenly was dead quiet as the announcer began to call the first name in the draft. No one was paying any attention to Jack and Gina. "You had them same clothes on yesterday. And look at you, what's wrong with your face and shit?" Gina said, pulling on his shirt.

She peered closer, sniffed him to pussy check, the way a woman does when she's on the verge of going the fuck off, searching for another female's scent or any other evidence. The rowdy crowd in the front room yelled as a picture of Rasheed flashed across the screen, along with a few other athletes that the commentator said had a very slim chance of getting drafted.

"Nigga, you got me twisted if you think I don't know when something is up with you," Gina said.

"Chill, Ma, a nigga been on the grind tryna make shit happen," Jack said, grinding his teeth and rubbing the spot where she had just pinched the shit out of him.

Grandma Hattie looked up at them as she wiped her hands on her apron. The thick creases in her forehead expressed concern. She ambled over. Her mahogany skin was lined so deep with age that some of her wrinkles overlapped each other. She knew they were fighting. Her weary mouth smiled, but her eyes didn't.

"Y'all be nice, you hear?" she said sweetly and then placed a comforting hand on Gina's shoulder. "She's much betta. Child still needs some rest, but you can take her home now. She done ate me outta house and home." Grandma Hattie laughed, causing Gina to smile at the old woman. Jack just ground his teeth with an urge for a beer so bad it was driving him crazy. Grandma Hattie's expression changed as she shrugged her small narrow shoulders. "Boy, you take good care of dis girl. All she needs is some rest and a lot of love now." The old woman didn't tell Jack that, more than likely, Gina would walk with a limp for the rest of her life.

There was some commotion at the door. Everyone turned to see Lieutenant Brown walking through with two cases of beer. The noise level got even louder. A few women yelled out his name. Drunken J.T. staggered. "Man, somebody give dis nigga a quarter or somethin'. How'd you know I was thirsty bro?" Everybody cracked up at J.T.'s crazy ass. Brown smiled and walked past him in his royal blue sweat suit. His thick, curly hair shined as a glint of sunlight danced off of it. He spoke to everyone in the house, people who had known him most of his life. The females sang his name in chorus with a few flirtatious invitations. Shit, he was a prime catch as far as the ladies were concerned. He was good looking and had a job with benefits.

Rasheed looked up from the television as Anthony reached out his fist. "Good luck, dawg." Rasheed gave him a dap. For a moment, Rasheed thought about the man who used to be his mentor, how he had taken him to his first basketball game. A lot had changed since Anthony had started working for the beast. He stepped over a red fire truck Lil' Malcolm was playing with on the floor. He playfully ruffled the child's hair as he bent down to play with him, teetering with both cases of beer stacked under one arm.

In the dining room Gina stood stunned as she looked at the handsome cop. Her heart raced in her chest. A riot of emotions went off in her head as he walked straight toward her. The last time she had seen him she was busting caps at his dome and fleeing the scene of a double homicide with a bullet in her leg. Now she felt trapped. She would have run away, but she couldn't. She hadn't told Jack that he was the cop that she shot at. She didn't know his name until now.

Jack shuffled his feet as Anthony walked up and pecked Grandma Hattie on the cheek, causing the old woman to blush like a school girl. He then set the boxes of beer on the table as they exchanged pleasantries. Anthony reached into one of the boxes and retrieved a can of beer as a woman walked over and said something to him. He ignored her and instead looked over at Jack and Gina. Embarrassed, the woman grabbed a can of beer and walked away hoping nobody saw how she got played. The expression on Anthony's face changed like a dark shadow had washed over it. Casually he strolled over, taking a drink from his beer.

"You look so much like your father it's a damn shame," he said, shaking his head as he talked to Jack and sticking his fist out so Jack could gave him a dap. Jack mopped his face with his weary hand, swallowed hard, trying not to stare at the beer. He had sworn to give up drinking and smoking. Game had taught him a lesson. Anthony then turned his attention to the pretty girl standing next to Jack. He remembered her being Jack's girl, but there was something about her that he just couldn't put his finger on. Her piercing green eyes held him, but there was something else.

"I'm still tryna figure out how my ole man ended up being a revolutionary and you a cop."

Anthony was still looking at Gina when he spoke. "It's simple. We were both pulled in two different directions to serve our people." He continued to stare at Gina, perplexed. Neither of them dared to break their optic standoff.

"Don't I ... know you from ..." Anthony said. The words trailed off his tongue like he was experiencing déjà vu. Jack stood between the two of them and watched the visual volley being exchanged as Brown furrowed his brow in an attempt to force his mind to remember something.

"Why you ain't at work today?" Grandma Hattie asked from the kitchen, sticking her head out the door. The woman who was trying to get his attention earlier walked past Anthony, attempting to make eye contact.

Jack watched as Anthony took another hearty drink of his beer and his mouth watered. That shit still had him buggin'. *What the fuck they put in them damn pills?* he wondered. He was grinding his teeth, except now it was getting worse. He was actually moving his jaw from side to side.

"I got suspended," Anthony said sourly. Somehow Rasheed overheard that part of their conversation.

"I told 'cha them crackas don't care about a nigga when he work for the beast. You'd come out better being a slave catcher." Anthony made a face and moved his lips as if to speak then changed his mind. Jack rubbed at his throat and said he needed some cold water.

Gina tore her eyes away from the cop and glowered at Jack. "His ass been up to something," she mumbled under her breath. Jack excused himself and walked off to the kitchen. He was dehydrated and then some!

With Jack gone and everyone huddled around the television, it seemed like it was just the two of them, Gina and the cop. He could have reached out and touched the silky baby hair that cascaded down the side of Gina's face, he was standing just that close to her. In some ways he could also see the innocence in her youthful beauty. He could also see the hood in her as her ponytail hung over her shoulder onto her breast, partially concealing a tattoo.

"So, Mr. Po-po, what did you get suspended fo'?" Gina asked, smiling devilishly as she limped over to the chair and sat down with great difficulty. Brown frowned as he watched her closely. Gina smoothed the wrinkles out of her dress with the palms of her hand.

An image flashed through Brown's mind. "How did you hurt yourself?" he asked with his eyebrows bunched together. This was now the detective in him talking.

"I was runnin' and I fell," Gina said, looking up at him with her hands still on her thighs. Her eyes matched his, almost inviting him to go along with the dialogue.

"Running from what?" Brown asked, never taking his eyes off the beautiful girl. Secretly Gina was enjoying the verbal sparring with the cop, all the while being conscious of the potential dangers that lurked like a deadly shark in knee-deep water.

"Didn't yo' momma teach you not to answer a question with a question?" Gina mimicked in a heavy New York accent that made Brown smile. "I'm saying, I asked you first. What was you suspended for?"

Brown pulled in his lips, thought for a second and reached over and pulled out a chair, straddling it backward.

"Excuse my language, but I was suspended for some bullshit," he said bitterly as he sighed. She could tell that he felt uneasy talking about it.

In the next room it had grown even more quiet, as more names were being announced. Rasheed sat in front of the television chewing his thumbnail as Monique sat by his side, her face resembling his, the pain built up from the stress of the unknown. The once jubilant mood was now somber, coated in heavy silence like a funeral home parlor.

"I'm sure you've heard of the Death Struck case," Anthony said. Gina shifted in her chair uncomfortably and stretched her legs, crossing one ankle over the other, catching Brown looking at her heart-shaped figure.

"No, I haven't," she lied with a straight face as she leaned forward in her chair expressing interest.

Anthony paused for a moment, apprehensive about telling her about the case. *Those eyes,* he thought.

"Well?" she said, attempting to stir him out of his deep thoughts.

He then looked around and saw Rasheed and remembered everyone was there for him. He was amongst people he considered family and she wouldn't be there, or even with Jack, if she weren't. He let his guard down and began speaking.

"Well, the disappearance of Damon Dice and the murder of his bodyguard have become very high profile cases. Not just in America, but all over the world. I didn't even know hip-hop was that big," Anthony said matter-of-factly, not telling her anything she didn't already know. "I have my suspicions who is behind it all but that's when I was pulled from the case and suspended."

"Really?" Gina asked, raising her eyebrows as she looked at him, pretending to be shocked. "It must be gang related or something," she said, trying to get more information from him. "You know, being a rapper and all."

"I don't think it's gang related," he said, dispelling that myth. "It's something deeper than that. I do know that it's just two people ... for now."

"Two people? Why do you say that?"

"Just my instincts," he said, trying not to give more information than necessary. "I do know that it's a male and female."

"A girl?" she said innocently.

"Yeah, and I think I'm this close to catching her." He gestured with his thumb and forefinger.

"Her," she pointed and hunched her shoulders. "Why so much emphasis on the woman, if you say it's a man and a woman?"

"Of course, I would like to catch both of them, but it's the woman who's killed two men in cold blood and then tried to kill me. It's personal now."

"Sounds like you need to be careful. The next time she shoots at you she might not miss."

Brown jerked his neck back as his eyebrows shot up. "How did you know that she shot at me?" Brown asked with a stern expression on his face, catching her completely off-guard.

"Huh, mmm, I think I read about it somewhere."

"You just told me that you never heard about the case."

Playing with fire, Gina was about to get burned. Brown was now looking at her so absorbedly that he frightened her. As she sat in the chair in front of him, she could feel her heart pounding so hard in her chest that she was sure he could see it.

Jack entered the room from the kitchen. He had a tall glass of ice water in one hand and a greasy chicken wing in the other. His pants sagged so low that his Glock was showing in his drawers. As soon as he joined them he looked at Gina and could sense that something was wrong.

"How long you been out the joint?" Anthony asked.

"Why, what you askin' for? This ain't cops and robbers day. Nigga, if you come as a friend, you askin' too many damn questions, know what I mean," Jack said as he continued to look back and forth between Anthony and Gina. Anthony saw the big-ass Glock in Jack's pants and read the warning expression on his face. Gina got up and walked into the next room. Jack followed as the female who had tried to strike up conversation earlier with Anthony walked back over and attempted to start another conversation with him. He never heard a word the woman said.

Rasheed stared at the television as Jack and Gina entered the room. The murmurs, muffled voices, and occasional giggles were now a scant reminder of the once festive mood. A few friends and family members had come, eaten the free food and drank the drinks, wished Rasheed good luck and left. Crazy-ass J.T. was cracking jokes about what it would be like if he were President. In all, the atmosphere now felt drained. Rasheed looked as if the very life had been sucked out of him. A man's dreams are often all he has in the ghetto, a dream of getting out. When you take that away from him you take away a part of the man.

Rasheed lowered his head, crestfallen, with his wide narrow shoulders slumped. Monique sat next to him and affectionately caressed the nape of his neck, cooing words of encouragement into her man's ear. A black woman's task is never easy.

They were announcing the final players who would be selected in the draft. The camera zoomed in on Isiah Thomas, President of the New York Knicks basketball association. He looked into the camera with a stoic expression and reached down to open the envelope for the Knicks' final pick of the draft. Feeling defeated, Rasheed raised his head to look at the television. Isiah announced with a slight smile on his face, "The New York Knicks would like to pick Rasheed Smith of the St. John Wild Cats. This year's AAA Champions."

The once somber room erupted in joyous clamor, with Monique being the loudest. "Thank ya, Jesus! Thank ya, Jesus!"

She jumped around so much she re-injured her ankle. Everyone was overcome with the kind of emotion that just fills you with beautiful euphoria as people celebrated in their own way.

As soon as she heard the noise, Grandma Hattie rushed out of the kitchen. Wiping her wet hands on her apron, she began to hobble over to Rasheed. He had pure shock written all over his face, as the reality of what had just happened started to come down on him. As Rasheed saw his grandmother nearing him, he stood and walked toward her. Once they met, he began to cry in sobs that racked his body as he hugged the black woman who had raised him. He held her tightly as she began to cry, too. The tears streaked down his face. He was overcome with emotions that he could not describe. It was like waking up one day struggling to feed your family and the next, being able to buy your child nice shoes or send them to a good school to get an education, the things that white folks took for granted and that blacks constant-ly struggled for.

There was a loud knock on the door and in walked the media, with lights so bright that they made Rasheed squint his eyes. A white woman shoved a microphone in his face and asked him to make a comment regarding being drafted right here, at home, by the New York Knicks. Lost for words, drunk-ass J.T. tried to take over the interview.

"I wanna give a shout out to all my niggas in the Tombs on lock down – Deemo, Tat Tat and dem."

While the reporters were in the house getting an interview, the crackheads were outside breaking into the news van.

Jack just looked on as he continued to grind his teeth, jaw clenching from side to side. He was elated that a nigga could eat and now feed his family, but there was one thing that Jack didn't like. Why was the nigga crying on national television? Niggas out of BK don't cry. *A nigga too thorough for that soft shit,* Jack was thinking.

From across the room Anthony was watching, happy for Rasheed. Suddenly his cell phone rang. With all the commotion he walked into the kitchen to take the call. To his surprise, it was Dr. Wong, the medical examiner. He talked urgently.

"I hear you got suspended," the doctor said in thickly accented English. "If you can find time, I need see you down here at the morgue."

"About what?" Anthony questioned as he raised his voice above the crowd and placed his finger in his ear.

"Captain Brooks, the man you fight with, he is here."

"What?!"

"Not just that. Guess who else?"

"Who?"

"Your boss. They looking at Damon Dice's body."

"Shit! They found him?"

"Sort of," Wong replied.

"What the fuck you mean, sort of?"

"They found him in dump without his head."

"Decapitated?"

"Yep. Come by tonight. I have something for you might help you solve the case." With that, Dr. Wong hung up the phone.

TWENTY-FIVE

Lieutenant Brown

The Brooklyn morgue was located on the south side of town next to the old cemetery. It was surrounded by an ancient twelve-foot gate with spiked points. At night the place looked like a haunted castle. When Brown arrived it was dark outside, heavy with dense patches of fog. Brown could barely see his hand in front of his face. The sound of his shoes echoed on the pavement as he briskly walked up the stairs. At the entrance of the morgue sat two lion head statues, as if guarding the door. As Brown walked up to the door, he was startled by a black cat that hissed and drew back its lips to expose its sharp teeth. As it brushed by his leg, skirting down the stairs, Brown jumped out of the way just as Dr. Wong opened the door.

"See what you did to kitty," Wong chided with a smirk on his face. Wearing a stained white smock, he held a sandwich in his hand.

Brown made a face at Dr. Wong and replied, "Damn cat is as big as a fucking dog."

Dr. Wong blinked, squinting at Brown in intervals. "Tom Cat big pussy. Maybe he no like you."

"Maybe I put bullet in ass," Brown retorted, mimicking Wong in broken English as he stepped inside the morgue. Together they walked down the long corridor. The place was eerie, old and damp.

They turned and walked into a room. Dr. Wong entered first and turned and waited for Brown. Every time he entered the room, it always reminded him of some type of death chamber, with its white porcelain autopsy tables that looked so old that they could have been donated to a science museum. The air was stale, tinged with an awful smell—death. The room temperature was refrigerator cold. Modern equipment appeared to be non-existent. Brown looked at all the electrical autopsy saws. On the table he saw a body with a white paper sheet covering it. On the table across from it was another body zipped up in a gray body bag. From the corner of the body bag a white substance was dripping on the floor. No matter how many times Brown viewed mutilated dead bodies, all the senseless killings, it gave him the creeps. He never had the stomach for it.

Dr. Wong took a bite out of his sandwich and began to talk with his mouth full of food. "I show you something to help you with Death Struck case," he said as he swallowed hard. "Body under sheet belong to Tommy Knight, the man known as Big Prophet. I about to perform eyetopsee," he spoke, pronouncing the word "autopsy" wrong. "The other body," Wong pointed, "belong to Damon Dice." Brown's jaw went slack and his eyes scrolled over to their corners as he looked over at the gray body bag. Damon Dice was in there, headless. "Which one you wanna see first?" Wong asked, gesturing with the sandwich still in his hand. Brown strolled over to Damon's body bag. With a slight nod he indicated to Wong to open it. Wong walked over and unzipped the bag with one hand.

The bag fell away from the deceased body like a husk. The horrible smell of rotten flesh was overwhelming. Brown took a step back, gagging as he placed a hand over his mouth. Wong took a bite out of his sandwich and walked over to a table and then came back. He passed Brown a face mask, which did little to help. Wong finished off the remainder of his sandwich, walked over to the sink, washed his hands, and put on a pair of latex gloves. All the while Brown stood his distance, looking at the headless body. Maggots were crawling all over Damon's genital area and large bugs were so plentiful that you could scoop them up by hand. Brown began to itch all over. He looked distressed as he scratched his neck.

"W … w … where did you find him?"

"Poor guy was at Brooklyn dump. One of the workers discover him," Wong spoke. "As soon as prints came back identify the body, Chief Daniels and Captain Brooks and his men were all over the place." As Wong spoke, Brown continued to peer at Damon.

"So, my boss Chief Daniels is the one tipping off Brooks," Brown said, talking to himself.

"What you say?" Wong asked.

"Nothing."

"I called you because I overhear your boss mention your name. He say something 'bout a cab and a lady with blond wig. They say together they work on case like team to find cab company and woman. He tell Chief Brooks, as favor, he let him make arrest. They both agree to keep you off case."

"Damn, you overheard that?" Brown asked as he scratched his chest. He should have figured it out, but he never would have thought it was his boss. That was truly fucked up. Now he wondered why they wanted him off the case. This was a high profile case, the kind that drew enough publicity to get a man promoted … or demoted.

Brown watched and scratched like he had fleas as Dr. Wong examined the body. "My bet is he had some kind of basilar skull fracture."

"A what?" Brown retorted.

"Trauma to the back of the head."

As Wong continued talking, Brown began to gag. "How in the hell can you say he had a skull fracture when he ain't got no head?" he said in a muffled voice as he scratched his neck.

Wong smiled with food stuck between his crooked teeth. "I say dat because there is blood in the airway. It's only one way that could have happened. Blood dripped down the back of the throat while he was breathing."

"You mean, he was alive when his head was cut off?"

Wong nodded his head.

"Damnit!" Brown exclaimed as he now scratched his jaw and took a timid step back from Wong. He had maggots crawling up his sleeve and his gloves were covered with them.

"I'm not sayin' he was conscious. He had a blood pressure, even if slight." Brown couldn't take it anymore. He turned away from the sight of the decapitated body and momentarily shut his eyes as he inhaled the horrible rancid smell of death.

After Wong washed his hands and changed his gloves, he walked over to Big Prophet's body. He pulled the sheet back exposing the badly burned corpse. "Sho' you somethin'. You eva watch eyetopsee before?" he asked and pointed to Big Prophet's chest. The markings were still visible, like a dead man talking from the grave, trying desperately to tell who his killer is. With his fingernail, Prophet had scratched initials that looked like "7C". The markings were unintelligible. As Brown peered down at the dead man, he now remembered seeing the markings at the crime scene. It had simply slipped his mind because so much had been going on.

"I also have somethin' else that may interest you," Wong said, blinking his eyes and turning to walk over to the x-ray machine. He pointed at some x-rays taken of Prophet's body. "Look." Wong pointed with a stubby finger.

Agitated, Brown scratched his forehead. "I don't know how to read an x-ray."

"You no hafta read, look, see bullet," Wong said, raising his voice and jabbing his finger at the x-ray. Brown leaned forward with his brow knotted, his eyes narrowed. In the rib cage area Brown saw what looked like tiny, luminous, star-shaped bullets.

"Bullets, the KTW Teflon armor-piercing Cop Killers," Brown muttered.

"Not just that," Wong added. "There another kind of bullet in the skull."

Brown raised his brow. "What kind?"

"I dunno, but we 'bout ta find out with eyetopsee," Wong said, blinking his eyes in intervals.

Barely five feet tall, Dr. Wong stood over Prophet as he carved the body with a scalpel. He swiftly cut a "T" incision, running the sharp blade from the shoulders to the sternum and down to the pelvis area, causing charred skin to peel away, exposing blood. The sound of flesh being cut was eerily slimy. Dr. Wong then used a pair of shears as he hacked through the sternum. Vomit rose in the back of Brown's throat, causing him to grab his stomach and almost barf up all of the food he had eaten earlier.

"Hey! You no look so good. Why don't you go stand over by the garbage can. You no vomit on floor." Wong pointed with the bloody shears in his hand. He then turned back around and stuck his hand inside the cavity of the body. The sound of his hand moving around inside the body cavity was gory. Brown winced and turned his head, placing his hand over his mouth. Wong removed a bullet and held it up to the light. Brown turned back around to face Dr. Wong. As he looked at the bullet, Brown's eyes watered as he struggled to keep his food down.

"What the fuck! The damn thing looks like an octopus," Brown said, looking at the bullet.

"It gets worse," Wong said, admiring the deadly bullet. "I found two different caliber bullets in the body."

"What?"

"The bullet that entered Prophet's cheek was from a .44," Wong said as he rinsed the bullet off in a weak solution of Clorox before bagging it.

"Why would someone want to use two different guns?" Brown asked out loud, perplexed. There just seemed to be too many missing pieces to this puzzle. Wong went back over to the body with an electric saw and began to saw on Prophet's skull. That did it. Brown couldn't take it anymore. He excused himself and headed for the exit door.

"You no wanna watch me do eyetopsee?" Wong yelled behind him.

◊ ◊ ◊ ◊

The next morning Brown awakened in his small, but com-

fortable, loft. Hauntingly, he remembered dreaming of dead bodies of beautiful women. It was Gina's face he saw in his dream ...
she chased him. He held his morning erection and thought about
her as a yawn tugged at the corners of his mouth. The clock on the
nightstand read 10:05 a.m. From his bedroom window a shy
morning sun shined across his bed. "Shit," he cursed as he sat up
in the bed and reached for the phone.

He waited patiently as the operator put him on hold.
Suddenly, Rodriguez came on the line. He sounded winded. In
the background, Brown heard the cacophony of loud voices in the
police station. Instantly it hit him just how much he missed work.

"Detective Rodriguez, how may I help you?" Rodriguez asked.

"Rodriquez, it's me, Brown. Just calling to find out what's
been going on with the Death Struck case."

Rodriguez lowered his voice to a conspiratorial tone. "Damn,
Lieutenant, we miss the shit out 'cha 'round here." He looked
around to see if anyone was listening to him and continued, "I got
some good news and some bad news." Brown rolled his eyes on
the other end of the phone as he planted his feet on the floor and
cupped his head in his hands. "What?"

"The good news is, you remember the jewelry store robbery
pictures of the woman with the blond wig?"

"Yeah."

"Well, Chief had the pictures sent to the FBI lab in
Washington. The pictures are much better. You need to see them.
We still don't have a make on the female, but these pictures gonna
damn sho' help."

Rodriguez took the phone away from his ear. Brown could
hear a struggle in the background. Someone was yelling, "Take
your fucking hands off me!"

Rodriguez called out, "Don't fuckin' put 'em in the holding
cell with the women. She's a he."

"Take your damn hands off me!" the voice repeated.

Rodriguez came back on the phone, "Shoo, fuckin' place is
like a mad house. Okay, where was I?"

"The bad news."

"Oh yeah, the bad news. The feds are trying to take over the case, saying it's gang related—"

"That's bullshit!" Brown said, interrupting Rodriguez. He stood and began to pace the floor in his boxer shorts.

"Have you seen the morning news? The story about Damon Dice's body being discovered headless is the talk of the media. Captain Brooks was on CNN with the Mayor talking about a special task force being set up to investigate and arrest rappers."

"You know what I find so damn amazing? When a rapper gets killed they almost never find the killer, but when a rapper gets in trouble they can't wait to lock 'em up." The two talked for a few more minutes. Before Brown hung up, Rodriguez agreed to keep him posted on anything that might be helpful about the case. As he got dressed to begin his day, he thought about the new picture of the woman from the jewelry store robbery.

TWENTY-SIX

Jack Lemon

Jack walked into the Tony building. Today he was conservatively dressed in a cream colored lambskin vest, white button-down cotton J. Lindeberg shirt, and black slacks with a pair of baby-soft Timberland boots. The diamond studs in his earlobes were as big as marbles. They were worth a fortune, but cost him nothing – thanks to Gina.

Today everything that he had ever done would come down to one moment – it was all or nothing. In a lot of ways he was entering the lion's den and he knew it. He had killed a man, forced his victim to watch and afterward shot the victim in the ass after making him take part in the murder of his friend.

Jack was about to step to G-Solo, the new acting CEO and President of DieHard Records. This was a dangerous move, especially if G-Solo had already flipped the script and went to them "folks." Jack could very well be walking into an ambush. Still, he had his trusty nine in his drawers. Jack had come for a take over, just like the corporate gangsters do. The timing was just right, what with Damon's body popping up without a head. *That should have put the fear of God in them niggas,* Jack thought. Now Jack was on some finesse time, just like the old heads in the joint had taught him.

On this day Jack was feeling himself. He was in that element that only a thug can describe. Almost three months out the joint, young nigga on the grind, twenty-six years old stacking major paper. He had over two million in cash and jewelry stashed. Plus his man Rasheed had just got drafted to the pros. The thug god was definitely shining on a nigga, but somehow Jack's mind drift-ed back to the white bitch Georgia Mae. One thing he had to admit, she gave some smoking head and ass. He wondered if she'd tricked Rasheed too with that fat ass of hers. One thing for sure, if she stayed around too long, Monique was in serious trouble.

Jack refocused his mind back on the matter at hand. His mind chimed like a song. "It's better to be feared than loved," Jack said over and over again. Finesse was a wise man's game, understood by a limited few, used by even less. The press move was dangerous. Too much pressure could burst an iron pipe and often the only way to find out if the press had backfired was if the vic went to the police.

As Jack walked on, he ignored the opulent wealth of the build-ing as well as some of the white faces that looked at him. Earlier that day he had called, pretending to be a reporter checking to see if G-Solo would be in his office. He was informed that he would be in the office giving interviews until two o'clock.

Up ahead Jack saw the security guard sitting at a booth. He was looking at a newspaper. Occasionally the guard would look up as he checked people's names off some sort of list before he gave them access to the elevator located behind him. "Shit," Jack cursed under his breath as his pace slowed. People continued to walk all around him with the hum of a busy work day. As Jack spied the elevator, he saw an attractive woman step out. She had a caramel complexion with a generous figure. Standing behind her was the biggest, blackest man that Jack had ever seen in his entire life. She strode by giving Jack a quick once over. He watched her ass wave from side to side.

"Bootylicious fo-reel, huh," Jack said out the side of his mouth, making her giggle girlishly as she strutted by. Her body-guard grilled Jack with the screw face as he walked by, making it his business to brush into him. Jack found himself once again refocusing back to the matter at hand – how to get past the secu-rity guard.

Casually Jack walked over to the directory and scanned the

names. DieHard Records was on the twenty-sixth floor. Jack heard the elevator door ding open. People stepped out. A fat woman with a briefcase on wheels walked over and said something to the security guard, causing him to turn his head. Jack made a beeline straight for the elevator. Now was the hard part – boldly walking into enemy territory. It was all or nothing. He pushed the button. The elevator went up, making his heart flutter as soft classical music piped through speakers.

At the twenty-sixth floor the door chimed open. Jack was instantly confronted by a mob of niggas. He reached for his strap. Someone in the crowd yelled, "Yo, son! Dat's my nigga! Dat's my nigga!"

Jack stood back and scanned the crowd, a sea of mean mug faces. His mind frantically tried to decide friend or foe before he pulled out his burner. A dark-skinned, well built man shoved his way through the crowd of what looked like a crew of over fifty people whose loyalty to him was written in the scowls on their faces.

Keyvon Jackson, better known to those around him as 40 smiled brightly, like a five hundred watt bulb. His smile was infectious as he walked up and bear hugged Jack.

"Nigga, wuz really good?" 40 said joyously as he firmly held Jack's shoulder with his hand. Jack fell back and kept his emotions in check, conscious that niggas had 40 on some celebrity type shit. True, he was that, but Jack knew the nigga back in the day when he was Keyvon and they was both flat feet hustling. It was important that 40 didn't get shit twisted. Jack was Jack, the same nigga he used to smoke trees with. It didn't take long for 40 to detect Jack's aloofness.

As they stepped back inside the elevator, his crew tried to follow. "Hold up," 40 said, throwing up his hand, the diamond and platinum bracelet sparkling like blue and white fire. "Let me holla at dis nigga for a sec. Me and dude go way back." As 40 spoke, the smile on his face dimmed like he was trying to read Jack's thoughts while the doors to the elevator closed. He pushed the button to make the car stop. He wanted to talk to his long time friend.

"Nigga, when you come home? Tell me what you need ... anything. I got the whole industry on lock." 40 was hyper, talking a mile a minute. However, he was conscious of the void, the huge gap that stood between them. Maybe it was just time, two friends being away from each other for too long. One thing 40 seemed to know for certain, Jack Lemon wasn't your average nigga. 40 had not sent Jack a dime while he was away. It was nothing intentional, shit was just moving too fast.

"Son, I'm tellin' ya, I got this bitch on blast. I'm the dopest rapper eva!" 40 bragged.

Jack looked at him and cocked his head to the side as if he wasn't impressed. "Yeah, Keyvon, you nice, got the game on lock, don't 'cha," Jack chided. 40 could sense the insincerity in Jack's statement. The moment suddenly became awkward as classical music played in the background.

Keyvon shrugged his shoulders, as if to throw the façade of "entertainer" away, so that he could come with the realness. His voice lowered a pitch as he pushed his lips forward with purposeful intent. "What da fuck is going on with you, nigga? I still got mad love for ya." Jack turned to face him, his mind searching for the right words. Keyvon exhaled deeply and continued, "You think a nigga done changed, huh? Well, let me tell you something. A nigga that say money don't change you is telling a damn lie, but I ain't never, never gonna forget where I come from. Word!

"When a nigga hit me up eight times you was da first muthafucka at my hospital bed." He pounded his fist hard inside the palm of his hand. "Hell, when I was on my dick, you gave a nigga his first work." He thought for a moment then started laughing as his eyes stayed on Jack. "We played hooky from school, use ta twist out bitches together. I remember the time with big booty Brenda. You pulled out the jammy and killed the poonaney. Horse-dick-ass nigga. By the time I went, it was like a truck had just drove through her." Keyvon laughed some more. Jack couldn't help but smile. Keyvon looked at his watch, chuckled and then turned serious again. "Yo, B, you need anything, car, clothes, cash, or hoes, holla at 'cha boy. "

"Yo, I'm good, son," Jack said, turning to face Keyvon, looking him in his eyes with an ice cold stare. "I got a problem, but money ain't one of them."

"Nigga, just tell me what you want, what your problem is."

Jack raised his voice as he cut his eyes into optic slants. "Nigga, you da problem!"

"What?" Keyvon frowned as his jaw dropped.

"Nigga, believe it or not, you the dopest rapper since Tupac and Biggie, but you're playin' right into these crackas' hands with all this beef shit you keep kickin' up with the home team."

"Nigga, what you talkin' 'bout? Big Dolla 'n dem niggas?" 40 said with a frown like he couldn't believe Jack was going to side with them, too.

"Word, son, I'm feelin' you, but that's why the East Coast, West Coast rivalry shit was invented in the first place, so they could make it look like black men killin' each other when in reality it's them crackas who got a hand in most of the killins. Like throwing a rock and hiding the hand. The bad part is, they gonna kill you, too."

"Whaaat?!" Keyvon gasped, looking at Jack like he had lost his fuckin' mind. Jack softened his voice to almost a plea.

"Yo, you a young man, both of us is, but it's power. Money is power. Hip-hop is power and the mic is powerful – powerful enough to affect an entire election, to change laws. Like it or not, you're the next emperor to the throne of hip-hop. Nigga, you gotta humble yourself. You can either bring us closer together or separate us further apart. Just think if we ran hip-hop like white folks run corporate America or Wall Street. A nigga ain't gonna get one of them ten-million-dollar-a-year jobs. They ain't gonna let a nigga make that kind of money cause they know how to play they position.

"White folks could be enemies and still find a way to come together to fuck us up, and then go back to being enemies.

Regardless of they beef, when it comes to breakin' bread with each other they gonna bond like fuckin' glue to make sure we don't get nothin' but fuckin' crumbs." As Jack spoke, 40 nodded his head like he was starting to get the point, then someone began banging on the elevator door. Jack lowered his voice, "My nigga, I'm tellin' ya what God love, the truth. A lot of niggas fitna come up missing, crackas too. Label executives, owners and just about everybody that got they hand in this shit and not helpin' our people."

Suddenly Keyvon's eyes shot wide open. "Damon Dice's body was found with his dome missing."

"Yep, it's gonna be a lot mo' just like that, know what I mean," Jack said with a straight face.

Keyvon nodded. "I never liked the nigga no way … and I feel what you tryna do, bring all the good cats together to take over the industry on a business level." He leaned up against the wood grain of the elevator, placing his foot up against the wall and pondered everything Jack had just said. With a deep breath, he began to speak. "Word, I'll find a way to place all my differences aside, let shit ride. Yo, I got a seed on the way," Keyvon said, thinking to the present. "This shit ain't all glamour. I miss dem days Jack, when a nigga used to be able to run carefree and wild."

Jack looked at his old friend, the bullet-proof vest, the armored cars and the fifty-man crew waiting for him on the other side of the elevator doors. Keyvon Jackson now lived within the fortress that his persona had built. He was trying to survive, a way to stay sucker free.

"Yo, where the fuck you get dem stones you got in your ears?" 40 asked, admiring Jack's diamonds as he pushed the button for the elevator door to open—his way of discreetly changing the subject and getting back into character.

As the door opened Jack said, "I might be working on a project soon. Might need your help. A nigga got a mil in the stash, wuz up?"

"That's enough for about five tracks," 40 bragged.

"Get the fuck outta here," Jack said, punching him in the

shoulder.

"Nigga, you betta ask somebody. You been gone too long, shit poppin'!" 40 extended his hand. "You fam, just make it happen and I'll work with ya." They hugged as 40's crew looked on. Afterward, they exchanged digits and Jack bounced down the hall to the next phase.

◊ ◊ ◊ ◊

Jack walked a short distance and came to a lobby and turned the corner. He was confronted by a cute secretary with short stylish hair, a pecan complexion and an pleasant oval face. She looked to be no older than eighteen with her small perky breasts and long golden acrylic fingernails accentuated with gold rings on each finger. She sat behind the handsome, large, oak desk, clearly fascinated with something on her computer screen. Jack spied the name on the door to her right, DieHard Records.

As he approached, he cleared his throat, startling the woman and causing her to look up. Her wide ebony eyes were the most beautiful shade of brown that Jack had ever seen, a teenage version of Toni Braxton. She pushed the ESC button on the computer, but not before Jack saw the porn she was looking at – two people having sex on the floor. With her crooked smile, she looked up as she held a wad of blue bubble gum in the corner of her mouth.

"I'm Mr. Baker from downstairs on the seventeenth floor. There's a package at the elevator for DieHard, that you?" Jack asked, pleased to watch the girl spring to her feet as her perky titties jiggled. She excused herself, pulled at her tight skirt and awkwardly walked by him in her high heels. Her little tooty booty, barely a handful, stuck out conspicuously. As soon as she turned the corner of the hallway, Jack adjusted his pants and walked through the door to DieHard Records. G-Solo was in for a big surprise.

◊ ◊ ◊ ◊

Stealthily Jack closed the door behind him. The inside of the office was decorated like a palace with expensive crystal and plush carpeting. The walls were adorned with gold and platinum records. A large, bigger-than-life picture window overlooked the city. *Damn!* Jack thought to himself once again. *These niggas livin' large.* Jack crinkled his nose as he smelled the sweet aroma of weed. He noticed a gray haze of smoke drifting toward the window like a miniature cloud.

He then heard the indistinguishable sound of slurping and sucking. It segued into lustful drones of "Ahhh, mmm, ohhh … that's it. That's it. Go faster, suck it, girl." It took only a second for Jack to recognize the passionate moans and groans. The sounds were coming from behind an impressive ivory and black marble wrought-iron desk with a matching La-Z-Boy loveseat. The chair was facing the opposite direction from Jack. He continued to creep forward, unbuttoning his vest for easy access to his strap.

"Emm, errr …" Jack cleared his throat. The chair quickly swiveled around to face Jack. G-Solo was nude except for the platinum chain around his neck and the diamond bracelets on his wrist. He had a smoldering blunt in his hand and one of the baddest chicks Jack had ever seen bent down, ass up, with his dick in her mouth.

She stood up so fast her conical breasts bounced like springboards. Her skin appeared flawless and was the color of maple syrup. There was a slight sheen of perspiration on her that glistened in the sunlight coming through the window. She had a slight Bugs Bunny overbite that gave her that ghetto fabulous sex appeal. With one had on her wide hip and the other over her mouth, she giddily blurted out a giggle. Her pop bottle figure was audaciously curved. The small bush between her legs was trimmed and shaped like a heart. She had a gap between her legs big enough to stick a fist through.

"Nigga, what da fuck you doin' in here?" G-Solo yelled through clinched teeth. He spoke as if they were superglued. Thanks to Jack's earlier handiwork, his jaw was wired shut.

"Calm the fuck down," Jack said, gesturing with his hand up like a cop stopping traffic.

"Fuck you mean, nigga? I'm calling the police." G-Solo

233

reached for the phone. Jack was now faced with his worst nightmare. This nigga was getting ready to make a bogus move and
force Jack to wet him and the chick up.

Jack's mind churned up old lessons learned in a cell, as his fingers instinctively inched toward his burner. *Better to be feared than
loved,* he remembered.

"Hello, I need the police here—"

"I'm a friend of a friend. They sent me," Jack said evenly, with
his hand under his vest. He was less than a second from killing G-
Solo and the chick.

Instantly, G-Solo froze. *Oh shit,* he thought to himself. *A
friend of a friend.* He knew what that meant. He thought back to
the night Big Prophet was killed and what the gunman had told
him. With Damon Dice's body recently discovered, minus a head,
it didn't take a rocket scientist to know these "friends," whoever
they were, were not playing games. Fear gripped G-Solo's body
like a gigantic hand. He slammed the phone down like he had
received an electrical shock.

"Oh shit, goddamn," G-Solo muttered, as the image of him
pulling the trigger and shooting his man Prophet in the face on
that dark and gloomy night flashed through his mind.

The whole time, the chick looked back and forth between the
two men with her finger pressed against her chin, leaning to one
side. She muttered as if talking to herself, "He's kinda cute."

G-Solo looked up at her annoyed. The broad was dingy as
hell. "Baby, get yo' shit and get outta here." She made a face, filling her rosy cheeks with air and expelling it as she folded her arms
over her breasts. It suddenly occurred to Jack just who the chick
looked like – Melyssa Ford, the broad that did all the videos. Jack
admired her nude body.

The door suddenly burst open and in walked the young secretary that Jack had earlier eluded. "You!" She pointed, still holding that wad of gum in her mouth. "The police are on their way."

"No! No! No!" G-Solo screamed as he jumped to his feet,
penis swinging. The secretary took one look at the scene and her

mouth flew open. The Melyssa Ford chick snickered at the secretary. The young girl had covered her eyes and was peeking through her fingers.

"I … I … I got everything under control. We don't need the police," G-Solo stuttered.

"But, you called security," the flustered secretary wailed.

"Leave!" G-Solo said as he pointed at the door.

The secretary's shoulders slumped as she backtracked her steps, mumbling something about telling mama.

"And your ass will be working at Chuck E. Cheese again!" G-Solo yelled behind her. He then cursed as he slung the blunt that he had still been holding at the desk after it burned his hand.

"Girl, put your clothes on. You gotta go," he said with a frown, his eyes focusing on Jack. G-Solo reached down and picked up a bundle of clothes and handed them to the woman. Jack did a double take, thinking about all the times in the joint he used to jack his dick on the *XXL* magazines with the sexy pictorials of the real Melyssa Ford, leaving his fingers sticky. Now as he watched her look-alike bent over, ass jiggling from side to side as she squeezed into a thong, he thought of all the things he could do to her that would make her sticky.

Jack forced his mind to other matters as he made an assessment of the situation – the dangers, the risks, the advantages and the disadvantages. One thing was certain, G-Solo sure in the hell wasn't mourning the death of his man Damon Dice. He was sitting in Dice's office smoking weed, getting his dick sucked by a broad that was a dime piece. In fact, it looked like the skinny nigga was celebrating Damon's death. Jack reached back into his mind and retrieved all the information he had forced out of Damon.

The broad continued to smile and flirt with Jack with her eyes as she was putting her clothes on. She licked the rim of her lips, showing off her tongue ring, a seductive dick tease. On her way out the door she caroled, "Haaaay G, call me tonight. If you like, bring a friend." She gave Jack her best "I wanna fuck you" eyes and strutted out the door.

G-Solo turned to face Jack, his eyes searching. The eleven false teeth inserted into G-Solo's mouth made him resemble a beaver and the wired braces made it almost impossible for him to open his mouth.

"Have a seat," Jack said as the two men stood considering each other. G-Solo frowned and pulled up his pants.

"Friend of a friend ... you killed Prophet?"

"No, he killed his muthafuckin' self doin' that dumb shit by talking slick out the mouth, selling death and conspiring with snitches. Dude was executed and you helped pull the trigger." Jack pointed at himself. "I had nothing to do with it."

"They made me pull the trigger," G-Solo said, breathing hard, face stricken with misery regarding what he had done. "Where's the gun?" G-Solo asked with more courage than he was actually feeling.

The blunt that G-Solo had flung on the desk just moments earlier caught Jack's attention. It was still burning, now with a long ash. Jack felt like he was having withdrawal. He wanted to hit it so bad that he could taste it, but since the episode with Georgia Mae, he was cool. You can learn a lot from a white woman.

Jack's mind went straight to press game mode. *It's better to be feared than loved.* Finesse was the key to manipulation in the press game. "I came to save your life," he said reassuringly, ignoring his question. "I'm your friend. I love your music. I was sent here to help you, but you're gonna have to keep it real with me. These people are cold-blooded killers," Jack said, running his press game.

"You came to help me?" G-Solo whined with his teeth wired shut. "Then help me get that gun back, pahleez man. If that gun gets into the wrong hands with my prints on it, I could get in big trouble."

"Yeah, I know," Jack said, feigning sympathy as he nodded his head. "You could also end up in the electric chair, but if you're lucky they'll just give you a couple of life sentences."

"Ohhh, nooo, you gotta help me!" G-Solo drawled with a

frown on his face like he was about to cry. He was a big ball of nerves.

"Nigga, didn't I tell ya that's what I'm here for?" Jack said, asserting himself. It was just like being a war daddy to one of them soft-ass niggas in the joint. As long as they felt you were going to protect them, the money kept coming.

"It really ain't all that bad. You're now overseeing DieHard's daily functions." G-Solo shot Jack a glare like he was crazy. "You seen this morning's news? Damon's body was found…" he paused for a second and said, "headless." G-Solo made a face. Jack slowly took a few steps then stood a few feet away from him. "You really don't seem to be too concerned about it. Your man's missing his wig, dead as a muhfuh, and you in here smokin' and getting your dick sucked by that video bitch." Lost for words, G-Solo moved his lips, but no words escaped.

"Listen, nigga, with Damon out the way all this is now yours," Jack said, spreading his arms. "The people that sent me got a master plan. Part of the plan is to make you rich beyond your wildest dreams." With that said, G-Solo leaned forward. Jack had his attention. "However, these people in high places, they also wouldn't mind seeing you and Phyllis dead." G-Solo's head snapped back like he had just received an upper cut and his eyes stretched damn near out the sockets.

"Phyllis, how my ole girl get into this?"

"Nigga, you know the rules. Your mama gotta go, too. These cats that sent me, they don't play!"

With tears in his eyes, G-Solo asked what Jack wanted him to do. Jack asked for the location of the financial records for DieHard's earnings.

"I'll hafta ask my sister, I mean my secretary, to get all the information off the computer." G-Solo grimaced and wiped his nose with the back of his hand.

The two stood and looked at each other, neither saying a word. Jack looked at the phone on the desk then back at G-Solo. He knew what that meant. He picked up the phone and told his secretary to gather all of the company's financial information and bring it to him. After hanging up the phone, he looked at the clock and began speaking. "I'm scheduled to have a meeting in a few minutes with the head of Tony Records, Michael Cobin. DieHard's contract expires this week. We're behind schedule with the albums of the other four groups on the label and Mr. Cobin is pressuring me to find a new CEO and President."

"Have you found anybody?"

"Nope, and I don't know what to do. I'm scared, man. I'm only twenty years old." G-Solo's voice cracked and his eyes slid to the floor as he looked at Jack for help.

"Tell you what," Jack said, taking a seat across from G-Solo. "Every man got a mission, a purpose in life. Know what I mean. You make music; I make men, like iron sharpens steel. I was born into this shit. I'm the son of a revolutionary, so I was born ta die. I'ma take you unda' my wing," Jack said, spitting game like flavor in your ear as he stared at the frightened man-child sitting across from him. For the first time, G-Solo's face brightened up. A glint of hope shined in his eyes as he bobbed his head up and down.

"Together, you and I fitna put this rap game on lock, make it so we can open doors for mo' cats that's hungry. I'ma teach 'cha how to think big. Now, I know you wonderin' if a nigga preachin' this black man conscious shit, why I'm rollin' wit' a team of killas? Simple, these sell-out niggas like some fuckin' disease, like cancer. They snitchin' and workin' against our people to help the man.

"Son, these niggas have to be dealt with. Black folks made twelve billion dollars last year. We gave ninety-five percent of it away. We think we pimpin', but we gettin' pimped by the system. White folks, Asians, Arabs and Indians got liquor stores, beauty supply shops, gas stations and shit in our hood, and they don't spend one fuckin' dime with us. They keep one hundred percent of their wealth in their communities to send their children to the best schools, to uplift their culture, fo-reel, fo-reel, they don't give a fuck 'bout us," Jack said with so much emotion that he grimaced in a hateful scowl.

"Nigga, you gotta have love fo' your people if you gonna roll with me," Jack said as the secretary sashayed across the carpet with her tooty booty wagging. She rolled her eyes at Jack, causing him to laugh dryly. She then placed the information he had asked for on the desk and walked back out the door.

Jack picked it up and thumbed through the reports hungrily. It listed various categories: Annual earnings, Budgets, Revenues. *Revenues?* Jack scanned the section detailing DieHard's revenues. The combined earnings overseas and in the United States came to a total of forty-seven million dollars. Jack whistled through his teeth. He was impressed with last year's earnings. Then he frowned as he looked up from the paper. "You only made five hundred grand this year?" he asked G-Solo.

"Yep, and I still owe Mr. Cobin eighty G's."

"How's dat?" Jack asked.

"I have to pay for the limo, security and some other bills."

Jack shook his head, something wasn't right.

"Where's yo' lawyer?"

"What lawyer? We use Mr. Cobin's lawyer. His name is David Steel. I trust him."

Hearing that, Jack tossed the papers into the air. He was livid. What was with this nigga, G-Solo? Was he that stupid? "Never trust a cracka, period! You wanna know why?"

G-Solo shrugged his shoulders. "Why?"

"Crackas don't trust each other, so you know damn well that after all that hideous shit they do to niggas they don't really expect us to trust them, and when they find one of them turn- the-otha-cheek-ass niggas, they teach him a lesson, too. Just like Cobin is doin' you," Jack said, barely able to contain himself. Jack thought for a second with his fingers interlocked under his chin. "I'm going to that meeting with you. You gonna tell Cobin I'm your choice for the new CEO of DieHard."

"But, you don't have no experience."

"Nigga, don't worry 'bout that. I got more than you. Besides, I got a feelin' this Cobin dude would rather have two dumb niggas in charge than one."

"But he's gonna want to know 'bout your past."

"Don't worry 'bout dat. Just have the papers drawn up with me on salary. Where is the meeting s'pose ta be?" Jack asked eagerly.

"Down the hall," G-Solo replied dubiously, like he wasn't feeling the plan. Jack spent the remaining minutes schooling G-Solo on what to say to the white man, Mr. Cobin.

◊ ◊ ◊ ◊

G-Solo attended the meeting with Jack by his side. G-Solo was shaking like crooked dice in a crap game full of killers. Jack played his position, stayed on the sidelines, low key. The office was spacious, with plaques and lots of pictures of rappers on the walls. Mr. Cobin had a long hatchet face, narrow shoulders and a slim, willowy build. His blue eyes seemed to always be watchfully alert – like a man who was sure of himself. They were all seated around his desk. Another man was in the room, David Steel, one of Tony's attorneys. He specialized in record contracts. He wore a perpetual smirk along with a pencil thin mustache. He was dressed in a three-thousand-dollar pinstriped suit.

So, this is corporate AmeriKKKa, home of the real gangsters, Jack thought to himself as he soaked up the scene. Mr. Cobin and his henchmen lawyer whispered to each other from time to time. Jack swore he could read their minds. Something about the two white men just wasn't right. Cobin started off with some drawn out act about his condolences for his dead friend Damon Dice. He then went on to talk about how the music industry was going to surely miss him.

Finally, Cobin cut his eyes at Jack as he inquired about him and, just as they rehearsed, G-Solo went over the spiel about Jack being the man to take over Damon Dice's position as CEO and President of DieHard Records. Cobin grinned slyly. He had worked with urban blacks since rappers Run DMC came on the scene in the 80s, so he knew it wasn't nothing unusual for an ex-felon or street hustler to take over a hip-hop record label and make it successful.

One thing that Cobin did find interesting about Jack Lemon was that he exuded an air of confidence that you didn't see in most young black men. It didn't really matter though. By the time his lawyers got finished manipulating the figures, most of the artists in the business were lucky to break even. G-Solo was one of them. If he picked a CEO for DieHard Records, the man had to be just as dumb as he was, Cobin figured, as he looked at Jack with a smirk.

For the first time, Jack wished he had a lawyer as he listened to the terms of DieHard's new contract agreement. G-Solo would be given a million dollar signing bonus and each one of the artists on the label who renewed their contracts would receive five hundred thousand. The contract had all kinds of incentives. If G-Solo sold over five million copies of his CD, they would give him five dollars of each sale, plus he could renegotiate the terms of the entire contract, with the right to buy it out at the cost that Tony had originally paid for it.

However, if G-Solo failed to meet the terms of his contract, he would only be given sixty cents of each record and his bonus would be reduced to four hundred thousand dollars. The million dollar signing bonus would become null and void, meaning he would be forced to pay back all additional monies. The same would apply to each artist on the DieHard label.

"I'm not signing that!" G-Solo huffed, barely understandable through all of the wire in his mouth.

"You stand to gain just over seventy-five million if you can complete the terms. Your last CD sold over two million. I have faith in you. I think it's a good contract with a good artist," Michael Cobin said as he glanced over at the lawyer for approval. The lawyer nodded like a puppet.

"I'm still in doubt from the last album. If I fail I'll be even more in debt with you," G-Solo complained in a whiny voice that irritated Jack.

"That's even more reason to sign the contract – to get out of debt," Cobin said.

Jack was all eyes and ears. Cobin was convincing and slick just like any hustler on the Brooklyn streets, only Cobin wore a suit and tie. Jack reached over and took the contract out of G-Solo's hand. The two white men watched him closely, the way a fox watches the chickens.

Jack took a deep breath and looked up from the paper. In the pit of his gut he knew he should have had a lawyer going over the documents with him. "So, basically, what you're saying is, if our sales are over five million dollars, DieHard Records will receive five dollars of each sale, plus we'll be able to buy back our contract if we decide to take an offer from another record label?"

"Exactly," Michael Cobin said, smiling for the first time as he folded his arms on the desk. "However, as I stated earlier, if you fail to meet the terms of the contract, there is a forfeit clause in the contract. Did I mention that?" Cobin shrugged his shoulders and chuckled. "If you fail to meet the terms of this very gracious contract, DieHard Records will become the sole possession of Tony Records. That is, until you can repay the defaulted monies back at nineteen percent interest."

"We'll lose the company if we don't sell the records?" Jack asked.

"The company, the artists, the rights to use the name and all royalties." As Cobin listed all the things they could lose, G-Solo noticeably cringed.

"We stand to gain over seventy-five million?" Jack asked.

"Yes, and more if you go on tour and sales go well. The last album did extremely well overseas."

"Sign it," Jack said, never taking his eyes off Cobin.

"No, I'm not signing that!" G-Solo screeched.

"Sign it now!" Jack raised his voice.

Hesitantly, G-Solo signed the document with a gold pen that Cobin's lawyer had shoved in his face. Cobin looked on, pleased. After G-Solo signed the contract, the lawyer quickly snatched it up.

"Glad to have you on board," Cobin said, extending his hand to Jack. "I love a man with balls and integrity, not afraid to take a chance." Jack shook his hand firmly and kept his thoughts to himself. Cobin might as well have been telling him to bend over; he was about to fuck Jack with Vaseline. Afterward Jack was given an office down the hall from G-Solo's, as well as a salary based on the sales of the DieHard records. Jack let it be known that he would be bringing a team of lawyers, accountants, advisors and others to work with the artists as well. Cobin gave him a look of good riddance.

◊ ◊ ◊ ◊

Jack paced the floor with his hand cupped under his chin. They were back in G-Solo's office. The phone had been ringing like crazy. G-Solo's limo driver was waiting downstairs along with a bodyguard that had shown up late for work again.

G-Solo fired up the blunt on his desk. He was a nervous wreck. Jack stopped pacing and glanced over at him. The kid was barely twenty years old, and just like all the other rap artists before him who had been given their own independent record labels, and in most cases didn't have a clue about the business aspect of it, G-Solo spent most of his days hanging out at the mall signing autographs with his boys and hitting on chicks. If he wasn't doing that, he spent his time stunting around in the extra stretch Maybach limousine, fucking bitches and getting blowed.

As Jack looked at his baby face, G-Solo blew a thick cloud of smoke up at the ceiling. Jack's urge to hit the blunt was so bad he felt like a junkie in withdrawal. "Yo, son, from this point on we gonna stack some chips and stop making white folks rich off us. Just like how Master P. did," Jack said as he watched G-Solo pull deeply on the blunt and make a face before choking on the smoke. The phone rang again.

"Call me back later," G-Solo spoke into the receiver and hung up.

"I'm tellin' ya now, your whole crew, everybody from bodyguards to publicists are being fired. I'm bringing in a whole new

DieHard team. This cracka, Cobin, he thinks that we just some dumb-ass niggas," Jack said as he walked over to the window with its majestic view of New York City, where down below people looked like ants.

"I'm callin' in the big guns. The shit gonna be big. You're gonna work wit' Big Dolla and 40."

"That ain't gonna happen. Them niggas don't get along with each other," G-Solo confirmed.

Jack spun around from the window. "Can't you see, that's the beauty of it all? These niggas the home team. They the heart and soul of hip-hop. The trick is to bring them together." Jack's voice was filled with emotion as he spoke about a facet of his dream. "One thing I learned about us human beings is that everybody got a price," Jack said.

"Man, I don't know."

"Just do what the fuck I tell ya. I'm investing a mil of my own money on this project. You just hope that we can pull it off, 'cause if not, your ass hit, son."

"Hit? It wasn't my idea to sign that contract."

Jack had to exercise patience with him and not lose sight of using finesse with the kid. With a calm voice he spoke, "You're in a lot of trouble with the gun and all. I'm tryna to help you, but right now you need to focus all your attention on what you do best, which is writing rhymes and setting up studio time for long hours. I intend to have all the projects on this label finished within the next two months. In the meantime, I'm getting in contact with all the gym shoe corporations to ink us a deal, and we're going to get started on a line of DieHard clothing. Hopefully, we can do a soundtrack for a movie or two. Get ready, you're going to be working with 40's camp." With that said, Jack headed for the door. He knew it sounded good, but could it work? It had to. Jack was a hustler.

Within days Jack's new agent had inked a deal in a brilliant move with a woman by the name of Vickie Stringer. She had turned one of her best selling books, *Life*, into a motion picture, with an unheard of budget for an urban film – seventy-five million. Several big-name stars were to act in the movie. Michael Cobin would be in for a big surprise in the coming months.

TWENTY-SEVEN

Rasheed & Georgia Mae

Two months after Rasheed was drafted and had signed a deal with the New York Knicks, in a pre-season game for the NBA rookies, he was leading scorer. In that same game, he went up for a dunk and came down wrong on his leg, shattering his knee. The bone popped so loud that some said they could hear it all the way up in the top of the stands. Rasheed was rushed to the emergency room. The dunk was captured on film and ESPN's SportsCenter replayed the footage of Rasheed's injury over and over again every thirty minutes.

When Monique got the call all the way in California where she was modeling, she bugged out. Later she watched the replay on SportsCenter and cried again. No human being's legs were supposed to bend back that far. She wanted to fly home immediately, but she was scheduled to fly to Paris for her first big shoot for "*Gentlemen's Magazine.*" Plus, they were paying her ten thousand dollars a day. She was scheduled to stay for a week and a half, then she would be shooting in Brazil.

Everything had been going well for Monique. Not only did she get the job as a model for the illustrious "*Gentlemen's Magazine,*" but she also earned a position as centerfold in the magazine and sales for that month were at an all-time high. She called Rasheed from her hotel room. Monique was already packed and ready to catch her flight with the rest of the girls on a private jet, courtesy of the founder and owner of Gentlemen's Enterprises.

Rasheed answered on the fourth ring. He sounded winded. "Hello."

"Ra, are you alright? I saw what happened on television—"

"It's torn up pretty bad. When are you coming home?"

"I ... I'm going to try to get there as soon as I get back from Paris."

"Paris? Mo, baby, I'm having second thoughts about you taking that job. We hardly ever see each other, and oh, some of the fellas on the team have seen your photo spread in the magazine."

Silence.

"Listen, baby," Monique said with a small voice. "This is my first assignment. Out of thirty-eight women I am the only sista. These people have paid me a lot of money. For me to back out now could hurt my career."

"Your career?" Rasheed raised his voice. "What about my fuckin' leg, what about me and the baby?"

"Ra, I'm sorry. I hoped that you could understand. I promise to make it back as soon as this is over with." She could hear him breathing on the phone. What she had to say next she knew would sound as if she were more concerned about their finances than him, but she had to ask, it was important. "Ra, baby, did you sign the insurance policy like I asked you to?" She could hear him sigh audibly as he muttered something under his breath.

"Uhh, hmm, next year I'm renewing my contract ... baby, when you comin' home?" Rasheed said, sounding disgruntled as he skirted around her question.

"So you didn't sign the policy," Monique said with grit in her voice. Rasheed writhed in pain as he sat on the couch in the plush confines of the condo he had just purchased. He shifted uncomfortably. The cast on his leg was all the way from his ankle to his upper thigh. Doctors had installed four rods. He would need several more surgeries just to be able to walk normally again.

"I need you," he spoke into the receiver, not answering her question. He shifted as he spoke. "Mo ... I'll put the key under the mat on the front. Baby, please come back tonight. They don't need you. I do."

Monique's heart broke at the sound of his plea, but he still hadn't answered her question. "What about the insurance policy, Rasheed?" she spoke with more force in her voice.

"How can you even think of an insurance policy at a time like this? Damnit, Mo, everything is 'bout fuckin' money with you now, just because you make about as much as me."

"No, it's just that the new house you bought Grandma Hattie and all the cars and the condo, everything is in your name and ..." Monique couldn't finish her statement. She hated when he made her feel this way. He had turned the tables like it was all her fault, like she didn't care. So, in the end they both avoided acknowledging the possibility of Rasheed not being able to ever play again. The rest of their conversation, all two minutes of it, was a strained dialogue. He hung up without saying goodbye. Afterward Monique cried and convinced herself that maybe she was overreacting.

One thing was certain – she needed to get back home as soon as possible to cater to her man. Then she had an idea. Still sniffling, she picked up the phone and called her girl Georgia Mae. They had become best friends. Sympathetically, Georgia Mae assured Monique that everything would be okay. The two friends chatted for hours. Before hanging up the phone, Georgia Mae assured Monique that she'd go by and check on Rasheed. That's what real girlfriends are for. Right?

◊ ◊ ◊ ◊

It wasn't two hours after Georgia Mae got off of the phone with Monique that she showed up at Rasheed's condo dressed provocatively. She wore a skin-tight, fire-red sequined mini dress that revealed lots cleavage. When she moved, her butt shook like drug store jelly. Georgia Mae was a woman on a mission. NBA players weren't plentiful these days. She pushed up her bosom and rapped on the door. Moments later Rasheed appeared, looking haggard and weary. He was teetering on crutches. Georgia Mae gasped like she was in total shock.

"Forgive me, but I had to come by and check on you and Monique. I heard about your injury on the news. Rasheed, I'm so sorry," Game said on the verge of tears.

Something about her kindness deeply touched him as he answered, "Monique isn't here."

"Nooo," Georgia Mae animatedly droned as she laced her hand over her mouth, shaking her head somberly. "I can't believe Monique isn't here for you at a time like this. You need somebody to look after you," Georgia Mae said as she walked through the door.

"She's in California 'bout to fly to Paris for some damn photo shoot," Rasheed spat bitterly as he watched Georgia Mae strut by, her eyes roaming over the handsome décor of the condo. Rasheed had hired an interior decorator to set his place up.

Georgia Mae spun on her heels as Rasheed limped toward her.

"Poor baby," she cooed like a sex kitten, lips pushed forward like she was about to give him a sultry, wet kiss. With her chest pushed forward she said, "Monique is wrong! She needs to be here for you."

Rasheed dropped his head. "You're right. I was thinking the same thing. It's like, all she thinks about is money now-a-days."

"Humph, they say money is the true test of a relationship, makes people change."

He nodded his head in agreement and sat down on the couch. Georgia Mae sat down next to him, placing her hand on his thigh, fingers twirling.

"I still can't believe Monique would choose her career over you. This just ain't right," she said as if she were really upset with Monique. Her hand stalled on Rasheed's lap, making tiny circles. "You look like you're in pain. Did they give you any pain medicine?" she asked.

"Yeah." He threw his head back on the couch and closed his eyes as her fingers crawled closer. "They gave me some shit, but it's not working all that well," he said, sighing.

"I got somethin' betta fo' ya," Georgia Mae said in a husky voice dripping with seduction. She inched closer, her nipple brushing against his chest. She unzipped his pants, but Rasheed opened his eyes and grabbed her hand. "Go ahead, stop me. Stop me from doing all the things that Monique should be here doing, loving you and taking care of you," Georgia Mae said as she slowly got down on her knees. He just looked at her with a raised brow as she moved his hand and with her teeth unzipped his fly, her lipstick staining his pants.

His enormous erection was throbbing as she pulled his penis out. She licked her lips and slowly she licked the head around the rim like it was a delicious tootsie pop, all the while her eyes watched him. He grabbed hold of the couch cushion as she placed the head in her mouth, slowly taking him in. He was thick, long and large. She would have to use both hands and all the muscles in her mouth.

He palmed the back of her head, aiding her mouth to take him deeper, and to his surprise, she did. She went much deeper as she found a rhythm. She hummed with his dick in her mouth. That seemed to excite him more, the way she made her mouth vibrate as her long tongue salivated, licking, sucking and playing with his balls. She made him arch his back off the couch to meet her deep in the back of her throat. Then her pace increased along with the suction of her mouth. Like a thief that was determined to steal his seed, she masterfully used the juices of her mouth, her tongue and her lips to deep throat him to the brink of ecstasy. Suddenly she stopped, stood up and shed her clothes like some exotic snake shedding its skin.

"Let me fix you something to drink. I got some coke, too. It'll make you feel good, make all your pain go away. Then I can finish freakin' you. You like how I suck dick?" Game licked her lips.

All Rasheed could do was nod his head in submission as his dick stood straight up like a black cobra about to strike. The next few nights he would spend sleepless with Georgia Mae. She did things to his body that he had only imagined.

TWENTY-EIGHT

DieHard Records

The crew waited in the hallway. Mr. Cobin sat perched behind his desk as if he had been waiting on them. There were also three other men in the room. Jack only recognized one, David Steel. The other two men sat to Cobin's right. They watched Jack with such an intense glare that it spooked him. Something definitely wasn't right. It was as if the two men were studying Jack. Cobin spoke slow and deliberately.

"I want you to meet a couple of my close associates, Mr. Springer," he pointed to his right, "is with the FBI agency here in New York, and beside him is Captain Brooks. He's with NYPD."

"Damnit!" Jack cursed under his breath, regretting that he hadn't brought one of his high-powered lawyers to the meeting.

"However, I first want to congratulate you on the success of the album," Cobin said with a fake smile. The other four acts on the label are also doing well, better than I had ever expected. And the whole New York thing you did with G-Solo's album, brilliant move." As Cobin talked Jack made a face that said, "cut the bull-shit." Cobin read Jack's body language and went straight to the point. He exhaled deeply and said, "I'm afraid we're going to have to renegotiate the contract. We've got a major problem. Agent Springer has been investigating DieHard Records for some time now. There appears to be some type of tax violation. Isn't that right, Mr. Springer?"

The agent nodded his head. He was neatly dressed in a gray suit, starched white cotton shirt and matching tie. The man looked to be no older than thirty. He had a bad case of acne on both of his hollow cheeks. As he cleared his throat, he spoke with polished English. "It appears that one million dollars was used in the production of the album and taxes for this amount were never reported to the IRS. Since your name is on the label as CEO and President of DieHard Records, the government is prepared to hold you accountable. However, this matter can be resolved. In order to avoid having any charges pressed against you, you must withdraw your name from the contract and allow Mr. Cobin to renegotiate."

Jack stood up before the white men, stunned beyond belief. There was no better cross than the double cross. The white men were putting the press game on Jack and it wasn't just that, Jack's lawyers had hidden the million dollars in a mountain of paperwork. The money had come from his pocket to help pay 40 and the rest of the rappers. Jack had a gut feeling that someone had tipped the feds off. He had only told one person.

The agent continued, "Hopefully, we can get this straightened out today, without the government having to freeze all of DieHard's assets. It's also my understanding that you have an athletic shoe contract, and a deal for the movie soundtrack to *Life*. Those too will have to be thoroughly investigated." Jack thought he detected a hint of a smile on the white man's face. He could feel his heart thumping in his chest as he now realized how foolish it was for him to come into this so-called meeting without his lawyers.

Captain Brooks cut in. "I knew your father," he said, unable to mask the venom in his voice as he twisted his thin pale lips like he wanted to spit. Jack cut his eyes over to G-Solo. Somehow he had distanced himself from Jack as he stood on the carpet chewing on his bottom lip, eyes cast to the floor. That's when Jack noticed that the door was slightly ajar. The MTV cameramen were filming the meeting.

"Your father, Jack Lemon, Sr., was one of them damn militants. He stirred up trouble for the good coloreds that didn't want to have nothing to do with that black and proud nonsense." Brooks stopped talking and made a face that indicated his hate.

"Now you tryna act just like your father."

"What the hell my father got to do with this?" Jack raised his voice, taking a step forward.

"I was right there when they killed him. Gunned him down like a mad dog," Brooks said with a satisfied grin on his face. Jack frowned as he looked at him. What Jack didn't know was that Brooks was terrified of him. He was the spitting image of his father, the man whose head he put a bullet in. Now, like some cruel and evil joke straight out of the twilight zone, Jack Senior was back.

Carefully, with a pained expression, Jack looked at each man in the room long and hard. It was then that he noticed that the room was short two chairs, purposely done to make Jack and G-Solo stand. Jack stood up and firmly placed his hands on the desk, knocking over one of Cobin's family portraits. Then he slowly leaned down, inches from Captain Brooks' face. Jack spoke with a menacing scowl, a deep timbre that sent chills through Brooks.

"Keep my ole man's name out 'cha fuckin' mouth. Okay."

It took Brooks a second to gather his thoughts. The resemblance was so uncanny. Brooks snapped out of whatever trance he was in and sprang to his feet with surprising quickness for a man his size.

"Nigger, don't you ever fucking threaten me!" Brooks shouted. "You'll end up just like your father! I run this city!" Brooks said, pointing a trembling finger in Jack's face.

It took everything in Jack's power to hold his tongue. That old white man had called him a nigger to his face. Jack prayed that the MTV crew was filming Brooks' racist tirade. Jack then moved to the side to give the cameraman a clear view. With steely calmness, Jack spoke from his heart, a voice that was foreign to him, his father's voice. "Yeah, I guess you would kill me, just like you killed my father, and his father, and his father before that. The cycle just keeps going on and on, until my son finds himself standing in front of you." Jack stopped talking and stood straight up. His voice cracked with emotion. "Shit gonna have to change. Know what I mean? Somebody other than black folks is gonna hafta start dying. The only thing a nigga want is to be respected and treated like a human being. I came in here almost three months ago, signed a contract that was weighted heavily against DieHard, but we succeeded. Y'all …" Jack bunched his face up with anger. "Now y'all want to try this guerilla shit."

"Mr. Lemon, all we're trying to do is help you," Cobin said with a nervous twitch in his face. Things had not been going as he had intended. "It's really quite simple, one of my accountants made a clerical error, and obviously you have too with the million dollars used to pay off the artists. I'm giving you a chance to kill two birds with one stone. All we want you to do is simply allow us to restructure the contract. That way you would have assistance out of the looming tax evasion charge and a possible lawsuit." As Cobin talked, Jack noticed his jittery motions as a ball of sweat rolled from his forehead down to his long beak-like nose. He wiped at the sweat with his thumb and continued to talk a mile a minute.

"Surely you can understand my position. Come on, let's see if we can work something out." Cobin smiled like cracked glass. "I need that contract back!" Cobin said, raising his voice.

"How much money you willing to pay to get it back?" Jack asked. He could feel the burning stares of everyone in the room.

"How much money you want, pal?" Cobin responded.

"About sixty-five mil along with the rights to buy out the contract and retain the label's name, and a cancellation of all debts owed to you," Jack said.

Cobin laughed a strained chuckle. Brooks had taken his seat. He mumbled something under his breath. "That's ridiculous," Cobin retorted, losing his composure.

"Take it or leave it," Jack shot back with a straight face.

"Damnit, don't fuckin' play games with me. My offer is twenty million and you walk away with everything – copyrights, royalties, artists and the label's name." As Cobin spoke Jack shook his head angrily with his jaw clenched tightly.

"Fuck, you think a nigga stupid? Twenty million is nothing compared to the money that you're going to make off of DieHard. Last year the hip-hop industry made over three billion dollars off the artists and the artists received less than one percent. The people that work the hardest get paid the least," Jack vented.

Cobin snarled with disdain as he realized his blunder in making Jack the CEO of DieHard. He had seriously underestimated the Brooklyn thug.

With his lips pressed tightly together, Cobin spoke against his teeth as the right side of his face twitched uncontrollably. "Either you renegotiate the terms of the contract on my terms or I'll have that money tied up in the courts so long you'll grow old and gray before you get it."

"Oh, you gonna up dat money?" Jack said. He was losing his temper. "We signed a contract."

"Fuck a contract! The only way you get that money is over my dead body."

Jack fumed with a deadly calm. "Be careful what you ask for."

"Get the hell out! Get out!" Cobin stood, pointing at the door. The two men stared each other down with deep hatred.

Finally Jack said to G-Solo, "Yo, G, let's go." Jack turned and headed for the door.

Cobin shrieked, "Leonard! This is the thanks I get after all I've done for you and your mother?" Cobin voiced a desperate plea. G-Solo stood in the middle of the floor. The moment lulled as Cobin tugged at G-Solo's conscience. "Don't walk out."

G-Solo exchanged glances with the FBI agent and then looked back and forth between Cobin and Jack. He looked like a frightened child standing in front of an oncoming train. To Jack's horror, G-Solo took a timid step toward Cobin, causing the lawyer, with his pencil thin mustache, to smile. Without G-Solo, one of the originators of the street concept of DieHard, the star, the heart and soul of the label gone, Jack would have nothing. Even the million dollars of his own money that he had invested would be lost.

With pensive brown eyes, G-Solo looked over at Jack and

shrugged his shoulders, his way of telling Jack to leave without him. G-Solo was staying with the white man, Mr. Cobin. Regardless of what Jack said about him, in G-Solo's eyes Cobin had been more than good to him and his family.

Jack made a face like a silent threat as he fixed his hand into a mock gun and aimed it at G-Solo—"POW!" G-Solo caught on quick. Jack was imitating G-Solo putting a bullet into Prophet. It was Jack's way of reminding him that the gun was still out there. Jack leaned toward G-Solo and said out the side of his mouth, "Yo, playa, if you wanna chill with the po-po dat's cool. I can make it happen, nigga."

G-Solo's eyebrows shot up in fear as his body did some kind of jerky motion and shifted gears as he walked over to Jack. Jack exhaled, not realizing that he had been holding his breath. *What the fuck kind of time is G-Solo on?* he thought. He had taken the nigga under his wing, showed him how to stack bank, and the nigga just tried some shit like that. Jack walked to the door as Cobin yelled, irate, "I promise both you niggers, you'll never—"

Jack opened the door wide as Cobin's lawyer grabbed his arm when he looked in horror at the film crew.

"What the fu—" Brooks muttered.

"Hey, you! Come here with that fucking camera!" Cobin yelled. Jack shoved G-Solo out the door and they all took off for the elevator. The secretary was nowhere in sight. One thing Jack learned from the meeting, G-Solo could not be trusted. The nigga had totally flipped the script. Now with the feds watching, Jack had no choice but to plan his exit out the game before it was too late. Not only that, he was deadly certain about one thing—Cobin was a wrap! Cracka was trying to take his grind and because of that, he had to be dealt with … in the way only Jack could deal.

◊ ◊ ◊ ◊

The next day the media was flooded with the news of Captain Bill Brooks and record executive and mogul Michael Cobin's tirade – blatantly calling the two young black males niggers. Every hour on the hour Cobin and Brooks' faces were seen on news broadcasts in America and in other parts of the world. The public, along with a few social activists, were asking for an investigation. The broadcast touched the hearts of millions of people, crossing the racial boundary. One part in particular that was played over and over again across black radio stations and TV was the very heart-felt statement that Jack Lemon made, with what looked like tears in his eyes, *I guess you wanna kill me like you killed my father, his father ... until my son finds himself standing in front of you.*

Somehow, the entire racist confrontation had sparked a fire of debate across America, especially when it was reported that music mogul executive Michael Cobin was attempting to balk on a contract worth an estimated eighty million dollars. It wasn't long before hip-hop celebrities got involved and eventually ignited a movement that created a chain reaction.

Due to all of the media exposure, the sale of DieHard recordings skyrocketed. *Thug's Paradise* was still number one on the charts. Shoe sales also increased by its largest margin ever due to sales of the DieHard athletic shoe. DieHard and its artists were becoming a household name. Some began to call Jack Lemon a young genius. Not only did he get the New York rappers to come together and put their animosities to the side, but they made music together.

It was decided that all the rappers would come together to do a free summit. It was going to be called the Future of Our Children Summit. It would be a three-day event to debate race relations as they related to hip-hop and rap music, as well as to donate toys and clothes to the children. Homeless children were even being flown in from Africa and other impoverished parts of the world.

Pretty soon word spread and more artists joined the cause. The children's summit was going to be one of the biggest events since the Million Man March. It was scheduled to be held at Madison Square Garden in New York. East Coast, West Coast and the Midwest all agreed to come together in unity. The Bloods, the

Crips, the G.D.s and the Latin Kings. Rappers from everywhere all agreed to be part of one of the most beautiful moments in history. It was similar to the vibrant movements of the 60s and 70s, a special kind of history in the making.

Meanwhile in Manhattan, the Police Department was being besieged with angry, picketing protesters who demanded the resignation of Captain Bill Brooks. Finally the Mayor was forced to hold a news conference in which he openly chastised Captain Brooks for using the "N word." He promised the angry crowd that Brooks would be suspended pending an investigation.

On the other side of town in a smoked-filled hotel room, Brooks conspired with Michael Cobin to have Jack Lemon killed and to make it look like a rivalry killing. Brooks knew just how to set the rapper up. However, what Brooks didn't know was that the feds were a lot closer to solving the Death Struck case than they were letting on. They now had a valuable inside informant named G-Solo. The old chain gang proverb was true, "Too much pressure will burst a pipe."

TWENTY-NINE

Lieutenant Brown

Brown had returned to duty from his suspension for striking Captain Brooks. Still, he wasn't back at full capacity. He was reprimanded, taken off the homicide division and given a desk job, where occasionally he was assigned to the field – mostly cases that were hard, if not impossible, to solve. He was also given strict orders to stay away from the Death Struck case. As of late, the case was starting to grow cold, but not with Brown. It tormented him like a demon, to the point that he sometimes acted possessed.

The only good news recently was the Future of Our Children Summit. Jack had quickly become a big name in the city, so much so that he had started taking security measures to protect his life. He had good reason to.

Brown shook his head as he smiled to himself thinking about the film that had run on all the major news stations. The spectacle of his nemesis, Captain Brown, and Michael Cobin during a malicious tirade spitting out racist epithets at Jack Lemon and the rapper G-Solo secretly pleased him. Maybe there was a God in heaven. "Vengeance is mine, said the Lord."

Captain Brooks was in so much trouble that there was a public outcry that threatened to become a riot with angry blacks storming the police station daily. The Mayor quickly distanced himself from Brooks like he had the Plague. Now it was Brooks who was suspended and very likely going to be kicked off the force.

Many thoughts about the case ran through Brown's mind, especially the woman in the blond wig.

"Anthony ... Anthony ... ANTHONY!"

Brown snapped out of his reverie to the sound of his name being called. It was 12:15 on a Friday night. Brown lounged at his crib. He was accompanied by a sexy young redbone with a bangin' body. She was twenty-three years old and fresh out the police academy. Brown had been trying to date her for a minute and with a little persistence, fate finally shined his way.

Keyshia accepted an invitation to see a movie. Tempestuous thunderstorms rained through the night, so they decided to go to his place to chill. Keyshia, with her curvaceous body and coal black, naturally curly hair, sat at the other end of the loveseat with her legs crossed. She had gotten tipsy off two peach wine coolers, but that didn't stop her from working on her third. She could not understand why Brown hadn't made a move on her yet. One of the reasons why she was attracted to him was because he was older, and older men had maturity and experience. But Brown's mind seemed to be elsewhere.

They watched a Dave Chappelle DVD on his 52" plasma screen TV while caustic laughter resonated throughout the room. As Keyshia giggled and laughed the swells of her large breasts jiggled. Her skirt rose up her thigh with each excited laugh followed by a giddy sigh that ended with a breathy feminine purr. Suddenly, emboldened by the drinks, she eased her body to the end of the couch, causing her skirt to rise even farther up her thigh. She leaned forward planting a kiss on Brown's cheek. "Lieutenant, you act like you got something else on your mind. You got any orders you wanna give me?" she drawled, the sound of her voice filled with seduction as her double D breasts pressed against his arm. Brown could smell the irresistible redolence of her sweet perfume mingled with the peach drink on her breath.

"Naw, I'm alright," he lied as he looked at her, their faces only an eyelash away from each other. She knew that he was lying, as only a woman would know. They had never had sex, but she wanted to, bad. She had practically waved a white flag telling him to come get the kitty. Keyshia wobbily leaned forward even farther and kissed him gently on his lips. He returned the favor. Soon their savoring turned into lip boxing and exploded into a passionate kiss as her tongue darted into his mouth.

She totally surprised him as her tongue fervidly lashed around inside his mouth with the promise of wild lovemaking. She unbuttoned his fly. He unbuttoned her blouse and reached inside her bra. A tender, supple breast overflowed in his palm. Her body felt like a human inferno. He maneuvered her bra and both breasts freed themselves. Greedily he lowered his head, slobbering and sucking, squeezing her breasts. She moaned a lustful tune as her hands frantically tried to tear away at his stubborn zipper.

He pushed her back on the couch as his sultry tongue, skilled and determined, trailed the erect contours of her nipples, causing a small explosion in her panties. He continued to lower his head, anxiously taking a trek down south to taste her goodies. She gasped as he eased his hand inside her wet panties. She obliged by lifting her hips up as he took a finger and pulled them down to her ankles.

She kicked her panties off and spread her legs ... wide. He lowered his head and his tongue drove for home, down her midriff, stopping only for a nibble at her belly button. She arched her back at the feel of his hot lava-like saliva, titillating her, invigorating her, causing her to throw one leg over the top of the couch in an effort to get in an "all the pussy you want" pose. He continued his mission like a prowler. Both of her hands found the nape of his neck and urged him to go to her spot as he licked and kissed, her pubic hairs tickling his nose. He eased one finger inside of her, then two ... three ...

"Ohhh, yesss baby ... yesss!" she exhorted with enticement and wanton lust. He was driving her wild. She scooted up, pushing his head down. He spread her vagina with his forefingers and thumbs as his tongue lapped at her juices.

Then a mechanical voice chimed, "You've got mail." Brown raised his head. He had been awaiting an email from the Medical Examiner's office.

"I've got to read that."

"Nooo!" Keyshia droned, still grabbing for his head.

A mustache of cum ringed around his mouth. Playfully he tried to kiss her, but she made a face as she turned her head. The kiss smudged her cheek as her arm flailed, reaching out to grab him as he pulled away.

"Daamn, shiiit!" she cursed as Brown walked over to his computer and sat down.

He logged on to check his e-mail. The first e-mail was from Dr. Wong:

> TO: *Brownson@aol.com*
> FROM: *DrWong@co.medicalexaminer.ny.us*
> DATE: *September 1, 2005, 12:49 a.m.*
> SUBJECT: *Woman with blond wig*

> *I know that you have been removed from the Death Struck cases. It's no secret, like myself, you too are fascinated with the murders and anxious to see the case solved.*

> *The information I am sending you is for your eyes only!!!*

> *I just happened to come into possession of 22 pictures at various angles of the armed female that robbed the jewelry store. As you will see, the pictures have been greatly enhanced due to FBI technology. I am also sending you some enhanced markings of the body of Prophet. If you will pay close attention, the markings look like "C7." A C with a line underneath it and a seven.*

After reading the e-mail Brown hit "REPLY" and typed quickly:

> *You're going too fast. I have not had a chance to review the photos of the female robbery suspect yet.*

Dr. Wong responded:

This was your case from the start. I'm just trying to help you. You're a good cop, my friend. I am forwarding you everything they have. I know that you can solve this case. I just wish that I could decipher what the scratches on the dead man's body are trying to say. He's trying to tell us something. What? Bye for now.

Dr. Wong logged off, leaving Brown to stare at his screen. Brown turned and looked over his shoulder at Keyshia. She had begun to put her bra back on. The comedian Dave Chappelle said something that made her laugh out loud, causing her pendulous breasts to sway from side to side.

As instructed, Brown clicked on the attachments that Dr. Wong had sent him. All of the pictures appeared on his screen. His mouth dropped open as he stared at the first picture. With his mouse he singled the photo out and clicked on it to enlarge it. The woman with the blond wig, sunglasses and baseball cap seemed to come to life. Brown could feel his heartbeat thumping in his chest as he looked at the photos. One particular picture grabbed his attention. It was of the woman crouching down aiming, firing a gun.

What really caught his attention was her face. She had a determined grimace as she let loose a shot. Orange fire flashed from the muzzle of the gun. Brown leaned forward in his seat, not breathing, not blinking, eyes bulging wide. He meticulously went over each picture, each angle. What the FBI lab had done with the photos was nothing short of brilliant.

Again, he went back to the first photo. Using his mouse, he enlarged the photo even more. The woman was crouched down, but barely visible was a tattoo on her breast. A partial shirt collar blocked it, but as Brown strained his eyes he could see it, yellow like some type of fruit design. Maybe a lemon? The tattoo haunted him, causing him to frown.

"Babeee, hurry up!" Keyshia cajoled with a slight slur. From the sound of her voice Brown could tell she was irritated.

He threw up one finger. "One minute," he said as he continued to frown at the screen. He had seen the tattoo somewhere before, but where? He stared at the screen as if in a trance and then momentarily closed his eyes. The woman appeared larger than life in his mind, like some cinematic fantasy, only it seemed too real. She was the same woman he had been dreaming about.

"How'd you hurt yourself?"

"Running."

"Running from what?"

"You need to be careful. The next time she shoots at you she might not miss."

Brown felt a cold chill. He was seeing the gun aimed at him, orange fire.

"Anthony Brown!" Keyshia called out with so much grit in her voice that it startled him, causing him to turn around. "I just know you didn't call me to your place to play with that damn computer. I can assure you that I've got better things to do with my time than to spend it with someone that I can assume doesn't have a clue what to do with me," Keyshia sassed with her hand placed on her round hip. Her bottom lip was slightly pouted.

"Go fix me another glass of E&J and get comfortable. Get ready to get your boots knocked off." Brown tried to sound hip, but Keyshia made a face at him as she shook her head dismissively.

"That was old and corny. You need to hurry up," she said as she headed for the kitchen. Brown's attention went back to his computer. He looked at the next document that Dr. Wong had sent to him. He pulled another picture up. It was the horrifically charred body of Prophet.

It was a struggle for Brown not to turn his head away from the screen as he remembered the smell of burnt flesh in the morgue the night Dr. Wong showed him the burned corpse. On the computer screen Dr. Wong had traced the scratches using some type of white marker, so the marks outlined on Prophet's chest looked like "C7," a C with a line underneath and a seven next to it. Brown scratched his head as he read the notations Dr. Wong had made next to the markings. It read: *Still can't figure this out.*

"Neither can I," Brown said to himself as he massaged his temples. He was clueless. Then he accidentally did something with his mouse and the markings turned upside down. It hit him like a ton of bricks – a dead man talking from the grave. Brown looked at the screen and the marking upside down looked like 'JL.' "Holy shit!" Brown cursed. "The killer's initials are JL."

"I'm back," Keyshia caroled, with fresh drinks in both hands. "Mr. Man, you need to get your ass over here, right now," she said with steel in her voice like a last warning.

"I'm on my way. Just let me jot these notes down." Brown heard her huff as she sat down on the couch. He reached for his pencil and wrote down what might be the clues that would crack the Death Struck case:

1. *Female has bright tattoo on left breast, possible lemon or some kind of fruit.*
2. *The same woman that picked up money from Damon Dice's mother could possibly be the same woman that robbed the jewelry store and killed two people during the heist.*
3. *Possibly woman and man working as a team.*
4. *Scratches on Prophet's chest could be "JL"?*
5. *Cab driver still not located.*
6. *Suspected woman walks with a limp and wears a blond wig.*
7. *Armor piercing bullets known as Cop Killers found at the scene of both killings.*

As Brown wrote down his note, Keyshia strolled up behind him. "Look, this is not working for me. I didn't come over here to watch you work," she said, putting on her blouse and giving him a look of disgust.

He stared at her lavender satin Victoria's Secret bra as one of her breasts threatened to fall out as she hurried to leave. Brown stood up opening his arms and walked toward her. Keyshia's voice was muffled against his chest. "I thought I would enjoy dating an older man. Maybe you could teach me a thing or two ..."

"Shhh," Brown whispered. "You made the right choice, let me show you why." He stood back and first unbuttoned her blouse and then his shirt. She instantly fell in love with his muscular, hairy chest. Next he stepped out his pants then his boxer shorts. Keyshia stretched her eyes at his organ as it dangled long. Brown walked up to her, his penis poked upward toward her breasts. Keyshia exhaled deeply into a soft groan. She took his dick and held it firmly in both of her hands.

As she stroked him she said, "God, you're big. I knew it would be the first time I saw you." Her breath was a murmur across his hairy chest. He unzipped her skirt, allowing it to fall to the floor in a heap. Taking her hand, he pulled her to the carpet.

"W ... what are you doing?"

"I'm finishing where I left off. Don't act like you ain't never had a man give you head on a carpeted floor before."

She shrugged, her face indicating she had never done it before. He gently lay her on the floor and got between her legs. He nibbled on her navel. She giggled. He then took his tongue and drove it all the way downtown to her anus, exploring every crevice and curve, making her body tingle in parts she didn't even know existed. She was suddenly overcome with a sensation she had never felt before in her life. *What is he doing down there?* she thought. Within minutes he turned her body into a waterfall in his mouth as she came in gushes without end. She moaned and groaned as her toes splayed wide while his fervid tongue molested her body. Brown closed his eyes and enjoyed himself as he made love to the young woman, the woman that walked with a limp. The woman who would attempt to kill him again ... one day soon.

THIRTY

Jack Lemon and the Blood Bath

A few weeks before the summit, a media blitz like never before hit New York City. TV journalists from all over the world were present. It was the first time that all the rappers had come together in unison. Some said it couldn't be done.

Jack sat in the spacious office he had rented in downtown Brooklyn. He was surrounded by a team of prominent entertainment attorneys and a civil suit attorney, in addition to two consultants and his PR people. G-Solo's album was already double platinum and was expected to reach eleven million in sales worldwide. Two records were already on the top ten list. Everything was looking lovely.

The murmur of soft voices filled the room. Jack's new secretary entered, causing a few heads to turn. She handed Jack an envelope with a bright gold seal on it.

"S'cuse me a second," Jack said as he looked at the envelope and opened it. It was from 40:

> *Jack,*
> *So, this is the respect I get? I don't think you have learned to appreciate the value of my work or me as an artist. When we were shorties, I used to look up to you. You had my back then, but now I'm tired of putting cats onto you and you turning around and spitting in my face. I think the latest move you made was a bitch move, something said for pure shock value. Now you're turning against me just like the rest of them fake-ass niggas.*

You talk about guns. We got them too and an army of loyal niggas that don't mind bleeding to wet your ass up. I did twelve tracks on G-Solo's album, helped you ink a deal with that chick, Vickie Stringer, for the soundtrack to the book that they just turned into a movie, Life. As you have failed to recognize, now-a-days I'm a force to be reckoned with. You shall learn.

Do me a favor and stay away from the summit. If you don't, I promise you I'll teach you a lesson about not staying loyal.

Till we meet, pistols poppin'
Fake-ass nigga!

After Jack read the letter he was baffled as to what the hell 40 was talking about. 40 was his man. He was like fam. Jack pushed it out his mind, making a mental note to get back at him. Jack figured, more than likely, somebody had just dropped some salt on him. Jack continued with his meeting, though his mind continued to drift back to 40's letter: *Pistols poppin... fake-ass nigga ...*

On the other side of town, 40 was baffled as well. Just yesterday, he had received a letter signed by Jack. In the letter Jack was calling him a punk-ass nigga, stating that he was going to check him and that the twelve tracks that 40 had done on the album wasn't shit. Jack and DieHard Records was going to blow up without his help. The letter went on to say that Jack was going to clap 40 if they ever crossed paths.

The ironic thing was that neither one of the men had written the threatening letters. Once again, like the hand that throws the stone and then hides itself, two black men were about to kill each other in a war instigated by the powers that be – the System.

◊ ◊ ◊ ◊

Jack left the meeting in a mental funk. It was like his mind was trying to tell him something, but he wouldn't listen. Jack walked briskly in the parking lot to his big body Benz. For the last few days, Jack had felt the weight of the world on his shoulders. He had a gut feeling that he couldn't describe, but all real hustlers knew when something wasn't quite right. It was just up to him to act on it.

There was a small voice in the back of his head telling him to take the money and get ghost. Jack had been informed by one of his attorneys that Cobin, true to his word, had gone to his own attorneys and filed a lawsuit. The judge had frozen all incoming funds from the sale of DieHard records. Still, the business account had over twenty-six million in it—money that Jack had access to. Too many people had families to feed. They were relying on his guidance. There was no way he could pull a stunt like that. Jack prided himself on the very concept of Black owned and operated. Besides, Cobin probably wanted him to take that money and run, that way the lawsuit would be settled.

On the highway, Jack drove past plush green scenic pastures while he listened to his all-time favorite classic old school joint by Mary J. and Method Man, "*You're All I Need.*" He boomed the customized fifteen-thousand-dollar system as he zoomed between lanes headed for a destination to see his lady Gina. He had found a nice spot a long time ago in a rural area just outside of town. Old habits are hard to break, from his hustlin' days to now being legit. A nigga ain't comfortable if he don't have a honeycomb hideout – a stash spot for a nigga to get missin'. To some it would have been considered country as hell, but to cats in the game, they knew it as a gangsta's retreat.

Jack still longed for Philly blunts packed with dro and something to sip on but he still wasn't fuckin' with it. Game had schooled him good but Jack had plans for her slick ass, too. He ruminated as he drove down the highway. If only he would have taken the time to look in his rearview mirror, he would have seen his assassins, sent on a mission to murder him.

THIRTY-ONE

Monique Cheeks

Monique arrived back from London and took a cab directly to Rasheed's condo. It was in the wee hours of the morning. It had been a week since Rasheed had injured his knee in the basketball game. She found the key under the mat just as he had said in their last conversation. *Well, I guess he ain't that mad at me,* she thought to herself.

She opened the door with her arms full of Louis Vuitton luggage and hands full of gifts for her man and her child. Her job as a model had been all that she had expected and more. For one thing, she had no idea just how stressful and tiring the job would be, but it was a lot better than being a stripper and the pay was excellent. *More than ten thousand dollars a day. It was worth it,* she thought.

After she placed her luggage on the floor, she swept over the elegance of the décor in Rasheed's newly furnished condo. There was a cozy fireplace, cathedral ceilings, Afrocentric paintings on the walls and plush carpeting so thick that Monique had to remind herself to pick up her feet when she walked. She padded across the living room toward the master bedroom. She thought her nose picked up a faint whiff of something. Her heart fluttered as she thought about Rasheed being home alone, suffering with a broken leg, and not being able to get home to him in time to be by his side. It deeply disturbed her, but it was her first job assignment and there was no way that she could come home without the risk of ruining her career.

Monique opened the door to their bedroom and a foul odor

hit her in the face, a musky odor that no woman could deny – sex. On the other side of the room, music played softly as she adjusted her eyes to the dim lights. What Monique saw made her knees buckle. Game was straddling Rasheed in bed as she tossed her hair back, riding, galloping like she was on a wild stallion as he palmed her ass, thrusting in her and causing her neck to snap back. Game moaned a love song. Her long blond hair rose and fell. Monique just stood there frozen as her eyes began to water. It felt like she was melting, losing a vestige of her womanhood, as she watched another woman make love to her man.

"RA-SHEEEED!" she screamed, rising on the balls of her feet, fists clenched tightly. The thin expensive leather strap on her purse fell off her shoulder. Game looked back at Monique and dove off Rasheed, taking the cover with her, leaving his dick to dangle crookedly like a bent flagpole. Monique turned on the light. On the nightstand was a plate full of coke and all over the room were empty beer bottles. In the back of Monique's mind she thought about the desperate phone call she had made to Game, asking her to check on her man. Game stared at Monique with the covers pulled up to her chin. The normally talkative Game was quiet.

"I can explain everythang, Mo," Rasheed said, high off coke, geeking with his eyes wide open like a wild man about to have a massive heart attack.

"Explain! Explain what? How my man and my so-called best friend are in my muthfuckin' bed fuckin'!" Monique screamed. She was livid.

Game propped her feet on the floor as she pushed a ringlet of hair from her face with the back of her hand. She muttered, barely audible, "I'm sorry, Fire—"

"Bitch, I bet you are sorry," Monique interrupted. "Sorry enough to want to steal my man! I knew you wanted a black man, but I never thought you would stoop so low as to want mine," Monique said angrily as tears ran down her cheeks.

Game stood and began to put on her jeans. Monique walked over to the dresser, picked up a lamp and hurled it at Rasheed.

Barely missing him, it crashed over his head. Game had the nerve to turn and give Monique a defiant look as she leered at her from the corner of her eyes.

"Rasheed! How can you do this to us, to our baby? This bitch, she ... she don't love you, not like I do," Monique cried.

Again, Game muttered, "I'm sorry." She walked over to the other side of the room, retrieved a credit card from her purse and began to scoop the cocaine off the plate into a plastic bag.

Monique wiped her nose with the back of her hand. "Junkie bitch, you'd fuck a snake if it was black," Monique hissed.

Rasheed struggled to get his leg on the floor. He grunted in pain as he threw a smoldering look Monique's way. He said to her, "It's all your fault."

"My fault?" Monique retorted, snaking her neck as she pointed a finger at herself.

"When I hurt my leg you could have taken the time from your precious job to come home and check on me."

Monique clenched her teeth as she looked between both of them with pure hatred. It dawned on her, he was jealous of her career. "Nigga, please, you're just a dumb-ass nigga. A white woman's dream is to have an NBA player. You can have him, you trifling-ass hoe," Monique spat as she narrowed her teary eyes at Game. Monique mopped at her eyes as she had a second thought. "Both of y'all got ten minutes to get the fuck out my muthafuckin' house ... or I'm callin' the police."

Rasheed looked at her in amazement. "This ain't yo' shit in here. I paid for it."

"We'll see 'bout that when the police get here then," Monique quipped.

They began to argue back and forth as Game walked around the room gathering her things, mostly drug paraphernalia. Monique thought she saw something that looked like a crack pipe. Monique quickly thought, *Fuck that!* She had a trick or two for her ass. She knew the white girl knew that Bruce Lee shit with her feet, but Monique was way too deep into her feelings. "I ain't gonna tell you no muthafuckin' mo', get your shit and go with yo' slut-trash, hoe-ass."

Game momentarily looked at Monique and glared with a facial expression that said "you better watch your mouth." The two women stared at each other with piercing glares. Monique could see the confidence in Game's face, like "I just fucked your man, get over it." Besides, she knew that Monique, being smaller, was no match for her.

"You were the one who told me to check on him because you were too busy with your job, flying around the country," Game said sarcastically. Her statement caught Monique completely off-guard.

This bitch was jealous of me all this time, Monique thought to herself. "I never told you to fuck my man," Monique huffed.

"Well, maybe if you had been giving him what he needed, instead of trying to imitate a model, he would not have had to come to me," Game sassed, heaving her breasts forward.

Monique's mouth dropped wide open with that statement as she watched Game walk over to Rasheed and say, "Give me a call when you get things straightened out around here."

"No, she didn't just try me like that," Monique fumed as she stood rigid, seeing blood. She stood in front of the bedroom door with no intentions of moving as Game walked toward her to exit the room. With all her might and all the strength she could muster she reached back and hit Game in the face, causing her head to violently hit the door frame. Two more blows and one hard punch had Game on the floor as blood rushed from her mouth and the back of her head. Monique quickly danced out the way and reached into her purse removing the key chain with the knife attached.

"Bitch, so help me God, I'ma cut 'cha if you don't get the fuck out my house ... and take that sorry-ass nigga with you!"

"Monique, girl, why did you hit her like that?" Rasheed yelled, eyes wild like he was having a bad coke experience. He hobbled over and stood between the two women. Game's nose continued to pour blood, staining the white carpet. She was still bent over, semi-conscious. Rasheed caressed her back, then suddenly from somewhere deep in Game's chest a sigh gave birth to a sob that crescendoed into a high pitched wail as she began to cry. She held her hand over her face to stop the bleeding. It only seemed to get worse.

Monique looked at the two pathetic people who used to be a big part of her life. She had a black woman's scorn written all over her face, lips pressed tightly across her teeth. Her pain was that of a young woman who had been exposed to so much hurt that her eyes narrowed into tiny slits, Brooklyn-born wrath. She kicked Rasheed in his leg, the broken one with the two hundred and eight stitches and all kinds of pins and steel in it. He fell like a rag doll.

"Nah, nah, muthafucka," she pointed in his face as he lay on the floor in a heap holding his leg. "So help me God, I'ma kick you again if you don't get the fuck out!" Monique threatened.

"Okay, okay," Rasheed said, grimacing in pain as he held his hand out in front of him to ward off her next blow. As he looked up at her, he was baffled as to where black women store all that pent-up rage. Monique was acting like a deranged maniac as she raced around the house grabbing all of Rasheed's clothes and other personal items, throwing them out into the hallway.

Moments later, after Monique had called a cab, Rasheed hobbled out the door with Game. The pair was a sight to behold. His reconstructed knee would more than likely have to have surgery all over again.

THIRTY-TWO

As Jack pulled his car into the circular driveway, he was still bumping the joint by Meth and Mary J. The plush green surroundings were enough to have a serene, relaxing effect on his mind. The five-acre home that he and Gina had rented was situated in an enclave of beautiful trees and brush. There was a fabulous cobblestone driveway lined with bushes and exotic flowers.

As Jack pulled up, he noticed Gina's Jeep parked in the drive. He grabbed his Glock from the seat and looked up to see her smiling at him from the large picture window. Jack exited the car, still looking up at her.

With his Glock in hand he saw the smile die on her face, only to be replaced by a frantic look as she pounded the window, gesturing for him to look behind him. The glass was too thick for Jack to hear what she was saying, but he did catch on to her warning. It was too late!

He spun around with his burner up. The masked gunman stepped out the bushes about ten yards away and fired three shots. The blast lifted Jack off his feet. In the distance he could have sworn he heard Gina scream or perhaps it was an angel, his mother. His whole life flashed before his eyes as he lay on his back helpless, powerless to move. He saw the shadow and heard a car come to a screeching halt. A passenger door opened, a voice yelled, "Make sure he's dead!" As Jack lay on his back he thought about 40, and he thought about Cobin. He thought about how somebody had caught him slipping.

The gunman walked over to Jack and stood over him and at

close range. He fired three more times into his chest, causing his lifeless body to jump like a rag doll. Afterward the gunman ran toward the waiting car. A salvo of shots rang out, "KA-BOOOM! KA-BOOOM! KA-BOOOM! KA-BOOOM!" Gina was bustin' the big ole .44 out the window, spraying glass everywhere. The big gun nearly knocked her down, but somehow she managed to hit the assassin. The impact of the bullet flipped him, taking a large chunk out of his back. The driver managed to reach out of the car and pull his dead partner inside the vehicle before he sped off.

Gina ran out the house barefoot and crying as Jack lay on the ground. She kneeled beside him, weeping. She cried as she reached down to cradle his body in her arms. "Help meeee! Somebody pleeeezz, help meeee." Her sobs racked her body as she swayed from side to side with Jack in her arms. As her tears wet Jack's face, his eyes suddenly fluttered and opened. He was struggling to breathe as he took long, anguishing gulps of air. Gina looked down at him in shock that he was still alive. It was then that she noticed that he was motioning with his hand, trying to tell her something. Abruptly, she cut short her cries of despair and placed her ear to his mouth.

He muttered, "My … chest …" as he continued to gasp for air he writhed in her arms in agony. Gina unbuttoned his shirt. To her utter surprise Jack was wearing a bullet-proof vest. She had forgotten he told her that he was going to start taking extra security measures. Gina laughed through her tears and began to frantically peck Jack's face with slobbering kisses as she held him in her arms. He winced in pain, struggling to breathe as he tried to push her away with a weary forearm.

"Baby, you're alive … you're alive!" she cried with joy as she held him to her bosom, her body slightly rocking back and forth. "I'ma call an ambulance."

"No!" Jack muttered and winced in pain as he continued to try to catch his breath. The impact of the bullets had knocked the wind out of him. Next to him, on the ground, was a trail of blood. Gina saw Jack glance down at it. She read his thoughts.

"I got 'em, baby. I blew his whole fuckin' back out." She smiled, teary-eyed with a sneer, her top lip curled upward.

"You ... gotta ... take me to Grandma Hattie's ... house," Jack managed to say. Gina nodded her head and attempted to lift him to his feet. Jack howled in pain as he held onto Gina's neck. Excruciating pain ricocheted throughout chest.

◊ ◊ ◊ ◊

After the draft and receiving his signing bonus, Rasheed bought his grandma a house on the east side of Brooklyn. Rasheed and Jack had not spoken to each other since the day Rasheed had called Jack to tell him about the tragedy of his broken leg. Rasheed also told Jack that he and Monique had broken up. At the time Jack didn't think nothing of it. Rasheed and Monique always fought and broke up, but when Rasheed asked to borrow ten grand, a light went off in Jack's head. Because his man had gotten picked so late in the draft he only signed a one-million-dollar contract which, by NBA standards, really wasn't a lot of money.

Rasheed picked up his phone on the third ring. His voice sounded groggy, weak, like maybe he was high off something. Jack quickly filled Rasheed in on the attempt made on his life. In the back of his mind, as he talked to his old friend, he could tell something was not right. He then heard a voice that he would never forget ... Georgia Mae.

"Yo, son, who is the broad I hear in the background?" Jack raised his voice and felt a sharp pain in his chest as he absent-mindedly rubbed the area that hurt the most.

Silence came from the other end of the phone, then a muffled sound, like someone had their hand over the receiver.

"Damn, nigga, who's dat in the background?" Jack inquired again.

"It's Game," Rasheed finally answered.

Silence.

Jack held onto the phone tightly, only his heavy breathing could be heard on the other end. Jack was enraged. "Nigga, what da fuck you got that slut over there for? You got a woman and a child!" Jack exploded.

"You ... you don't understand," Rasheed exclaimed. "Game was here for me when nobody was. Fuck dat bitch Monique! All she cares 'bout is her damn career. She don't love me no mo'."

Jack shook his head as he held the phone. "Listen, B, not the family, yo. Stay sincere to the family. That's all we got as black men, know what I mean? A man's family is his prized possession. Once he gives that up, what's the sense in livin'?" Jack lowered his voice to a gravelly tone. "Dat white bitch ain't no good. Word is bond!" Jack could hear Rasheed smack his lips over the phone.

"You know what? I'm sick of people telling me what's good for me. Since we was shorties your head been fucked up with that racist shit. I think all you niggas be jealous when you see a nigga with a white chick. Jealous because you can't have her."

"What?!"

"Yeah, you know it's the truth. Well, I'ma do me. Game came into my life at a time when I was in a lot of pain. It's just that you got so much hatred for white folks that you think all white folks is bad."

"Nigga, I ain't never said that. What she do to ya, suck yo' dick and blow up in yo' ass? I dogged her ass—"

Click!

Rasheed hung up the phone. Jack was irate. Fuck going to Grandma Hattie's house. He let Gina wrap his chest with a gauze bandage, took a few of her pain killers and suited up for war. Jack was preparing to bring the pain in the worst way. Fuck everything! Someone had made an attempt on his life ... but they had failed.

Jack got on the phone then went to his old hood, recruited two of the most grimy niggas he could find, cats that was loyal to the streets. Mayhem and murder was the order of the day. Jack didn't simply want to kill; he wanted to make an example by massacring a bunch of muthafuckas in cold blood—to send a message to the streets. Within four days he and his clique of thugs would go on a killing spree that would equal the number of killings for the rest of the United States that year. He set his sights on the big wigs first, the rich crackas in corporate America.

◊ ◊ ◊ ◊

On a warm Tuesday night, Michael Cobin and his lawyer went out to celebrate. One of his confidants had informed him that Jack Lemon had been taken care of, shot several times in the chest at close range. They went out to one of Cobin's favorite eateries, an Italian restaurant on Arthur Avenue. With Jack gone and G-Solo under his thumb, Cobin and his lawyer made a toast to more money as they sat in the back of the restaurant that had for years refused to serve blacks. However, it did that day.

As his lawyer, David Steel, anxiously looked over some forged documents, Cobin rubbed his hands together with glee. Never again would he make a mistake like that, under-estimating one of those young thugs. Making Jack Lemon the CEO and President of DieHard with total control was a very bad business move that could have cost him millions of dollars. Cobin looked up to the sound of commotion coming from the front of the restaurant. A waitress scurried by, panic-stricken. He thought he heard shrieks of, "They've got guns, run."

Cobin and Steel exchanged glances as they looked up from the booth. Three masked gunmen approached and demanded their money and jewelry. Unafraid, Cobin looked up at them with contempt as he complied with their request by taking off his Rolex watch and giving them his wallet, which contained credit cards and about twelve hundred in cash. *Just some petty-ass niggers,* he thought. *Give them what they want and they'll go away.*

A hoarse voice growled as one of the gunmen leaned over him, "Cracka, I told 'cha to be careful what you ask fo'. You said the only way you would pay me would be over your dead body." As Jack spoke Cobin could see the slits of his white eyes as he recognized the voice.

Cobin mumbled his last words, "Jack Lemon." The first bullet tore through his right eye, then the double barrel let loose, knocking him out of the booth.

With a stricken face, the frightened lawyer looked on in horror. "Please, don't kill me. I got a wife and child." A fusillade of bullets pushed his body to the other side of the booth. Gun smoke smoldered like fog as a river of blood ran. The three armed gunmen calmly walked out of the restaurant, hopped into a waiting black Chevy and sped off.

Each day the reign of violent terror continued to seize the city. The next day, on September 21st, Platinum Records CEO, Richard Wright, sauntered into the barber shop in New York's affluent Sheraton Hotel. He strolled over to chair No. 7, his lucky number. Two seats down from him sat a man who resembled Dick Clark. They exchanged greetings as the barber fitted a white smock around Wright's neck. Today Wright wanted a special cut, something that would make him look younger. Tonight was the big award show. He was to present the award for best new artist of the year. He couldn't help but smirk as he studied himself in the mirror. He thought about Mariah Carey's tight little ass and felt a slight erection. He sure hoped he would be seated next to her this year.

Just as the barber was covering his face with shaving cream, three masked gunmen strolled in the shop with pistols leveled at his head. They let loose with explosions that sounded like Fourth of July fireworks as they riddled the record executive's body with bullets. The gunmen continued to drill bullets into the body to make a statement. The final blast of the twelve gauge lifted the dying man's body from the seat, causing the footrest to go flying in the air. Ears ringing to the sound of death, they exited the shop. The Dick Clark look-alike had a heart attack. From his hospital bed he told authorities he saw "NOTHING." Witnesses stated that the gunmen disappeared into the pedestrians on 7th Avenue.

On September 23rd in the Mayor's Ballroom, over two hundred people, mostly rich record label executives and owners, were in town attending an annual big gala event. It was a festive gathering of who's who in the business. Three men entered. They were sharply dressed in expensive double-breasted black tuxedos and were wearing Presidential masks of the late President Ronald

Reagan.

At first, every one at the gala thought it was part of some type of show, that was until the masked men pulled out sub-machine guns with long clips from underneath their jackets and ordered all the men in the ballroom to line the walls. They were then stripped of their cash and valuables. All seventy-two men were then violently cut down with machine gun fire as wives and girlfriends screamed, affronted by death. Miraculously, thirteen men survived to tell what had happened during the slaughter that rocked the city.

For days the killings continued. Some said it was the mob, since they had their hand in the music industry in a major way. Some said it was the work of hit men, but the streets knew—it was Jack Lemon and his niggas starting to gear up for war. Next, one of 40's people got shot coming out a club, then word quickly spread on the streets that something big was about to go down in terms of a body count. Now it was about to be a real bloodbath, with mothers crying and pallbearers at funerals carrying coffins filled with young black men. Jack Lemon was Death Struck, understanding zero!

THIRTY-THREE

Lieutenant Brown

When the killings had first started, the Chief of Police, Brown's boss, had pulled him from his desk job and immediately placed him back on duty to his old job in the homicide division. Brown was one of the first at the murder scene. The place was a bloody mess.

Cops were stepping all over the evidence. There was already a superior officer there in charge. For the first time in Brown's career he saw the law from another side. He knew the only reason why his boss put him back on the job was because some so-called "important white people" had been gunned down. Brown took one look at the two deceased victims as he listened to the know-it-all white cop declare to the other officers that the motive for the murders was a botched robbery attempt. Brown knew better, but kept his mouth shut. Someone had set it up to look like a robbery attempt.

The music executive had his brains blown out. Brown knew an execution when he saw one. Brown noticed the spent shell casing on the floor and bent down to examine it. It was a KTW. Brown muttered under his breath, "Cop Killers." He rose and just walked out the restaurant, leaving all of the noise and the commotion behind him. The woman was on his mind again.

For the next few days the media had a feeding frenzy. There were so many killings of white folks that it practically stretched the entire police force thin. Brown didn't care about the bodies any more; he was numb. He just wanted to catch the killers ... the woman.

◊ ◊ ◊ ◊

A few days later the killings were still going strong. Over a hundred Black males had been questioned and the police still had made no arrests, nor did they have any leads. As Brown approached his office the rookie cop, Keyshia, stood out front in his doorway. She pivoted on her toes with pure delight when she saw him walking her way. They both exchanged sly smiles. Brown got the impression that if she had been a kitten she would have rubbed against his leg. She wore her uniform skin tight as her breasts strained against the material.

"I was on my way to target practice and I decided to drop by and check on you to remind you of our date for tonight. I'll cook dinner," she said with an arched eyebrow as if waiting for an answer.

He looked at her breasts, wondering if it was her bra that had her ample breasts so perky or if she was so aroused by seeing him that her nipples became erect. "I'll bring the peach wine coolers," he said with a smirk.

"Oh, you wanna get me drunk so you can seduce me again, huh?" she giggled. They both laughed.

"Uhm, err," Rodriguez cleared his throat to get Brown's attention. "Lieutenant, sir, I need to talk to you."

"Yeah, sure," Brown said, turning away from Keyshia with an embarrassed expression on his face.

Keyshia mouthed, "Six o'clock," and walked off.

Both men watched her butt sway from side to side. Rodriguez glanced at Brown, giving him a knowing look. Rodriguez took a deep breath and tilted his head slightly. "We got a major problem brewing," he said as people passed them in the hall. Brown nodded toward his door, indicating that they should step inside his office. With the door closed a muffled murmur of noise could still be heard outside.

"It started last night. The hospital is overflowing with gunshot victims and, not just that, one of my best pad snitches is telling me that all throughout Brooklyn boroughs, Vanderveer Projects,

Crown Heights, Franklin Avenue, Marcy Projects and Gun Hill Road, they warring big time. Somehow the Latin Kings, the Ñetas, the Bloods, the Folks and the Disciples have gotten involved. It's as far away as Chicago and California. It has something to do with that summit for the kids."

Brown frowned in disbelief. "What do you mean? That can't be. That's the biggest event the city of New York has ever scheduled," he said with a pained expression as he listened quietly as Rodriguez filled him in. Somehow, mysteriously, from the East Coast to the West Coast, including the Midwest, turmoil was mounting like a dark, violent thunderstorm about to break and New York City was going to be the killing ground. Over the years there had been fisticuffs at the Source Awards and other events, only now it was decided that different gang leaders would step it up a notch with a real demonstration of a gang war.

The word on the streets was the Madison Square Garden, where the Future of Our Children Summit was going to be held, was going to be turned into the killing ground. 40 and Jack Lemon were at each other's throats talking about serious gun play. There had already been an exchange of bullets where several people in 40's clique had been shot. Things started to escalate from coast to coast. Rodriguez shook his head somberly after he had finished telling Lieutenant Brown everything he had heard from the streets.

Brown walked to the other side of his desk, sat down, loosened his tie and unbuttoned his shirt from the top. Exasperated, he cursed, "Muthafucka!" and slammed his heavy fist down so hard on the desk that it made Rodriguez flinch.

"Why the hell is it that every time we take one big step forward, we take two giant steps back?" Brown looked at Rodriguez with smoldering rage. "We got all these celebrities coming to the city, not to mention all the millions of dollars that have been donated for all the homeless Black children and struggling parents. For God's sake, there are going to be children flown in from some of the poorest countries in Africa and other parts of the world and over ten thousand children from just this city alone. Fuck!" Brown sat back in his seat and sighed, blowing air through his teeth.

He continued with his mind deep in thought. "Certain people are going to get a big kick out of this. This city had a chance to make history, now I might be forced to make hundreds of arrests or risk having this thing blow up in our faces," Brown said, interlocking his fingers under his chin.

His mind drifted off to another time, another place, but it was always the same scenario, Black folks trying to overcome insurmountable odds. Just like decades ago, the East Coast and the West Coast had started warring with each other, mysteriously right around the time they were starting to come together in brotherhood. Blacks learned of the deeper lot in the 60s and 70s. The source of the friction turned out to be federal government agents, who intentionally set out to undermine one of the most beautiful Black movements the world had ever seen – The Civil Rights Movement. Spies, bugging and break-ins. All types of tactics were used.

This was at a time when Blacks used to protest and march every time a Black man was killed in cold blood by the police. The youths would smash and loot white owned businesses. Blacks were starting to control their communities, create their own destinies. There were Black activist groups like the Black Liberation Army, the Black Panthers and more. There were even a few white militant groups that stood up for Blacks.

But eventually, with the influx of illicit drugs flooding into the ghettos along with the work of the Government, a lot of Black leaders became addicted. It was exactly like the crack cocaine epidemic that seized the ghettos across America in the 80s. The devastation, deaths, and lengthy prison sentences that it caused Black people could only be compared to the Slave trade. It may even have been worse than the terror of slavery.

"I gotta go talk to Jack Lemon," Brown said, rising from his chair.

"Talk to him about what?" Rodriguez asked with a raised brow.

"His father was my best friend back in the day. He was a revolutionary, but it cost him his life. The same thing that they're doing to our youth today, they tried to do back then. It worked. Jack Lemon is headed for destruction. If a man can't navigate his present or his past, then history becomes a lie agreed upon by slave masters and their offspring." Brown picked up the phone and made a few calls.

THIRTY-FOUR

Murder Was The Case

Jack arrived at his office with a crew of battle-tested niggas. Cats that sported tattoo tears in place of ghetto fears. They toted big guns and they had all done long stretches in the pen. The kind of niggas that enforced fuck or fight rules on white boys and soft-ass, wanna-be ganstas. Cats whose loyalty was mounted like trophies and medals by tombstones.

The sound of metal armor clinked as they all mobbed into the office, twenty-six deep. Jack didn't believe in bodyguards, but he did believe in the home team. He had made his mind up. If them niggas were talking about letting shit pop off, then so be it. Someone had already made an attempt to do him in and failed.

Jack didn't give a fuck about the Future of Our Children Summit or nothing else. Too many niggas was selling death, talking that killer talk. They had Jack fucked up with somebody else. The rapper Curtis Smith had even sent a threatening letter, talking 'bout if niggas out of Cali saw him at the summit, they was going to take his diamond studded, platinum DieHard chain. Jack had made his mind up to strike first. They was going to bomb on them niggas with serious ammo as soon as they reached their hotels. There was no doubt whatsoever in Jack's mind that he was going to draw first blood – take the crime to them niggas first, Brooklyn style.

G-Solo looked up with trembling fear in his eyes as all the thugs trailed in and lined the wall like mafia hitmen about to bring the pain. Suddenly, he had a severe urge to move his bowels. He had been waiting in Jack's office to talk to him about the death of Cobin.

Jack took in G-Solo's appearance. His eyes were red and swollen, half his hair was braided, the other half nappy, like he had slept on it. His clothes, a DieHard sweat suit, were wrinkled. G-Solo had his mouth open as if searching for the proper speech to plead for his life. He just knew Jack had found out that he was trying to set him up with the feds.

Gina strode in last. As usual she was dressed to a T. She wore a gangsta Chanel outfit with matching fedora and Isaac Mizrahi shoes with a Hermes bag. Her twenty-thousand-dollar attire was her normal shine. She was a gangsta's girl. Ever since she hit the big lick with the diamonds, Jack kept her laced with the finest of everything. Gina would be the queen bee of the posse of killers on that day ... and she would love every minute of it. They rode in a caravan four cars thick.

Jack took one look at G-Solo and thought, *Coward-ass nigga. I wonder why he so damn scared?* "Word, B, you gonna be a'ight, dis my peeps. They fam, know what I mean," Jack said to G-Solo, assuring his star artist it was all good.

Gina walked with a slight limp to the other side of the room. If G-Solo recognized her without the blond wig and sunglasses from the night of the murder, he made no indication of it. One of Jack's men walked over to the window and peered out. The bulge underneath his coat was visible; the man had a Thomson sub-machine gun strapped to his body. A slight ripple of voices stirred as words were exchanged in hushed tones across the room.

After G-Solo realized that they had not come for him, his mind quickly turned back to mourning the loss of Mr. Cobin. He struggled to talk and his face twisted like a man who was having a seizure. None of the heads in the room were paying attention. They were too busy planning how to bomb on niggas at the summit that was quickly approaching.

"M ... M ... Mr. Cobin is dead ... that man was good to me and my whole family," G-Solo whined. His facial expression made Jack want to smack the shit out of him. Exasperated, Jack's nostrils flared as he huffed and blew out air.

"Fuck dat cracka! You all on dat cracka's dick even after I done showed you how he been scheming and frauding a nigga out his chips. He stole a lot of money from DieHard and you, you brain-dead-ass nigga. You need to be happy for him. Crackas always braggin' 'bout goin' ta heaven with its streets paved with gold. Cobin's bitch ass got a first class ticket there," Jack said, causing Gina to chuckle as she reached into her Hermes bag and took out a Black & Mild cigar and freaked it. Jack peeked his chrome-plated nine. He was about to say something when the phone rang.

G-Solo picked it up, "Uh ... uh ... uh ... ah, nooo!" he said, alarmed with his eyes stretched wide as he looked at Jack. He put his hand over the receiver. "The police is out in the hall," G-Solo whispered. All the heads in the room were straight buggin' at the announcement of the infamous police. Zippers unzipped, buttons unsnapped, a big commotion started in the room. The door suddenly swung open and in walked Lieutenant Brown with the secretary clamoring behind him.

"Hey! You just can't walk in here," she complained.

"I just did," he responded over his shoulder, his long trench coat twirling around as he turned around looking at the angry mob of faces that said he was not welcome there. Brown recognized each and every person in the room. He was shocked to find the crème de la crème of New York City's criminal elite all huddled up in the room with haggard, but smug, faces. These were men he knew would, at this very moment, kill him.

Jack walked up to him fuming mad. He tried to abate his anger with a tightly clenched jaw as he said to his secretary, "It's a'ight, let him stay." The secretary opened her mouth to say something but decided against it, turned and walked out the door. Gina eased open her bag and slid her hand inside.

"What's up Stone, Lindsey, Legend? What you fellas up to today?" Brown asked with a nod of his head. The only sounds returned were grunts, along with the shuffling of feet.

"What kinda fuckin' shit is dis?" Stone asked, giving Jack a cold stare. Jack glowered back at him as a few other heads in the room looked about with panicked expressions. On the other side of the room Gina shuffled her feet uncomfortably with her hand still buried in her bag.

"What the fuck you want, cop?!" Jack barked as he walked up on Brown. Jack winced slightly in pain because his chest still hurt from the attempt made on his life. He cracked his knuckles as he rolled the toothpick in his mouth from one side to the other. The rest of the heads in the room was straight buggin'. Cats in the room had arrest warrants, pending indictments and some mo' shit.

"Listen, man, I know what y'all fitna do. It's not worth it."

"You couldn't know what we about ta do, cop. You just come strollin' up in this piece. You could lose yo' muthafuckin' life," Jack spat with a scowl on his face that said he meant business. Brown took a tentative step back to regroup his thoughts. Evidently things were a lot more serious than he thought they were.

"Please, just hear me out and I'ma leave," Brown said, gesturing with both his hands, palms out.

Jack shook his head like "do you believe this shit?"

Stone yelled from the other side of the room, "Let the nigga talk and GO!"

Jack exhaled and made a face. A few of the crew had already started sweating the window, checking the spot below. The room was one big electric volt of tension. Brown knew he ran the risk of getting shot, killed even. He swallowed hard with the facial expression of a man that just wanted to make a solemn plea. "Back in the sixties and seventies we gave birth to one of the most beautiful struggles the world had ever seen. This was during the time brothas just got tired of having dogs sicced on them and their children, simply because someone didn't like the color of their skin. Young people your age, dared to stand up and fight back." As Brown talked his lip trembled with emotion. "They demanded to be treated as equals, like human beings. Y'all sorta remind me of that time with this thing you're doing with the Future of Our Children Summit."

Impatiently, Jack looked at his watch. "Yo, if you come in here wit' dat Officer Friendly rap, save it."

"Damnit, let me finish!" Brown raised his voice with a frown so intense it disturbed Jack, but forced him to listen.

"Your father was the head of the Black Panther branch right here in Brooklyn. They had a breakfast program every morning. They would feed the hungry black children, babies of all ages. There'd be a line a block long. The college sistas used to volunteer they time, the brothas too. Each and every one of them children went to school with a full belly. They also built a clinic to administer medical help to the old folks and pregnant black women. They did it right on the streets or in the neighbors' houses, young black men and women y'all age." Brown pointed at each person in the room as he bunched his lips tightly together like he was holding back some kind of pain.

His voice tremored when he spoke next. "I don't know ... but the white authorities hated your father something bad for what he was doing for the Black community. White America has never fully understood why black folks would want to fight back. White institutions created the ghetto and maintained it in such a way that it's nearly impossible for a black man to get out. Your father knew this. The BLA, Black Liberation Army, the Black Panthers and a host of other organizations were nothing but young people like yourselves, barely in their twenties. They became a threat to the government."

Brown continued, "Huey P. Newton started the Black Panther program out in California and it quickly spread throughout the United States. Here in New York a brotha by the name of Eldridge Clever was over the Harlem branch. At the time he and Newton were the best of friends. Soon COINTELPRO started sending threatening letters and phone calls to each man as if the other had done it. Pretty soon, not just Newton and Eldridge, but the entire East and West Coasts were beefing and had started killing each other, and not before long, so many black men were dying that it stirred a national outcry.

"White folks started calling for Black men to stop killing each other, saying that at the rate they were going, it wouldn't be long before they would be on the endangered species list. That was also during the time that tons of heroin was deliberately placed throughout the ghettos." Brown stopped talking and wet his lips and made a face at Jack. "Did you receive a threatening phone call, letter or was an attempt made on your life?"

Jack furrowed his brow and swallowed the dry lump in his throat.

Stone asked with urgency in his voice, "Yo, did 'ja?"

Jack cupped his chin, thought for a second, while the roar of hoarse voices seemed to challenge Jack to answer the question.

"Mr. Po-po, why didn't ya join the movement, since it was all that?" Gina chimed in. Brown looked over at her. Their eyes locked. There was something about Gina's emerald eyes that enchanted Brown, holding him spellbound. It wasn't just that, it was her style and grace. She carried herself with a certain air. She had flawless skin like LisaRaye and a body like Alicia Keys. It took everything in his power to tear his eyes away from her. With his mouth slightly agape he watched as she limped to the other side of the room to take a seat.

"My … my family was doing bad; it was hard times. It was decided that I should join the service. I ended up doing a double tour of duty. When I came home everybody was dead, strung out on drugs, or gone to prison … just like they are doing all over again to young black men," Brown said, and then refocused his attention on Jack. "The sista Adia Shakur," he looked at Jack, "do you remember when she saved your life?"

Jack didn't answer, but he noticeably flinched with the memory of the beautiful woman with the big afro. Brown continued as he now purposely jogged Jack's memory to a period he thought he had forced out of his mind – the death of his father. "The day that the police ambushed the Panther branch on 63rd Avenue she saved your life by placing you in that metal filing cabinet." Jack closed his eyes and swallowed hard as he relived the vivid scene all over again. The bullet, the blood, his father sprawled on the floor. "I came here to help you, but you gotta help me."

"Fuck dat! You're on dem crackas' side," a disgruntled voice said.

Brown spun around to face the voice. "Look at y'all! Y'all killin' each other all over again. Young black men dying for nuthin'. If old dudes like myself can't save y'all, who the fuck can?" Brown asked, as he walked over to mean faces.

Silence.

"Have I ever busted any of you or taken you to jail? I'm sure I've caught each and every one of you at one time or another with dope or guns, but I always took the stuff from you and let you go. If that's being a bad cop, then so be it. Maybe you would rather have a white cop protecting your communities. If y'all don't care, I won't anymore," he shrugged his shoulders. "The only things I'm concerned about from now on are the Death Struck cases."

He turned back around and faced Gina and Jack. "Before y'all start killin' each other, don't do something y'all will regret. That summit is going to be broadcast all over the world. Most white folks always see us killin' each other and expect us to keep doing so. And the sad thing is, we keep doing it. Get on the phone, call 40, call them brothas on the West Coast."

With that said, Brown looked at Gina long and hard. "You never did tell me how you hurt your leg," he said, looking at the tattoo of a lemon with the initials JL on her chest. Her mouth flew open as she watched him walk out the door. No one seemed to be paying the least bit of attention to him or her, but Gina knew without a shadow of a doubt that she was going to have to kill him.

As soon as Brown walked out the door, everyone started talking at once. Brown had got them all to thinking. Stone stepped up to Jack. He was stocky with wide shoulders and had a perpetual menacing grimace on his face. His naturally gray eyes were known to change colors during his violent mood swings. His neatly cropped wavy hair was trimmed so low you could see his scalp. He had a dirty cinnamon complexion with a thin mustache that connected with his goatee. He stepped to Jack with two pistols in his drawers.

"Yo, son, call them niggas. Find out if they tryna make it happen. I ain't tryna to get caught up in some FBI, secret squirrel bullshit like dem niggas back in the day, know what I mean?"

G-Solo spoke up for the first time. "I got 40's number on speed-dial. I can put him on the speakerphone."

"Hell yeah, let's get dat nigga on the line and see what he has to say," a voice intoned.

They all huddled around the phone like Ali Baba and the Forty Thieves. After a few minutes G-Solo was finally able to get 40 on the phone. The sound of a beat machine blared in the background.

40 put G-Solo on blast. "Is this G-Solo?"

"Yeah, it's me."

"You gonna learn what niggas to fuck with and what niggas not to fuck with. One of my dudes died this morning. One of your niggas burned him coming out the club. Now this shit is personal, so you realize there's gonna be some retribution." 40 was speaking with calm steel in his voice. "Yo, that nigga Jack sellin' me death. Leavin' bitch-ass messages on my phone. Tell yo' man a nigga ain't hard ta find. I ain't new to this. I'm true to this."

In the background a voice could be heard saying, "Da nigga get out the joint, take over that weak-ass label and think he can't be touched." Cats in the room with Jack was looking at each other, some with screw faces like they wanted to get at 40's camp. Others were thinking maybe what the cop was saying had some truth to it. All were uneasy.

Jack sat on the desk with his forehead knotted in intense concentration as he looked at the small beige speakerphone. He took the toothpick out his mouth. "Word, nigga, I ain't never wrote you no letter. I ain't had a message sent to you. Come on man, you know me better than that," Jack said with his mouth twisted.

Quiet. The beat machine turned off on the other side as hushed voices could be heard in the background of 40's camp.

Jack continued, "Somebody tried to wet a nigga up, caught me slippin'. I took five or six shots to the chest. Luckily a nigga had on a vest." Jack heard a rustle of noise on the other end of the phone. "Yo, B, I got a letter too, signed by you. Talkin' 'bout pistols poppin' when we meet."

"Listen, Jack, I don't write letters. I serve a nigga to his face, know what I mean. If you didn't write no letter, and I damn sure didn't write no letter, then who the fuck did?" 40 asked with grit in his voice.

Jack shook his head and growled, "Dem fuckin' crackas, the feds."

"Word?" 40 asked. Suddenly everyone was talkin'. 40 cut in, "Somebody dumped on my nigga. I'm payin' for funerals on this end."

"Yo, B, I told 'cha somebody tried to do me. I took a lot of slugs to the chest. I'm still havin' trouble walkin'.'"

"Tell me what the fuck is goin' on," 40 barked, heated.

Jack went on to fill him in as best he could as 40 listened. Jack explained the little he knew about the dynamics of COINTEL-PRO. After Jack had finished talking, the rooms of both camps hummed with a deadly silence. If 40 refused to believe Jack's unbelievable tale of white and black men who worked for the government to cause confusion, then mayhem and murder was 'bout to happen. Nothing short of a war.

40 could be heard puffing on something on the other end of the phone, then he sipped on a drink and smacked his lips. "This rap shit, hip-hop, making too much money. We ain't never had to cross over to them. Corporate America crossed over to us. Jack, my nigga, I feel what you sayin'. When I received that bullshit with your name on it, sellin' me death, I had a gut feelin' somethin' wasn't right. Niggas don't send letters. That shit ain't gangsta." 40 took another long sip of something and belched loudly.

"I'ma put a joint out tonight on wax. You know hip-hop is the CNN of the streets. Niggas be bangin' my joints all the way in Germany. We only got a few days before the big summit so I'ma put out my first message and let the streets know 'bout this Con–Tel bullshit. We gotta try to squash this shit. You gonna hafta fall all the way back."

"Why is that?" Jack asked with concern in his voice.

"Them niggas, Curtis Smith and the Bloods, tryna get at you too."

"Man, I ain't never did nothing—"

"Son," 40 interrupted, "somebody put out some vicious rumors on you threatenin' a nigga if he show up at the Summit. You must ain't had your ear to the ground."

"No, B, when a nigga tried to slump me I made a statement, but I'ma tell you this, and on everything I love, if a nigga do some dumb shit, if one child, one sista gets hurt at the Summit I'ma fuckin' snap!"

"Naw, yo, son, you need to chill. I'ma go on the radio stations and put the word out that everything gravy, but it's going to take a miracle for shit not to pop off. A lot of things have already been set in motion. Jack, niggas really tryna send you to the big caddy in the sky."

"Nigga, the feelin' is mutual," Jack responded. 40 laughed loud and throaty. Jack smiled and both camps fed off the jubilant vibe as they erupted in laughter, the kind of laughter that comes like a release of too much built up tension. Afterward they still made security plans and they all left, except G-Solo. He picked up the phone. It wasn't over yet. It was only the beginning.

THIRTY-FIVE

The Summit

The first day of the Future of Our Children Summit was spectacular. It was one of the biggest Black events since the Million Man March. It was so huge that it had completely shut down the entire metropolitan city of New York. All the hotels had been filled days in advance as people from all over the world made the trip to the city. To the unsuspecting, the unknowing, underneath the camaraderie, a war was still brewing.

Outside Madison Square Garden the streets were cluttered for miles with traffic moving at a snail's pace. Black folks camped out and barbecued in the streets. White folks were pissed. For the festive occasion, dozens of eighteen-wheelers filled with toys and bicycles, which had been bought with one million dollars raised by various rappers, were given away to the children.

That morning, for the first time that Jack could remember, he prayed to a God that he felt hardly ever answered the prayers of black folks. He prayed for the children and the beautiful black women attending the Summit. He prayed because he knew the end was near. It had to be. God's law says so. You live by the sword, you die by the sword, and Jack had killed many men.

◊ ◊ ◊ ◊

A rainbow of brilliant light bulbs burst into a kaleidoscope of colors inside Madison Square Garden. The crowd of black folks was loud enough to raise the roof. Teenage girls could be heard screaming and yelling their favorite rapper's name, some even cried hysterically as all the rappers and other celebrities sat at various tables with microphones perched in front of them. Even Big

Dolla and 40 were sitting across from each other.

Gina nudged Jack to get his attention, but he was too busy doing his own security with his eyes. Curtis Smith and the Bloods sat up front in the audience. They had been making faces at Jack. On the other side of the audience were the Crips. On one side of the stage were all the old school rappers, and all the new artists who had just come into the game sat to the far right. They joked and played around as video cameras from different countries filmed the occasion.

When the charismatic leader of the Nation of Islam took the podium the noisy crowd quieted to a stir of whispers. He thanked Allah for the occasion. For the next couple of hours, different rappers took turns talking about topics that ranged from teenage pregnancy to drug addiction and Black self-empowerment. It was agreed upon that a lot of the rappers would start to run their own record labels. The entire time Jack scanned the audience, looking for any signs of drama. The kids were enjoying themselves, but the ganstas had all eyes on Jack, especially the Bloods.

Again it was the Nation of Islam leader's turn to speak. To everyone's shock, he gave praise to DieHard's CEO and President for his brainchild, the first Future of Our Children Summit, where all the rappers could come together. The entire stadium gave Jack a standing ovation, with Gina applauding the loudest. He told his mouth not to smile, but his lips would not obey, and instead he grinned. The speaker went on to give one of the best speeches of his life.

"Black people are far from being economically and politically, as well as educationally competitive with whites and we are going to have to stop placing the blame on them. It's a damn shame ... a damn shame, when two white men alone are worth more than seventy billion dollars. That's more than all the money that the forty million black folks have put together in Ameri-Ka. Weee," he drawled, "built this country!" He shook his fist in the air as he gnawed at the compassion for everyone in the packed stadium.

"We built this country with our blood, sweat and tears – our mothers and fathers. Our median income is far less than the Asians, the Hispanics, people who haven't been in this country thirty years. We have been in this country since they brought us here against our will as slaves and we still have nothing. Well, Mr. White Man, we ain't slaves no damn more. That's why we have come here for the Future of Our Children. Fight back, black men!" he yelled and the crowd went wild.

He continued, "And to you gang bangers, don't you fall for the okey-doke. It has come to my attention that each of y'all have received threatening letters and phone calls in the night, saying harm was going to come to you. And now, right now, as I speak y'all can't wait to kill each other – shed some black blood." Jack's jaw went slack.

"This system was meant to make you kill your brother, kill yourself, but not today. Listen to me closely. It was the powers that be that killed Malcolm, that killed Martin, and if you let it, it will kill you, too. To you brothers that received the death threats, the threat came from your government. Please, I implore you, for the babies, there can be no more killings, not today, not ever again." Curtis Smith was the first to rise to his feet, then about three hundred Bloods rose, then the G.D.s and the Crips, and all the gangs that had come to do bodily harm stood.

Jack rose, too, teary-eyed and tired. A lot of people in high places were disappointed. The Future of Our Children Summit was a big success. The summit closed with a speech to the young black women, and the blatantly disrespectful way that rap music portrayed them – scantily dressed in the videos, humping the camera, and how it made women of color be looked upon and treated with little respect. Afterward everyone went to the clubs and had a nice time ... everyone except G-Solo.

THIRTY-SIX

Last Call
Jack Lemon

Jack lay in bed in the wee hours of the morning as Gina lay next to him snoring lightly. They were at the country house that Jack renovated. He had once thought of the place as his honeycomb hideout, but since the last attempt on his life it had proven there was no sense trying to hide out. It didn't really matter now anyway.

Who would have thought a gangsta for life would have come up with such a brilliant idea to bridge the gap of the East Coast, West Coast rivalry all through their love for helping children, as well as encouraging people to become entrepreneurs? All the greedy white record executives had backed up, giving the younger hip-hop heads a chance to make some money. That was Jack's work.

Jack listened to the crickets chirp along with Gina's snoring as the soft wind wailed against the windowpane. Then Jack heard a twig break. He reached for his strap under the pillow and quietly tiptoed out of the bed to look out the window. The cloudless sky was black. Dawn was just starting to peek over the horizon. *They're already outside,* Jack thought as his heart pounded so fast in his chest that he had to struggle to breathe. He took deep pulls of air like he was drinking from a straw. For the first time in a long time, Jack Lemon was scared. He saw a shadow in the bushes ... then another. His palm with the gun in it started to sweat.

Gina stirred in her sleep and reached out for him. "Boo, why you standing over there?" she asked groggily.

"Uhm ... uh ... I'm not feeling too good. You gotta get up

and get out," Jack said, as he spied out the window again.

"Whaaat?" She frowned at him, still trying to adjust her eyes to the darkness.

"Listen, I left some important papers back at the office. Some of them are papers for the DieHard video game. We're scheduled to have the meeting later on today. I also have papers to put the business in your name, just in case—"

"Just in case of what?" Gina's voice screeched, interrupting him.

Jack didn't answer. She sighed and glanced at the clock on the vanity. It was 6:01 a.m. It was over an hour's drive back to Brooklyn. Gina sniffled and yawned and looked at Jack. Then it dawned on her, she needed to go back to the city anyway. She had some unfinished business with Lieutenant Brown. She was sure it was only a matter of time before he figured her out, if he hadn't already. Gina knew he wanted to sex her. She could tell by the way his hungry eyes roamed the curves of her body. She had a plan to seduce him into vulnerability and then kill him.

She showered and changed clothes. Jack was pacing the room. "The sooner you get back, the sooner I'll be able to prepare for the meeting." As Jack spoke, Gina realized something was deeply troubling him. It caused her to have a premonition. Gina walked up to Jack as she was about to leave. She hugged him tightly and quickly pulled away.

"Jack, you're trembling." She raised her voice in utter shock. "What's wrong with you?"

Jack took a timid step back. "Didn't I tell you I was sick? Damn! I'm just not feeling well. Now GO!" Jack demanded, not daring to look at her. He knew this would be their last time seeing each other. He needed to get her out of the house before them folks came. She turned after failing to read what was really on his mind.

"Gina!" She stopped in her tracks, not bothering to look back. "I love ya, Ma." His voice had lowered to almost a whisper.

She bit her lip and exhaled deeply, "I love you, too!" Her voice cracked with emotion with her back still to him. She walked out of the door and out of Jack's life for the last time.

Jack looked out the window and prayed that they would let her go. The morning sun was starting to rise as a large terry-cloth cloud floated over, casting a shadow over the house. Gina walked to her Jeep, chirped the alarm and got in.

With his gun poised in his right hand, Jack checked the landscape as he watched Gina pull out of the driveway. The dense foliage around the house was clustered too thick for Jack to detect any movement. Suddenly G-Solo's red Lamborghini Murciélago pulled up in the driveway. The sun gleamed off the hood of the car as Jack wondered what the hell he was doing there.

Jack greeted his number-one-selling artist with graciousness. "My nigga, what brings you all the way out to the boondocks?" Jack asked as they bumped fists and hugged before G-Solo could answer. As they stood in the doorway Jack looked behind G-Solo and whispered in a conspiratorial tone, "Did 'ja see anything out there? A nigga feel like Scarface right about now. I can't sleep at night. I could have sworn I seen the po-po in the bushes and some mo' shit," Jack confessed as he shut the door after peering out one last time.

Nervously, G-Solo took the time to assure Jack that there was nothing out there, saying he had checked thoroughly. Jack somewhat relaxed, maybe his mind was playing tricks on him. They walked into the living room and got comfortable.

G-Solo sat on the couch. "I ... I ... I need to talk to you, man," G-Solo stammered, moving his hands like he was a bundle of nerves.

"Talk about what?" Jack asked with concern as he stood over G-Solo.

"The gun that you used to kill Prophet with, I need it back," G-Solo said as he fondled his shirt.

Jack looked at him and raised his brow. "You mean the gun that you used," he corrected. G-Solo fidgeted even more. "Chill, son. You came all the way out here to ask me that?" G-Solo nodded. Jack felt a pang of sympathy for him. "Haven't I been like a big brotha to ya?" G-Solo nodded his head and bit down on his bottom lip. "I got your paper straight with the label. You don't have to work another day in yo' life if you don't want to. You can live off your royalty checks, not to mention the shoe deal and the clothing line. Nigga, you still got the number one album in America."

G-Solo grimaced and pulled at his shirt again.

Jack strode over to the window and talked to his reflection. Something suddenly dawned on him. He turned around and looked at G-Solo and asked, "How did 'ja get my address?"

"Uhm ... uhm ... uhm, I got it from your secretary," G-Solo said.

Jack turned back to the window, and it hit him. He glanced up into the horizon and saw a helicopter hovering in one spot. Jack turned around to face G-Solo. "None of my friends know where this place is. Only my enemies."

Silence.

G-Solo moved his mouth, but no words came out. Jack continued, "Damn, you came all the way out here to set me up."

G-Solo flinched like he had been slapped. He balled his face up and began to cry. "You told me they was going to give me the gas chamber. You said the best I could get was one or two life sentences. I was scared. I ... I ain't never been in trouble before." G-Solo wept. Jack walked away from the window just as a Tactical Assault Team truck pulled up into the driveway.

Jack touched his temple with two fingers, his mind heavy with thought. *Too much pressure ... The finesse game ... It is better to be feared than loved.* All the wisdom that he had learned in the joint now seemed to come back and haunt him. Gina's beautiful face flashed before his eyes. Jack glanced out the window and saw the SWAT truck as heavily-armed men scurried out of it.

"They ... they told me if I cooperated the most time I would get was twenty years," G-Solo muttered between sobs. Jack walked away from the window just as a marksman had placed a cross on the back of his head.

"You gotta be the dumbest muthafucka on the planet."

"No … no … Captain Brooks, he came to help me. He helped me make a deal with the feds."

Jack shook his head. "You wearing a wire?" he asked. G-Solo cried harder as he nodded his head "yes." Jack cursed under his breath as G-Solo was now damn near hysterical.

Jack walked over and patted G-Solo on the back with sympathy. He felt the wire running the length of his back. G-Solo only seemed to sob harder. "I'm sorry, Jack. I'm sorry."

Jack made a face and hugged him. "Yeah, yeah, everything's gonna be a'ight. I know you couldn't help it. You did what you had to do," Jack said soothingly as G-Solo cried on his chest.

A deep voice that Jack recognized all too well bellowed loudly through a bullhorn, "JACK LEMON, COME OUT WITH YOUR HANDS UP!" The same voice that had commanded his father to do the same thing. Closing his eyes, Jack could see his dead father's face. A lone tear trickled down his cheek.

"It's over for me, I'm giving up," Jack spoke pensively, for the benefit of the wire. He knew them folks was listening.

For the first time, G-Solo smiled. "Yeah, they'll probably work a deal for you, too."

"Yeah." Jack pointed with his chin. Together they slowly walked to the door.

The voice bellowed again, "THIS IS YOUR LAST WARNING! COME OUT WITH YOUR HANDS ABOVE YOUR HEAD!" The voice seemed to taunt Jack, maybe the same way it did his father, and not just that, wasn't Brooks supposed to have been suspended? Fired?

Jack opened the door, the bright sun momentarily blinding him. G-Solo stepped out first, with his hands held in the air. All of a sudden, in one swift motion, Jack grabbed him by the back of his shirt collar. He yanked G-Solo close to him, making a human shield. Jack shoved the muzzle of his nine-millimeter to the back of his head.

Through clenched teeth Jack raved, "Pussy-ass crackas, I ain't never goin' back to yo' 10 by 12 cage. Keep your fuckin' rats away from me." *POW!* Jack pulled the trigger, shooting G-Solo in the back of the head. Blood splattered in Jack's face as G-Solo's body slumped to the porch floor. Jack rushed back inside, slamming the door shut. "Is that gangsta enough for yo' ass?" Jack yelled out loud as a salvo of bullets rained on the house. Jack raced to the arsenal of heavy assault weapons he had stored in his bedroom closet. It was enough to hold an army of police at bay.

THIRTY-SEVEN

Gina Thomas

Gina was about thirty miles up the road, deep in thought, when she looked up into her rearview mirror and saw the flashing blue light. An unmarked police car was right on her bumper. Furtively, she eased the small two-barrel .357 Derringer out of her purse and placed it underneath the dashboard in a secret compartment. As she pulled her vehicle over to the shoulder of the road, she fought to keep her composure. After she had come to a complete stop she watched the two burly white cops get out of their car and approach her vehicle with caution. As one officer approached, the other stood to the side.

"Ma'am, could you please get out of your vehicle?" he said with an authoritative tone that hinted at being polite.

"Step out my car? For what? I wasn't speeding or anything," Gina said with an attitude as she snaked her neck at the officer.

"Ma'am, your vehicle was observed leaving the residence of a murder suspect," the officer said, stone-faced.

Gina's eyebrows shot up. It felt like her heart had been slammed against her rib cage. She tried to play it off, but failed miserably. "S'pose I don't want to?"

"Then I'm going to have to forcibly remove you from your car and take you down to the station," the officer said, just as an eighteen-wheeler whooshed by, stirring up dirt and debris.

Gina thought about stepping on the gas pedal and hauling ass as she looked up to see the other cop at the passenger door peering inside her car. The moment lingered. "Am I being arrested?" she asked, feeling her legs shaking on the gas pedal.

"No, we just want to ask you a few questions about your boyfriend, Jack Lemon."

Gina killed the ignition, grabbed her purse and exited her Jeep. The other cop walked up and asked if she'd mind if he searched her vehicle.

"Yeah, I mind," Gina said with contempt, as she arched her brow.

The other officer then said, "Come on and have a seat in the back of the car for a second." Gina sucked her teeth as she followed him. A lone car passed. Gina squinted against the ardent sun as she turned back to see the other officer who had asked to search her car. He now had her door open. Just as she was about to say something, she heard the sporadic crackling of the police radio.

"All units, all units, be advised, shots fired! I repeat, shots have been fired. Two officers and a civilian are down, critically wounded. Gunman randomly firing shots from powerful assault weapon at officers, possible automatic AK-47. Need assistance from all units in the area." Gina listened as the policeman hurriedly gave the location. Gina's legs buckled, forcing her to grab hold of the police car for support. She knew the location well.

Jack was having his trial on the street. The two police officers looked at each other in disbelief. The one officer who was about to search Gina's Jeep looked at his partner as they both scrambled to get into his car.

"We already had enough help, with SWAT and the feds to take down an army, Bob. What the hell's going on back there?"

The other officer swung the police door open, nearly hitting Gina. "Young lady, we'll get back to you soon."

As the patrol car made a U-turn in the middle of the road, burning rubber, Gina stood in the dust on the side of the road as her hair fluttered in the wind. It then dawned on her, she would never see Jack again. "Damnit!" She began to sob as she ran back to her Jeep.

THIRTY-EIGHT

Last Stand
Jack Lemon

   Nightfall, ten hours later, Jack had the artillery barking like he was in Vietnam. He was putting up a fierce gun battle. Inside the home he had an arsenal of deadly weapons, an AK-47, a Mac-11 and an AR-15 with an infrared scope on it. Outside, Brooks was irate. Not only was he no longer Captain, he had been demoted to Lieutenant all because of a black man. He had done everything in his power to flush Jack Lemon out of the house, including having the electricity and water turned off. They had fired dozens of canisters of tear gas into the house as well. And yet, like some crazed lunatic, Jack strategically went from window to window, room to room, letting loose rounds of deadly ammunition, making it extremely difficult for the tactical assault unit to storm the house because they couldn't pinpoint his location.

   Overhead the media, along with a police helicopter, hovered. Jack also fired at them, along with virtually everything that moved. The entire footage of the standoff aired on national television as a breaking news report. All the boroughs throughout New York watched and waited. The federal prisoners that were fortunate enough to have CNN watched the drama unfold. Some of them even claimed to know Jack Lemon personally. Gina, just like everyone else at the scene, was held behind a police barricade where she was forced to watch and listen to the varying news reports of what was unfolding right in front of her eyes. With her heart broken, she cried frantically. For the first time in her life there was nothing she could do to help Jack.

◊ ◊ ◊ ◊

Finally, Brooks had enough. Three officers had been shot and, tragically, G-Solo's body still lay slumped on the front porch. Brooks ordered one of his men to bring in an incendiary device. It was a small container that held a lethal flammable combustion material.

Jack continued to shoot bursts of rounds from his AR-15, making the police scatter. Brooks gave the nod as federal agents stood by. Today would be the day he would get his arrest and afterward, the feds would pick up the case in a change of jurisdiction. At least, that was the plan. It didn't seem to be working.

The flammable canister was shot into the house. Instantly, the house burst into flames. Gina watched it all with the rest of the viewers. She wasn't the only one crying now. All the heads who knew and loved Jack watched, hoping that maybe he would come running out of the burning inferno. Then there was an explosion that rocked the ground. As fire licked at the sky, the flames roared. Piece by piece the house started to collapse.

Some would later say that Jack Lemon lived how he died, that he was ruthless to people who betrayed their own people but loving and caring to the needy. With him, his dream for a thug revolution died. By the time the fire department put out the fire, the house was nothing but smoldering ruins. Like the father, the son, too, perished at the hands of Bill Brooks.

THIRTY-NINE

Days later, police authorities finally discovered what was thought to be Jack's remains, and his skull. Gina was still being harassed by the police, as well as the media. Jack had named her as predecessor if something happened to him and suddenly she found herself as the new CEO of DieHard Records. Jack's closed-casket funeral was held on a Monday. Thousands of people attended. Rasheed showed up with Game. They had set a date to get married at the end of the year. Game was pregnant, but it wasn't Rasheed's child. He still walked with the aid of crutches. His basketball career was uncertain.

Monique showed up at the funeral, too. She was still devastated by the loss of Rasheed, but refused to let him know it. Gina didn't have a eulogy or a preacher. She knew how Jack would have felt about that. She simply played his favorite song, a song that he had dedicated to her. Mary J. and Method Man's *"You're All I Need."*

◊ ◊ ◊ ◊

One Month Later
Gina

As Gina sat outside the precinct in her new Mercedes SLK55 AMG, she waited for Lieutenant Brown to emerge. He agreed to meet her after she had given him a proposition he couldn't refuse. He informed her that his shift ended at midnight, so there she waited. The night was clear and the dark sky was lit with millions of stars. Gina focused on one star. It was bigger than the rest. She thought about Jack's last words to her, *I love ya, Ma,* and a lone tear trickled from her eye, cascading down her cheek.

As she looked at the clock on her dashboard, she had three more minutes. She thought about all she had learned from Jack. She had learned from the best. One minute left. Gina unlocked the briefcase that sat on the passenger side and smiled as she looked at the contents. She closed the lid, leaving it unlocked. She got out of her car and began her countdown. *Three ... two ... one.*

Lieutenant Anthony Brown appeared at exactly midnight. He looked around and finally spotted her and began walking toward her eagerly. He loved how she looked leaning against her car. He had been doing nothing but thinking of her. When he was close enough, he noticed that her suit jacket was unbuttoned revealing her supple cleavage, including the tattoo she had on her breast. He was hoping to see, up-close and personal tonight, what the tattoo was. When he spoke to her, he was immediately drawn into those emerald eyes. As if in a trance, he told her to follow him. She nodded and got into her car.

As Anthony walked to his car, Gina opened her briefcase and retrieved her blond wig. She shook it, placed it on her head, finger combed it and smiled at herself as she began to follow the good lieutenant.

◊ ◊ ◊ ◊

Lieutenant Anthony Brown

As Anthony drove, he thought of all the things he would do with Gina tonight. It had been a long time coming. He smiled as he looked through his rearview mirror as she followed him. An old school tune by Jodeci played on the radio and his dick hardened as he thought about how well he was going to punish her. The ringing of his cell phone pulled his thoughts away from what would be happening at his loft in a few minutes.

"Hello," he said irritated.

"Hello, Brown. It's Wong. You sitting down?"

"Actually I'm almost home. You got something for me?" He slowed as he made a left turn onto his street.

"I just receive the report from the DNA samples taken at the burned house, suppose to be Jack Lemon's."

"And?" Brown said as he parked his car in his usual parking spot. Gina found a space two cars down from him. Anthony got out of the car and began to walk toward her car. Just as he neared, Wong continued.

"The skull we found belong to Damon Dice, not Jack Lemon." As he reached out to open Gina's door, Wong said, "It seem like Jack pulled a fast one on you and Brooks. It look like he still alive."

"Jack's alive?" he said as he opened Gina's door.

◊ ◊ ◊ ◊

Jack Lemon

Thousands of miles away on a tropical island, women sashayed by in thongs while two men sat in the sand barefoot. As Jack watched the women, his thoughts drifted back to New York and all that had happened. It turned out several big-name rappers started one of the biggest music companies in the world and Tony, as well as other companies, filed a lawsuit for discrimination claiming their hiring practices didn't hire enough whites. The tables had turned, and that was the first time that had ever happened in history, thanks to Jack.

"Damn yo, you gonna suck up all the weed?" Jack complained in a disgruntled voice.

"Nigga, you said you didn't smoke weed no mo'."

"I said, I *had* stopped smoking weed 'cause of this white bitch name Game, but it's a whole new day. Now pass the blunt, Pac."

"I see now I'ma hafta hurry up and get yo' ass off this island. Auntie Adia said you was on some thug revolutionary shit, but you need to bring your own weed if you a real weed head. Ain't enough room for two weed heads on this little-ass island."

"Just chill, Pac, I see you livin' easy," Jack said as he sucked on the blunt and coughed. Tupac shook his head at Jack and reached for the blunt just as three dark-skinned women walked by, making eye contact. Jack's mind drifted to Gina and he smiled. He knew Gina would always hold it down for him, but Brooks had to be dealt with. When he least expected it, he would experience Jack's wrath, only it would be worse than anyone could imagine. Taking a deep pull off of the blunt now, Jack held the smoke in his lungs and didn't cough. He passed it back to Pac as he got up, ran to the ocean and dived in, catching a big wave. As the wave accepted him, his thoughts drifted back to Brooks. *It ain't ova,* he thought. *It ain't ova.*

Pac smiled, "Thug revolutionary, huh? What's the world coming to?"

ACKNOWLEDGEMENTS

I would like to extend my sincerest gratitude to the following family members and friends whose encouragement and support helped me through difficult times and greatly assisted me with my writing and publication of my books.

To **Taya R. Baker**, my dear friend and personal disputant. We argued and fell out about this book and other troubling matters, but you have never let me down. Thank you for being the preliminary co-editor and typist on this project. You are my confidant; our friendship is priceless.

To my Auntie, **Antoniate Sullivan.** Ever since we were small children, you always doted on me. When Mom ran off and took me away, after all those years you found me in the most difficult time of my life. Makes a brother wonder…could God be a Black woman in disguise? I am so happy to have you back in my life. Thank you, Auntie!

Leo Jr. Murphy, you have to believe in yourself. Stand strong and confident. Discipline and perseverance in determination are the keys to life. You must exercise patience! Son, I got you. To my step-dad, **Samuel R. Ates,** Sir, you call yourself a Christian. I have two questions for you: What would my mother have wanted, and what would Jesus do?

To my beautiful daughters **Jasmine**, **Desiree**, **Lamaya** and **Christie Murphy**…I love you all very much. I will do everything in my power to make sure that you all grow up to be respectable, intelligent young ladies. As for **Frankie Murphy**…young lady, I would like to talk to you before you kill something. **Dr. Mutulu Shakur**, you are my mentor, and I will never forget you…Never! It was you who molded my mind, taught me how to think about Black love and our struggle. The conscious aspects of my work wouldn't be possible if it weren't for you. I love you very much and look forward to seeing you liberated.

Alicia Sullivan, **Ariah Boyitt**, **James Sullivan**, my family...I look forward to spending some quality time with you. **Alicia**, I promise as soon as you graduate from college, I'll help you write some motion pictures.

Jimmy Smith, thank you for your support and being there for me during trying times and for so many years. And a big thank you to **Marvin Johnson** and your beautiful queen **Key-Key**...I hope you like this one. To my brotha **Leon Blue**, dude, did we brainstorm on this one or what!?

Ms. Vickie Stringer, I feel so fortunate to be blessed with the most beautiful and business-minded boss in the entire industry. To be part of the largest urban publishing company in the United States is no doubt a dream come true. I still recall the day I received the card from you welcoming me to the Triple Crown family. Blew my mind! Ms. Stringer, though we often don't agree on certain things (like book titles), I still think "To Kill a Chicken Head" was a very good title. You really don't have to curse at me! (Joke.) Being a novice, I know I'm a pain in the butt, but now that I finally see the panoramic view of your dynasty as your dream unfolds, I recognize a modern day Madame C.J. Walker, the first self-made millionaire Black woman. While she made her fortune from hair and beauty products, you are building yours with the cinder blocks of words, one book at a time. Thank you for allowing me to be a part of your legacy, and I enjoyed the hell our of your book, *Dirty Red*. I think it is your best work.

To my brother **K'wan Foye**, I feel I was remiss for not including you in my first book. After all, you were the embryo that germinated offspring such as myself. Thanks for giving Ms. Stringer that push. The tale of you two is a bestseller in itself, believe it or not!

Mia McPherson, Editor-in-Chief, whenever I call, you always brighten my day with your sweet, giddy voice. You truly are a jewel in the Crown. You always make me laugh, or at least smile.

Remember when you said the title "To Kill a Chicken Head" wasn't such a bad title and then asked where did I come up with these titles? Love ya, Ma-Mia! Thanks to all the rest of my family at Triple Crown, past and present: **Kaori Fujita**, **Aaron Johnson**, **Benzo Stringer** and my girl, **Tammy Fournier**. To my special editor, the heart and soul of my writing, **Ms. Cynthia Parker,** it's a damn shame editors don't get the props they deserve. A writer is nothing without a good editor. In my case, you've been with me from the jump, turning excess verbiage into elegant prose. I want you to know that I appreciate your hard work and dedication. It is you who breathes life into our work. May God bless you and your family.

TO THE FOLLOWING AUTHORS

Ms. Kashamba Williams at Precioustymes Entertainment is a gifted writer and mother, a counselor to young ladies and an advocate and entrepreneur. I will always be in your debt. You know what you did. Thank you from the bottom of my heart, and also for your support and helpful insights into this shady-ass business. I enjoy the hell out of your books, especially *Court's Mercy*. I gotta send you a kite tonight.

To my gorgeous label-mate **Toy Styles**, the Benevolent One and author of several bestsellers, including *A Hustler's Son* and *Black and Ugly*. You were the first person in this industry to truly embrace me caringly. You always ask what do I want, do I need anything…that's gangsta. I can't wait to meet you in person. I look forward to working with you on our project in '08. It seems like you're the only author willing to work with me.

Michael Covington, author of *Chances* on TCP, and my homie, please get at me. Holla at you, boy. Let's make it do what it do! And to the rest of the authors who languish behind enemy lines: we are strong as our weakest link. Meaning, when one of us does good, it reflects on all of us, and people will want to read more of TCP.

To my sista, **Tanika Lynch**: I truly enjoyed your book *Whore*.

Great shock value! Brotha **Quentin Carter** and his book *Hoodwinked.* Son, you're a beast! You killed 'em with that joint. **Darrell DeBrew**, you're a very talented writer. I think the ending in *Keisha* was Da-Bomb! The book was an awesome read from start to finish. **Jason Poole** and **Victor Martin** are both trailblazers and now have books out. To my homie in Chi-town **Victor Woods** and his book *A Breed Apart.* Fresh out the joint, and Simon & Schuster gave you a million dollars. Must be nice. Get at me, dawg! **Wendell Shannon**, author of *Business as Usual*, I'm going to give you a call. **Hellema** and her publishing company: Damn, Boo, how long you gonna be mad at me?

TO ALL THE REAL SOLDIERS IN THE STRUGGLE

The baby of the family, **Varro "Lateef" Brooks,** and the most important person in his life, **Tiarra**, his daughter, and his mom, **Cheryl**, and **Mai**. **Adrienne Green**, girl, you may not be a gold-digger, but you sure like dudes with gold…or platinum…and lots of money. To my step-children, **Fabian** and **Bianica Greene**. **Ms. Stephanie Grir** and her daughter **Amber**. Good luck on your new business, "The Blessings" Beauty Salon. I really look forward to getting to know you. You could be the one. **Rasta 16**, respect. **Crucial and Cecil**. **Kaylon Bailey**. **Bianca**, **Kacy Colleen**, Queen of Washington, D.C. **Raymond Gurges**. **Gregory Rudd** and his book. It's hot, too! Somebody need to get at dude to publish "C.R.E.A.M." To my folks in Edgefield, S.C. C.O. Smitty, if you liked the last one, you'll love this one. **Robert Lee**. **Reynolds II Audy Perez**, **Jeremy Graham**. **Ms. Yolanda Bringhan**, love ya, ma! **Mario** from Thomasville. **Tory R. Taylor** and **Queen Cheryl Taylor**. Will the real Jack Lemon please stand up? Well, here's his sista, **Tajuana Hardison**. If I spell your name wrong again, you're going to kill me! This is a big shout out for pushing all them 5's and to your book club "Just Us Girls" from Greensboro, NC: **Teresa Woods**, **Sharon Milton**, **Michelle Woods**, and **Tracy Jarman**. To my dude **Andrew "Boony" Fletcher**: Yeah, I'm still killin' rats. **Mark Tolliver**, **Steve White**, big smoke rings, huh? **BGB Hymme**, Champaign, Illinois. **G. Folks**, the hometeam. **Steve & Dwanda Skillern El**. **Jonathan Winters, B.K.A. Miami Overtown**. **Nob** from V.I. **Ra'shaan Rodgers**, Greenville, NC. Good luck on your writing. **James (J-Rock) Brady**, Simple City Crew, S.E. **Mark Dennis**, No. 57358-019, aka **Mr. Bankhead**. **Eric Benson/Lavon Wright**, Inside/Out Productions, album coming soon: "Living with a Curse." **Ya Boy**, Serious-n-da- Beast. To **Travis Strord** and his attractive sista **Crystal Strord**. To my brotha **Chue** from Greenville and **Shawn Harris** aka **Black Gucci**. Twun. To **Benita Litmon** and **Shani Johnson**. Thank you for your support.

TO THE SARASOTA HOMETEAM

Lolonda White, girl, if I could go back in time, I would have never let you go. Miss you to death! **Roosevelt Smiley, Joe L. Burt** and **Hodo**, everybody there in that beautiful town, I'm trying to put it on the map. To **Anthony Glenn** and the White Brotha, **Ray Levasseur**, ten years later I have not forgotten you. You said I couldn't do it. If you see me and a bear fighting, pour honey on me. To my sista **Efia**, thank you for all your hard work. **Tony Walker**, with God's speed, something has to give. **David Brown, Gregory S. Jones, Marcus Sanders**. Thought I forgot...**Ernest Spann**. Dude, I'm waiting on you. **James Isum** and family down there at Coleman Pen. Thank you, brothers, for the sympathy card! **Johnny Reed, Clifford Senter** and his beautiful sister **Laurita Senter**. Also, my friend, **Ms. Linda Tillman**, I wish you and your family the best. Look forward to seeing you soon!

TO ALL THE LITERARY HEADS

I read all my reviews and sincerely appreciate my fans going to such great lengths. Seriously, you all truly amaze me. ARC Book Club, AALBC.com. Raw Sistaz Book Review. Booking Matters Magazine. To my Rasta Brotha **Iras** at Atlanta's WRFG-FM 89.3, playing all the conscious joints. I will continue to support you. I wish you would do the same by realizing that urban lit is a part of hip-hop. To **Ms. Monique Patterson**, editor at St. Martin's Press, I received your discourse concerning my first novel, *Life*. It came too late…

<u>TO MY FANS</u>

As a show of appreciation, I want you all to visit my website online at www.leosullivan.com for free books, T-shirts and to be able to download my next book, which is not yet titled. I don't know what the future holds for me, but I do know that the same people you meet going up, you'll see them coming down. If I missed anyone in the acknowledgements, don't worry, you are with me in my heart. For now, I just have to keep it conscious and gangsta. Too many of our people have died and sacrificed their lives for me not to. The man-made debacle of the storm Katrina should have served as a wakeup call. How can you allow men, women and children to go six days without food and water?

You may write Leo directly at:
Leo Sullivan #10024-017
PO Box 150160
Atlanta, GA 30315

UNITED WE STAND

ORDER FORM

Triple Crown Publications
PO Box 6888
Columbus, Oh 43205

Name: _____

Address: _____

City/State: _____

Zip: _____

	TITLES	PRICES
	Dime Piece	$15.00
	Gangsta	$15.00
	Let That Be The Reason	$15.00
	A Hustler's Wife	$15.00
	The Game	$15.00
	Black	$15.00
	Dollar Bill	$15.00
	A Project Chick	$15.00
	Road Dawgz	$15.00
	Blinded	$15.00
	Diva	$15.00
	Sheisty	$15.00
	Grimey	$15.00
	Me & My Boyfriend	$15.00
	Larceny	$15.00
	Rage Times Fury	$15.00
	A Hood Legend	$15.00
	Flipside of The Game	$15.00
	Menage's Way	$15.00

SHIPPING/HANDLING (Via U.S. Media Mail) $3.95 1-2 Books, $5.95 3-4 Books add $1.95 for ea. additional book

TOTAL $_____

FORMS OF ACCEPTED PAYMENTS:
Postage Stamps, Institutional Checks & Money Orders, all mail in orders take 5-7 Business days to be delivered.

ORDER FORM

Triple Crown Publications
PO Box 6888
Columbus, Oh 43205

Name: _____

Address: _____

City/State: _____

Zip: _____

	TITLES	PRICES
	Still Sheisty	$15.00
	Chyna Black	$15.00
	Game Over	$15.00
	Cash Money	$15.00
	Crack Head	$15.00
	For The Strength of You	$15.00
	Down Chick	$15.00
	Dirty South	$15.00
	Cream	$15.00
	Hoodwinked	$15.00
	Bitch	$15.00
	Stacy	$15.00
	Life	$15.00
	Keisha	$15.00
	Mina's Joint	$15.00
	How To Succeed in The Publishing Game	$20.00
	Love & Loyalty	$15.00
	Whore	$15.00
	A Hustler's Son	$15.00

SHIPPING/HANDLING (Via U.S. Media Mail) $3.95 1-2 Books, $5.95 3-4 Books add $1.95 for ea. additional book

TOTAL $_____

FORMS OF ACCEPTED PAYMENTS:
Postage Stamps, Institutional Checks & Money Orders, all mail in orders take 5-7 Business days to be delivered.

ORDER FORM

Triple Crown Publications
PO Box 6888
Columbus, Oh 43205

Name: _____

Address: _____

City/State: _____

Zip: _____

	TITLES	PRICES
	Chances	$15.00
	Contagious	$15.00
	Hold U Down	$15.00
	Black and Ugly	$15.00
	In Cahootz	$15.00
	Dirty Red *Hard Cover Only*	$20.00
	Dangerous	$15.00
	Street Love	$15.00
	Sunshine & Rain	$15.00
	Bitch Reloaded	$15.00
	Dirty Red *paperback*	$15.00
	Mistress of the Game	$15.00
	Queen	$15.00
	The Set Up	$15.00
	Torn	$15.00

SHIPPING/HANDLING (Via U.S. Media Mail) $3.95 1-2 Books, $5.95 3-4 Books add $1.95 for ea. additional book

TOTAL $_____

FORMS OF ACCEPTED PAYMENTS:
Postage Stamps, Institutional Checks & Money Orders, all mail in orders take 5-7 Business days to be delivered.